The Wind in the Willows

Eric Kincaid

Peter Pan

Classic Stories

The Jungle Book

Alice In Wonderland

BRIMAX

Introduction

CLASSIC STORIES are tales that have stood the test of time. Stories which we pass down to our children, as they were passed down to ourselves. Stories which will always retain their power to enchant and stimulate.

In this collection we bring together some of the best in children's literature; from the inspiring story of Mowgli's courage in his Jungle Book adventures, to the wonderfully whimsical characters in The Wind in the Willows. From Alice's fantastical journey and all the bizarre creatures she meets in Wonderland, to the danger, excitement and thrills of Peter Pan's Neverland.

Eric Kincaid has been illustrating books for children since 1972, and he is, in his own right, a celebrated classic illustrator. His stunning interpretations of these characters bring together delicacy with detail, atmosphere with clarity, and excitement with beauty.

Brimax is proud to bring together this stunning collection, which will be enjoyed time and again, by children and adults alike.

First published in Great Britain in 2001 by Briamx
an imprint of Octopus Publishing Group Ltd
2-4 Heron Quays, London E14 4JP
© Octopus Publishing Group Ltd

ISBN 1-8585-4409-2

Printed in China

Peter Pan

by

J.M.Barrie

Introduction

James Barrie's masterpiece about Peter Pan, Wendy and the Lost Boys on the island of Neverland has thrilled and enchanted generations of children.

There never was a more mischievous or cockier lad than Peter, the boy who never grew up. His story is an exciting voyage into the vivid make-believe world of every child's imagination. Grown-ups have long forgotten where Neverland is. But to the Darling children, Wendy, John and Michael - and every young reader - its dangers and adventures are all too real.

The Darling family, of course, lived at No 14. They were a very ordinary family, even though Mr and Mrs Darling had a large dog called Nana to nurse the children. Yet Nana was so clever. It was she who sensed danger the night Peter Pan flew into the children's bedroom, taught them how to fly and tempted them away to Neverland. There on the island lived the sad Lost Boys, who had never had a mother. It was also home to the Redskins, strange mermaids, a jealous fairy called Tinker Bell, a huge crocodile and Peter Pan's sworn enemy, the terrifying pirate, Captain Hook.

When Captain Hook captures Wendy and the children, they all seem doomed to walk the plank of the Jolly Roger. Will Mr and Mrs Darling ever see their children again?

CHAPTER ONE

Peter Pan's Arrival

All children, except one strange little boy, grow up one day. Wendy knew she would have to grow up when she was just two years old. She was playing in the garden and picked a flower for her mother. Mrs Darling saw her daughter running towards her and smiled because Wendy looked so enchanting. 'Oh, why can't you remain like this for ever!' she cried.

Wendy understood then that she wouldn't always be two. It was the beginning of the end, really. Some day, she too would be a grown-up.

Mrs Darling was a perfect mother with a kind face and the prettiest mouth you ever saw. It was full of kisses. Mrs Darling loved to kiss her children, yet there always seemed to be one special kiss which Wendy could never get. There it was, plain enough, on the right-hand corner of Mrs Darling's mouth. One day someone would steal that kiss.

When Mrs Darling was just a girl herself, all the boys fell in love with her. They ran to ask her to marry them. But clever Mr Darling beat them all because he took a taxi and got there first. So Mrs Darling married George. But even he could not get that special kiss.

Mr and Mrs Darling lived in a tree-lined street, and their house was No 14. They had three children. Wendy was the first to be

born, followed soon after by John and then Michael. The Darlings adored them all.

Mr Darling worked in the city. No one was quite sure what he did, but he knew about stocks and shares, and those sorts of things. Each morning he went off to work, looking very important with his brief case and umbrella. One thing about Mr Darling was that he liked to keep up with his neighbours. Next door they had a nanny for the children, so the Darlings got one, too.

But as the family was so poor, the nanny the Darlings found was a prim Newfoundland dog called Nana. She had not belonged to anyone in particular before. The Darlings first spotted her in London's Kensington Gardens, where Nana was forever peeping into prams to make sure the babies were being looked after properly.

Nana might have been a rather unusual nanny, but she was indeed a treasure. She was so good with the children at bath-time, and up at any moment of the night if the children made the slightest cry. She slept in a kennel in the nursery.

Nana was so clever. She always knew if a child's cough was something which needed medicine. She believed in old-fashioned remedies like rhubarb leaf, and hated all the new-fangled talk of germs.

You should have seen Nana taking the children to school. She walked quietly by their side when they were well-behaved, or butted them in the back if they were naughty. When John was playing football she never forgot his sweater, and she usually carried an umbrella in her mouth in case of rain.

The children went to Miss Fulsom's Kindergarten. In the afternoon Nana would join the other nannies waiting for the children to finish school. They sat on benches while Nana lay on the floor, but that was the only difference. The nannies took no notice of Nana because they thought her very inferior. Nana in turn ignored them because of their silly gossip.

Everyone in the family loved Nana, except for Mr Darling. He wondered uneasily if the neighbours talked about them, for having such a strange nanny. After all, he did have his position in the city to consider. Mr Darling also suspected that Nana did not admire him as much as he thought she should.

But all in all the Darlings were a happy family. In fact there never was a happier family until the coming of Peter Pan.

* * *

I don't know whether you have ever seen a map of a person's mind. Doctors can sometimes draw maps of other parts of you, but they could never draw a map of a child's mind. It's like a chest of drawers, full of strange bits and pieces; childish secrets, memories of your first day at school and thoughts about when mother is going to serve your favourite chocolate pudding for tea.

Hidden in a corner of all that jumble is the make-believe world of Neverland. It has a special place in every child's mind. Neverland is almost always an island and it has coral reefs and boats, redskins, and lonely hideouts. It's a place where gnomes live and caves have rivers running through them. Somewhere on the island there is aways an old lady with a crooked nose.

Of course, the Neverlands vary a lot in each child's mind. John's Neverland, for instance, had a lagoon with flamingoes flying over it, while Michael, who was very small, had a flamingo with lagoons flying over it. In John's Neverland he lived in an upturned boat, Michael in a wigwam and Wendy in a house of leaves sewn together. John had no friends, Michael had friends at night and Wendy had a pet wolf which had been left by its mother.

On the magical shores of Neverland children are forever beaching their boats to play. We have all been there and we can still hear the sound of the surf breaking on the island shore. But some of us will never land there again because we are grown up now.

The Neverland is not a frightening place by day when children are at play. But just before you go to sleep, it can become all too real. That's why some mothers put night-lights by the bedside to stop children becoming frightened.

Mrs Darling often tried to look into her children's minds last thing at night, hoping to find out what they were thinking. Sometimes she discovered things in their heads which she could not understand. Quite the most baffling of these was the word Peter. She knew of no Peter and yet he was there in John and Michael's minds, while the name was written all over Wendy's mind.

'Who is he, my pet?' asked Mrs Darling, kneeling beside Wendy's bed.

'He is Peter Pan, mother,' answered Wendy.

Mrs Darling, who had her own Neverland as a child, recalled vague memories of a Peter Pan who was said to live with the fairies. She remembered odd stories about him. Wasn't he the

boy who, when children died, went part of the way with them so they wouldn't be frightened? She had believed in Peter Pan then, but now she was grown up, married and far too sensible. She doubted whether there was any such person. 'Besides,' she said to Wendy, 'he would be grown up by now.'

'Oh, he isn't grown up,' said Wendy, who by now was nearly ten years old. 'He is the same size as me.' She didn't know how she knew. She just knew.

Later, Mrs Darling mentioned Peter Pan to her husband. But he pooh-poohed the whole idea. 'Mark my words,' he said, 'it's some nonsense Nana has been putting into their heads. It's just the sort of idea a dog would have. Leave it alone and the children will soon forget it.'

But it did not blow over and soon the troublesome boy gave Mrs Darling quite a shock. It was Wendy who gave her the strange news. Some leaves from a very strange tree had been found on the nursery floor, leaves which certainly hadn't been there when the children went to bed.

'I do believe it is Peter again,' said Wendy.

'Whatever do you mean, Wendy?' asked her mother.

'The leaves must have stuck to his shoes,' said Wendy, who was a very tidy girl. 'It was naughty of him not to wipe his feet before he came in.'

Wendy explained in a quite matter-of-fact way that she thought Peter Pan sometimes came into the nursery at night and sat at the foot of her bed, playing music on his pipes. Unfortunately she never woke, so she couldn't explain to her mother how she knew. She just knew.

'What nonsense you talk, precious,' said Mrs Darling. 'No one can get into the house without knocking.'

'I think he comes in by the window,' said Wendy.

'My love, the nursery is three floors up.'

'Weren't the leaves at the foot of the window, mother?' said Wendy proudly.

Mrs Darling did not know what to think. Later she examined the leaves closely. They were skeleton leaves and she was sure they did not come from any tree that grew in England. Had some strange boy been in the room? She searched for any strange footprints and even rattled the poker up the chimney to make sure he wasn't hiding there. She found nothing. 'Wendy must be dreaming,' said Mrs Darling.

But Wendy had not been dreaming, as the very next night showed. It was the night on which the extraordinary adventures

of the children began. It was Nana's night off and the children were all in bed. Mrs Darling sang to them and, one by one, they let go of her hand and slid away into the land of sleep.

They all looked so cosy in bed and Mrs Darling forgot her fears as she settled into a chair to do some sewing. The nursery was dimly lit by the three night-lights and the fire was warm. Very soon she fell asleep.

While Mrs Darling slept, she had a dream. She dreamt that the Neverland had come too near and that a strange boy had appeared. He did not alarm her. But in the dream he had drawn aside the hazy curtain which always hides Neverland.
Mrs Darling saw Wendy, John and Michael peeping through the gap.

The dream itself might have meant nothing, but while she was dreaming the window of the nursery blew open and a boy dropped down onto the floor. He was accompanied by a strange tiny light, no bigger than your fist. It darted around the room like a living thing, and it must have been this light which woke Mrs Darling.

She jumped up with a cry, and saw the boy. Somehow she knew at once that he was Peter Pan. He was a lovely boy, dressed in skeleton leaves. But the most delightful thing about him was that he still had all his baby teeth.

He saw Mrs Darling was a grown-up and gnashed his pearly little teeth at her.

CHAPTER TWO

Peter Pan's Shadow

Mrs Darling screamed. Hardly had the sound left her mouth than Nana returned from her evening out and ran into the nursery. She growled and sprang at the boy, who escaped through the window. Again Mrs Darling screamed, but this time she was worried what had happened to the boy. She ran down to the street to look for his little body which she expected would be lying on the ground. But it was not there. She looked up and in the black night she could see nothing but a shooting star.

She returned to the nursery to find Nana with something in her mouth. It was the boy's shadow. As he leapt through the window, Nana had closed it, too late to catch the boy, but quickly enough to stop his shadow escaping. Slam went the window and snapped the shadow off.

Mrs Darling examined the shadow carefully, but really it was quite a normal sort of shadow.

Nana had no doubt what was the best thing to do with the shadow. She hung it out at the window, sure that the boy would return for it later. But Mrs Darling could not leave it hanging there. It looked like she had hung the washing out and what would the neighbours think? She rolled up the shadow and put it away carefully in a drawer. There it would stay until she could find a good time to tell Mr Darling all about it.

Her chance came a week later, on a Friday, a never-to-be-forgotten Friday. It was the day that Mr and Mrs Darling had been invited to dine at No. 27. As evening came and they dressed for the dinner, everything was as normal in the Darling household. Nana put the water on for Michael's bath and was carrying him on her back to the bathroom.

'I won't have a bath. I won't go to bed,' shouted Michael in protest. 'It isn't six o'clock yet. I shan't love you any more Nana if you make me. I won't be bathed. I won't!'

Then Mrs Darling came in wearing her white evening gown. She had dressed early because Wendy loved to see her in the gown. She was also wearing Wendy's bracelet on her arm. Wendy was so proud to lend the bracelet to her mother.

Mrs Darling found Wendy and John playing a favourite game, mothers and fathers, pretending that they were Mr and Mrs Darling and Wendy had just been born. 'I am happy to tell you, Mrs Darling, that you are now a mother,' said John.

Wendy danced with joy, just as Mrs Darling must have done when Wendy was really born. Wendy and John had just got to the part of the game where John was born when Michael returned from his bath and said he wanted to be born as well. But John replied heartlessly: 'We don't want any more children.'

Michael nearly cried. 'Nobody wants me,' he said.

Mrs Darling, looking on, could not bear it. 'I do want another child,' she said. 'I so want a third child.'

'Boy or girl?' asked Michael, not too hopefully.

'Oh a boy,' said Mrs Darling. 'Certainly a little boy just like you.'

Michael leapt into his mother's arms in delight and was still locked in embrace when Mr Darling rushed in. In his hand was a tie and he was looking furious. 'What's the matter, dear?' asked Mrs Darling.

'Matter?' he yelled. 'This tie is driving me mad. This tie will not tie. Not round my neck! Round the bedpost! Oh yes, twenty times I have tied it round the bedpost. But round my neck? Oh, no.'

Mrs Darling smiled to herself at the sight of her husband in such a tantrum. He had always had a short temper, 'I warn you, mother,' he stormed, 'unless this tie is round my neck soon, we won't go out to dinner tonight. And if I don't go out to dinner tonight, I will never go to my office again. And if I don't go to the office, you and I will starve, and our children will be flung out on the streets.'

'Come dear,' said Mrs Darling, 'let me try.'

It was done in a trice and Mr Darling forgot his rage at once, and was soon dancing round the room with Michael on his back. All the children joined in. Nana, hearing all the fuss, wandered in, too. Unluckily she brushed against Mr Darling's new trousers, covering them with her hairs. He was so angry and once more said how stupid it was to have a dog for a nanny.

'Nana is a treasure,' said Mrs Darling, brushing off the hairs.

'I think she looks on the children as puppies,' snapped Mr Darling.

'Oh, no, dear,' said Mrs Darling. 'I'm sure she knows they are different.'

Just then Mrs Darling had a thought. Perhaps now was the time to tell her husband about the boy and his shadow. So she did. He laughed at first, but became very thoughtful when she showed him the shadow.

'It is nobody I know,' he said, examining it carefully, 'but he does look like a scoundrel.'

Nana returned with some cough medicine for Michael. She poured it into a spoon, but Michael couldn't bear to drink the dreadful stuff. 'I won't take it,' Michael cried naughtily. 'Won't! Won't!'

'Be a man,' said Mr Darling. 'When I was your age I took medicine without a murmur.'

Wendy joined the conversation. 'Father has to take medicine even now, and it's much nastier than Michael's, isn't it, father?'

'Ever so much nastier,' said Mr Darling. 'I would take mine now if I hadn't lost the bottle.'

He had not exactly lost his medicine. In the dead of the night he had climbed to the top of the wardrobe to hide it. But Liza, the Darling's faithful servant, had found it and put it back beside Mr Darling's bed.

'I know where the medicine is,' cried Wendy, always glad to be helpful. 'I'll bring it.' She ran off before he could stop her and Mr Darling's spirits sank. It was such beastly medicine.

Wendy returned with the medicine in a glass. Mr Darling frowned. 'Michael, you take yours first,' he mumbled.

'No father, you first,' said Michael, who was suspicious by nature.

'I shall be sick, you know,' said Mr Darling. 'Besides, there's more in my glass than there is on your spoon. It isn't fair.'

'I thought you said you could easily take your medicine,' said Wendy.

'Father, I'm waiting,' said Michael.

'It's all very well to say you are waiting,' said Mr Darling. 'So am I waiting.'

'Father's a cowardy custard.'

'So are you a cowardy custard.'

'I'm not frightened,' said Mr Darling.

'Neither am I frightened,' said Michael.

'Well, then, take your medicine.'

'Well, then, you take yours.'

Wendy came up with the answer. 'Why don't you both take it at the same time?'

'Certainly,' said Mr Darling. 'Are you ready, Michael?'

Wendy gave the words; one, two, three. Michael took his medicine, but Mr Darling slipped his behind his back. There was a yell of rage from Michael.

'Stop that row, Michael,' said Mr Darling. 'I meant to take mine, but . . . I think I've taken mine already today.'

The children all gave their father shaming looks and he thought he would try to make a joke out of the whole thing. 'I shall pour my medicine into Nana's bowl and she can drink it. She'll think it's milk.'

The children did not share their father's sense of humour and there were no smiles as he poured the medicine into the bowl. He patted Nana when she returned from cleaning up the bathroom. 'Good dog,' he said, patting Nana's head. 'Look, there's some milk in your bowl.'

Nana wagged her tail, ran to the bowl and began lapping the medicine. She gave Mr Darling such a look. It wasn't an angry stare, just a very sad one. Then she crept into her kennel. Wendy immediately went over and gave Nana a big cuddle.

Mr Darling knew he should not have done it, but he could not give in. 'It was only a joke,' he said, growing angry again. 'I will not allow that dog to lord it in my nursery for an hour longer,' he said. 'The proper place for that dog is in the yard, and there it will go to be tied up this instant.'

The children wept and Nana ran to Mr Darling, but he waved her away. Mrs Darling did her best. 'Remember what I told you about the boy,' she said. 'Remember how Nana chased him away. You must not punish Nana.'

Mr Darling would not listen because he was determined to show that he was the master of the house. He seized Nana and dragged her from the nursery. He was ashamed of himself but he still did it. When he had tied Nana to a chain in the backyard,

he went and sat in the passage feeling rather sad and guilty at what he had done.

Meanwhile Mrs Darling put the children to bed and lit their night-lights. They could all hear Nana barking and John whispered: 'It's because she has been tied up.'

Wendy was wiser. 'That is not Nana's unhappy bark,' she said. 'That is her bark when she smells danger.'

'Danger!' started Mrs Darling. 'Are you sure?'

'Oh yes,' said Wendy.

Mrs Darling shivered a little and went to the window. It was securely shut. She looked out and saw that the night sky was peppered with stars. It was as if the stars were crowding round the house to see what was happening inside. But Mrs Darling did not notice that, nor that one or two of the smaller stars winked at her. Yet she felt frightened. 'Oh, how I wish that I wasn't going out to dinner tonight,' she said.

Even Michael, already half asleep, knew she was worried. 'Can anything harm us after the night-lights are lit?' he asked.

'Nothing, precious,' she said. 'Night-lights are the eyes a mother leaves behind to guard her children.'

She sang lullabies to the children until they were all asleep and then she crept from the room.

*   *   *

No. 27 was only a few yards further up the street. Mr and Mrs Darling closed the door of No. 14 and walked out into the silent street which had been covered by a slight fall of snow. They were the only people to be seen and all the stars were watching. That's all stars can do. They cannot take an active part in anything. It is punishment put on them for something they did so long ago that no star remembers what it was.

The stars are not really friendly to Peter because he has a mischievous way of creeping up on them and trying to blow out their lights. But they are so fond of fun that they were on his side on this special night and anxious to get the grown-ups out of the way. So as soon as Mr and Mrs Darling entered No. 27 and the door closed, there was a sudden flurry of activity in the heavens.

The smallest of all the stars screamed out: 'Now, Peter!'

CHAPTER THREE

Come Away, Come Away

After Mr and Mrs Darling left the house, the night-lights by the beds of the three children continued to burn brightly for a moment. Then, one by one, they blinked, yawned and went out. There was another light in the room now, a thousand times brighter than the night-lights.

In no time at all the light had flashed around the room, looking in all the drawers for Peter's shadow, searching in the wardrobe and turning every pocket inside out. It was not really a light because when it came to rest you saw it was a fairy, no taller than the length of a hand. It was a girl called Tinker Bell and she was perfectly dressed in a skeleton leaf gown.

A moment after the fairy's arrival, the window was blown open by the breathing of the little stars and Peter Pan dropped in. He had carried Tinker Bell part of the way and his hands were still covered in fairy dust.

'Tinker Bell,' he called out softly, after making sure that the children were asleep. 'Tink, where are you?'

Tinker Bell was busily playing in a jug. It was great fun because she had never been in a jug before.

'Oh, come out of that jug,' said Peter. 'Have you found out where they put my shadow?'

A tinkle of golden bells answered him. It was fairy language and Peter understood it. Tink said that the shadow was in the big box. She meant the chest of drawers, but Peter guessed what she was saying. He jumped at them, scattering their contents on the floor. In a moment he found his shadow and shut the drawer. He was so happy again that he forgot that he had shut up Tinker Bell inside.

If Peter ever thought at all, and I don't think he ever did, he would have imagined that he and his shadow would have joined up quite naturally again. But they did not. He tried to stick it on with soap from the bathroom, but that also failed. Peter thought he would never be able to join his shadow ever again. He sat on the floor and cried.

His sobs woke Wendy and she sat up in bed. She was not alarmed to see a stranger on the floor. She was indeed quite interested. 'Boy,' she said politely. 'Why are you crying?'

Peter could also be very polite. He stood up and bowed to Wendy quite beautifully. She was delighted and bowed in return. 'What's your name?' Peter asked.

'Wendy Moira Angela Darling. What's yours?'

'Peter Pan.'

Wendy had already guessed that this must be Peter Pan. 'Where do you live?' she asked.

'Second to the right,' said Peter, 'and straight on till morning.'

'What a funny address.'

'No it isn't,' he said.

Wendy did not want to be rude. 'Sorry,' she said. 'I mean, is that the address they put on your letters?'

'Don't get letters,' said Peter.

'But surely your mother does?'

'Don't have a mother,' he said. Not only did Peter not have a mother, he had no wish to have one. He thought them very silly things.

'Oh, Peter,' said Wendy sadly, getting out of bed to comfort him. 'No wonder you were crying.'

'I wasn't crying about mothers,' said Peter rather indignantly. 'I was crying because I can't get my shadow to stick on. Besides I wasn't crying.'

And if you believe Peter Pan, and some people don't, he would always tell you he never cried or slept.

Wendy saw the shadow on the floor and felt terribly sorry for Peter. 'How awful,' she said, but she could not help smiling when she saw how he had tried to stick it on with soap. How

Wendy saw the shadow on the floor
and felt terribly sorry for Peter.

exactly like a boy! 'I know what to do. I'll sew it on,' she said.

'What's sew?' asked Peter.

'You're dreadfully ignorant,' said Wendy.

'No, I'm not'.

'Never mind. I will sew it on for you, my little man,' she said, although he was as tall as herself. 'It might hurt a little.'

'Oh, I shan't cry,' said Peter.

Wendy got out her sewing bag and, as Peter clenched his teeth, she sewed the shadow onto his foot. He was delighted and jumped around in glee, quickly forgetting who had helped him regain his shadow. 'How clever I am,' he crowed. 'Oh, the cleverness of me.'

There never was a more cockier boy and Wendy had never heard such a cocky crow.

'I suppose I did nothing?' said Wendy.

'You did a little,' Peter said, and continued to dance.

'In that case,' she said a little haughtily, 'if you have no more use for me, I will go back to bed.'

Wendy got back into bed and covered her head with the blankets. Peter tried to get her to look up by pretending he was going, and when that failed, he tapped her gently with his foot. 'Wendy,' he said. 'I can't help it, I can't help crowing when I'm pleased with myself.'

Wendy still wouldn't look up, but she was listening closely. 'Wendy,' he continued with the angelic voice he put on for special occasions. 'Wendy, one girl is more use than twenty boys.'

Peter's charm worked. She peeped out from beneath her bedclothes. 'Do you really think so?'

'Yes, I do.'

'In that case I think you are very sweet,' she declared, 'and I'll get up again.'

She sat with him on the side of the bed and said she would give him a kiss if he liked. But Peter did not know what she meant, and he held out his hand to receive the kiss. 'Surely you know what a kiss is?' she said.

'I shall know when you give it to me,' he replied stiffly, holding out his hand.

Wendy did not want to hurt Peter's feelings over not knowing what a kiss was. So she gave him a thimble instead.

'Now,' said Peter, 'Shall I give you a kiss?'

'If you please,' said Wendy, sad that Peter had clearly never been kissed.

She did not know whether to expect a kiss or not, so she put
her cheek closer to him, but he merely took an acorn button
from his coat and put it into her hand. She said that she would
wear his kiss on the chain round her neck. It was lucky that she
did put it on that chain, because later on it would save her life.

Wendy asked Peter how old he was, but he did not know.
'I think I am quite young,' he said. 'I ran away the day
I was born.'

Wendy was surprised at his words and told him to sit closer.
'It was because I heard father and mother talking,' he explained
in a low voice. 'They were talking about what I was to be when
I became a man. I don't ever want to be a man. I want always to
be a little boy and have fun. So I ran away to Kensington
Gardens and lived a long time among the fairies.'

Wendy was fascinated and asked so many questions about the
fairies. Her interest quite surprised Peter because he thought
the subject of fairies rather boring. In fact he found them so
troublesome that sometimes he had to give them a hiding. Still
he liked them on the whole and he told Wendy how the
fairies began.

'You see Wendy, when the first baby laughed for the very first
time, its laugh broke into a thousand pieces, and they all went
skipping about, and that was the beginning of the fairies.'

Wendy listened wide-eyed as he continued. 'You know, there
ought to be a fairy for every boy and girl.'

'Ought to be?' said Wendy. 'Isn't there?'

'No. You see, children know such a lot these days, they soon
don't believe in fairies. And every time a child says "I don't
believe in fairies", there is a fairy somewhere that falls down
dead.'

Peter Pan thought he had said enough about fairies and began
to wonder where Tinker Bell was. 'I can't think where she has
gone to,' he said.

He got off the bed and called Tink by name. Wendy's heart
fluttered with excitement. 'Peter,' she cried, clutching his arm.
'You don't mean to tell me there is a fairy in this room!'

'She was here just now,' said Peter. 'You don't hear her,
do you?'

'The only sound I can hear,' said Wendy, 'is like a tinkle
of bells.'

'That's Tink,' said Peter. 'That's fairy language. I think I can
hear her, too.'

The sound came from the chest of drawers and Peter began to

smile. No one could ever look quite so merry as Peter and he had the loveliest of gurgles for a laugh. 'Wendy,' he laughed. 'I do believe I have shut her up in the drawer!'

Peter let poor Tink out of the drawer and she flew about the nursery screaming with fury. Peter said he was sorry. 'How could I know you were in the drawer?' he said.

'Peter,' said Wendy, 'if only she would stand still and let me see her.'

Now fairies hardly ever stand still, but for a moment Tinker Bell came to rest on the cuckoo clock. 'Tink,' said Peter to the fairy. 'This lady says she wishes you were her fairy.'

Tinker Bell snapped an answer in fairy talk. She was still very angry and Wendy asked what she had said.

'She is not being very polite,' he said. 'She says you are a great ugly girl and that she is my fairy. But she knows she cannot be my fairy because I am a gentleman and she is a lady.'

Tink turned in disgust. 'You silly ass,' she said to Peter and disappeared into the bathroom. Tink always called people 'You silly ass'. It was her favourite expression.

'She is quite a common fairy really,' said Peter. 'She's called Tinker Bell because she mends the pots and kettles, like gypsy tinkers do.'

Wendy and Peter Pan were now sitting in the armchair and she was still full of questions. 'If you don't live in Kensington Gardens now . . .'

Peter Pan interrupted her. 'Sometimes I still do . . .'

'But where do you live mostly now?'

'With the lost boys,' answered Peter.

'Whoever are they?' said Wendy.

'They are the children who fall out of their prams when their nurses are looking the other way. If they are not claimed in seven days, they are sent far away to the Neverland. I'm their captain'.

Wendy thought what fun it must be, but she could not see how cunning Peter Pan was. He said Neverland was rather lonely because there were no girls. 'They are far too clever to fall out of their prams,' he said. 'So they never get lost and never come to Neverland.'

Wendy was so pleased to hear Peter Pan's words. 'I think,' she said, 'it is perfectly lovely the way you talk about girls. My brother John over there hates girls.'

Peter leapt from the chair and kicked John out of bed, blankets and all. John was so deeply asleep he didn't even wake

up, but continued dozing on the floor. Wendy told Peter off for
kicking her brother. 'You are not the captain in this house,'
she said.

But Wendy realized that Peter only meant to be kind to her
and told him he could kiss her. 'I thought you would want it
back,' he said a little bitterly, offering to return the thimble.

'Oh dear,' said Wendy, still not wanting to hurt Peter's
feelings. 'I don't mean a kiss, I mean a thimble.'

She kissed Peter on the cheek to show him how. Immediately
he said he would also give her a thimble. But before he could
kiss her, Wendy let out a screech. Someone was pulling her hair.

It was Tink. She was angrier than ever and Peter had never
seen her so naughty before. Before flying off in a flash of light,
the fairy spoke to him sharply.

'Tink says she will do that every time you give me a thimble,'
explained Peter.

Wendy asked why and Peter questioned Tink. 'You silly ass,'
was all Tink would say. Peter did not understand, but Wendy
somehow knew what was wrong. Tinker Bell was jealous of her
giving thimbles to Peter.

Peter soon forgot about Tinker's fury and began telling
Wendy why he came to the nursery window. It was not to see
her, but to listen to the stories Mrs Darling read to the children.
'You see,' said Peter, 'I don't know any stories. Nor do any of
the lost boys.'

'How awful,' said Wendy.

'Do you know,' Peter asked, 'why swallows build nests in the
eaves of houses? It is to listen to the stories children are told at
night. That reminds me, your mother was telling a lovely story
the other night.'

Wendy asked which one it was and Peter said it was about
a prince who couldn't find the lady who wore the glass slipper.
'Oh, that was Cinderella,' said Wendy. 'The prince found her,
and they lived happily ever after.'

Peter seemed delighted to hear the story had a happy ending
and he rushed towards the window. 'Where are you going?'
asked Wendy.

'To tell the other boys what happened to the prince.'

'Don't go, Peter,' she begged. 'I know lots of stories.'

That was exactly what Wendy said, so there can be no doubt
about it. Wendy first put the idea into Peter's head. 'Come with
me then, Wendy,' he said. 'Come with me to Neverland and tell
your stories to the lost boys.'

He began to pull her towards the window.

'No. No. I can't. Think of mummy! Besides I can't fly.'

'I'll teach you,' said Peter. 'I'll show you how to jump on the wind's back and then away we go.'

'Oo! How lovely to fly,' said Wendy.

'Wendy, Wendy,' said Peter. 'When you are sleeping in your silly bed, you could be flying about with me saying funny things to the stars.'

'How lovely,' said Wendy.

'And, Wendy, there are mermaids.'

'Mermaids! What, mermaids with tails?'

'Such long tails,' said Peter.

'Oh,' cried Wendy, 'to see a mermaid.'

Peter Pan was being so cunning. He was saying everything to tempt Wendy into coming away with him. 'You could tuck us in at night. You could darn our clothes and make pockets for us. None of us has any pockets.'

Everything he said excited her so much. 'Oo! To fly! To see mermaids with tails!' she cried. 'Peter, would you teach John and Michael to fly too?'

'If you like,' said Peter, without much interest, and Wendy ran and shook her brothers awake.

'Wake up,' she cried. 'Peter Pan has come to teach us to fly.'

John rubbed his eyes. 'Then I shall get up,' he said. Of course, he was already on the floor. 'Hallo,' he said. 'I am up!'

Michael was up, too. But then Peter Pan suddenly signalled to everyone to be quiet. They listened but could hear nothing. Everything must be right. No, stop! Everything was wrong. Nana, who had been barking all evening, was quiet now. It was her silence they had heard.

'Quick! Hide!' cried John. They were just in time.

Nana burst into the nursery dragging the servant Liza behind her. Liza glanced around and the nursery looked its old self. You would have sworn its three wicked inmates were sleeping angelically, when they were really artfully hidden behind the window curtains.

Liza was in a bad mood. She had been making Christmas puddings in the kitchen and had been forced to leave her work because Nana had been barking so much. 'There, you suspicious brute,' she said, looking around the darkened room and hanging on to the rope holding Nana. 'The children are perfectly safe. The little angels are sound asleep in bed.'

Nana tried to free herself from Liza's clutches because she

knew all was not right. She could hear the children breathing behind the curtains. But Liza hauled the dog away. Unhappy Nana was tied up again. 'Any more barking,' said Liza, 'and I'll go and get the master to whip you.'

Nana cared little whether she was whipped or not, as long as her children were safe. She barked and barked, and strained and strained at the chain . . .

*   *   *

John was the first to emerge from behind the curtains. 'Peter,' he said. 'Can you really fly?'

Peter did not answer but took off and flew once around the room. 'How wonderful,' said John.

It looked so easy that the children all tried it. But they always went down instead of up. 'How do you do it?' asked John.

'You just think wonderful thoughts,' explained Peter, 'and they lift you into the air.'

Of course, Peter was trifling with the children, for no one can fly unless fairy dust has been blown on them. Fortunately Peter's hands were still covered in fairy dust from carrying Tinker Bell and he blew some on the children. 'Now just wriggle your shoulders and let go,' said Peter.

They were all on their beds and gallant Michael let go first and immediately he soared towards the nursery ceiling.

'I flew!' he screamed, while still in mid-air.

John and Wendy also let go and soon they were soaring towards the bathroom.

'Oh, lovely,' said Wendy.

'Oh, ripping,' said John.

'Look at me,' cried Michael.

'Look at me!' they all shouted.

They could not fly so well as Peter, their heads kept bobbing against the ceiling. Peter tried to help Wendy but he had to stop because Tinker Bell grew so angry.

'I say,' cried John. 'Why don't we all go out?'

Of course this was what Peter Pan had been planning, but Wendy still hesitated. Peter knew what to do. 'Mermaids!' he said again.

'Oo,' said Wendy, so excited.

Michael was ready. He wanted to see how long it took to fly

a billion miles.

'And there are pirates,' added Peter for good measure.

'Pirates!' shouted John, seizing his Sunday hat. 'Let us go at once.'

* * *

Meanwhile Nana had been desperately pulling at the rope tied to the chain in the yard. At last it broke. In a moment she had run to No. 27, burst through the front door and galloped into the dining room. Her paws were raised to the heavens.

Mr and Mrs Darling knew at once that something terrible was happening in the nursery and, without another thought, rushed into the street.

They looked up to the nursery window and saw that it was still safely shut. But the room was ablaze with light, and the most heart-gripping sight of all, they could see in shadow on the curtain three figures in night attire circling round and round, not on the floor but in the air.

But wait! Not three figures, four!

The Darlings opened their front door but even as they were coming up the stairs, the stars once more blew the nursery window open and the smallest star of all called out: 'Watch out, Peter!'

Peter knew there was not a moment to lose. 'Come,' he cried and soared out into the midnight sky, followed by John, Michael and Wendy.

Mr and Mrs Darling and Nana rushed into the nursery too late. The birds had flown.

CHAPTER FOUR

The Flight to Neverland

'Second to the right, and straight on till morning.' That, Peter had told Wendy, was the way to Neverland. But even birds, carrying maps and looking at them at windy corners, could not have found their way with those directions. Peter, you must understand, often said anything that came into his head.

At first Wendy, John and Michael trusted Peter completely, and so great were the delights of flying that they wasted time circling round church spires and any other tall objects which took their fancy.

Wendy was the first to worry about how long they had been gone from No. 14. John began to think, too. They were flying over a sea and he could not decide whether it was their second sea or their third night. Sometimes it was dark, sometimes light. Sometimes they were cold because they were in their nightclothes. Sometimes they were hot. Did they feel hungry at times, or were they merely pretending because Peter had such a wonderful way of feeding them?

He chased birds which had food in their mouths and snatched it from them. Then the birds would follow and try and snatch it back. They happily chased each other for miles.

Certainly they did not pretend to be sleepy. They were sleepy, and that was dangerous. The moment their eyes closed, down

they fell. The awful thing was that Peter thought it so funny.

'There he goes again,' he would cry out in delight, as Michael suddenly dropped like a stone.

'Save him. Save him,' shouted Wendy. Eventually Peter would dive through the air and catch Michael just before he hit the sea. He always waited until the very last moment, and you felt it was his cleverness which interested him and not the saving of a human life.

Peter could sleep in the air without falling by simply lying on his back and floating, but then he was so light that if you got behind him and blew he went faster.

Peter loved playing games. Sometimes he would fly close to the water and touch each shark's passing tail, just like children running their fingers along iron railings in the street.

'Tell him to stop showing off,' said John.

Wendy said they should be nice to Peter in case he left them, but Michael thought they could always go back.

'How could we ever find our way back without him?' said Wendy.

'Well, then, we could go on,' said John.

'That is the awful thing,' said Wendy. 'We would have to go on because we don't know how to stop.'

The truth was that Peter had forgotten to tell them how to stop.

John said that if the worst came to the worst, all they had to do was to go straight on. The world was round, he said, and in time they must get back to their nursery window.

Wendy asked how they were going to feed themselves but John said that he had already nipped a bit of food from an eagle's mouth. 'After the twentieth try,' said Wendy, 'and besides see how we keep bumping into clouds.'

Indeed they were always bumping into things. They could now fly straight, although they still kicked too much. But if they saw a cloud in front of them, the more they tried to avoid it, the more certain they were to bump into it.

If Nana had been there she would have had a bandage around Michael's head by now.

* * *

Sometimes Peter forgot all sorts of things. He would go so fast
that he would suddenly shoot out of sight, to have some
adventure by himself. He would return, laughing over something
fearfully funny he had been saying to a star, but had already
forgotten what it was. Or he would come back with mermaid
scales still sticking to him, and yet not be able to say for certain
what had happened.

'If he forgets things so quickly,' warned Wendy, 'we can't be
sure that he won't forget us.'

Indeed sometimes when he returned he did not remember
them, at least not well. Once even Wendy had to tell him her
name. He just told her to keep reminding him if he did forget in
future.

But Peter did not forget to teach them to sleep in the air,
showing them how to lie out flat on a strong wind that was going
their way. The children found they could sleep quite safely.
They would have slept more but Peter quickly tired of sleeping
and he would cry out in his captain's voice: 'We get off here.'
Then the children would wake and change winds to head off
towards their destination.

So with occasional arguments, but on the whole plenty of
laughing and rollicking, they came close to the island of
Neverland. It was many moons before they reached it and their
finding it was not so much due to Peter or Tink's guidance, but
because the island was out looking for them. No one can find
the magic shores unless the island finds them.

'There it is,' said Peter calmly.

'Where, where?' the children cried.

'Where all the arrows are pointing,' said Peter.

A million arrows of light from the sun were pointing out the
island to the children. The sun wanted them to be sure of their
way before leaving them for the night.

All three children stood on tiptoe in the air to get their first
sight of the island. Strange to say they recognised it at once.
It looked like a friend they knew so well.

'John,' cried Wendy, 'there's the lagoon!'

'I say, John, I see your flamingo,' said Michael.

John could see Michael's cave and Michael spotted Wendy's
orphan wolf. Michael also saw the redskin camp and John asked
him where because he wanted to see if the braves were on the
warpath. 'I see now,' he said. 'Yes, they are on the warpath
right enough.'

Peter was a little annoyed that they seemed to know so much

about the island. He wanted everything to be his big surprise. But soon they needed his help again. Night fell, leaving the island in gloom. In the old days at home the Neverland had always begun to look a little threatening by bedtime and the children were always glad when mother put the night-lights on. As darkness fell they had liked Nana saying that Neverland was all make-believe.

Of course Neverland had been make-believe in those days, but it was real now. There were no night-lights, and it was getting darker every moment. And where was Nana?

They flew close to Peter and saw that his careless manner had gone. They were now over the fearsome island, flying so low that sometimes a tree top grazed their faces. They could not see anything horrid in the air, yet flying grew harder, as though they were pushing their way through enemy forces. Sometimes they hung in the air until Peter had beaten back the air with his fists. 'They don't want us to land,' he explained.

'Who are they?' Wendy whispered with a shudder.

But Peter could not or would not say whether it was the fairies fighting them. Instead he asked John: 'Do you want an adventure now, or would you like to have tea first?'

Wendy and Michael wanted 'tea first', but John asked what sort of adventure.

'There's a pirate asleep in the grass below,' said Peter. 'If you like we could go down and kill him.'

'What! Do you kill many?' asked John.

'Tons,' said Peter. 'I have never known so many pirates on the island before.'

'Who is their captain now?' asked John.

'Hook,' said Peter, his face becoming very serious as he said the hated name.

'James Hook?' asked John, nervously.

'Aye,' said Peter.

Michael began to cry, and even John could only speak in gulps, for they both knew of Hook's infamy. 'He was Blackbeard's bo'sun,' John whispered. 'He is the most terrible of all the pirates.'

'How big is he?' asked John.

Peter surprised him by saying that Hook was not as big as he had been. 'I cut a bit off him,' said Peter.

'What bit?' asked John.

'His right hand.'

'Then he can't fight now?' said John, much relieved.

'Oh, can't he just,' said Peter. 'He has an iron hook instead of a right hand, and he claws with it.'

'Claws!' shuddered John.

'Yes. And there is one thing you must promise me. If we meet Hook in open fight, you must leave him to me.'

'I promise,' said John, loyally.

At that moment they were not too worried about Hook and the other dangers which lurked below because Tink was flying with them. They could see each other in her light. She could not fly as slowly as the children and had to go round and round them in circles. So the children were travelling down a brightly lit tunnel. Wendy quite liked this until Peter pointed out a problem.

'Tink tells me that the pirates sighted us before darkness came and they got Long Tom out.'

'The big gun?' asked John.

'Yes,' said Peter, 'and of course they must see Tink's light. They are sure to fire at us.'

'Tell Tink to go away,' said the three children together.

Peter refused. 'She is also rather frightened. You don't think I would send her away all by herself in such a state.'

Just then someone gave Peter a loving pinch.

'Then tell her to put out her light,' suggested Wendy.

Peter said that she could not do that. 'That is about the only thing fairies can't do. It just goes out by itself when she falls asleep, same as the stars.'

'Then tell her to go to sleep at once,' John ordered.

'She can't sleep except when she's sleepy. It is the only other thing fairies can't do.'

'Seems to me,' yawned John, 'sleeping is the only thing worth doing.'

This time it was John's turn to get a mysterious pinch, but it was not a loving one.

'If only one of us had a pocket to put her in,' said Peter.

They all searched but they could not find a pocket between them. Then Peter solved the problem. Tink could travel in John's hat. Tink agreed and they flew on in the dark with Wendy carrying the mischievous fairy in the hat. Tink hated being carried by Wendy.

As they flew on everything fell silent. It was the quietest silence they had ever heard, broken only by a distant lapping sound. Peter explained it was wild beasts drinking. A little later they heard a sound like branches of a tree rubbing together.

'It's the redskins sharpening their knives,' said Peter.

Everything was too quiet for Michael. 'If only someone would make a real noise,' he said.

'BOOM!' The air was shattered by a tremendous crash. The pirates had fired on them with Long Tom. The blast from the explosion sent everyone flying across the heavens. No one was hit but Peter was carried far out to sea, John and Michael found themselves alone in the darkness, while Wendy was blown upwards with no companion but Tinker Bell. It would have been wiser if Wendy had dropped the hat then and there.

I don't know whether the idea came suddenly to Tink, or whether she had planned it on the way, but she popped out of the hat and began to lure Wendy to her destruction.

Tinker was not all bad. It's just that she was all bad just then. Sometimes she was all good. Fairies have to be one thing or the other, because being so small they only have room for one feeling at a time. Just then she was full of jealousy over Wendy.

Tink flew back and forth, signalling to Wendy to follow her. What else could Wendy do? She called out to Peter and John and Michael, but only received echoes in return. She did not know that Tink hated her at that moment, and followed the fairy to her doom.

CHAPTER FIVE

The Island of Neverland

Whenever Peter Pan returns to Neverland, the island wakes up again. When he is not there, the fairies take an hour longer to get up in the morning, the redskins never stop eating, and when the pirates and the lost boys meet they never bother to fight each other. When Peter returns the whole island comes to life.

On the night of Peter's return everyone was on the move. Put your ear to the ground and you can hear the whole island buzzing with activity.

The lost boys were out looking for Peter, the pirates were out looking for the lost boys, the redskins were looking for the pirates, and the beasts were looking out for the redskins. They were all going round and round the island, but they did not meet because they were travelling at the same speed and in the same direction.

All wanted blood except the lost boys. They liked blood normally, but tonight they are out to greet their captain, Peter Pan. As all the different groups follow each other tonight, let us take a look at them one by one.

The number of boys on the island varies. It depends on who's been killed and who's growing up, which is against Peter's rules. He thins them out from time to time. Tonight there are six boys. Let us watch them as they pass by in single file, each with a dagger in his hand.

They all wear the skins of bears which they have killed themselves. Peter makes sure they all wear the skins, because no one is allowed to look like him.

First of all there is Tootles, the gentlest and saddest of the boys. He is also rather brave but has had fewer adventures than the other boys. It is just that when things happen, he always seems to have just stepped round the corner to do something. When he comes back from collecting sticks, or whatever, the other boys would be sweeping up the blood. But he had better watch out tonight because Tinker Bell is bent on mischief and she needs help. Tink thinks he's the most easily tricked of the boys.

Next comes Nibs, a cheerful lad, and then there is Slightly, who always thinks he can remember when he was a baby in the days before he was lost. He cuts whistles out of tree branches and dances to his own tunes. He is the most conceited of the boys.

Now here is Curly. He is forever in trouble, often taking the blame for other boys' naughtiness. If Peter ever asks, 'Who did this?' then Curly is the one who will step forward.

Finally there are the Twins. We cannot describe what they are like for fear of describing the wrong one. They are so alike. Peter never quite understood what twins were and because his band were never allowed to know anything he did not know, no one knew much about the twins.

As the boys vanish into the gloom, not far behind them come the pirates, always singing the same dreadful song:

'Avast below, yo ho, heave to,
A-pirating we go,
And if we're parted by a shot,
We're sure to meet below!'

There never was a more villainous-looking lot, armed to the teeth with pistols, cutlasses and daggers. There was the handsome Italian Cecco, with great arms bare and pieces of eight in his ears as ornaments. He had once cut his name in letters of blood on the back of the prison governor at Goa.

Behind Cecco is the gigantic Blackamoor, followed by Bill Jukes, who has tattoes all over him. Cookson, said to be the evil Black Murphy's brother, is next.

Then comes Gentleman Starkey, once a high-born schoolboy but now a man with many a dainty way of killing his enemies.

There never was a more villainous-looking lot,
armed to the teeth with pistols, cutlasses and daggers.

Behind him comes Skylights and the Irish bo'sun Smee, a strangely friendly man who often apologised to any man he was about to kill.

Noodler, a man who always looked as though his hands were fixed on backwards, comes next, closely followed by Robert Mullins, Alf Mason and other ruffians well-known and dreaded on the Spanish Main.

In the middle of this gang of villians, resting in a rough chariot pulled by his men, is the blackest and most terrifying of all the pirates, James Hook. Instead of a right hand, he has an iron hook which he raises into the air to get his men to travel more quickly. He treats them like dogs and as dogs they obey him utterly.

Hook is a huge man with a dark evil face and hair dressed in long curls, just like old King Charles II. His blue eyes can look quite sad, but when he plunges his hook into anyone, two red spots appear in them. His eyes light up terribly. The most awful thing about Hook, apart from his grim hook, is that the more villainous he becomes, the more politely he behaves.

Tonight he lies in his chariot smoking two cigars at once in a gadget he invented himself.

Yet, he is a breed apart from his men. It is rumoured he went to the most famous school in England before he became a pirate. He is a man of great courage and they say the only thing which frightens him is the sight of his own blood, which is thick and strangely coloured. But there is one other thing which terrifies Captain James Hook. We will learn about that later.

But before the pirates disappear into the dark in search of the boys, let us kill a pirate to show how Hook works. Skylights will do. As they travel on, Skylights accidentally lurches against Hook and ruffles his lace collar. Hook is furious. His hook shoots out, there is a tearing sound and a single screech. Then the body is kicked aside and the pirates move on. Hook has not even taken the cigars out of his mouth.

Such is the terrible man against whom Peter Pan must pit his wits.

On the trail of the pirates, stealing silently down the war-path, come the redskins. They carry tomahawks and knives, and their naked bodies gleam with paint and oil. They are the Piccaninny Tribe and, strung around their bodies, are the scalps of boys as well as pirates. Leading is the brave Great Big Little Panther, who has so many scalps that they are weighing him down. At the end of the column comes Tiger Lily, the most beautiful redskin princess.

The redskins pass by in a ghostly silence. They are so clever they can step on a broken twig without making a sound. The only noise is their heavy breathing because they are still so fat from eating too much while Peter was away.

Coming out of the shadows after the redskins are the beasts, a procession of lions, tigers, bears and other savage animals. Their tongues are hanging out tonight because they are hungry.

When they have passed, there is still one more creature to come, a gigantic crocodile.

* * *

So the island and its inhabitants are on the move. All are keeping a sharp look out at the front, but no one suspects that the danger may be creeping up from behind.

The first group to fall out of the moving circle were the boys. They sat down on the grass close to their underground home, and began to talk about when they thought Peter would return.

'I do wish he would come back soon,' said the boys, who although they obeyed their captain without question, were all larger than him.

'I am the only one who is not frightened of the pirates,' said Slightly, 'but I wish he would come back and tell us whether he has heard anything more of Cinderella.'

Tootles was sure that Cinderella must be very much like his mother. It was only when Peter was away that they could talk about their mothers. Peter said mothers were silly and should not be spoken of.

The boys' talk suddenly came to a halt when they heard a chilling distant sound. It was a grim song they knew too well:

> 'Yo ho, yo ho, the pirate life,
> The flag of skull and bones,
> A merry hour, a hempen rope,
> And hey for Davy Jones.'

Now, where are the lost boys? Rabbits could not have disappeared more quickly. All the boys, except Nibs who had gone off to look for the pirates, had disappeared into their underground home. But how did they get in? Look closely and you may see seven trees, each with a hollow trunk as large as a boy. These are the seven entrances to the home which Hook has been searching for many a moon.

As the pirates advanced, the quick eye of Starkey saw Nibs disappearing through the wood. He had his pistol out in a flash. But quicker still was Hook's iron claw, which snapped around Starkey's shoulder.

'It was one of the boys you hate,' said Starkey. 'I could have shot him dead.'

'Put that pistol back,' snarled Hook threateningly. 'The sound of your shot would have brought Tiger Lily's redskins on us. Do you want to lose your scalp?'

Smee jumped forward. 'Shall I after him, captain?' he said. 'I'll tickle him with my Johnny Corkscrew.' Smee had names for everything and his gleaming cutlass was called Johnny Corkscrew because he wiggled it in the wound. One could mention some lovely habits of Smee. For instance after killing someone he would wipe his spectacles instead of his cutlass.

'Not now,' said Hook darkly. 'That was only one of the boys. I want to capture all seven. Now! Scatter and look for them.'

The pirates disappeared into the trees and Hook was left alone with Smee. 'There are seven of them,' said the black captain. 'But the one I really want is Peter Pan. 'Twas he who cut off my arm. I've waited long to shake his hand with this. Oh, how I will tear him apart.'

Hook devilishly brandished the hook.

'I have often heard you say how useful the hook is,' said Smee. 'Didn't you say once that if you were a mother you would want all your children born with a hook instead of a hand.'

Hook looked proudly at his hook and then his black look returned. 'Peter flung my arm,' he said wincing, 'to a passing crocodile.'

'I have often noticed,' said Smee, 'your strange dread of crocodiles.'

'Not of crocodiles,' said Hook. 'But of that one crocodile. It liked my arm so much, Smee, that it has followed me ever since, from sea to sea, and from land to land, licking its lips for the rest of me.'

'In a way,' said Smee, 'that is a sort of compliment.'

'I want no compliments,' barked Hook. 'I want Peter Pan, who first gave the brute its taste for me. But then I do have an advantage over it. It once swallowed a clock which goes tick inside it. So before it can reach me I hear the tick and run off.'

Hook laughed deep and long and sat down on a large mushroom. 'Some day that clock will run down,' said Smee, 'and then the crocodile will get you.'

Hook wetted his dry lips. 'Aye. That's the fear that haunts me.'

Suddenly Hook stood up. 'Odds, bobs, hammer and tongs!' he shouted. 'I'm burning!'

He examined the mushroom he was sitting on and found it was hot. Hook kicked it and it fell over. Beneath it was a hole and smoke was billowing out of it.

The pirates looked at each other and both exclaimed: 'It's a chimney!' Not only was smoke coming out, but also the sound of children's voices. They knew at once they had discovered the lost boys' home. They bent down and listened to the boys chatting cheerfully below.

They listened for a few moments before replacing the chimney, noticing at the same time the seven entrances to the hollow trees. Each one looked far too small for either Hook or Smee to get down. 'Did you hear them say Peter Pan was still away?' asked Smee.

Hook nodded and stood for a long time, lost in thought. Then at last a blood curdling smile lit up his swarthy face. 'We will return to the ship and cook up a large rich cake with green sugar on it,' he sneered. 'We will leave it on the shores of the mermaids' lagoon for the boys to find.'

Hook knew the boys had no mothers so they would not know how dangerous it was to eat such a special cake. 'They will gobble it up,' he laughed, 'and they will all die. Ho, ho, ho.'

The two pirates celebrated the idea by breaking into song again:

> 'Avast below, when I appear,
> By fear they're overtook,
> Nothing's left upon the bones when you,
> Have shaken claws with Hook.'

But another tune stopped them in their tracks. 'Tick! Tick! Tick! Tick!' Hook stood shuddering and shaking in fear, one foot in the air.

'The crocodile,' he gasped and bounded away.

The crocodile had passed the redskins and was now on the trail of Hook.

Soon after, the boys emerged into the open to find Nibs rushing back towards them, pursued by a pack of wolves. 'Save me. Save me,' he cried, falling on the ground.

'What would Peter do?' said one boy.

'He would turn his back on them and look through his legs,' said another.

One by one they bent over and looked through their legs at the approaching wolves. Victory came quickly. The wolves took one look at the boys, dropped their tails and fled.

Now Nibs rose from the ground and, looking to the sky, shouted: 'I have seen a wonderful thing. A great white bird is flying this way.'

'What is it?' cried the other boys.

'I don't know,' said Nibs, 'but it looks so weary and it keeps saying "Poor Wendy".'

'I remember,' said Slightly, pretending he could still remember his babyhood, 'there are birds called Wendies.'

'Here it comes,' said Curly.

Wendy was now overhead and the boys could hear her cries. But louder still came the shrill voice of Tinker Bell. The jealous fairy was pinching Wendy at every chance.

'Hallo, Tink,' welcomed the boys.

Tink's reply rang out for all to hear. 'Peter wants you to shoot the Wendy.'

No boy would ever disobey Peter. All but Tootles, who already had his bow and arrow in hand, popped down their trees to find weapons.

'Quick, Tootles,' screamed Tinker Bell. 'Shoot the Wendy bird. Peter will be so pleased.'

Tootles fitted an arrow into his bow, took aim and fired. It flew true and straight. Wendy fluttered to the ground with an arrow in her breast.

CHAPTER SIX

The Wendy House

oolish Tootles was standing like a conqueror over Wendy's body when the other boys sprang, armed, from their trees.

'You are too late,' he said proudly. 'I have shot Wendy. Peter will be so pleased with me.'

Overhead Tinker Bell shouted 'Silly ass!' and flew off. The others did not hear her as they crowded round Wendy. A terrible silence fell upon the wood and if Wendy's heart had been beating, they would have all heard it.

'This is no bird,' said Slightly. 'I think it must be a lady.'

'And we have killed her,' said Nibs.

Every boy took off his hat as a mark of respect there and then. 'Now I see,' said Curly, sadly. 'Peter was bringing her for us.'

'A lady to look after us at last,' said one of the twins, 'and Tootles has killed her.'

They were sorry for Tootles, but sorrier for themselves. Tootles' face was very white. 'I did it,' he said. 'When I dreamed of ladies I used to think my mother had come. But when at last she did come, I shot her.'

He moved sadly away, but, feeling sorry for Tootles, they called him back. 'No, I must go,' he said. 'I am so afraid of Peter.'

It was at this tragic moment that they heard a sound which brought their hearts to their mouths. It was Peter crowing.

'Hide her!' whispered the boys, gathering around Wendy. But Tootles stood aside.

Then Peter was down beside them. 'Greetings, boys,' he said, and they all saluted him in silence. Peter frowned. 'I am back. Why don't you cheer? I have some great news. I have at last brought a mother for you all. Have you seen her?'

Tootles spoke so quietly. 'I will show her to you. Stand back boys. Let Peter see.'

Peter looked at the figure of Wendy, knelt down and removed the arrow from her breast. 'Whose arrow?' he asked.

'Mine, Peter,' said Tootles, who sunk to his knees.

Peter raised the arrow in the air ready to strike the poor boy. Tootles, who thought he should die for what he had done, bared his chest and told Peter to strike him dead. But as hard as he tried, Peter could not bring the arrow down. Something stopped him.

'Look!' said Nibs. 'It's the Wendy lady. Look at her arm.'

They looked and saw that Wendy had raised her arm. As Nibs bent down, two whispered words came to her lips: 'Poor Tootles.'

'She lives,' said Peter, kneeling down beside her. That's when he saw the acorn button which he had given Wendy in the nursery. She had hung it on the chain around her neck. 'See!' he cried. 'The arrow struck against the button. It is the kiss I gave her. It has saved her life.'

'I remember kisses,' said Slightly. 'Let me see that button. Yes, that is definitely a kiss.'

Peter begged Wendy to get better. 'Remember,' he said. 'I must show you the mermaids.'

Just then there was a cry in the sky. 'It's Tink,' said Curly. 'She is crying because Wendy lives.'

The boys then had to tell Peter of Tink's crime and he looked up into the sky in fury. 'Listen, Tinker Bell,' he said. 'I am your friend no longer. Be gone for ever.'

Tinker Bell flew down onto his shoulder and begged to be forgiven. Peter brushed her off. But when Wendy moved her arm again he forgave Tink a little. 'Well, not forever, but for a whole week.'

Tink left and the boys said they should move Wendy to their home to recover. But Peter said it was not right to carry a lady anywhere. 'We will build a house round her,' he announced.

In a moment they were scurrying round making Wendy more comfortable, preparing a bed and building a fire. As they worked John and Michael appeared. They were so tired they dragged their feet behind them, falling asleep at one step and then waking at the next.

'Hello, Peter,' they said.

'Hello?' said Peter, who had quite forgotten them.

'Is Wendy asleep?' they asked.

Peter said she was and continued measuring Wendy to see how big the house would have to be. 'Curly,' he said. 'Make sure that these two boys help with the new house.'

'Build a house?' asked John.

'For the Wendy,' said Curly.

'For Wendy,' John said in disbelief. 'Why, she is only a girl.'

'That,' explained Curly, 'is why we are her servants.'

'You? Wendy's servants!' said John and Michael together.

'Yes,' said Peter, 'and you will be, too. To work with you. We'll make a table and some chairs first and then build the house round them.'

'Yes,' said Slightly, 'that is how a house is built. It all comes back to me now.'

The astonished brothers were dragged away to cut wood and carry while Peter ordered Slightly to go and find a doctor. Slightly disappeared, wondering where he would find a doctor. He scratched his head and came up with an idea. He returned a few moments later wearing John's hat and looking very serious, just like a doctor would do.

'Please, sir,' said Peter, approaching Slightly, 'are you the doctor?'

The difference between Peter and the other boys was that they knew when something was make-believe or not, while to Peter make-believe and true were exactly the same. This worried the boys because sometimes they had to eat make-believe suppers, and Peter would always rap their knuckles if they did not pretend to make-believe properly.

'Yes, I am the doctor,' said Slightly. 'I will put a glass thing in the patient's mouth.'

Peter waited anxiously as Slightly put a glass thing in Wendy's mouth and then removed it. 'How is she?' asked Peter.

'I think it has cured her,' said the doctor.

'Good,' said Peter.

'I will call again this evening,' said Slightly, 'but in the meantime you must give her beef tea from a cup with

a spout on it.'

Then, with a very polite good-bye to Peter, the doctor left. Slightly heaved a sigh of relief that Peter had really believed he was the doctor.

By the time the doctor had finished his business, all the materials for Wendy's house were ready. 'But what sort of house would Wendy like?' wondered Peter. Just then Wendy moved and began to sing very quietly:

> 'I wish I had a pretty house,
> The littlest ever seen,
> With funny little red walls,
> And roof of mossy green.'

Everyone was delighted and that is how they built Wendy's house. They were so happy, they sang as they worked.

> 'We've built the little walls and roof,
> and made a lovely door
> So tell us, mother Wendy,
> What are you wanting more?'

Wendy answered them with another verse:

> 'Oh, really, next I think I'll have,
> Gay windows all about,
> With roses peeping in, you know,
> And babies peeping out.'

There were not any roses, babies neither. So they completed the house with make-believe and sang a little more:

> 'We've made the roses peeping out,
> The babies are at the door,
> We cannot make ourselves, you know,
> 'Cos we've been made before.'

When all was done, Peter, seeing that the house was such a good idea, immediately pretended that it was his own, marching up and down ordering all sorts of finishing touches. Tootles gave up the sole of his shoe for a knocker and John's hat, with the top knocked through, made for a very good chimney. And as if to agree, the hat immediately began to smoke.

Now all that was left to do was to knock on the door and ask who was inside. 'You must always look your best when you knock at someone's door,' said Peter, smartening himself up.

Then, as Tinker Bell sneered from a nearby branch, Peter knocked on the door and all the boys wondered who would come out. The door did open and a lady did come out. It was Wendy and they all lifted their hats to her.

'Where am I?' she asked.

'You are in the house we built for you,' said Slightly.

'It's a lovely, darling house,' said Wendy.

'And we are your children,' cried the twins.

Then they all went on their knees and begged Wendy to be their mother. 'I'm only a little girl,' said Wendy, 'but I do feel that a mother is exactly what I am.'

'You are! You are!' they all cried.

'Very well,' she said. 'I will do my best. Come inside, you naughty children, and before I put you to bed, I just have time to finish the story of Cinderella.'

In they all went. I don't know how there was room for them, but you can squeeze very tight in Neverland. That was the first of many happy evenings they had with Wendy.

Later that night she tucked them up in the great bed in their home under the ground, but she herself slept in the little house. Outside Peter kept watch with his sword drawn because he could hear the pirates singing far away and he knew the wolves were on the prowl.

The little house looked so cosy and safe in the darkness with a bright light showing through the blinds, the chimney smoking beautifully and Peter standing guard outside.

Of course, Peter did not stay on guard very long. He was soon asleep and the fairies of the night took great delight in tweaking his nose as they passed by on their way home to their nests in the tops of the trees.

CHAPTER SEVEN

The Home under the Ground

The first thing Peter did the next day was to measure Wendy, John and Michael for hollow trees. Peter thought it safer for John and Michael to live with the boys in the home under the ground, although Wendy slept in her own house at night. Each tree had to fit exactly the person who was to use it and each person had to have his own tree. No two people were quite the same size.

Once you fitted a tree you drew in breath at the top and down you went at exactly the right speed, while to come up, you breathed in and out alternately and wriggled up. Once you mastered the art it was easy.

Peter measures people as carefully as for a suit of clothes. The only difference is that clothes are made to fit you, while you have to be made to fit the tree. If you are bumpy in awkward places or the only available tree is an odd shape, then Peter does some things to you, and after that you fit. Wendy and Michael fitted their trees at the first try, but John had to be altered a little.

After a few days' practice they could all go up and down as gaily as buckets in a well. And how they came to love their new home, especially Wendy.

It consisted of only one room and on the floor grew stout
mushrooms which were used as stools. A Never tree tried to
grow in the centre of the room, but every morning the boys
sawed the trunk through, level with the floor. By tea-time it had
always grown two feet high again and then they put a door on
top of it, so making a table. As soon as things were cleared
away, they sawed off the trunk again to make more room
to play.

There was an enormous fire-place which could be lit in almost
any part of the room you chose. Wendy dried the boys' clothes
over it. The bed leaned against the wall by day and was let down
in the evening. It filled nearly half the room. All the boys except
Michael slept in it, lying like sardines in a tin. There was a strict
rule against turning around in the night. The person who wanted
to roll over had to give a signal, and then they would all turn
over at the same time.

Michael should have used the bed, but Wendy would insist on
having a baby, and as he was the littlest he was hung up in
a basket.

There was one small opening in the wall, no larger than
a bird-cage. This was the private apartment of Tinker Bell.
It could be shut off from the rest of the home by a tiny curtain,
which Tink, who was most fussy, always kept drawn when
dressing or undressing. No woman, however important or rich,
could have had a more beautiful bedroom. There were different
bedspreads to match the fruit-blossom of the season, wonderful
carpets and rugs and even a twinkling chandelier, although of
course she lit the room herself.

Tink was very vain about her appearance and spent a lot of
time looking in her fine mirror. All in all the room was so smart,
it gave the appearance of having a permanently turned-up and
very snooty nose.

Wendy was kept so busy by the boys, cooking, sewing,
darning and telling stories. Really, there were whole weeks
when she never went above ground during the day. The cooking
in particular kept her nose to the pot. Their main food was
roasted bread-fruit, yams, coconut, baked pig, mammee apples,
tappa rolls and bananas washed down with calabashes of poe-
poe. But you never knew whether there would be a real meal or
just make-believe. It all depended on Peter's whim. He could
eat, really eat, but make-believe was so real to him that he got
fatter even if the meal was not a true one.

Now, do you remember Wendy's pet wolf? Well, it soon

discovered that Wendy had come to the island and found her. They fell into each other's arms like old friends. Afterwards it followed her everywhere.

As the time passed, Wendy did think about her mother and father at No. 14. She did not really worry because she was absolutely sure they would always keep the nursery window open for her return. What did disturb her at times was that John remembered his parents only vaguely, like people he had once known. Michael, still so young, was quite happy to believe that Wendy was his real mother.

These things frightened her and she tried to get them to remember their old lives by setting examination papers on it. The questions were quite ordinary – 'What was the colour of your Mother's eyes? Who was taller, Father or Mother? Was Mother blonde or brunette? Write an essay of How I Spent My Last Holiday. Describe Mother's laugh. Describe Mother's party dress. Describe the Nursery Kennel and its occupant.'

When they could not answer a particular question Wendy put black marks on the paper. What a dreadful number of black marks John had. But worse still, Slightly wanted to reply to every question too and he was sure he would come first in the exam. Sad Slightly came out last.

* * *

Adventures for the lost boys and the children were a daily event, but Peter also invented a new game which fascinated him a great deal. He pretended to have the sort of adventures which Wendy, John and Michael had at their real home.

He would sit on a stool throwing a ball to the others, playfully run around the house pushing everyone about or even go out for walks, pretending they were good for his health. He would return without having so much as killed a grizzly bear. But Peter could not do such boring things for long.

He often went out alone and when he came back no one was sure whether he had had an adventure or not. Sometimes he might have forgotten what he had done, and when you went out you found the body. On the other hand he might tell about a great adventure and you never did find the body.

Sometimes he came in with his head bandaged and Wendy would bathe the wound in lukewarm water. She was never quite sure what he had been up to.

But there were adventures which had to be true because the children were involved in them. To describe them all would take a huge book, so the most we can do is to give an example of an average hour on the island. Should we tell the story of the brush with the redskins at Slightly Gulch? That was the day Peter decided to change sides in the middle of the fight.

With victory still in the balance, Peter called out to Tootles: 'I'm a redskin, what are you?' Tootles followed his captain, as did the others. They all became redskins. The fight would have ended there had not the real redskins joined in with Peter's game and agreed to be lost boys for that one time.

But there were other adventures. There was the night attack by redskins on the home under the gound. That was when several redskins got stuck in the hollow trees and had to be pulled out like corks.

Then there was that poisonous cake the pirates cooked to give to the lost boys. They placed it in one cunning spot after another, but Wendy always found it first and snatched it from the hands of her children. Eventually the cake became rock hard and Captain Hook used to trip over it in the dark.

Tinker Bell was involved in one particular adventure. While Wendy was asleep she and some other fairies lifted her onto a large leaf and let her float away from the island towards the mainland. Luckily the leaf sank and Wendy woke and swam back to safety.

There was the day Peter challenged lions to attack him. He drew a circle around him on the ground with an arrow and defied the beasts to cross it. Though he waited for hours, with the boys looking on breathlessly from nearby trees, not one lion dared cross the line.

On another occasion, a Never bird built a nest in a tree overhanging the lagoon. Then the nest with its eggs fell into the water, but it kept floating. The mother bird would not leave her eggs and she continued to sit on the nest, floating wherever the tide took her. Peter, who it must be said used to take great pleasure in tormenting the bird, ordered that she should not be disturbed in future. The Never bird would reward Peter for his kindness one day.

But the most exciting adventure concerned Peter Pan and Tiger Lily, the beautiful redskin princess. It all took place at Mermaids' Lagoon.

The children often spent long summer days on the lagoon, swimming and trying to play with the mermaids. You must not think the mermaids were friendly, on the contrary. Wendy never had a pleasant word with any of them. She would creep up to Marooners' Rock where the mermaids loved to sun themselves, combing out their hair in a lazy way which quite irritated her. But as soon as Wendy got close, they dived into the water, splashing her with their tails, not by accident, but on purpose.

The mermaids treated all the boys in the same way, except, of course, Peter. He chatted with them at Marooners' Rock and even sat on their tails when they were cheeky. He did give Wendy one of their combs.

The most haunting time at which to see the mermaids is in the evening when the moon slowly rises into the sky and the mermaids howl with the strangest cries. The lagoon is a dangerous place for mortal beings then. Wendy had never been by the lagoon at that time because she had a strict rule that all the boys should be in bed by seven o'clock.

But one day Wendy and the boys were all on Marooners' Rock. She was doing some sewing while most of the boys were snoozing in the sunshine.

As she stitched, a change came over the lagoon. Little shivers ran over it, the sun vanished and dark shadows stole across the lagoon. It turned cold and so dark that Wendy could not see what she was doing any longer. When she looked up the lagoon was not the friendly place she had known.

It was not, she knew, that night had come, but that something as dark as night had come. She should have woken the children immediately, but she did not. Even when she heard the sound of muffled oars, and her heart was in her mouth, she did not wake them.

Wendy was frozen to the spot, remembering only how Marooners' Rock had got its name. On that rock, evil captains had left sailors to drown. For when the tide rises, the rock is soon under water.

It was lucky for the boys that there was one among them who could sniff danger even in his sleep. Peter Pan sprang up wide awake and stood absolutely still with one hand to his ear, listening.

'Pirates!' he cried.

*The most haunting time at which to see the mermaids
is in the evening . . .*

CHAPTER EIGHT

The Mermaids' Lagoon

Peter Pan's cry of 'Pirates!' woke all the other boys and they gathered round him. A strange smile came to Peter's face and when Wendy saw it she shuddered. She knew he was looking forward to another great adventure. While that smile remained on his face, no one dared say a word. All they could do was to stand ready to obey. The order came sharply: 'Dive!'

Everyone dived in the water, leaving the lagoon seemingly deserted. Marooners' Rock stood alone in the forbidding waters, almost as if it was marooned itself.

The boat drew nearer. It was the pirate dinghy with three figures aboard – Smee, Starkey and none other than Tiger Lily. Her hands and ankles were tied and she knew her fate. She was to be left on the rock to drown, a death more terrible than by fire or torture because her tribe believed that there is no path through water to the happy hunting-ground. Yet her face did not show any fear. She was the daughter of a chief and she would die honourably as a chief's daughter.

The pirates had caught Tiger Lily creeping around their ship with a knife in her mouth. No watch was kept on the ship because it was Captain Hook's boast that just the sound of his name was enough to keep people away. So she had easily slipped aboard.

In the gloom the two pirates did not see the rock until they crashed into it. 'Luff, you lubber,' cried Smee. 'Here's the rock. Now, then, what we have to do is to put the redskin on it, and leave her to drown.'

The princess was brutally thrown onto the rock.

Quite near the rock, but out of sight, two heads bobbed up and down in the water, Peter's and Wendy's. Wendy was crying because it was the first tragedy she had seen. Peter had seen many tragedies, but he had forgotten them all. He was just angry that it was two against one; two pirates against the beautiful Tiger Lily, the redskin Princess he now meant to save.

Peter could have waited until the pirates had gone, but he was never one to choose the easy way. As usual he had a plan. He would imitate the voice of Hook.

'Ahoy there, you lubbers,' he called. It was a marvellous imitation.

'The captain!' said the pirates, staring at each other in surprise.

'He must be swimming out to us,' said Starkey, when they had looked for him in vain. Then Smee called out to tell his captain that they had put Tiger Lily on the rock.

'Set her free,' came the astonishing answer.

'Free?' The pirates scratched their heads in amazement.

'Yes, cut her bonds and let her go.'

'But, captain . . .'

'At once, do you hear,' shouted Peter, 'or I'll plunge my hook into you.'

'This is strange,' gasped Smee.

'Better do what the captain orders,' said Starkey, a little nervously.

'Aye, aye,' said Smee, and he cut Tiger Lily's ropes. She immediately slipped into the water.

Wendy thought Peter had been so clever, but she also knew he would be so cock-a-hoop at his own success in fooling the pirates that he would crow out in delight. So she covered his mouth with her hand.

Peter may have been about to crow but his lips puckered into a whistle of surprise when suddenly he heard Hook's voice. 'Boat ahoy!' came the shout over the water. It was not Peter speaking. The real Captain Hook was also out and about on the lagoon.

Hook was swimming to the boat and his men raised a lantern to show him the way. In the light Wendy saw his hook grip the

boat's side. For the first time she saw the evil swarthy face as Hook rose dripping from the water. Quaking in fright, she would have liked to swim quickly away. But Peter would not move. He was just too full of himself. 'Am I not a wonder? Am I not a real wonder?' he whispered. 'Now let's listen to what Hook has got to say.'

The two pirates were very curious to know why their captain had come, but he just sat with his head on his hook looking deeply miserable.

'Captain, is all well?' they asked. Hook did not answer, but his moans and sighs could be heard clearly.

'He sighs,' said Smee.

'He sighs again,' said Starkey.

'And yet a third time he sighs,' said Smee. 'What's up, captain?'

'The game's up,' he cried. 'Those boys have found a mother.'

Frightened though she was, Wendy was proud to hear Hook's words.

'A mother?' cried Starkey. 'This is indeed a bad day.'

'What's a mother?' asked the ignorant Smee.

Wendy could not believe Smee did not know what a mother was. She always said afterwards that if you could have a pet pirate, Smee would be her one.

Just then Peter pulled Wendy beneath the water because he thought Hook had spotted them. 'What was that?' cried Hook, hearing the water ripple.

'I heard nothing,' said Starkey, raising the lantern over the waters. As the pirates looked they saw a strange sight. It was the floating nest of the Never bird and she was sitting on it.

'See,' said Hook, his voice breaking softly as if he was remembering his more innocent days as a boy. 'That is a mother. The nest must have fallen into the water, but would she desert her eggs? Never!'

Smee gazed at the bird in amazement, but Starkey was more suspicious. 'If that bird is a mother, perhaps she is hanging around here to help Peter.'

Hook winced. 'Yes, that is the fear which haunts me.'

Just then Smee suggested something which cheered Hook greatly. 'Captain,' he said, 'why don't we kidnap the boys' mother and make her our mother?'

'It's a princely scheme,' cried Hook. 'We will seize the children and carry them to the boat. We will make the boys walk the plank and she can be our mother.'

It was too much for little Wendy. 'Never!' she blurted out.

'What was that?' cried the three pirates together.

They looked but could still see nothing. It must have been the wind, they decided as the boat gently bumped into Marooners' Rock. Hook suddenly remembered Tiger Lily. 'Where is the redskin?'

Hook had a mischievous sense of humour sometimes and the two men thought he was joking with them. 'It's all right, Captain, we let her go,' said Smee.

'Let her go!' roared Hook.

''Twas your own orders, captain,' said Smee, beginning to worry.

'You called over the water to us. You told us to let her go,' said Starkey.

'Brimstone and gall,' thundered Hook. 'What mischief is afoot here.' His face had gone black with rage, but he could see that his two men were not lying. 'Lads,' he said. 'I gave no such order.'

'Then something very odd's been going on here,' said Smee.

Hook's voice quivered a little as he turned towards the lagoon. Beads of cold sweat glistened on his brow. 'Spirit that haunts this dark lagoon tonight,' he cried. 'Do you hear me?'

Of course Peter should have kept quiet, but he didn't. He immediately answered in Hook's voice. 'Odds, Bobs, hammer and tongs, I hear you.'

Hook did not blink, but Smee and Starkey clung to each other in terror. 'Who are you stranger? Speak,' Hook demanded.

'I am James Hook,' replied the voice, 'Captain of the Jolly Roger.'

'You are not. You are not!' Hook cried hoarsely.

'Brimstone and gall,' the voice answered. 'Say that again and I'll spike you with an anchor.'

Hook changed his tack. 'If you are Hook, who am I?'

'A codfish,' came the reply. 'Only a codfish.'

'A codfish!' Hook echoed. He saw the two men draw back, looking at him most strangely. They were wondering whether their captain really was a codfish.

Hook began to think he was losing his mind. But he was not beaten yet. He began a guessing game. 'Hook,' he called out. 'Have you another voice?'

Peter could never resist a game and he answered quite naturally in his own voice. 'I have.'

'And another name?'

'Aye, aye.'

'Vegetable?' asked the real Hook.

'No.'

'Mineral?'

'No.'

'Animal?'

'Yes.'

'Man?' asked Hook.

'No!' said Peter indignantly.

'Boy?'

'Yes.'

'Ordinary boy?'

'No!'

'Wonderful boy?' asked Hook.

Wendy winced as Peter answered: 'Yes.'

Hook was still puzzled. 'You ask him some questions,' he said to the others, wiping the chilling sweat from his brow. The pirates could not think of anything to ask.

'Can't guess?' crowed Peter. 'Can't guess? Do you give up?'

Peter had given the pirates their chance. 'Yes, yes, we give up.'

'Well, then,' he cried proudly. 'I am Peter Pan.'

Pan! Peter Pan! In a moment Hook was himself again. 'Now we have him,' he shouted. 'Take him, dead or alive.'

Hook dived into the lagoon at the very moment Peter cried out: 'Are you ready boys?'

'Aye, aye,' came the reply from all around the lagoon.

'Then let's have at them,' cried Peter, seeing the boys burst from all corners of the lagoon.

The fight was short and sharp. First to draw blood was John, who bravely climbed into the boat and attacked Starkey. There was a fierce struggle as John tore his cutlass from him. Starkey wriggled overboard and John leapt after him as the dinghy drifted away.

Tootles led the attack on Smee and was slightly wounded in the ribs by the pirate's corkscrewing cutlass. But Smee himself was bloodied by Curley. Further from the rock, Starkey had escaped from John and was now battling Slightly and the twins. When Starkey swam off again, the boys found themselves surrounding Hook.

They were all brave boys and should not be blamed for backing away from the pirate captain as his swirling iron claw made a circle of dead water round him. The boys fled like fishes.

But there was one who did not fear him; there was one prepared to enter the circle. But strangely Peter and Hook did not meet in the water. Hook clambered onto the rock to catch his breath and at that moment Peter climbed on at the other end. The rock was slippery and they had to crawl rather than climb. Neither knew that the other one was coming.

Each feeling his way in the darkness, it was not until they actually grabbed each other's arm by accident and came face to face, that they met.

Peter was not scared. He gnashed his teeth with joy at meeting his enemy. Thinking very quickly, he snatched a knife from Hook's belt and was about to drive it home, when he saw that he was higher up the rock than his foe. It would not have been fair, so he gave the pirate a hand to help him up.

It was then that Hook bit him. It was not the pain but the unfairness of it which dazed Peter, especially after he had helped Hook up the rock. The shock of Hook's unfair play made him quite helpless. Twice the iron hand clawed him. Peter seemed doomed to die by the dreaded hook.

'Tick! Tick! Tick! Tick!' Hook heard the familiar sound with dread. A few moments later the boys saw Hook in the water striking out wildly for the ship. There was no look of triumph on his face, just pure fear. The crocodile was on his tail!

Normally the boys would have swum alongside cheering, but now they were searching for Peter and Wendy, calling out over the lagoon.

There was no answer, just the mocking laughter of the mermaids. 'They must be swimming back, or flying,' the boys decided. They were not worried because they had such faith in Peter. They just chuckled, knowing they would be late for bed; and it was all Mother Wendy's fault.

*   *   *

When the voices of the boys had died away, a cold silence came over the lagoon, and then a feeble cry was heard. 'Help! Help!'

Two small figures were in the water beside the rock. Wendy had fainted and lay in Peter's arms. With one last effort Peter pulled her up on the rock and then lay down beside her. He saw that the water level was rising fast and knew they would soon be drowned. Peter Pan would be no more.

As they lay side by side, a mischievous mermaid caught

Wendy by the feet, and began pulling her softly into the water. Peter, feeling her slip from him, was just in time to drag her back. But he had to tell her the truth.

'We are on the rock, Wendy,' he said. 'But it is growing smaller. Soon the water will cover it. We must go.'

'Yes,' said Wendy quietly. 'Shall we swim or fly, Peter?'

'Could you swim or fly as far as the island without me?' he asked.

She had to admit that she was too exhausted and Peter's head sunk at the answer. 'I can't help you,' he said. 'Hook wounded me. I can neither swim or fly.'

'Do you mean we will both be drowned?'

They put their hands over their eyes to avoid looking at the rising water. As they waited for the end, something brushed against Peter. It was as light as a kiss and it stayed on his cheek, as if to say: 'Can I help?' It was the tail of a kite which Michael had made a few days earlier. In a high wind it had torn itself out of his hand and floated away.

'Michael's kite,' said Peter, looking up at the fluttering object. 'If it lifted Michael off the ground, why should it not carry you?'

'Both of us,' said Wendy.

'It can't lift two,' said Peter. 'Michael and Curly tried.'

'Let us draw lots,' said Wendy bravely.

But Peter was already tying the tail of the kite round her. At first she refused to go without him, but then with a 'Goodbye' he pushed her from the rock. In a few minutes she was carried out of his sight. Peter was alone on the rock.

The rock was a very small one now and soon it would be under water. Pale rays of light tiptoed across the lagoon and Peter heard the saddest and most musical sound in the world, the mermaids calling to the moon.

The sound even frightened Peter a little. But that did not stop him from standing up and boldly saying: 'To die will be a very big adventure.'

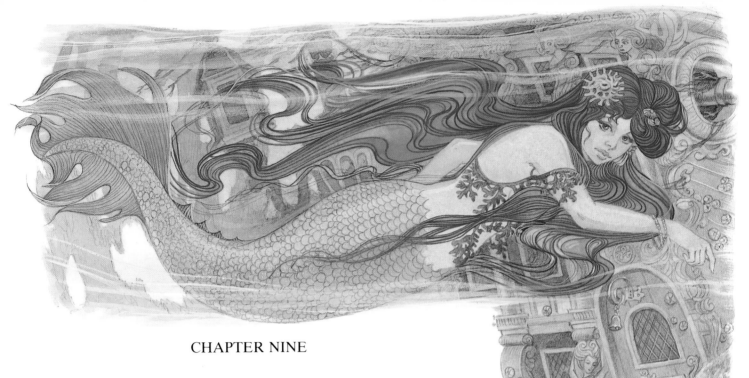

CHAPTER NINE

The Never Bird

Peter was quite alone on Marooners' Rock and he saw the mermaids, one by one, swimming off to their bedchambers. They spend the night in coral caves, and the door to each one has a tiny bell on it. Every time the doors open or shut the bell rings out. Peter heard the bells ring from the sea bottom as the mermaids went off to bed.

The water around Marooners' Rock rose until it was lapping at Peter's feet. To pass the time until he was finally swallowed up, Peter watched the only thing moving on the lagoon. He thought it was a bit of floating paper, perhaps part of the kite. He wondered idly how long it would take to drift ashore.

But soon after he noticed an odd thing. Whatever was moving out there had a purpose because it was fighting the tide. Peter, always happy to support the underdog, could not help clapping each time the piece of paper gained a few yards against the tide. It was such a brave piece of paper.

It was not really a piece of paper; it was the Never bird, sitting on her nest, making desperate efforts to reach Peter. By flapping her wings, she was somehow able to guide her strange boat. By the time Peter saw her she was absolutely exhausted. She had come to save him, even if it meant losing the eggs she was sitting on. It was the bird's way of thanking Peter for ordering everyone to leave her in peace when the nest fell in the water.

The Never bird called out to Peter, trying to tell him what she was doing. Peter shouted back, asking what she was doing. Now, many people think that birds and strange boys like Peter can understand each other's languages, but the truth must be told. Not only could they not understand each other, they also forgot their manners.

'I . . . want . . . you . . . to . . . get . . . into . . . the . . . nest . . .,' the bird called, speaking as slowly and distinctly as possible. 'I . . . am . . . too . . . tired . . . to . . . bring . . . it . . . any . . . nearer . . . Can . . . you . . . swim . . . to . . . me?'

'What are you quacking about?' said Peter.

The Never bird became irritated. They do have very short tempers. 'You dunderhead little boy,' she screamed. 'Why don't you do as I tell you?'

Peter was sure she was calling him names and shouted at her again. Then they both snapped at each other.

'Shut up!'

'Shut up!'

Nevertheless the Never bird was determined to save Peter and with one last mighty effort, she paddled herself to the rock. Then up she flew, deserting her eggs.

At last Peter understood and clutched the nest and jumped aboard, waving his thanks to the bird which now fluttered overhead. Like a worrying mother, she wanted to see what he did with her eggs.

There were two large white eggs and Peter lifted them up. The bird covered her face with her wings. She could hardly bear to see what happened to her eggs, but she could not help peeping through her feathers.

Peter was busy thinking. He had seen the old pole which had been driven into Marooners' Rock long ago to mark the site of buried treasure. The children had discovered the glittering hoard and, when in playful mood, used to fling showers of diamonds, pearls and pieces of eight at the gulls. Thinking it was food, the gulls would pounce on the gems and then fly away in a rage at the scurvy trick which had been played on them.

But the pole was still there and on it Starkey had hung his wide-brimmed tarpaulin waterproof hat. Peter put the eggs in the hat and pushed it out onto the lagoon. It floated beautifully.

The Never bird saw at once what he was up to and flew down and once more settled snugly on her eggs. Meanwhile Peter got into the nest, took the pole as a mast and hung up his shirt for a sail.

*Meanwhile Peter got into the nest, took the pole
as a mast and hung up his shirt for a sail.*

The Never bird drifted in one direction and he floated off in another, both cheering each other for being so clever, though Peter thought he had been especially smart.

When Peter reached dry land, he left the nest where the Never bird would quickly find it. But the hat was such a fine nest that she abandoned the nest altogether.

In days to come when Starkey walked by the shores, he would look out jealously at the bird sitting in his hat. And, strange to tell, all Never birds now build their nest in the shape of a broad-brimmed hat.

* * *

There was great rejoicing when Peter reached the home under the ground. Wendy had got back already and every boy had adventures to tell. Perhaps the best thing was that all of them were several hours late for bed. In fact they tried everything to stay up even later, demanding bandages for make-believe wounds.

Wendy, who was so happy to have everyone at home again, would have none of it. 'To bed! To bed!' she ordered in a voice that had to be obeyed.

Next day, however, she let them have their way. She gave out bandages to everyone, and they played until bedtime at a special game of limping about and carrying their arms in slings.

CHAPTER TEN

The Happy Home

The most important result of the adventure on Mermaids' Lagoon was that the redskins became the boys' greatest friends and allies. Peter had saved Tiger Lily from a dreadful fate, and now there was nothing she and her braves would not do for him.

All night they sat above the home under the ground, guarding everyone against the big attack by the pirates, which clearly was going to come very soon. In the meantime they smoked their peace pipes.

They called Peter the Great White Father, and almost worshipped him. Peter liked this tremendously. 'The Great White Father,' he would say, 'is glad to see the Piccaninny warriors protecting his wigwam from the pirates.'

'Me Tiger Lily,' the princess would say. 'Peter Pan save me, me his best friend. Me no let pirates hurt him.'

'It is good,' Peter would say. 'Peter Pan has spoken.'

That meant that it was time for the redskins to shut up. And they always obeyed. But they did not treat the other boys with such respect. They looked on the boys as very ordinary braves and said 'How-do?' to them and things like that. The boys did not like it, but Peter thought it quite right that they should be treated in a less important way.

Secretly Wendy sympathized with the boys a little, but she was too loyal a housewife to listen to any complaints against father. 'Father knows best,' she always said. But her private opinion was that the redskins should not call her squaw.

The redskins were at their posts above the home one evening when the children were having their evening meal. Peter had gone out to find the time for Wendy. The way you got time on the island was to find the crocodile and then stay near it until the clock struck the hour.

The meal happened to be a make-believe tea, and they all sat round the table guzzling everything they could imagine. They were in a boisterous mood, chattering and playing about. The noise was deafening. If Wendy had said 'Silence!' once, she had said it twenty times.

Sometimes there were disputes between the boys. But it was a golden rule that no one could hit back during meals. Instead they had to shout, 'I complain of so-and-so', and Wendy would settle the argument.

'Have you finished your milk, yet?' she asked Slightly.

'Almost,' said Slightly, looking into his imaginary mug.

'No, he hasn't,' said Nibs. 'He hasn't even begun to drink it.'

That was enough to cause a fight and Slightly seized his chance. His hand shot into the air. 'I complain of Nibs,' he cried.

John's hand, however, was up first. 'May I sit in father's chair?'

Wendy was shocked. 'Certainly not. Only father can sit there.'

'He is not really our father,' said John. 'He didn't even know what a father was until I told him.'

The twins decided John was grumbling far too much. 'We complain of John,' they cried.

Tootles held up his hand. 'I don't suppose I could be father,' he said very quietly.

Wendy was always very gentle with Tootles. 'No, I'm afraid you can't.'

Tootles said very little, but once he had said something he had a silly way of going on. 'Then, if I can't be father, I don't suppose, Michael, you would let me be baby?'

'No, I won't,' said Michael, who was already in his hanging basket.

'If I can't be a baby,' said Tootles, 'can I be a twin?'

'No,' replied the twins. 'It's awfully difficult to be a twin.'

Tootles did not give up. 'If I can't be anything important,

would any of you like to see me do a trick?'

'No!' they all replied.

Then they all set about each other, shouting, arguing, squabbling and, of course, complaining.

'I complain of the twins.'

'I complain of Nibs.'

'I complain of Curly.'

So much noise, so much fun. 'Oh. Oh dear,' said Wendy at last. 'I'm sure I sometimes think that children are more trouble than they are worth.'

Wendy told the boys to clear away and sat down at her work basket. There was a huge collection of socks to darn and every pair had holes in the toes.

Then it was Michael's turn to grumble. 'Wendy,' he said. 'I'm too big for this cradle.'

'You must stay there,' said Wendy. 'You are the smallest boy here and there must always be a baby in a cradle in every house.'

That put Michael in his place and the other boys began to dance. It was such a happy scene which met Peter on his return. He brought nuts for the boys and the right time for Wendy. 'You really spoil the boys,' she said.

'Aye, old lady,' said Peter.

'It was me who told Peter mothers are called old lady,' said Michael.

'I complain of Michael,' said Curly instantly, thinking he was boasting. But there was no time to listen to his complaint because the first twin went up to Peter and said everyone wanted to do some more dancing.

'Dance away, my little man,' said Peter, who was in great spirits.

'But we want you to dance,' said the twin.

Peter was really the best dancer of all but he was in playful mood. 'What, me!' he cried. 'My old bones would rattle.'

'But it's Saturday night,' said Slightly. 'You must dance.'

It was not really Saturday night. At least it might have been, but they had long lost count of the days. But if anyone wanted to do something special they always said it was Saturday night.

'Of course it is Saturday night, Peter,' said Wendy.

So they all danced that night and later, as the boys got ready for bed, Peter and Wendy talked. 'I was just thinking,' he said. 'It is only make-believe that I am their father?'

'Oh, yes,' said Wendy.

'You see,' he went on, 'it would make me seem so old if I was
their father.'

'But the boys do belong to us,' said Wendy. 'They are yours
and mine.'

'But not really,' said Peter, a little worried.

'Not if you don't want them to be,' answered Wendy, hearing
Peter sigh with relief. 'But what do you really think of me?'

'I am your devoted son,' said Peter.

Wendy had guessed as much. Peter would always be a boy,
even if she would have liked him to grow up. Peter's mother she
would have to be.

'It's very odd,' said Peter. 'You are the same as Tiger Lily.
She doesn't want to be my mother either. Perhaps Tinker Bell
will be my mother.'

Tink had only one answer. 'You silly ass.'

Wendy had heard Tink say the words so often that she now
knew what they meant. 'I almost agree with her,' said Wendy.

When the children were ready for bed, they had more dances.
Wendy sang a song and it was such a haunting tune that the
children danced, pretending to be afraid of their own shadows.
Little did they know that other more frightening shadows would
soon be on them.

But for that moment all was to be fun. They danced, sang,
fought with pillows and tried to tell stories.

Even Slightly tried to tell a story that night, but the beginning
was so terribly dull that even he found it boring. 'Yes, it is a dull
story,' he confessed. 'Let's pretend my beginning is the end.'

And then at last they all got into bed to listen to Wendy's
story. It was the story the boys loved best, and the one Peter
hated most. Usually when she began this story he left the room
or put his hands over his ears. If he had done either, things
might have turned out differently. But tonight, the Night of
Nights as they came to call it, he remained on his mushroom
stool to listen.

CHAPTER ELEVEN

Wendy's Story

'Listen then,' said Wendy, settling down to tell her story with Michael at her feet and the other boys in bed. 'There was once a gentleman . . . '

'I wish it was a lady,' interrupted Curley.

'I wish he'd been a white rat,' said Nibs.

'Quiet!' said Wendy. 'There was a lady, too.'

'I hope she isn't dead,' said Tootles.

'Oh, no, she's not dead,' said Wendy.

'A little less noise from you, children,' called out Peter, who was determined that Wendy should finish the story, however boring he thought it was.

'The gentleman's name,' continued Wendy, 'was Mr Darling, and her name was Mrs Darling.'

'I think I knew them once,' said Michael, a little unsure.

'They were married, you know,' said Wendy, 'and what do you think they had?'

'White rats,' cried Nibs, inspired.

'No,' said Wendy. 'They had three children and those three children had a faithful nurse, a dog called Nana. But Mr Darling was angry with Nana one day and chained her up in the yard, and so all the children flew away. They flew away to the Neverland where the lost children are.'

'I thought that's what they did,' said Curly, excitedly. 'I don't know how, but I just knew they did.'

'Oh, Wendy,' cried Tootles. 'Was one of the lost children called Tootles?'

'Yes, of course he was.'

Tootles was overcome with excitement. 'I'm in a story, Nibs. I'm in a story!'

'Hush,' said Wendy. 'Now I want you to think how unhappy Mr and Mrs Darling were after their children flew away. Think of the empty beds.'

'It's terribly sad,' said one of the twins.

'I don't see how this story can have a happy ending,' said the second twin. 'Do you Nibs?'

Wendy went on. 'If you know how great a mother's love can be, you should not be frightened how this story will end.'

Peter hated talk of mothers, and he really disliked this part of the story. 'You see,' said Wendy, 'the heroine of this story knew that her mother would always leave the nursery window open so the children could fly back in. That's why these children stayed away for years and had a lovely time.'

'Did they ever go back?' asked Slightly.

Wendy was not ready to give the ending of the story away so quickly. 'Let's take a peep into the future,' she said. 'The years have rolled by and who is this elegant lady I see. I don't know how old she is but I see her getting off a train at London station . . .'

'Oh, Wendy, who is she?' cried Nibs excitedly, as if he didn't know.

'Can it be,' said Wendy, screwing up her eyes to look closer. 'Can it be . . . yes . . . no . . . yes . . . it is Wendy.'

Cries of delight echoed from the big bed.

'And who are the two noble gentlemen I see with her?' continued Wendy. 'Can they be John and Michael? They are!'

'Oh,' cried the boys.

'You see, dear brothers,' she said looking at John and then Michael. 'The window was still open. The children were right to trust in their mother's love. The children flew back to their mother and father and I cannot describe how happy the scene was.'

That was Wendy's story and everyone except Peter enjoyed it. He let out a sad groan.

'What is it, Peter?' asked Wendy.

'It's a pain,' he said.

'What kind of pain is it?' said Wendy.

Peter Pan said it was not so much a pain as an ache in his heart. 'Wendy,' said Peter. 'You are wrong about mothers.'

What Peter said frightened the children and they all gathered around him to hear something he had never told them before. 'Long ago,' he said, 'I thought like Wendy. I thought my mother would always keep the window open for me. So I stayed away for moons and moons before flying back. But I found the window was barred. My mother had forgotten all about me and there was another little boy sleeping in my bed.'

Now, whether this was true is another matter. But at that moment Peter thought he was telling the truth. 'Are you sure mothers are like that?' asked the boys.

'Yes, indeed,' answered Peter.

'Mothers are toads then,' said the boys.

John and Michael cried out as one. 'Wendy, let us go home.'

'Yes,' she said, clutching both of them in her arms.

'No, not tonight,' said the lost boys.

'Yes, we must go at once,' said Wendy. 'Perhaps mother already thinks we are never coming back.'

The sudden sadness at that thought made Wendy forget Peter's feelings, and she said to him quite sharply: 'Peter, will you make the necessary arrangements?'

'If you wish it,' he replied, as coolly as if she'd asked him to pass the nuts. He was not going to show he cared if Wendy didn't.

There was not so much as a "sorry-you're-going" from either of them. But of course he cared very much. Peter was feeling very angry about grown-ups who, as usual, seemed to be spoiling everything. 'I'll go and make the arrangements,' said Peter, hurrying to his tree. Once inside he took a series of quick breaths. In the Neverland there is a saying that every time you breathe a grown-up dies. Peter was killing them off as fast as he could.

When Peter left, the lost boys began to panic about losing Wendy. 'We can't let her go,' said one.

'Let's keep her prisoner,' said another.

'Aye. Chain her up.'

Wendy turned to Tootles for help. He might have been the silliest boy but he knew what to say. 'I am just Tootles, and nobody ever listens to me. But the first boy who does not behave like a gentleman towards Wendy will have a bloodied nose from me.'

The others stood back uneasily and just then Peter returned. They knew they would get no support from him. He would never keep a girl in the Neverland against her will.

'Wendy,' he said, striding up and down unhappily, 'I have asked the redskins to guide you through the wood, as flying tires you so much.'

Wendy thanked him and Peter gave Nibs orders to wake Tinker Bell. Nibs had to knock twice before he got an answer, though Tink had really been sitting up in bed listening for some time.

'You are to get up, Tink,' said Nibs. 'Peter wants you to take Wendy on a journey.'

Tink had been delighted to hear that Wendy was going, but she was jolly sure that she wasn't going to be the one to take her. So she snapped angrily at Nibs and pretended to go to sleep again.

Peter heard what had been going on and marched to the young fairy's bedroom. 'Tink,' he said, 'if you don't get up and dress at once, I will open the curtains and then we will all see you in your night-dress.'

That made Tink leap to the floor. 'Who said I wasn't getting up?' she cried.

Meanwhile the boys were looking sadly at Wendy, John and Michael, now ready for the journey. They were sad and dejected, not just because they were about to lose their mother, but also because they thought she was going off somewhere nice, somewhere they had not been invited.

Wendy felt a tear coming into her eye. 'Dear ones,' she said. 'If you all come with me, I'm sure my father and mother would adopt you. You could all stay at my house.'

The invitation was meant especially for Peter, but each of the boys was thinking just of himself. They jumped at the invitation. 'Peter, can we all go?' they asked.

'All right,' said Peter, bitterly. 'You can go.' The boys rushed away to get their things packed, leaving Wendy and Peter together.

Wendy was determined to give Peter some medicine before they all set off. She loved to give the boys medicine and really gave them far too much. It was only water but she poured it from the kernel of a fruit and counted out the drops. This made it always seem like real medicine.

Wendy was ready to give it to Peter when she saw such a sad look on his face. 'Come on Peter,' she said. 'Pack your things and we'll be away.'

'No,' he replied. 'I'm not going with you, Wendy. Who
knows, if I did, I might be forced to grow up. I want to stay
a boy and have fun.' Then he skipped up and down the room,
pretending to play merrily on his pipes. She actually had to run
after him to say one more thing.

'We could find your mother,' she said softly.

Now, Peter, if ever he really did have a mother, no longer
missed her. He could do very well without one, and he said so.
Wendy tried to persuade him once more but it was no good.
Peter's mind was made up. 'Peter isn't coming,' she explained to
the lost boys.

Each now carried their things, wrapped in a bundle tied to the
end of a stick. 'If you find your mothers,' said Peter, 'I hope
you'll like them. Now then, no fuss or crying, good-bye.'

Wendy had to shake his hand as there was no sign he would
prefer a thimble. 'You will remember to keep your clothes
clean, Peter,' she said. 'And make sure you take your medicine.'

An awkward pause followed and Peter broke the silence by
calling for Tink. 'Are you ready, Tinker Bell?'

'Aye, aye,' replied Tink.

'Then lead the way.'

Tink darted up the nearest tree, but no one had the chance to
follow because it was at that moment that the pirates made their
attack on the redskins. The air was filled with shrieks and the
clash of steel.

Below there was dead silence as everyone listened open-
mouthed to the battle above. Then Wendy fell on her knees and
turned to Peter. Everyone else turned to Peter as if asking him
not to desert them now.

As for Peter, he seized his sword. The excitement of battle
was in his eye.

never do up. Which ever way they tried, there never seemed
enough rope to go round him. When they tried to pack Slightly
in one part, he bulged out in another.

Hook came over to see why Slightly was causing so much
trouble. 'Aha,' he cried in triumph, 'I have discovered his
secret.'

The truth was that Slightly loved to drink water so much that
his stomach had blown up out of all proportion to his proper
size. Without telling any of the other boys, he had carved away
his tree to make it fit him, rather than reducing himself to fit the
tree. Now his tree had been hollowed out enough for even a
grown man to slip down. 'That tree will fit me nicely,' sneered
Hook.

Slightly was finally tied up and Hook thought for a moment
how he would carry all the children away. 'Ho,' he said, looking
at the house the boys had built for Wendy. 'That will do.'

The children were thrown into the house and four stout
pirates raised it on their shoulders. Then, with the other pirates
marching behind and singing their hateful pirate chorus, the
procession set off through the wood. Just as the little house
disappeared into the forest, the tiny chimney let out a brave
little column of smoke as if defying Hook to the last.

Hook saw it as he went about his dastardly business. He
tip-toed to Slightly's tree and listened. Not a sound. Was Peter
asleep, wondered Hook, or was he waiting at the foot of
Slightly's tree with a dagger in his hand? There was no way of
knowing except by going down. Hook took off his cloak, slipped
into the tree and descended into the unknown.

He arrived at the foot of the tree and in the dim light looked
into the room. There on the great bed lay Peter, fast asleep.

Peter had been unaware of the tragedy above. After the
children left, he played gaily on his pipes for a while,
determined to prove to himself that he did not care a jot about
them leaving Neverland. Then he had gone to bed, lying on the
top of the cover rather than snugly underneath. He only did that
to spite Wendy because she always tucked him up in case the
night turned chilly. He saw the medicine that Wendy had left
him and he ignored that too.

In truth Peter felt like crying as he began to doze, but he
thought it would annoy Wendy more if he laughed instead. So
he let out a deep laugh and fell asleep in the middle of it. One
arm dropped over the edge of the bed and a leg arched into the
air. The unfinished part of his laugh was still on his wide-open

He tip-toed to Slightly's tree and listened.

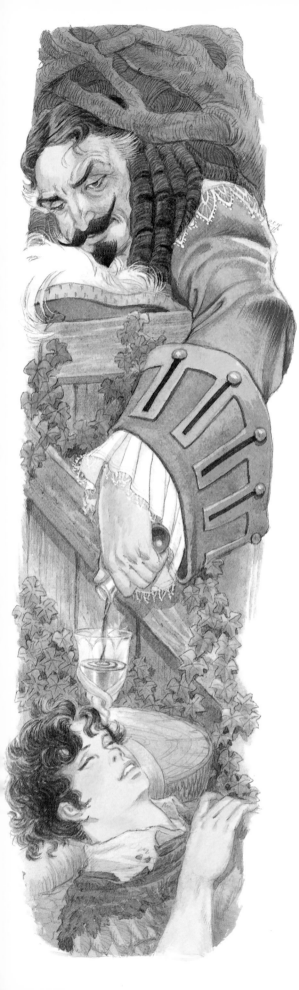

mouth, his pearly teeth gleaming brightly.

Hook looked on and thought for a brief moment what a pretty scene it made. Just sometimes Hook revealed another side to his character. It's said that he liked flowers and gentle music. The man was not all evil. If the nicer side of Hook had been in control then, he might have left Peter to sleep on so peacefully. But he looked again.

Hook saw Peter's smiling open mouth. 'Odds bods,' thought Hook, his black heart taking charge again. 'Pan is so cocky! He's even cocky when he's asleep!'

A light from the lamp shone dimly on the bed, but Hook stood in darkness himself. He stepped forward and found something in his way; the door of Slightly's tree. It did not completely fill the doorway and Hook had been looking over the top of it. Searching for the catch to open it, Hook found to his fury that it was too low down to reach. Angrily he rattled the door and pushed himself against it. It would not budge. Was his enemy to escape him after all?

That was the moment Hook saw Peter's medicine. It was just within reach and an idea came to him. Hook always carried a small bottle containing a deadly poison, just in case he should ever be captured alive. He would rather die by his own hand. Now Hook put five drops of the poison into Peter's medicine glass.

He took one long triumphant look at his victim, as if to say victory was his, and slid up the tree. Donning his hat and wrapping his cloak around him, Hook vanished into the trees muttering to himself in delight at what he had done.

Peter slept on. But just before ten o'clock by crocodile time, he was woken by a gentle tapping on the door of his tree. 'Who's that?' he asked, reaching for his dagger.

There was no answer and he called out once more. Again there was no answer. He got up and went to the door. 'I won't open the door unless you speak,' said Peter.

Then at last he heard a lovely bell-like voice. It was Tink and he quickly undid the door. 'Whatever has happened?' asked Peter.

Tink took a deep breath and, in one long unbroken sentence, told how Wendy and the boys had been captured by the pirates. 'Poor Wendy. I'll rescue her,' cried Peter.

Before setting out he decided to do something to please Wendy. He would take the medicine she had left him. He reached for the glass. 'No!' shrieked Tinker Bell, who had heard

Hook muttering as he sped through the forest. 'Hook has poisoned it.'

'Don't be silly,' said Peter. 'How could Hook have got down here? He's far too big to get down one of our trees. Besides I never fall asleep.'

'I don't know,' said Tink in desperation. 'But he has definitely poisoned your medicine. He has. He has.'

Peter would not listen. He raised the cup and was about to swallow the deadly contents when Tink, in one lightning movement, flew between his lips and drained the glass herself. 'How dare you drink my medicine,' he snapped.

But Tink did not answer. She was already feeling very ill. 'What is the matter with you?' asked Peter.

'It was poisoned,' she said softly, 'and now I am going to be dead.'

'Oh, Tink,' said Peter. 'You drank it to save me. Why?'

Her wings would scarcely carry Tink now, but in reply the adoring fairy dropped onto his shoulder and gave his chin a very loving bite. She whispered in his ear, 'You silly ass' and then fluttered weakly to her room and lay down on the bed.

Peter's head almost filled Tink's room as he looked in and saw that her light was fading. If it went out he knew she would be no more. Peter began to cry huge tears and Tink thought they were so beautiful that she put out her fingers and let the tears flow over them. Then she tried to speak.

Her voice was so low that Peter could hardly hear her. 'Peter,' she said, 'I think I would get well again if the children of the world believed in fairies.'

Peter flung out his arms and called out to all the children: 'Do you believe in fairies?'

Tink sat up in bed to hear her fate. She fancied she heard the children say 'Yes!' But Peter was not sure. He called out again. 'If you believe in fairies, clap your hands. Don't let Tink die.'

This time the sound of distant clapping filled the skies above the house. A few little brats did hiss, but most of the world's children seemed to be clapping that night.

The sound stopped as quickly as it had started, as if every mother had rushed into their children's nursery to discover what on earth was going on. But Tink had already been saved.

Tink's light grew brighter, she sprang from her bed and flashed through the room as cheekily as ever. She did not give a thought to thanking the clapping children who had saved her. And who knows what she would have done if she had got her

hands on the children who hissed.

'Now!' said Peter. 'To rescue Wendy.'

Peter scuttled up his tree. Outside again, he saw that the moon was riding high and snow had fallen on the ground.

He could not be sure where the children had been taken because the snow had hidden all the footprints, and the island was now filled with a deathly silence. He would have liked to wait until morning and daylight, but time was running out.

Just then the crocodile passed him, but not another living thing moved. He knew well that sudden death might be waiting for him at the next tree, or even stalking him from behind.

But nothing could frighten him on this night, and he swore a terrible oath: 'Hook or me this time.'

Peter thought about flying but he did not want to give himself away to anyone. So he decided to travel like the redskins. He crawled forward like a snake, leaping up now and again to dart across a clearing on which the moonlight was shining. He dashed along with one finger pressed on his lip and a dagger at the ready. Peter Pan was as happy as could be.

CHAPTER THIRTEEN

The Pirate Ship

One dim, grim light flickered over Kidd's Creek, which is near the mouth of the Pirate River. There lay the brig, the Jolly Roger. She was an evil, dirty-looking ship whose masts and rigging had been repaired with pieces from other ships. The Jolly Roger was a cannibal of the high seas.

The ship was almost silent, except for the sound of the ship's sewing machine at which the hard-working Smee was sitting. A few of the pirates were leaning on the side of the ship drinking rum, and others were playing dice or cards, using rotten barrels for tables. Some pirates, who were sleeping, had taken up positions as far away as possible from Hook's reach, in case he should claw them in passing.

Hook was on the main deck deep in thought. It was his moment of triumph. Peter was dead and all the other boys were on the ship, about to walk the dreaded plank. Yet he was not happy because he was so alone. Hook never felt more alone than when he was with his ragged mob of men. He hated them and they had no great love for him. 'No little children love me either,' he thought.

Hook was not a man to be envied. You could almost feel sorry for him at times.

Hook looked with envy at Smee. Now, there was a man who always thought that every child lived in fear of him. Fear him! Fear Smee! There was not a child on board who did not already love the man. Smee had said horrid things to the children and gently cuffed them with the palm of his hand, because he would not hit with his fist. The children had only liked him more, and Michael had even tried on his spectacles.

Hook would have loved to tell Smee how much the children liked him. But it would be too cruel a thing to do. How could Hook say that to a man who was quite sure he was the most frightening pirate.

Hook's oddly gentle thoughts were interrupted when some of the men started to dance. 'Quiet, you scugs,' he cried, 'or I'll throw the anchor at you. Are all the children chained, so they cannot fly away?'

'Aye, aye,' the pirates replied.

'Then bring them up from below,' said Hook.

All the sad prisoners, except Wendy, were dragged from the dark hold and lined up in front of Hook. 'Now then, me bully boys,' he said. 'Six of you will walk the plank tonight, but I need two cabin boys. Which of you will it be?'

Wendy had told all the boys not to upset Hook, so Tootles stepped forward politely to explain his problem. 'You see, sir, I don't think my mother would like me to be a pirate. Would your mother, Slightly?'

Slightly did not think his mother would like him to be a pirate either. Nor did any of the other boys who stepped forward.

Hook grew angry. 'You, boy,' he said, speaking to John. 'You look as if you have pluck. Did you ever want to be a pirate, my hearty?'

John had indeed. 'I once thought of calling myself Red-handed Jack,' he answered.

'That's a good name, too,' said Hook. 'That's what we'll call you if you join us.'

Michael did not want to be left out. 'What would I be called if I joined?' he asked.

'Blackbeard Joe,' said John, much to Michael's delight. But then Hook told them that they would have to swear 'Down with the King' if they joined. 'Then I refuse,' said John, and Michael said the same.

'Rule Britannia,' squeaked Curly.

Hook's black face turned red with anger. 'That seals your doom. Bring up their mother, get the plank ready.'

They were only young boys and they went white when they saw Jukes and Cecco preparing the plank. But they tried to look brave when Wendy arrived on deck.

No words can describe how Wendy hated those pirates. The boys could at least see some glamour in being a pirate, but all Wendy saw was a ship which hadn't been scrubbed for years. The port holes were so grimy you could scrawl 'Dirty Pig' on every one with your finger. And Wendy had written it several times already.

'So, my beauty,' said Hook. 'You are to see your children walk the plank.'

'Are they all to die?' she asked.

'They are,' he snarled. 'You have time for a few last words with them.'

Wendy told them to be brave. 'Your real mothers would hope that you died like true English gentlemen,' she said.

'We will,' they all cried. Even the pirates were awed by their bravery.

'Tie Wendy to the mast!' cried Hook.

Smee tied Wendy to the mast and when it was done, he whispered: 'I'll save you if you promise to be my mother.' But Wendy replied that she would rather have no children at all.

The boys shivered as Hook, smiling through clenched teeth, took a step towards them. Their time had come.

'Tick! Tick! Tick! Tick! Tick! Tick!'

Everyone heard it, pirates, boys and Wendy. Hook stopped dead in his tracks. He listened in terror for a moment and then fell into a heap, his iron claw lying limply beside him. He began to crawl along the deck, trying to get as far away from the dreaded ticking noise as possible. 'Hide me!' he cried to his men.

They gathered round him, every man's eyes turned away from the terrible creature which was about to come aboard. They did not even think of fighting. If a crocodile was coming, then that was their fate.

Only when Hook was hidden by a circle of pirates did the boys' curiosity lead them to look over the side of the ship to see the crocodile. They got the surprise of their lives. There was no crocodile. It was Peter.

Peter put his finger to his lips to tell them to keep quite. Then he went on ticking.

CHAPTER FOURTEEN
'Hook or Me This Time'

As Peter climbed up the side of the ship, he was thinking how clever he had been. When he left the home under the ground, he had seen the crocodile pass by. It was not until he was in the forest that he suddenly realized that the crocodile had stopped ticking. The clock had finally unwound itself and stopped.

The poor crocodile had lost its tick, its closest friend. Peter decided to put the creature's misfortune to his own use. He started ticking so that the other dangerous creatures of the forest would think he was the crocodile and let him pass safely.

He ticked very well indeed, but there was one unexpected result. The crocodile followed him all the way, probably thinking Peter had stolen its tick. But Peter stayed well ahead of the creature, thinking all the time: 'Hook or me this time'.

He had swum out to the ship and clambered up the side. He was thinking so hard about the battle ahead that he had forgotten to stop ticking. The idea of frightening Hook out of his wits by ticking had not crossed Peter's mind at all. But when he saw the pirates cowering in a corner, he understood what had happened.

He decided at once that, after all, he had thought up the idea. 'How clever of me,' he said to himself, indicating to the boys that it would not be a good idea to burst into applause just then.

It was at this moment that Ed Teynte, the ship's quartermaster, emerged from his cabin and came along the deck. Peter leapt into action, striking true and deep with his dagger. John clapped his hands on the ill-fated pirate's mouth to hide his dying groan. He fell forward and four boys caught him to prevent the thud on the deck. Peter gave the signal and quickly the body was cast overboard.

'That's number one gone,' said Slightly, who had begun to count.

Hook and the pirates heard the splash of the body hitting the water, and, thinking the crocodile had gone, turned around again. The boys were still there but Peter had already tip-toed into a cabin.

'The crocodile has gone,' announced Smee.

'Then I'll raise a cheer to Johnny Plank,' said Hook, raising himself to his full height and breaking into song.

> 'Yo ho, the frisky plank
> You walks along it so,
> Till it goes down and you goes down.
> To Davey Jones below.'

To frighten the boys even more he danced along an imaginary plank. 'Do you want a touch of the cat o' nine tails before you walk the plank?' he smirked.

'No, no,' they all cried. The hideous pirate just smiled and called on Jukes to fetch the dreaded whip. 'It's in the cabin.'

The cabin! Peter was in the cabin! The children stared at each other.

'Aye, aye,' said Jukes and marched into the cabin. The boys watched him go as Hook continued his song:

> 'Yo ho, yo ho, the scratching cat
> In tails of nine, you know,
> and when they are writ upon your back . . .'

What the last line was will never be known because there was a sudden screech from the cabin, followed by a familiar crowing sound. The boys knew whose crow that was.

'What was that?' said Hook.

'Number two,' said Slightly, very solemnly.

The Italian pirate Cecco rushed into the cabin and then came out almost immediately. 'What's the matter with Bill Jukes,

you dog,' hissed Hook, towering over the terrified Cecco.

'The matter with him,' said Cecco, 'is that he's dead, stabbed. But worse still the cabin's as black as a pit, and there is something terrible in there. It's crowing.'

The boys were looking far too cheerful at this stage and Hook saw their mischievous faces. 'Cecco,' he said in his most stately voice, 'go back in that cabin and fetch me that cock-a-doodle-doo.'

Cecco, bravest of the brave, shivered in his boots and cried: 'No! No!'

'Did you say you would not go?' said Hook, stroking his claw.

Cecco went and no sooner had he entered the cabin door than there was another deathly screech and again a crow. Nobody spoke except Slightly. 'Three,' he said.

'Death and odds fish,' thundered Hook. 'Who is to bring me that cock-a-doodle-doo?'

Starkey suggested they should wait for Cecco to come out, but Hook suggested that Starkey might volunteer to go in. 'No, by thunder,' said Starkey.

'By my hook,' said the captain. 'I think you did volunteer because I wouldn't want you to see how playful this hook can be.'

Starkey was determind not to go in and said he would rather swing from the rigging. The other pirates agreed with him completely.

'Is it mutiny, then?' asked Hook, so very politely. 'And Starkey is the ring-leader, is he?'

Every pirate knows that death is the only sentence for mutiny, and Starkey called for mercy. 'Shake hands, Starkey,' said Hook, advancing with his hook all of a twitch.

Starkey looked round for help but none came. He saw the red sparks in Hook's eye and took the only way out. With a despairing shout, he leapt into the sea and vanished.

'Four,' said Slightly.

Hook seized a lantern and swung his claw viciously in the air. 'Now,' he said. 'I'll bring out that cock-a-doodle-doo.' With that he disappeared into the cabin.

'Five.' How Slightly wanted to say the number. It was already on his lips when Hook came out again.

'Something blew my light out,' he said a little nervously. The pirates could see that their captain was not keen to go back into the cabin and talk of mutiny began again.

All pirates are superstitious and Cookson cried: 'They do say that a ship is cursed when there's one more on board than there should be. Is there a stranger on board?'

'Stranger or whatever,' said Mullins. 'Has this something in the cabin got a tail?'

'Has it got a hook?' asked another.

One by one the pirates began to panic and cry: 'The ship is doomed.' At that the children could not resist raising a cheer. Hook had almost forgotten his prisoners, but on looking round a smile lit up his face. 'Lads,' he cried to the crew. 'Here's an idea. Open the cabin door and drive the children in. Let them fight the cock-a-doodle-doo for us. If they kill him, we're so much the better. If he kills them we're none the worse.'

The pirates cheered their captain again and obeyed him instantly. The boys, pretending to struggle, were pushed into the cabin and the door closed.

'Now, let's listen,' said Hook. They all listened but none dared face the door. They turned their backs in fear. In the cabin Peter found the key to the boys' chains and quickly freed them. Then, armed with what weapons they could find, the boys crept out of the cabin.

Peter waved his hand, telling them all to hide, and then flew to the mast and freed Wendy. At that moment nothing could have been easier for them all than to fly away to safety, but one thing stopped Peter; his oath: 'Hook or me this time.'

He whispered to Wendy and she went off to hide with the others while he took her cloak and draped it around himself. Then he stood by the mast, pretending to be her, and took a deep breath and crowed.

The pirates, who still had their backs to the cabin, were panic stricken. Had the unknown creature killed all the boys now? 'Never mind the boys,' whispered Hook. 'I've thought it out. There's a Jonah aboard.'

The pirates all knew what a Jonah was. It was the name they gave to any person who brought bad luck and destruction to a ship. 'Aye,' they said, still feeling in mutinous mood, 'it's probably a man with a hook, and a name the same.'

'No, lads, no,' said Hook. 'It's the girl. A girl always brings bad luck to a pirate's ship. We'll be all right when she's gone.'

The men agreed and Hook told them to fling Wendy overboard. They rushed at the figure by the mast and Mullins cried out: 'no one can save you now!'

'There's one,' came a voice from beneath the cloak.

'Who's that?' said a very puzzled Mullins.

'Peter Pan the avenger,' came the terrible answer. As Peter spoke, he flung off the cloak. Every pirate gasped. So here was the terrible cock-a-doodle-doo.

Hook was speechless for a moment, but then he cried: 'Cleave him to the brisket, lads.'

The children could not imagine what that meant, but when Peter called out, 'Down boys and at them!' they rushed from their hiding places to attack. The pirates were so surprised that they ran in all directions, striking out wildly at anything. Man to man the pirates were stronger, but because they fought while running backwards, the boys could hunt them in pairs and choose which one to attack.

Some of the pirates leapt into the sea and others tried to hide. Slightly ran about with a lamp showing where they were. The pirates were half blinded in the light and quickly fell victim to the other boys' swords.

There was little to be heard except for the clang of weapons, an occasional screech or splash, and Slightly counting '-five-six-seven-eight-nine-ten-eleven.' The last of the pirates were no more when Hook was finally surrounded by a group of the boys. They kept coming closer and closer but all the time he kept them at bay with his swirling hook. One boy who got a little too close was caught by the hook and the captain used him as a shield.

Then another figure, who had just finished off Mullins, sprang into the circle. 'Put up your swords, boys,' cried the newcomer. 'This man is mine.'

Hook found himself face to face with Peter, and the others drew back. The two enemies looked at each other for a long time. Hook shuddered slightly, but there was a smile on Peter's face. 'So, Pan,' said Hook, at last. 'This is all your doing.'

'Aye, James Hook,' Peter answered, 'it is all my doing.'

'Then prepare to meet your doom, my cocky boy,' snarled Hook.

'Have at you,' cried Peter, and the fight began.

Peter was a superb swordsman. He moved so quickly, defending himself against any thrust by Hook with dazzling speed. But the boy was so much smaller than Hook that he could never quite reach the target with his sword.

Hook, not quite so nimble on his feet, was Peter's equal as a swordsman. Yet he was astonished how Peter managed to turn away all his thrusts. The captain began to use his hook as well. It flashed time and time again through the air, nearly slicing the

boy in two. Hook closed in for the kill.

The hook descended once more. But this time Peter doubled up, letting the dreaded weapon race past above his head. Then he darted forward and pierced Hook in the ribs with his sword.

Hook, you will remember, only feared one thing; the sight of his own blood. When he saw the wound in his ribs he dropped his sword in horror. He was at Peter's mercy. 'Now!' cried all the boys.

But Peter wanted to see fair play. He told Hook to pick up his sword again. Hook did not hesitate, but then he looked at Peter with a very worried eye. Until then Hook had thought he was fighting an ordinary fiend, but now he was beginning to wonder.

'Pan,' he said. 'Who and what are you?'

'I'm youth, I'm happiness,' Peter answered. 'I'm a little bird that has broken out of an egg.'

It was nonsense, of course, but it was proof to the unhappy Hook that Peter did not know who or what he was. 'To swords again,' cried Hook.

Hook now fought with true desperation, his sword sweeping through the air with such violence that it would have cut any man in two. But Peter moved so quickly, darting in now and then to prick his enemy once more in the ribs.

It was too much for Hook. He saw he was beaten and rushed off to the barrel where the pirates kept the gunpowder. Quickly he drew a light and lit a fuse. 'There!' he shouted. 'In two minutes the ship will be blown to bits.'

But it was no use. Peter flew to the barrel and threw the fuse overboard. It was a sign for the other boys to take to the air. They flew through the rigging and above the decks tormenting Hook with their swords. The captain staggered about, blindly lashing out at the boys who always stayed just out of reach.

Peter advanced on Hook again, cornering him at last. Hook leapt onto the side of the ship, ready to throw himself into the sea. It was the end. Hook knew it. But there was one thing he could still do to save his honour. As Peter flew towards him, Hook cried out: 'Don't waste you sword on me, just kick me into the water.'

That is what Peter did.

It was Hook's final triumph because everyone knows it is unfair to kick someone. 'That was unfair,' cried Hook as he tumbled towards the water.

Of course, Hook did not know that the crocodile was waiting for him below.

So died Captain James Hook.

'Seventeen,' sang out Slightly, but he was not quite correct with his figures. Fifteen pirates died, two escaped to shore. Starkey was captured by the redskins and forced to be a nurse to all their children. Smee escaped too, and he spent the rest of his days saying he was the only man that James Hook had feared.

Wendy took no part in the fight, but now she congratulated everyone. Then she took them into Hook's cabin and pointed to the clock. 'It's half past one,' she said. 'Time for bed.'

She put them all to bed in the pirates' bunks and then went to find Peter. He had been walking up and down the deck until he fell asleep by the Long Tom gun. He had been dreaming and was crying in his sleep. Wendy held him tight.

CHAPTER FIFTEEN

The Return Home

The morning after the fight everyone was up and about early because the pirate ship was rising and falling in a heavy sea. Tootles decided he was going to be bo'sun, the man in charge of the ship's sails and rigging. He set to his new job with enthusiasm, chewing tobacco like every good pirate. In fact they all put on pirates clothes, trousers cut off at the knee and red handkerchiefs for caps.

It does not need to be said who was captain, but Nibs and John were his first and second mate. There was one woman aboard as you might have guessed, but the rest were jolly jack tars, ordinary seamen. They lived in the fo'c'sle at the front of the ship.

Peter had already lashed himself to the wheel like every skipper did in rough weather, and he piped all his crew together to tell them what he expected of them.

'I know you are all pirate scum from the darkest dives of Rio and the Gold Coast,' he barked, as any good captain would. 'But you must do your duty like gallant hearties.'

The crew cheered him loudly as he shouted out a few sharp orders and then they turned the ship around, away from the island, and set a course for the mainland and home.

Captain Pan looked at his charts and calculated that if the good winds lasted, they should reach the Azores about June 21st. After that it would save time to fly.

The crew were a little undecided what sort of ship they wanted. Some wanted it to be a good and honest ship, but others felt they should keep it as a pirate ship. Whatever they thought, Peter was always in charge and had to be obeyed. He treated his men like dogs, just like Hook had, and he demanded instant obedience, just like Hook. Now, what was going on?

The general feeling was that Peter was running a good and honest ship. But was he just pretending so that Wendy would not become suspicious about his real plans? Certainly Wendy did not like it when Peter asked her to make him a new suit out of some of Hook's old clothes. But she did, and when he wore them he seemed to become more like Captain James Hook every day.

At night he would wear the suit in his cabin and smoke two cigars at once with Hook's cigar-holder. Strangely, he would clench one of his hands tightly, leaving just one finger to wriggle free. When he held the hand up against the light of his cabin lamp, an eerie shadow appeared on the wall; it was just like Hook's hook.

* * *

But now we must leave Peter and his friends playing pirates to return to No. 14 and the nursery. After all, the children who belong in the nursery are on their way home. We must check that the beds are aired and that Mr and Mrs Darling have not gone out for the evening. Then again, perhaps it would serve the children right if the beds weren't aired and their parents had left for a weekend in the country. Perhaps they need a lesson for leaving home so selfishly.

But, of course, Mrs Darling would not want that. She still loved her thankless children. The beds were aired, and in fact she had not left the house since they had vanished. And the nursery window? Yes, it is open.

Looking through the window we can see that the only change in the nursery rooms is that Nana's kennel is not there. Between the hours of nine o'clock in the morning and six o'clock at night the kennel is never there any more.

When the children flew away, Mr Darling felt he was to blame for what had happened. He was the one who had chained Nana up in the yard. He at last admitted that Nana was perhaps wiser than him. Mr Darling punished himself by getting down on all fours and crawling into the kennel. Mrs Darling tried everything to get him to come out, but he always said: 'No, this is the place for me.'

He swore that he would not come out until his children returned. The once proud Mr Darling was now a very humble man indeed as he sat in the kennel.

Nana often tried to get into the kennel too, but he would not allow it. But he followed Nana's wishes in every other matter.

Every morning Mr Darling got into the kennel. Then it was put into a taxi which took him to his office. He returned the same way at six o'clock. In the past he had always worried what the neighbours thought. Now he held his head high, even when people laughed at him in the kennel. He did not lose his manners either. He would lift his hat politely to any lady who looked inside.

People slowly came to understand why he would not leave the kennel and they felt sorry for him. Crowds followed the cab in the morning, cheering him on. Young girls climbed up to get his autograph. Journalists came to interview him. Rich people asked him to supper, adding: 'Do come in the kennel.'

One Thursday night Mrs Darling was in the nursery waiting for Mr Darling to return from work. Her eyes were filled with sadness. All the happiness of earlier times had vanished because she had lost her children.

As Mrs Darling falls asleep, it would be so nice to whisper in her ear that the children are coming back. They are just two miles away from the window and all are flying strongly. All we need to do is whisper that they are on the way. Let's.

It is a pity we did because we have woken her up. 'O Nana,' said Mrs Darling, to the faithful dog lying beside her. 'I dreamed that the children had come back.' Tears came to Nana's eyes and she put a paw gently on Mrs Darling's lap.

They had not moved when the kennel was brought back. Mr Darling leaned out to kiss his wife. Outside the crowd were still cheering him. 'Listen to them,' he said. 'They are very kind.'

Mrs Darling was beginning to wonder about her husband. He had put himself in the kennel as a punishment, but now could it be that he was enjoying the crowds following him every day? 'Are you sure you are not enjoying it?' she asked.

'My love,' he answered. 'Of course not.'

Mrs Darling said she was sorry for thinking such a thing, but

still believed she was right.

Mr Darling was tired after his day's work in the kennel and curled up like a puppy to go to sleep. 'Play me a tune on the piano to help me sleep,' he said.

Mrs Darling got up and walked towards the piano. It stood in the daytime area of the nursery, away from the beds. 'My dear,' said Mr Darling, 'can you close the window. I feel a draught.'

Mrs Darling was horrified. 'Never ask me to do that,' she said. 'The window must always be left open for them. Always, always.'

It was Mr Darling's turn to apologize as she began to play on the piano. Soon he was asleep.

While he slept Peter Pan and Tinker Bell flew into the room. Where were the children? Surely the plan they discussed on the ship was for Wendy, John and Michael to arrive home first.

Peter's first words tell all. 'Quick, Tink,' he said. 'Close the window. Bar it.'

Tinker Bell did as she was told and Peter continued: 'Good, now we must hide. When Wendy comes she will think her mother has locked her out. She will have to come back with me to Neverland.'

Peter had planned it all along. If he had been pretending to be Captain Hook when they were on the pirate ship, now he was showing all of Hook's cleverness. He did not want to lose Wendy and he was determined that she should return to Neverland.

Peter peeped at Mrs Darling on the piano. 'It's Wendy's mother,' he said to Tink. 'She is a pretty lady, but not as pretty as my mother. Her mouth looks like a thimble, but my mother's looks like many thimbles.'

Of course, Peter knew nothing about his mother, but he always did like to boast about her.

Peter listened to Mrs Darling playing. It was "Home Sweet Home" and, although he did not recognize the tune, he knew it was saying, 'Come Back, Wendy.'

'The window is barred,' said Peter, very pleased with himself as he looked at Mrs Darling. 'You will never see Wendy again.'

Mrs Darling finished playing and Peter saw two large tears in her eyes. 'She wants me to undo the window,' he thought. 'But I won't. Not I.'

He peeped again and saw that the tears were beginning to fall onto her cheek. 'She is very fond of Wendy, I can see that,' thought Peter, getting quite angry. 'I'm fond of her, too.

We can't both have her.'

Peter was irritated and decided not to look at Mrs Darling any more. He skipped about and made funny faces, but somehow he could not get her unhappy face out of his head. It was as if Mrs Darling was inside him, knocking and asking him to let Wendy come home.

'Oh, all right,' he sulked to Tinker Bell, 'we don't want any silly mothers, do we? I'll let Wendy come home if she must.'

With that they unbarred the window and flew out. Just a second later Wendy, John and Michael flew in. They were so pleased the window was open, and never thought for a moment that perhaps they did not deserve to find their way home so easily.

They landed on the floor, quite unashamed at running away from home for so long. Michael had even forgotten this was his home. 'John,' he said, 'I think I have been here before.'

'Of course you have, silly,' said John. 'There is your old bed.'

'So it is!' cried Michael.

'Look!' cried John. 'It's the kennel.' He dashed across to look into it.

'Perhaps Nana is inside,' said Wendy.

But John whistled out aloud. 'Hello? Hello? There's a man inside,' he said.

'It's father!' cried Wendy.

'Let me see,' begged Michael, taking a peep. 'He's not as big as the pirate I killed.'

Wendy and John were puzzled to find their father in the kennel. 'He didn't used to sleep in the kennel,' said John.

'Perhaps we don't remember our old life as well as we thought,' replied Wendy.

It was then that Mrs Darling began to play the piano again. 'It's mother!' cried Wendy, looking at Mrs Darling from behind a bed.

Michael was puzzled now. 'Then, Wendy,' he said, 'you are not really our mother?'

Wendy smiled, realizing that if they had not returned then, Michael would have completely forgotten everything about his old life.

John suggested they should creep in and surprise Mrs Darling by putting their hands over her eyes. Wendy thought they should break the happy news more gently. 'Let's all slip into our beds,' she said, 'and be there when she comes in, just as if we had never been away.'

So when Mrs Darling finished playing and walked back across the nursery, all the beds were fully occupied. The children waited for her cry of joy, but it did not come.

Mrs Darling had seen them, but she could not believe they were there. She saw them in their beds so often in her dreams. Mrs Darling was sure she was still dreaming.

She sat down in the chair by the fire, the place where in the old days she had nursed her children. Wendy was worried and could not understand what was happening.

'Mother!' she cried.

'That's Wendy's voice,' thought Mrs Darling.

'Mother!' said John.

'That's John's,' she thought.

'Mother!' cried Michael. He remembered who she was now.

'And that's Michael's voice,' she thought, dreamily stretching out her arms to hold the three little children. Now what's this? The children had slipped out of bed and now stood right in front of her.

This was no dream. Mrs Darling's arms slipped round Wendy, then John and finally Michael. All three children were back in her arms.

'George! George!' she cried, when she had found her voice again.

Mr Darling awoke to share her delight, and Nana came rushing in too. There could not have been a happier scene, and there was no one to see it; except one strange boy who was staring in at the window.

Poor Peter Pan. He had enjoyed a million adventures in his life, but what he was looking at through the window was one joy which could never be his.

Alice in Wonderland

by

Lewis Carroll

Introduction

Lewis Carroll was the pen-name of mathematics lecturer Charles Dodgson, when writing his nonsense poems and books. He was born 27th January 1832 and was educated at Richmond School, Rugby School and Christ Church, Oxford, where he taught mathematics for 26 years until 1881.

His best-known book is *Alice's Adventures in Wonderland* which he wrote specially to amuse the daughter of the Dean of Christ Church. Her name was Alice Pleasance Liddell. The book was first published in 1865 and has since become one of the most famous and best-loved children's stories ever written.

In this story, Alice follows the White Rabbit down the rabbit-hole into an amazing wonderland where creatures hold never-ending tea-parties, dance the 'lobster quadrille' and play the strangest game of croquet ever seen.

CHAPTER 1

Down the Rabbit-hole

Alice was beginning to get very tired of sitting by her
sister on the bank, and of having nothing to do; once or twice
she had peeped into the book her sister was reading, but it had
no pictures or conversations in it, "and what is the use of
a book," thought Alice, "without pictures or conversations?"

So she was considering in her own mind (as well as she
could, for the hot day made her feel very sleepy and stupid),
whether the pleasure of making a daisy-chain would be worth
the trouble of getting up and picking the daisies, when
suddenly a White Rabbit with pink eyes ran close by her.

There was nothing so *very* remarkable in that: nor did Alice
think it so *very* much out of the way to hear the Rabbit say to
itself, "Oh dear! Oh dear! I shall be too late!" (When she
thought it over afterwards, it occurred to her that she ought to

have wondered at this, but at the time it all seemed quite natural); but when the Rabbit actually *took a watch out of its waistcoat-pocket*, and looked at it, and then hurried on, Alice started to her feet, for it flashed across her mind that she had never before seen a rabbit with either a waistcoat-pocket or a watch to take out of it, and burning with curiosity, she ran across the field after it, and was just in time to see it pop down a large rabbit-hole under the hedge.

In another moment down went Alice after it, never once considering how in the world she was to get out again.

The rabbit-hole went straight on like a tunnel for some way, and then dipped suddenly down, so suddenly that Alice had not a moment to think about stopping herself before she found herself falling down what seemed to be a very deep well.

Either the well was very deep, or she fell very slowly, for she had plenty of time as she went down to look about her, and to wonder what was going to happen next. First, she tried to look down and make out what she was coming to, but it was too dark to see anything: then she looked at the sides of the well, and noticed that they were filled with cupboards and book-shelves: here and there she saw maps and pictures hung upon pegs. She took down a jar from one of the shelves as she passed: it was labelled "ORANGE MARMALADE," but to her great disappointment it was empty: she did not like to drop the jar for fear of killing somebody underneath, so managed to put it into one of the cupboards as she fell past it.

"Well!" thought Alice to herself. "After such a fall as this, I shall think nothing of tumbling down-stairs! How brave they'll all think me at home! Why, I wouldn't say anything about it, even if I fell off the top of the house!" (Which was very likely true.)

Down, down, down. Would the fall *never* come to an end? "I wonder how many miles I've fallen by this time?" she said aloud. "I must be getting somewhere near the centre of the earth. Let me see: that would be four thousand miles down, I think–" (for, you see, Alice had learnt several things of this sort in her lessons in the schoolroom, and though this was not a *very* good opportunity for showing off her knowledge, as there was no one to listen to her, still it was good practice to say it over) "– yes, that's about the right distance – but then

I wonder what Latitude or Longitude I've got to?" (Alice had not the slightest idea what Latitude was, or Longitude either, but she thought they were nice grand words to say.)

Presently she began again. "I wonder if I shall fall right *through* the earth! How funny it'll seem to come out among the people that walk with their heads downwards! The Antipathies, I think –" (she was rather glad there *was* no one listening, this time, as it didn't sound at all the right word: "– but I shall have to ask them what the name of the country is, you know. Please, Ma'am, is this New Zealand? Or Australia?" (and she tried to curtsey as she spoke – fancy *curtseying* as you're falling through the air! Do you think she could manage it?) "And what an ignorant little girl she'll think me for asking! No, it'll never do to ask: perhaps I shall see it written up somewhere."

Down, down, down. There was nothing else to do, so Alice soon began talking again. "Dinah'll miss me very much to-night, I should think!" (Dinah was the cat.) "I hope they'll remember her saucer of milk at tea-time. Dinah, my dear! I wish you were down here with me! There are no mice in the air, I'm afraid, but you might catch a bat, and that's very like a mouse, you know. But do cats eat bats, I wonder?" And here Alice began to get rather sleepy, and went on saying to herself, in a dreamy sort of way, "Do cats eat bats? Do cats eat bats?" and sometimes, "Do bats eat cats?", for, you see, as she couldn't answer either question, it didn't much matter which way she put it. She felt that she was dozing off, and had just begun to dream that she was walking hand in hand with Dinah, and was saying to her very earnestly, "Now, Dinah, tell me the truth: did you ever eat a bat?", when suddenly, thump! thump! down she came upon a heap of sticks and dry leaves, and the fall was over.

Alice was not a bit hurt, and she jumped up on to her feet in a moment: she looked up, but it was all dark overhead: before her was another long passage, and the White Rabbit was still in sight, hurrying down it. There was not a moment to be lost: away went Alice like the wind, and was just in time to hear it say, as it turned a corner, "Oh my ears and whiskers, how late it's getting!" She was close behind it when she turned the corner, but the Rabbit was no longer to be seen: she found

herself in a long, low hall, which was lit up by a row of lamps hanging from the roof.

There were doors all round the hall, but they were all locked; and when Alice had been all the way down one side and up the other trying every door, she walked sadly down the middle, wondering how she was ever to get out again.

Suddenly she came upon a little three-legged table, all made of solid glass: there was nothing on it but a tiny golden key, and Alice's first idea was that this might belong to one of the doors of the hall; but, alas! either the locks were too large, or the key was too small, but at any rate it would not open any of them. However, on the second time round, she came upon a low curtain she had noticed before, and behind it was a little door about fifteen inches high: she tried the little golden key in the lock, and to her great delight it fitted.

Alice opened the door and found that it led into a small passage, not much larger than a rat-hole: she knelt down and looked along the passage into the loveliest garden you ever saw. How she longed to get out of that dark hall, and wander about among those beds of bright flowers and those cool fountains, but she could not even get her head through the doorway: "and even if my head *would* go through," thought poor Alice, "it would be of very little use without my shoulders. Oh, how I wish I could shut up like a telescope! I think I could, if I only knew how to begin." For, you see, so many out-of-the-way things had happened lately, that Alice had begun to think that very few things indeed were really impossible.

There seemed to be no use in waiting by the little door, so she went back to the table, half hoping she might find another key on it, or at any rate a book of rules for shutting people up like telescopes: this time she found a little bottle on it ("which certainly was not here before," said Alice), and tied round the neck of the bottle was a paper label, with the words "DRINK ME" beautifully printed on it in large letters.

It was all very well to say "Drink me," but the wise little Alice was not going to do *that* in a hurry. "No, I'll look first," she said, "and see whether it's marked '*poison*' or not"; for she had read several nice little stories about children who had got burnt, and eaten up by wild beasts, and other unpleasant

*She knelt down and looked along the passage into the loveliest
garden you ever saw.*

things, all because they *would* not remember the simple rules their friends had taught them: such as, that a red-hot poker will burn you if you hold it too long; and that, if you cut your finger *very* deeply with a knife, it usually bleeds; and she had never forgotten that, if you drink much from a bottle marked "poison", it is almost certain to disagree with you, sooner or later.

However, this bottle was *not* marked "poison", so Alice ventured to taste it, and finding it very nice (it had, in fact, a sort of mixed flavour of cherry-tart, custard, pineapple, roast turkey, toffee, and hot buttered toast), she very soon finished it off.

*   *   *   *   *

"What a curious feeling!" said Alice. "I must be shutting up like a telescope!"

And so it was indeed: she was now only ten inches high, and her face brightened up at the thought that she was now the right size for going through the little door into that lovely garden. First, however, she waited for a few minutes to see if she was going to shrink any further: she felt a little nervous about this; "for it might end, you know," said Alice to herself, "in my going out altogether, like a candle. I wonder what I should be like then?" And she tried to fancy what the flame of a candle looks like after the candle is blown out, for she could not remember ever having seen such a thing.

After a while, finding that nothing more happened, she decided on going into the garden at once; but, alas for poor Alice! When she got to the door, she found she had forgotten the little golden key, and when she went back to the table for it, she found she could not possibly reach it: she could see it quite plainly through the glass and she tried her best to climb up one of the legs of the table, but it was too slippery; and when she had tired herself out with trying, the poor little thing sat down and cried.

"Come, there's no use in crying like that!" said Alice to herself rather sharply. "I advise you to leave off this minute!" She generally gave herself very good advice (though she very seldom followed it), and sometimes she scolded herself so

severely as to bring tears into her eyes; and once she
remembered trying to box her own ears for having cheated
herself in a game of croquet she was playing against herself, for
this curious child was very fond of pretending to be two people.
"But it's no use now," thought poor Alice, "to pretend to be
two people! Why, there's hardly enough of me left to make *one*
respectable person!"

Soon her eye fell on a little glass box that was lying under the
table: she opened it, and found in it a very small cake, on
which the words "EAT ME" were beautifully marked in
currants. "Well I'll eat it," said Alice, "and if it makes me grow
larger, I can reach the key; and if it makes me grow smaller,
I can creep under the door: so either way I'll get into the
garden, and I don't care which happens!"

She ate a little bit, and said anxiously to herself, "Which
way? Which way?", holding her hand on the top of her head to
feel which way it was growing; and she was quite surprised to
find that she remained the same size. To be sure, this is what
generally happens when one eats cake; but Alice had got so
much into the way of expecting nothing but out-of-the-way
things to happen, that it seemed quite dull and stupid for life to
go on in the common way.

So she set to work, and very soon finished off the cake.

*   *   *   *   *

CHAPTER 2
The Pool of Tears

"Curiouser and curiouser!" cried Alice (she was so much surprised, that for the moment she quite forgot how to speak good English). "Now I'm opening out like the largest telescope that ever was! Good-bye, feet!" (for when she looked down at her feet, they seemed to be almost out of sight, they were getting so far off). "Oh, my poor little feet, I wonder who will put on your shoes and stockings for you now, dears? I'm sure *I* shan't be able! I shall be a great deal too far off to trouble myself about you: you must manage the best way you can – but I must be kind to them," thought Alice, "or perhaps they won't walk the way I want to go! Let me see. I'll give them a new pair of boots every Christmas."

And she went on planning to herself how she would manage it. "They must go by the carrier," she thought; "and how funny it'll seem, sending presents to one's own feet! And how odd the directions will look!

> *Alice's Right Foot, Esq.*
> *Hearthrug,*
> *near the Fender*
> *(with Alice's love).*

Oh dear, what nonsense I'm talking!"

Just at this moment her head struck against the roof of the hall: in fact she was now rather more than nine feet high, and she at once took up the little golden key and hurried off to the garden door.

Poor Alice! It was as much as she could do, lying down on one side, to look through into the garden with one eye, but to get through was more hopeless than ever: she sat down and began to cry again.

"You ought to be ashamed of yourself," said Alice, "a great girl like you" (she might well say this), "to go on crying in this way! Stop this moment, I tell you!" But she went on all the same, shedding gallons of tears, until there was a large pool all round her, four inches deep and reaching half down the hall.

After a time she heard a little pattering of feet in the distance, and she hastily dried her eyes to see what was coming. It was the White Rabbit returning, splendidly dressed, with a pair of white kid-gloves in one hand and a large fan in the other: he came trotting along in a great hurry, muttering to himself as he came, "Oh! the Duchess, the Duchess! Oh! Won't she be savage if I've kept her waiting!" Alice felt so desperate that she was ready to ask help of any one: so, when the Rabbit came near her, she began, in a low, timid voice, "If you please, Sir——" The Rabbit started violently, dropped the white kid-gloves and the fan, and scurried away into the darkness as hard as he could go.

Alice took up the fan and gloves, and, as the hall was very hot, she kept fanning herself all the time she went on talking. "Dear, dear! How queer everything is today! And yesterday things went on just as usual. I wonder if I've been changed in the night? Let me think: *was* I the same when I got up this morning? I almost think I can remember feeling a little

different. But if I'm not the same, the next question is, 'Who in the world am I?' Ah, *that's* the great puzzle!" And she began thinking over all the children she knew that were of the same age as herself, to see if she could have been changed for any of them.

"I'm sure I'm not Ada," she said, "for her hair goes in such long ringlets, and mine doesn't go in ringlets at all; and I'm sure I can't be Mabel, for I know all sorts of things, and she, oh! she knows such a very little! Besides, *she's* she, and *I'm* I, and – oh dear, how puzzling it all is! I'll try if I know all the things I used to know. Let me see: four times five is twelve, and four times six is thirteen, and four times seven is – oh dear! I shall never get to twenty at that rate! However, the Multiplication Table doesn't signify: let's try Geography. London is the capital of Paris, and Paris is the capital of Rome, and Rome – no; *that's* all wrong, I'm certain! I must have been changed for Mabel! I'll try and say '*How doth the little——*'," and she crossed her hands on her lap as if she were saying lessons, and began to repeat it, but her voice sounded hoarse and strange, and the words did not come the same as they used to do:—

> *How doth the little crocodile*
> *Improve his shining tail,*
> *And pour the waters of the Nile*
> *On every golden scale!*
>
> *How cheerfully he seems to grin,*
> *And neatly spreads his claws,*
> *And welcomes little fishes in,*
> *With gently smiling jaws!*

"I'm sure those are not the right words," said poor Alice, and her eyes filled with tears again as she went on. "I must be Mabel, after all, and I shall have to go and live in that poky little house, and have next to no toys to play with, and oh, ever so many lessons to learn! No, I've made up my mind about it: if I'm Mabel, I'll stay down here! It'll be no use their putting their heads down and saying 'Come up again, dear!' I shall only look up and say 'Who am I then? Tell me that first, and then, if I like being that person, I'll come up: if not, I'll stay down here till I'm somebody else' – but, oh dear!" cried Alice, with a sudden burst of tears, "I do wish they *would* put their heads down! I am so *very* tired of being all alone here!"

As she said this she looked down at her hands, and was surprised to see that she had put on one of the Rabbit's little white kid-gloves while she was talking. "How *can* I have done that?" she thought. "I must be growing small again." She got up and went to the table to measure herself by it, and found that, as nearly as she could guess, she was now about two feet high, and was going on shrinking rapidly: she soon found out that the cause of this was the fan she was holding, and she dropped it hastily, just in time to save herself from shrinking away altogether.

"That was a narrow escape!" said Alice, a good deal frightened at the sudden change, but very glad to find herself still in existence. "And now for the garden!" And she ran with all speed back to the little door; but, alas! the little door was shut again, and the little golden key was lying on the glass table as before, "and things are worse than ever," thought the poor child, "for I never was so small as this before, never! And I declare it's too bad, that it is!"

As she said this her foot slipped, and in another moment, splash! she was up to her chin in salt water. Her first idea was that she had somehow fallen into the sea, "and in that case I can go back by railway," she said to herself. (Alice had been to the seaside once in her life, and had come to the general conclusion, that wherever you go to on the English coast you find a number of bathing machines in the sea, some children digging in the sand with wooden spades, then a row of lodging houses, and behind them a railway-station.) However, she soon made out that she was in the pool of tears which she had wept when she was nine feet high.

"I wish I hadn't cried so much!" said Alice, as she swam about, trying to find her way out. "I shall be punished for it now, I suppose, by being drowned in my own tears! That *will* be a queer thing, to be sure! However, everything is queer today."

Just then she heard something splashing about in the pool a little way off, and she swam nearer to make out what it was:

at first she thought it must be a walrus or hippopotamus, but then she remembered how small she was now, and she soon made out that it was only a mouse that had slipped in like herself.

"Would it be of any use now," thought Alice, "to speak to this mouse? Everything is so out-of-the-way down here, that I should think very likely it can talk: at any rate, there's no harm in trying." So she began: "O Mouse, do you know the way out of this pool? I am very tired of swimming about here, O Mouse!" (Alice thought this must be the right way of speaking to a mouse: she had never done such a thing before, but she remembered having seen in her brother's Latin Grammar, "A mouse – of a mouse – to a mouse – a mouse – O mouse".) The mouse looked at her rather inquisitively, and seemed to her to wink with one of its little eyes, but it said nothing.

"Perhaps it doesn't understand English," thought Alice. "I daresay it's a French mouse, come over with William the Conqueror." (For, with all her knowledge of history, Alice had no clear notion how long ago anything had happened.) So she began again: "Où est ma chatte?" which was the first sentence in her French lesson-book. The Mouse gave a sudden leap out of the water, and seemed to quiver all over with fright. "Oh, I beg your pardon!" cried Alice hastily, afraid that she had hurt the poor animal's feelings. "I quite forgot you didn't like cats."

"Not like cats!" cried the Mouse, in a shrill, passionate voice. "Would *you* like cats, if you were me?"

"Well, perhaps not," said Alice in a soothing tone: "don't be angry about it. And yet I wish I could show you our cat Dinah. I think you'd take a fancy to cats if you could only see her. She is such a dear quiet thing," Alice went on half to herself, as she swam lazily about in the pool, "and she sits purring so nicely by the fire, licking her paws and washing her face – and she is such a nice soft thing to nurse – and she's such a capital one for catching mice – oh, I beg your pardon!" cried Alice again, for this time the Mouse was bristling all over, and she felt certain it must be really offended. "We won't talk about her any more if you'd rather not."

"We, indeed!" cried the Mouse, who was trembling down to the end of its tail. "As if *I* would talk on such a subject! Our

"O Mouse, do you know the way out of this pool?
I am very tired of swimming about here, O Mouse!"

to Alice.

"Only a thimble," said Alice sadly.

"Hand it over here," said the Dodo.

Then they all crowded round her once more, while the Dodo solemnly presented the thimble, saying, "We beg your acceptance of this elegant thimble"; and, when it had finished this short speech, they all cheered.

Alice thought the whole thing very absurd, but they all looked so grave that she did not dare to laugh; and, as she could not think of anything to say, she simply bowed, and took the thimble, looking as solemn as she could.

The next thing was to eat the comfits: this caused some noise and confusion, as the large birds complained that they could not taste theirs, and the small ones choked and had to be patted on the back. However, it was over at last, and they sat down again in a ring, and begged the Mouse to tell them something more.

"You promised to tell me your history, you know," said Alice, "and why it is you hate – C and D," she added in a whisper, half afraid that it would be offended again.

"Mine is a long and sad tale!" said the Mouse turning to Alice, and sighing.

"It *is* a long tail, certainly," said Alice, looking down with wonder at the Mouse's tail; "but why do you call it sad?" And she kept on puzzling about it while the Mouse was speaking, so that her idea of the tale was something like this:—

"Fury said to a
mouse, That he
met in the
house,
'Let us
both go to
law: *I* will
prosecute
you. Come
I'll take no
denial; We
must have a
trial: For
really this
morning I've
nothing
to do.'
Said the
mouse to the
cur, 'Such
a trial
dear Sir,
With
no jury
or judge
would be
wasting
our
breath.'
'I'll be
judge, I'll
be jury,
said
cunning
old Fury:
'I'll
try the
whole
cause
and
condemn
you
to
death.'"

"You are not attending!" said the Mouse to Alice severely. "What are you thinking of?"

"I beg your pardon," said Alice very humbly; "you had got to the fifth bend, I think?"

"I had *not*!" cried the Mouse, sharply and very angrily.

"A knot!" said Alice, always ready to make herself useful, and looking anxiously about her. "Oh, do let me help to undo it!"

"I shall do nothing of the sort," said the Mouse, getting up and walking away. "You insult me by talking such nonsense!"

"I didn't mean it!" pleaded poor Alice. "But you're so easily offended, you know!"

The Mouse only growled in reply.

"Please come back and finish your story!" Alice called after it. And the others all joined in chorus. "Yes, please do!" But the Mouse only shook its head impatiently and walked a little quicker.

"What a pity it wouldn't stay!" sighed the Lory, as soon as it was quite out of sight. And an old Crab took the opportunity of saying to her daughter "Ah, my dear! Let this be a lesson to you never to lose *your* temper!" "Hold your tongue, Ma!" said the young Crab, a little snappishly. "You're enough to try the patience of an oyster!"

"I wish I had our Dinah here, I know I do!" said Alice aloud, addressing nobody in particular. "*She'd* soon fetch it back!"

"And who is Dinah, if I might venture to ask the question?" said the Lory.

Alice replied eagerly, for she was always ready to talk about her pet: "Dinah's our cat. And she's such a capital one for catching mice, you can't think! And oh, I wish you could see her after the birds! Why, she'll eat a little bird as soon as look at it!"

The speech caused a remarkable sensation among the party. Some of the birds hurried off at once: one old Magpie began wrapping itself up very carefully, remarking "I really must be getting home: the night-air doesn't suit my throat!" and a Canary called out in a trembling voice to its children "Come away, my dears! It's high time you were all in bed!" On various pretexts they all moved off, and Alice was soon left alone.

"I wish I hadn't mentioned Dinah!" she said to herself in

The speech caused a remarkable sensation among the party.

a melancholy tone. "Nobody seems to like her, down here, and I'm sure she's the best cat in the world! Oh, my dear Dinah! I wonder if I shall ever see you any more!" And here poor Alice began to cry again, for she felt very lonely and low-spirited. In a little while, however, she again heard a little pattering of footsteps in the distance, and she looked up eagerly, half hoping that the Mouse had changed his mind, and was coming back to finish his story.

CHAPTER 4

The Rabbit Sends in
a Little Bill

IT was the White Rabbit, trotting slowly back again, and
looking anxiously about it as it went, as if it had lost something;
and she heard it muttering to itself, "The Duchess! The
Duchess! Oh my dear paws! Oh my fur and whiskers! She'll get
me executed, as sure as ferrets are ferrets! Where *can* I have
dropped them, I wonder?" Alice guessed in a moment that it
was looking for the fan and the pair of white kid-gloves, and
she very good-naturedly began hunting about for them, but
they were nowhere to be seen – everything seemed to have
changed since her swim in the pool, and the great hall, with
the glass table and the little door, had vanished completely.

Very soon the Rabbit noticed Alice, as she went hunting
about, and called out to her in an angry tone, "Why, Mary
Ann, what *are* you doing out here? Run home this moment,

and fetch me a pair of gloves and a fan! Quick, now," and Alice was so much frightened that she ran off at once in the direction it pointed to, without trying to explain the mistake that it had made.

"He took me for his housemaid," she said to herself as she ran. "How surprised he'll be when he finds out who I am! But I'd better take him his fan and gloves – that is, if I can find them." As she said this she came upon a neat little house, on the door of which was a bright brass plate with the name "W. RABBIT" engraved upon it. She went in without knocking, and hurried up stairs, in great fear lest she should meet the real Mary Ann, and be turned out of the house before she had found the fan and gloves.

"How queer it seems," Alice said to herself, "to be going messages for a rabbit! I suppose Dinah'll be sending me on messages next!" And she began fancying the sort of thing that would happen: " 'Miss Alice! Come here directly, and get ready for your walk!' 'Coming in a minute, nurse! But I've got to watch this mouse-hole till Dinah comes back, and see that the mouse doesn't get out.' Only I don't think," Alice went on, "that they'd let Dinah stop in the house if it began ordering people about like that!"

By this time she had found her way into a tidy little room with a table in the window, and on it (as she had hoped) a fan and two or three pairs of tiny white kid-gloves: she took up the fan and a pair of the gloves, and was just going to leave the room, when her eyes fell upon a little bottle that stood near the looking-glass. There was no label this time with the words "DRINK ME," but nevertheless she uncorked it and put it to her lips. "I know *something* interesting is sure to happen," she said to herself, "whenever I eat or drink anything: so I'll just see what this bottle does. I do hope it'll make me grow large again, for really I'm quite tired of being such a tiny little thing!"

It did so indeed, and much sooner than she had expected: before she had drunk half the bottle she found her head pressing against the ceiling, and had to stoop to save her neck from being broken. She hastily put down the bottle, saying to herself "That's quite enough – I hope I shan't grow any more – As it is, I can't get out at the door – I do wish I hadn't drunk quite so much!"

Alas! it was too late to wish that! She went on growing, and growing, and very soon had to kneel down on the floor: in another minute there was not even room for this, and she tried the effect of lying down with one elbow against the door, and the other arm curled round her head. Still she went on growing, and, as a last resource, she put one arm out of the window, and one foot up the chimney, and said to herself "Now I can do no more, whatever happens. What *will* become of me?"

Luckily for Alice, the little magic bottle had now had its full effect, and she grew no larger: still it was very uncomfortable, and as there seemed to be no sort of chance of her ever getting out of the room again, no wonder she felt unhappy.

"It was much pleasanter at home," thought poor Alice, "when one wasn't always growing larger and smaller, and being ordered about by mice and rabbits. I almost wish I hadn't gone down that rabbit-hole – and yet – and yet – it's curious, you know, this sort of life! I do wonder what *can* have happened to me! When I used to read fairy-tales, I fancied that kind of thing never happened, and now here I am in the middle of one! There ought to be a book written about me, that there ought! And when I grow up, I'll write one – but I'm grown up now," she added in a sorrowful tone: "at least there's no room to grow up any more *here*."

"But then," thought Alice, "shall I *never* get any older than I am now? That'll be a comfort, one way – never to be an old woman – but then – always to have lessons to learn! Oh, I shouldn't like *that*!"

"Oh, you foolish Alice!" she answered herself. "How can you learn lessons in here? Why, there's hardly room for *you*, and no room at all for any lesson-books!"

And so she went on, taking first one side and then the other, and making quite a conversation of it altogether; but after a few minutes she heard a voice outside, and stopped to listen.

"Mary Ann! Mary Ann!" said the voice. "Fetch me my gloves this moment!" Then came a little pattering of feet on the stairs. Alice knew it was the Rabbit coming to look for her, and she trembled till she shook the house, quite forgetting that she was now about a thousand times as large as the Rabbit, and had no reason to be afraid of it.

dead silence.

Alice noticed with some surprise that the pebbles were all turning into little cakes as they lay on the floor, and a bright idea came into her head. "If I eat one of these cakes," she thought, "it's sure to make *some* change in my size; and, as it can't possibly make me larger, it must make me smaller, I suppose."

So she swallowed one of the cakes, and was delighted to find that she began shrinking directly. As soon as she was small enough to get through the door, she ran out of the house, and found quite a crowd of little animals and birds waiting outside. The poor little Lizard, Bill, was in the middle, being held up by two guinea-pigs, who were giving it something out of a bottle. They all made a rush at Alice the moment she appeared; but she ran off as hard as she could, and soon found herself safe in a thick wood.

"The first thing I've got to do," said Alice to herself, as she wandered about in the wood, "is to grow to my right size again; and the second thing is to find my way into that lovely garden. I think that will be the best plan."

It sounded an excellent plan, no doubt, and very neatly and simply arranged; the only difficulty was, that she had not the smallest idea how to set about it; and, while she was peering about anxiously among the trees, a little sharp bark just over her head made her look up in a great hurry.

An enormous puppy was looking down at her with large round eyes, and feebly stretching out one paw, trying to touch her. "Poor little thing!" said Alice, in a coaxing tone, and she tried hard to whistle to it; but she was terribly frightened all the time at the thought that it might be hungry, in which case it would be very likely to eat her up in spite of all her coaxing.

Hardly knowing what she did, she picked up a little bit of stick, and held it out to the puppy: whereupon the puppy jumped into the air off all its feet at once, with a yelp of delight, and rushed at the stick, and made believe to worry it: then Alice dodged behind a great thistle, to keep herself from being run over; and, the moment she appeared on the other side, the puppy made another rush at the stick, and tumbled head over heels in its hurry to get hold of it: then Alice, thinking it was very like having a game of play with a cart-horse, and expecting every moment to be trampled under its feet, ran round the thistle again: then the puppy began a series of short charges at the stick, running a very little way forwards each time and a long way back, and barking hoarsely all the while, till at last it sat down a good way off, panting, with its tongue hanging out of its mouth, and its great eyes half shut.

This seemed to Alice a good opportunity for making her escape: so she set off at once, and ran till she was quite tired and out of breath, and till the puppy's bark sounded quite faint in the distance.

"And yet what a dear little puppy it was!" said Alice, as she leant against a buttercup to rest herself, and fanned herself with one of the leaves, "I should have liked teaching it tricks very much, if – if I'd only been the right size to do it! Oh dear! I'd nearly forgotten that I've got to grow up again! Let me see – how *is* it to be managed? I suppose I ought to eat or drink something or other; but the great question is, 'What?' "

The great question certainly was, "What?" Alice looked all round her at the flowers and blades of grass, but she could not see anything that looked like the right thing to eat or drink under the circumstances. There was a large mushroom growing near her, about the same height as herself; and, when she had looked under it, and on both sides of it, and behind it, it occurred to her that she might as well look and see what was on top of it.

She stretched herself up on tiptoe, and peeped over the edge of the mushroom, and her eyes immediately met those of a large blue caterpillar, that was sitting on the top with its arms folded, quietly smoking a long hookah, and taking not the smallest notice of her or of anything else.

CHAPTER 5

Advice from a Caterpillar

The Caterpillar and Alice looked at each other for some time in silence: at last the Caterpillar took the hookah out of its mouth, and addressed her in a languid, sleepy voice.

"Who are *you?*" said the Caterpillar.

This was not an encouraging opening for a conversation. Alice replied, rather shyly, "I – I hardly know, Sir, just at present – at least I know who I *was* when I got up this morning, but I think I must have been changed several times since then."

"What do you mean by that?" said the Caterpillar sternly. "Explain yourself!"

"I can't explain *myself*, I'm afraid, Sir," said Alice, "because I'm not myself, you see."

"I don't see," said the Caterpillar.

"I'm afraid I can't put it more clearly," Alice replied very

politely, "for I can't understand it myself to begin with; and being so many different sizes in a day is very confusing."

"It isn't," said the Caterpillar.

"Well, perhaps you haven't found it so yet," said Alice; "but when you have to turn into a chrysalis – you will some day, you know – and then after that into a butterfly, I should think you'll feel it a little queer, won't you?"

"Not a bit," said the Caterpillar.

"Well, perhaps *your* feelings may be different," said Alice; "all I know is, it would feel very queer to *me*."

"You!" said the Caterpillar contemptuously. "Who are *you*?"

Which brought them back again to the beginning of the conversation. Alice felt a little irritated at the Caterpillar's making such *very* short remarks, and she drew herself up and said, very gravely, "I think you ought to tell me who *you* are, first."

"Why?" said the Caterpillar.

Here was another puzzling question: and, as Alice could not think of any good reason, and the Caterpillar seemed to be in a *very* unpleasant state of mind, she turned away.

"Come back!" the Caterpillar called after her. "I've something important to say!"

This sounded promising, certainly. Alice turned and came back again.

"Keep your temper," said the Caterpillar.

"Is that all?" said Alice, swallowing down her anger as well as she could.

"No," said the Caterpillar.

Alice thought she might as well wait, as she had nothing else to do, and perhaps after all it might tell her something worth hearing. For some minutes if puffed away without speaking; but at last it unfolded its arms, took the hookah out of its mouth again, and said "So you think you're changed, do you?"

"I'm afraid I am, Sir," said Alice. "I can't remember things as I used – and I don't keep the same size for ten minutes together!"

"Can't remember *what* things?" said the Caterpillar.

"Well, I've tried to say '*How doth the little busy bee*,' but it all came different!" Alice replied in a very melancholy voice.

"Repeat '*You are old, Father William*,' " said the Caterpillar.

Alice folded her hands, and began:—

"You are old, Father William," the young man said,
    "And your hair has become very white;
And yet you incessantly stand on your head –
    Do you think, at your age, it is right?"

"In my youth," Father William replied to his son,
    "I feared it might injure the brain;
But, now that I'm perfectly sure I have none,
    Why, I do it again and again."

"You are old," said the youth, "as I mentioned before,
    And have grown most uncommonly fat;
Yet you turned a back-somersault in at the door –
    Pray, what is the reason of that?"

"In my youth," said the sage, as he shook his grey locks,
    "I kept all my limbs very supple
By the use of this ointment – one shilling the box –
    Allow me to sell you a couple?"

"You are old," said the youth, "and your jaws are too weak
    For anything tougher than suet;
Yet you finished the goose, with the bones and the beak –
    Pray, how did you manage to do it?"

"In my youth," said his father, "I took to the law
    And argued each case with my wife;
And the muscular strength, which it gave to my jaw,
    Has lasted the rest of my life."

"You are old," said the youth, "one would hardly suppose
    That your eye was as steady as ever;
Yet you balanced an eel on the end of your nose –
    What made you so awfully clever?"

"I have answered three questions, and that is enough,"
    Said his father, "don't give yourself airs!
Do you think I can listen all day to such stuff?
    Be off, or I'll kick you down stairs!"

"That is not said right," said the Caterpillar.

"Not *quite* right, I'm afraid," said Alice, timidly: "Some of the words have got altered."

"It is wrong from beginning to end," said the Caterpillar decidedly, and there was silence for some minutes.

The Caterpillar was the first to speak.

"What size do you want to be?" it asked.

"Oh, I'm not particular as to size," Alice hastily replied; "only one doesn't like changing so often, you know."

"I *don't* know," said the Caterpillar.

Alice said nothing: she had never been so much contradicted in all her life before, and she felt that she was losing her temper.

"Are you content now?" said the Caterpillar.

"Well, I should like to be a *little* larger, Sir, if you wouldn't mind," said Alice: "three inches is such a wretched height to be."

"It is a very good height indeed!" said the Caterpillar angrily, rearing itself upright as it spoke (it was exactly three inches high).

"But I'm not used to it!" pleaded poor Alice in a piteous tone. And she thought to herself, "I wish the creatures wouldn't be so easily offended!"

"You'll get used to it in time," said the Caterpillar; and it put the hookah into its mouth and began smoking again.

This time Alice waited patiently until it chose to speak again. In a minute or two the Caterpillar took the hookah out of its mouth and yawned once or twice, and shook itself. Then it got down off the mushroom, and crawled away into the grass, merely remarking as it went, "One side will make you grow taller, and the other side will make you grow shorter."

"One side of *what*? The other side of *what*?" thought Alice to herself.

"Of the mushroom," said the Caterpillar, just as if she had asked it aloud; and in another moment it was out of sight.

Alice remained looking thoughtfully at the mushroom for a minute, trying to make out which were the two sides of it; and as it was perfectly round, she found this a very difficult question. However, at last she stretched out her arms round it as far as they would go, and broke off a bit of the edge with each hand.

"And now which is which?" she said to herself, and nibbled a little of the right-hand bit to try the effect: the next moment she felt a violent blow underneath her chin: it had struck her foot!

She was a good deal frightened by this very sudden change, but she felt that there was no time to be lost, as she was shrinking rapidly: so she set to work at once to eat some of the other bit. Her chin was pressed so closely against her foot, that there was hardly room to open her mouth; but she did it at last, and managed to swallow a morsel of the left-hand bit.

*   *   *   *   *

"Come, my head's free at last!" said Alice in a tone of delight, which changed into alarm in another moment, when she found that her shoulders were nowhere to be found: all she could see, when she looked down, was an immense length of neck, which seemed to rise like a stalk out of a sea of green leaves that lay far below her.

"What *can* all that green stuff be?" said Alice. "And where *have* my shoulders got to? And oh, my poor hands, how is it I can't see you?" She was moving them about as she spoke, but no result seemed to follow, except a little shaking among the distant green leaves.

As there seemed to be no chance of getting her hands up to her head, she tried to get her head down to *them*, and was delighted to find that her neck would bend about easily in any direction, like a serpent. She had just succeeded in curving it down into a graceful zigzag, and was going to dive in among the leaves, which she found to be nothing but the tops of trees under which she had been wandering, when a sharp hiss made her draw back in a hurry: a large pigeon had flown into her face, and was beating her violently with its wings.

"Serpent!" screamed the Pigeon.

"I'm *not* a serpent!" said Alice indignantly. "Let me alone!"

"Serpent, I say again!" repeated the Pigeon, but in a more subdued tone, and added with a kind of sob, "I've tried every way, but nothing seems to suit them!"

"I haven't the least idea what you're talking about," said Alice.

"I've tried the roots of trees, and I've tried banks, and I've tried hedges," the Pigeon went on, without attending to her; "but those serpents! There's no pleasing them!"

Alice was more and more puzzled, but she thought there was no use in saying anything more till the Pigeon had finished.

"As if it wasn't trouble enough hatching the eggs," said the Pigeon; "but I must be on the look-out for serpents night and day! Why, I haven't had a wink of sleep these three weeks!"

"I'm very sorry you've been annoyed," said Alice, who was beginning to see its meaning.

"And just as I'd taken the highest tree in the wood," continued the Pigeon, raising its voice to a shriek, "and just as I was thinking I should be free of them at last, they must needs come wriggling down from the sky! Ugh, Serpent!"

"But I'm *not* a serpent, I tell you!" said Alice. "I'm a—— I'm a——"

"Well! *What* are you?" said the Pigeon. "I can see you're trying to invent something!"

"I – I'm a little girl," said Alice, rather doubtfully, as she remembered the number of changes she had gone through that day.

"A likely story indeed!" said the Pigeon, in a tone of the deepest contempt. "I've seen a good many little girls in my time, but never *one* with such a neck as that! No, no! You're a serpent; and there's no use denying it. I suppose you'll be telling me next that you never tasted an egg!"

"I *have* tasted eggs, certainly," said Alice, who was a very truthful child; "but little girls eat eggs quite as much as serpents do, you know."

"I don't believe it," said the Pigeon; "but if they do, why, then they're a kind of serpent: that's all I can say."

This was such a new idea to Alice, that she was quite silent for a minute or two, which gave the Pigeon the opportunity of adding, "You're looking for eggs, I know *that* well enough; and what does it matter to me whether you're a little girl or a serpent?"

"It matters a good deal to *me*," said Alice hastily; "but I'm not looking for eggs, as it happens; and, if I was, I shouldn't want *yours*: I don't like them raw."

"Well, be off, then!" said the Pigeon in a sulky tone, as it

"But I'm not a serpent, I tell you!" said Alice.

settled down again into its nest. Alice crouched down among the trees as well as she could, for her neck kept getting entangled among the branches, and every now and then she had to stop and untwist it. After a while she remembered that she still held the pieces of mushroom in her hands, and she set to work very carefully, nibbling first at one and then at the other, and growing sometimes taller, and sometimes shorter, until she had succeeded in bringing herself down to her usual height.

It was so long since she had been anything near the right size, that it felt quite strange at first; but she got used to it in a few minutes, and began talking to herself, as usual, "Come, there's half my plan done now! How puzzling all these changes are! I'm never sure what I'm going to be, from one minute to another! However, I've got back to my right size: the next thing is, to get into that beautiful garden – how *is* that to be done, I wonder?" As she said this, she came suddenly upon an open place, with a little house in it about four feet high. "Whoever lives there?" thought Alice; "it'll never do to come upon them *this* size: why, I should frighten them out of their wits!" So she began nibbling at the right-hand bit again, and did not venture to go near the house till she had brought herself down to nine inches high.

CHAPTER 6
Pig and Pepper

F OR a minute or two she stood looking at the house, and wondering what to do next, when suddenly a footman in livery came running out of the wood – (she considered him to be a footman because he was in livery: otherwise, judging by his face only, she would have called him a fish) – and rapped loudly at the door with his knuckles. It was opened by another footman in livery, with a round face, and large eyes like a frog; and both footmen, Alice noticed, had powdered hair that curled all over their heads. She felt very curious to know what it was all about, and crept a little way out of the wood to listen.

The Fish-Footman began by producing from under his arm a great letter, nearly as large as himself, and this he handed over to the other, saying, in a solemn tone, "For the Duchess. An invitation from the Queen to play croquet." The Frog-Footman repeated, in the same solemn tone, only changing the order of the words a little, "From the Queen. An invitation for

the Duchess to play croquet."

Then they both bowed low, and their curls got entangled together.

Alice laughed so much at this, that she had to run back into the wood for fear of their hearing her; and, when she next peeped out, the Fish-Footman was gone, and the other was sitting on the ground near the door, staring stupidly up into the sky.

Alice went timidly up to the door, and knocked.

"There's no sort of use in knocking," said the Footman, "and that for two reasons. First, because I'm on the same side of the door as you are: secondly, because they're making such a noise inside, no one could possibly hear you." And certainly there *was* a most extraordinary noise going on within – a constant howling and sneezing, and every now and then a great crash, as if a dish or kettle had been broken to pieces.

"Please, then," said Alice, "how am I to get in?"

"There might be some sense in your knocking," the Footman went on, without attending to her, "if we had the door between us. For instance, if you were *inside*, you might knock, and I could let you out, you know." He was looking up into the sky all the time he was speaking, and this Alice thought decidedly uncivil. "But perhaps he can't help it," she said to herself; "his eyes are so *very* nearly at the top of his head. But at any rate he might answer questions – How am I to get in?" she repeated, aloud.

"I shall sit here," the Footman remarked, "till tomorrow——"

At this moment the door of the house opened, and a large plate came skimming out, straight at the Footman's head: it just grazed his nose, and broke to pieces against one of the trees behind him.

"—— or next day, maybe," the Footman continued in the same tone, exactly as if nothing had happened.

"How am I to get in?" asked Alice again, in a louder tone.

"*Are* you to get in at all?" said the Footman. "That's the first question, you know."

It was, no doubt: only Alice did not like to be told so. "It's really dreadful," she muttered to herself, "the way all the creatures argue. It's enough to drive one crazy!"

The Footman seemed to think this a good opportunity for repeating his remark with variations. "I shall sit here," he said, "on and off, for days and days."

"But what am *I* to do?" said Alice.

"Anything you like," said the Footman, and began whistling.

"Oh, there's no use in talking to him," said Alice desperately: "he's perfectly idiotic!" And she opened the door and went in.

The door led right into a large kitchen, which was full of smoke from one end to the other: the Duchess was sitting on a three-legged stool in the middle, nursing a baby: the cook was leaning over the fire, stirring a large cauldron which seemed to be full of soup.

"There's certainly too much pepper in that soup!" Alice said to herself, as well as she could for sneezing.

There was certainly too much of it in the *air*. Even the Duchess sneezed occasionally; and as for the baby, it was sneezing and howling alternately without a moment's pause. The only two creatures in the kitchen that did *not* sneeze, were the cook, and a large cat, which was lying on the hearth and grinning from ear to ear.

"Please would you tell me," said Alice, a little timidly, for she was not quite sure whether it was good manners for her to speak first, "why your cat grins like that?"

"It's a Cheshire-Cat," said the Duchess, "and that's why, Pig!"

She said the last word with such sudden violence that Alice quite jumped; but she saw in another moment that it was addressed to the baby, and not to her, so she took courage, and went on again:—

"I didn't know that Cheshire-Cats always grinned; in fact, I didn't know that cats *could* grin."

"They all can," said the Duchess; "and most of 'em do."

"I don't know of any that do," Alice said very politely, feeling quite pleased to have got into a conversation.

"You don't know much," said the Duchess; "and that's a fact."

Alice did not at all like the tone of this remark, and thought it would be as well to introduce some other subject of

conversation. While she was trying to fix on one, the cook took the cauldron of soup off the fire, and at once set to work throwing everything within her reach at the Duchess and the baby – the fire-irons came first; then followed a shower of saucepans, plates and dishes. The Duchess took no notice of them even when they hit her; and the baby was howling so much already, that it was quite impossible to say whether the blows hurt it or not.

"Oh, *please* mind what you're doing!" cried Alice, jumping up and down in an agony of terror. "Oh, there goes his *precious* nose!" as an unusually large saucepan flew close by it, and very nearly carried it off.

"If everybody minded their own business," the Duchess said, in a hoarse growl, "the world would go round a deal faster than it does."

"Which would *not* be an advantage," said Alice, who felt very glad to get an opportunity of showing off a little of her knowledge. "Just think what work it would make with the day and night! You see, the earth takes twenty-four hours to turn round on its axis——"

"Talking of axes," said the Duchess, "chop off her head!"

Alice glanced rather anxiously at the cook, to see if she meant to take the hint; but the cook was busily stirring the soup; and seemed not to be listening, so she went on again: "Twenty-four hours, I *think*; or is it twelve? I——"

"Oh, don't bother *me*!" said the Duchess. "I never could abide figures!" And with that she began nursing her child again, singing a sort of lullaby to it as she did so, and giving it a violent shake at the end of every line:—

> *Speak roughly to your little boy,*
> *And beat him when he sneezes:*
> *He only does it to annoy,*
> *Because he knows it teases.*

CHORUS

(in which the cook and the baby joined):—

Wow! wow! wow!

"If everybody minded their own business," the Duchess said,
in a hoarse growl, "the world would go round a deal faster than it does."

While the Duchess sang the second verse of the song, she kept tossing the baby violently up and down, and the poor little thing howled so, that Alice could hardly hear the words:—

> *I speak severely to my boy,*
> *I beat him when he sneezes;*
> *For he can thoroughly enjoy*
> *The pepper when he pleases!*

Chorus

Wow! wow! wow!

"Here! You may nurse it a bit, if you like!" the Duchess said to Alice, flinging the baby at her as she spoke. "I must go and get ready to play croquet with the Queen," and she hurried out of the room. The cook threw a frying-pan after her as she went, but it just missed her.

Alice caught the baby with some difficulty, as it was a queer-shaped little creature, and held out its arms and legs in all directions, "just like a starfish," thought Alice. The poor little thing was snorting like a steam-engine when she caught it, and kept doubling itself up and straightening itself out again, so that altogether, for the first minute or two, it was as much as she could do to hold it.

As soon as she had made out the proper way of nursing it (which was to twist it up into a sort of knot, and then keep tight hold of its right ear and left foot, so as to prevent its undoing itself), she carried it out into the open air. "If I don't take this child away with me," thought Alice, "they're sure to kill it in a day or two. Wouldn't it be murder to leave it behind?" She said the last words out loud, and the little thing grunted in reply (it had left off sneezing by this time). "Don't grunt," said Alice; "that's not at all a proper way of expressing yourself."

The baby grunted again, and Alice looked very anxiously into its face to see what was the matter with it. There could be no doubt that it had a *very* turn-up nose, much more like a snout than a real nose: also its eyes were getting extremely small for a baby: altogether Alice did not like the look of the thing at all. "But perhaps it was only sobbing," she thought, and looked into its eyes again, to see if there were any tears.

No, there were no tears. "If you're going to turn into a pig, my dear," said Alice, seriously, "I'll have nothing more to do with you. Mind now!" The poor little thing sobbed again (or grunted, it was impossible to say which), and they went on for some while in silence.

Alice was just beginning to think to herself, "Now, what am I to do with this creature, when I get it home?" when it grunted again, so violently, that she looked down into its face in some alarm. This time there could be *no* mistake about it: it was neither more or less than a pig, and she felt that it would be quite absurd for her to carry it any further.

So she set the little creature down, and felt quite relieved to see it trot away quietly into the wood. "If it had grown up," she said to herself, "it would have made a dreadfully ugly child: but it makes rather a handsome pig, I think." And she began thinking over other children she knew, who might do very well as pigs, and was just saying to herself "if one only knew the right way to change them——" when she was a little startled by seeing the Cheshire-Cat sitting on a bough of a tree a few yards off.

The Cat only grinned when it saw Alice. It looked good-natured, she thought: still it had *very* long claws and a great many teeth, so she felt that it ought to be treated with respect.

"Cheshire-Puss," she began rather timidly, as she did not at all know whether it would like the name: however, it only grinned a little wider. "Come, it's pleased so far," thought Alice, and she went on. "Would you tell me, please, which way I ought to go from here?"

"That depends a good deal on where you want to get to," said the Cat.

"I don't much care where——" said Alice.

"Then it doesn't matter which way you go," said the Cat.

"—— so long as I get *somewhere*," Alice added as an explanation.

"Oh, you're sure to do that," said the Cat, "if you only walk long enough."

Alice felt that this could not be denied, so she tried another question. "What sort of people live about here?"

"In *that* direction," the Cat said, waving its right paw around, "lives a Hatter: and in *that* direction," waving the

other paw, "lives a March Hare. Visit either you like: they're both mad."

"But I don't want to go among mad people," Alice remarked.

"Oh, you can't help that," said the Cat: "we're all mad here. I'm mad. You're mad."

"How do you know I'm mad?" said Alice.

"You must be," said the Cat, "or you wouldn't have come here."

Alice didn't think that proved it at all: however, she went on: "And how do you know that you're mad?"

"To begin with," said the Cat, "a dog's not mad. You grant that?"

"I suppose so," said Alice.

"Well, then," the Cat went on, "you see a dog growls when it's angry, and wags its tail when it's pleased. Now I growl when I'm pleased, and wag my tail when I'm angry. Therefore I'm mad."

"I call it purring, not growling," said Alice.

"Call it what you like," said the Cat. "Do you play croquet with the Queen today?"

"I should like it very much," said Alice, "but I haven't been invited yet."

"You'll see me there," said the Cat, and vanished.

Alice was not much surprised at this, she was getting so well used to queer things happening. While she was still looking at the place where it had been, it suddenly appeared again.

"By-the bye, what became of the baby?" said the Cat. "I'd nearly forgotten to ask."

"It turned into a pig," Alice answered very quietly, just as if the Cat had come back in a natural way.

"I thought it would," said the Cat, and vanished again.

Alice waited a little, half expecting to see it again, but it did not appear, and after a minute or two she walked on in the direction in which the March Hare was said to live. "I've seen hatters before," she said to herself: "the March Hare will be the most interesting, and perhaps, as this is May, it won't be raving mad – at least not so mad as it was in March." As she said this, she looked up, and there was the Cat again, sitting on a branch of a tree.

"Did you say 'pig', or 'fig'?" said the Cat.

"I said 'pig'," replied Alice; "and I wish you wouldn't keep appearing and vanishing so suddenly: you make one quite giddy!"

"All right," said the Cat; and this time it vanished quite slowly, beginning with the end of the tail, and ending with the grin, which remained some time after the rest of it had gone.

"Well! I've often seen a cat without a grin," thought Alice; "but a grin without a cat! It's the most curious thing I ever saw in all my life!"

She had not gone much farther before she came in sight of the house of the March Hare: she thought it must be the right house, because the chimneys were shaped like ears and the roof was thatched with fur. It was so large a house, that she did not like to go nearer till she had nibbled some more of the left-hand bit of mushroom, and raised herself to about two feet high: even then she walked up towards it rather timidly, saying to herself "Suppose it should be raving mad after all! I almost wish I'd gone to see the Hatter instead!"

CHAPTER 7
A Mad Tea-Party

THERE was a table set out under a tree in front of the
house, and the March Hare and the Hatter were having tea at
it: a Dormouse was sitting between them, fast asleep, and the
other two were using it as a cushion, resting their elbows on it,
and talking over its head. "Very uncomfortable for the
Dormouse," thought Alice; "only as it's asleep, I suppose it
doesn't mind."

The table was a large one, but the three were all crowded
together at one corner of it. "No room! No room!" they cried
out when they saw Alice coming. "There's *plenty* of room!"
said Alice indignantly, and she sat down in a large arm-chair at
one end of the table.

"Have some wine," the March Hare said in
an encouraging tone.

Alice looked all round the table, but there was nothing on it but tea. "I don't see any wine," she remarked.

"There isn't any," said the March Hare.

"Then it wasn't very civil of you to offer it," said Alice angrily.

"It wasn't very civil of you to sit down without being invited," said the March Hare.

"I didn't know it was *your* table," said Alice: "it's laid for a great many more than three."

"Your hair wants cutting," said the Hatter. He had been looking at Alice for some time with great curiosity, and this was his first speech.

"You should learn not to make personal remarks," Alice said with some severity: "it's very rude."

The Hatter opened his eyes wide on hearing this; but all he *said* was "Why is a raven like a writing-desk?"

"Come, we shall have some fun now!" thought Alice. "I'm glad they've begun asking riddles – I believe I can guess that," she added aloud.

"Do you mean that you think you can find out the answer to it," said the March Hare.

"Exactly so," said Alice.

"Then you should say what you mean," the March Hare went on.

"I do," Alice hastily replied; "at least – at least I mean what I say – that's the same thing, you know."

"Not the same thing a bit!" said the Hatter. "Why, you might just as well say that 'I see what I eat' is the same thing as 'I eat what I see'!"

"You might just as well say," added the March Hare, "that 'I like what I get' is the same thing as 'I get what I like'!"

"You might just as well say," added the Dormouse, which seemed to be talking in its sleep, "that 'I breathe when I sleep' is the same thing as 'I sleep when I breathe'!"

"It *is* the same thing with you," said the Hatter, and here the conversation dropped, and the party sat silent for a minute, while Alice thought over all she could remember about ravens and writing-desks, which wasn't much.

The Hatter was the first to break the silence. "What day of the month is it?" he said, turning to Alice: he had taken his

watch out of his pocket, and was looking at it uneasily, shaking it every now and then, and holding it to his ear.

Alice considered a little, and then said, "The fourth."

"Two days wrong!" sighed the Hatter. "I told you butter wouldn't suit the works!" he added, looking angrily at the March Hare.

"It was the *best* butter," the March Hare meekly replied.

"Yes, but some crumbs must have got in as well," the Hatter grumbled: "you shouldn't have put it in with the bread-knife."

The March Hare took the watch and looked at it gloomily; then he dipped it into his cup of tea, and looked at it again: but he could think of nothing better to say than his first remark, "It was the *best* butter, you know."

Alice had been looking over his shoulder with some curiosity. "What a funny watch!" she remarked. "It tells the day of the month, and doesn't tell what o'clock it is!"

"Why should it?" muttered the Hatter. "Does *your* watch tell you what year it is?"

"Of course not," Alice replied very readily: "but that's because it stays the same year for such a long time together."

"Which is just the case with *mine*," said the Hatter.

Alice felt dreadfully puzzled. The Hatter's remark seemed to her to have no sort of meaning in it, and yet it was certainly English. "I don't quite understand you," she said, as politely as she could.

"The Dormouse is asleep again," said the Hatter, and he poured a little hot tea upon its nose.

The Dormouse shook its head impatiently, and said, without opening its eyes, "Of course, of course: just what I was going to remark myself."

"Have you guessed the riddle yet?" the Hatter said, turning to Alice again.

"No, I give it up," Alice replied. "What's the answer?"

"I haven't the slightest idea," said the Hatter.

"Nor I," said the March Hare.

Alice sighed wearily. "I think you might do something better with the time," she said, "than wasting it in asking riddles that have no answer."

"If you knew Time as well as I do," said the Hatter, "you wouldn't talk about wasting *it*. It's *him*."

"I don't know what you mean," said Alice.

"Of course you don't," the Hatter said, tossing his head contemptuously. "I dare say you never even spoke to Time!"

"Perhaps not," Alice cautiously replied; "but I know I have to beat time when I learn music."

"Ah! That accounts for it," said the Hatter. "He won't stand beating. Now, if you only kept on good terms with him, he'd do almost anything you liked with the clock. For instance, suppose it were nine o'clock in the morning, just time to begin lessons: you'd only have to whisper a hint to Time, and round goes the clock in a twinkling! Half-past one, time for dinner!"

("I only wish it was," the March Hare said to itself in a whisper.)

"That would be grand, certainly," said Alice thoughtfully; "but then – I shouldn't be hungry for it, you know."

"Not at first, perhaps," said the Hatter: "but you could keep it to half-past one as long as you liked."

"Is that the way *you* manage?" Alice asked.

The Hatter shook his head mournfully. "Not I!" he replied. "We quarrelled last March – just before *he* went mad, you know——" (pointing with his teaspoon at the March Hare,) "——it was at the great concert given by the Queen of Hearts, and I had to sing

> *Twinkle, twinkle, little bat!*
> *How I wonder what you're at!"*

You know the song, perhaps?"

"I've heard something like it," said Alice.

"It goes on, you know," the Hatter continued, "in this way:—

> *Up above the world you fly,*
> *Like a tea-tray in the sky.*
> *Twinkle, twinkle——"*

Here the dormouse shook itself and began singing in its sleep "*Twinkle, twinkle, twinkle, twinkle——*" and went on so long that they had to pinch it to make it stop.

"Well, I'd hardly finished the verse," said the Hatter, "when

the Queen bawled out, 'He's murdering the time! Off with his head!'"

"How dreadfully savage!" exclaimed Alice.

"And ever since that," the Hatter went on in a mournful tone, "he won't do a thing I ask! It's always six o'clock now."

A bright idea came into Alice's head. "Is that the reason so many tea-things are put out here?" she asked.

"Yes, that's it," said the Hatter with a sigh: "it's always tea-time, and we've no time to wash the things between whiles."

"Then you keep moving round, I suppose?" said Alice.

"Exactly so," said the Hatter: "as the things get used up."

"But what happens when you come to the beginning again?" Alice ventured to ask.

"Suppose we change the subject," the March Hare interrupted, yawning. "I'm getting tired of this. I vote the young lady tells us a story."

"I'm afraid I don't know one," said Alice, rather alarmed at the proposal.

"Then the Dormouse shall!" they both cried. "Wake up, Dormouse!" And they pinched it on both sides at once.

The Dormouse slowly opened its eyes. "I wasn't asleep," it said in a hoarse, feeble voice, "I heard every word you fellows were saying."

"Tell us a story!" said the March Hare.

"Yes, please do!" pleaded Alice.

"And be quick about it," added the Hatter, "or you'll be asleep again before it's done."

"Once upon a time there were three little sisters," the Dormouse began in a great hurry; "and their names were Elsie, Lacie, and Tillie; and they lived at the bottom of a well——"

"What did they live on?" said Alice, who always took a great interest in questions of eating and drinking.

"They lived on treacle," said the Dormouse, after thinking a minute or two.

"They couldn't have done that, you know," Alice gently remarked. "They'd have been ill."

"So they were," said the Dormouse; "*very* ill."

Alice tried a little to fancy to herself what such an extraordinary way of living would be like, but it puzzled her too much: so she went on: "But why did they live at the bottom of a well?"

"Take some more tea," the March Hare said to Alice, earnestly.

"I've had nothing yet," Alice replied in an offended tone: "so I can't take more."

"You mean you can't take *less*," said the Hatter: "it's very easy to take *more* than nothing."

"Nobody asked *your* opinion," said Alice.

"Who's making personal remarks now?" the Hatter asked triumphantly.

Alice did not quite know what to say to this: so she helped herself to some tea and bread-and-butter, and then turned to the Dormouse, and repeated her question. "Why did they live at the bottom of a well?"

The Dormouse again took a minute or two to think about it, and then said "It was a treacle-well."

"There's no such thing!" Alice was beginning very angrily, but the Hatter and the March Hare went "Sh! Sh!" and the Dormouse sulkily remarked "If you can't be civil, you'd better finish the story for yourself."

"No, please go on!" Alice said very humbly. "I won't interrupt you again. I dare say there may be *one*."

"One, indeed!" said the Dormouse indignantly. However, he consented to go on. "And so these three little sisters – they were learning to draw, you know——"

"What did they draw?" said Alice, quite forgetting her promise.

"Treacle," said the Dormouse, without considering at all, this time.

"I want a clean cup," interrupted the Hatter: "let's all move one place on."

He moved on as he spoke, and the Dormouse followed him: the March Hare moved into the Dormouse's place, and Alice rather unwillingly took the place of the March Hare. The Hatter was the only one who got any advantage from the change; and Alice was a good deal worse off than before, as the March Hare had just upset the milk-jug into his plate.

Alice did not wish to offend the Dormouse again, so she began very cautiously: "But I don't understand. Where did

they draw the treacle from?"

"You can draw water out of a water-well," said the Hatter; "so I should think you could draw treacle out of a treacle-well – eh, stupid?"

"But they were *in* the well," Alice said to the Dormouse, not choosing to notice this last remark.

"Of course they were," said the Dormouse: "well in."

This answer so confused poor Alice, that she let the Dormouse go on for some time without interrupting it.

"They were learning to draw," the Dormouse went on, yawning and rubbing its eyes, for it was getting very sleepy; "and they drew all manner of things – everything that begins with an M——"

"Why with an M?" said Alice.

"Why not?" said the March Hare.

Alice was silent.

The Dormouse had closed his eyes by this time, and was going off into a doze; but, on being pinched by the Hatter, it woke up again with a little shriek, and went on: "——that begins with an M, such as mousetraps, and the moon, and memory, and muchness – you know you say things are 'much of a muchness' – did you ever see such a thing as a drawing of a muchness?"

"Really, now you ask me," said Alice, very much confused, "I don't think——"

"Then you shouldn't talk," said the Hatter.

This piece of rudeness was more than Alice could bear: she got up in great disgust, and walked off: the Dormouse fell asleep instantly, and neither of the others took the least notice of her going, though she looked back once or twice, half hoping that they would call after her: the last time she saw them, they were trying to put the Dormouse into the teapot.

"At any rate I'll never go *there* again!" said Alice, as she picked her way through the wood. "It's the stupidest tea-party I ever was at in all my life!"

Just as she had said this, she noticed that one of the trees had a door leading right into it. "That's very curious!" she thought. "But everything's curious today. I think I may as well go in at once." And in she went.

Once more she found herself in the long hall, and close to

the little glass table. "Now, I'll manage better this time," she said to herself, and began by taking the little golden key, and unlocking the door that led into the garden. Then she set to work nibbling at the mushroom (she had kept a piece of it in her pocket) till she was about a foot high; then she walked down the little passage: and *then* – she found herself at last in the beautiful garden, among the bright flower-beds and the cool fountains.

The Queen's Croquet-Ground

A LARGE rose-tree stood near the entrance of the garden: the roses growing on it were white, but there were three gardeners at it, busily painting them red. Alice thought this a very curious thing, and she went nearer to watch them, and, just as she came up to them, she heard one of them say "Look out now, Five! Don't go splashing paint over me like that!"

"I couldn't help it," said Five, in a sulky tone. "Seven jogged my elbow."

On which Seven looked up and said "That's right, Five! Always lay the blame on others!"

"*You'd* better not talk!" said Five. "I heard the Queen say only yesterday you deserved to be beheaded."

"What for?" said the one who had spoken first.

"That's none of *your* business, Two!" said Seven.

"Yes, it *is* his business!" said Five. "And I'll tell him – it was for bringing the cook tulip-roots instead of onions."

Seven flung down his brush, and had just begun "Well, of all the unjust things———" when his eye chanced to fall upon Alice, as she stood watching them, and he checked himself suddenly: the others looked round also, and all of them bowed low.

"Would you tell me, please," said Alice, a little timidly, "why you are painting those roses?"

Five and Seven said nothing, but looked at Two. Two began, in a low voice, "Why, the fact is, you see, Miss, this here ought to have been a *red* rose-tree, and we put a white one in by mistake; and, if the Queen was to find it out, we should all have our heads cut off, you know. So you see, Miss, we're doing our best, afore she comes, to———" At this moment, Five, who had been anxiously looking across the garden, called out "The Queen! The Queen!" and the three gardeners instantly threw themselves flat upon their faces. There was a sound of many footsteps, and Alice looked round, eager to see the Queen.

First came ten soldiers carrying clubs: these were all shaped like the three gardeners, oblong and flat, with their hands and feet at the corners: next the ten courtiers: these were ornamented all over with diamonds, and walked two and two, as the soldiers did. After these came the royal children: there were ten of them, and the little dears came jumping merrily along, hand in hand, in couples: they were all ornamented with hearts. Next came the guests, mostly Kings and Queens, and among them Alice recognised the White Rabbit: it was talking in a hurried nervous manner, smiling at everything that was said, and went by without noticing her. Then followed the Knave of Hearts, carrying the King's crown on a crimson velvet cushion; and, last of all this grand procession, came THE KING AND THE QUEEN OF HEARTS.

Alice was rather doubtful whether she ought not to lie down on her face like the three gardeners, but she could not remember ever having heard of such a rule at processions, "and besides, what would be the use of a procession," thought she, "if people had all to lie down on their faces, so that they couldn't see it?" So she stood where she was, and waited.

When the procession came opposite to Alice, they all

hedgehog, which seemed to Alice an excellent opportunity for croqueting one of them with the other: the only difficulty was, that her flamingo was gone across to the other side of the garden, where Alice could see it trying in a helpless sort of way to fly up into a tree.

By the time she had caught the flamingo and brought it back, the fight was over, and both the hedgehogs were out of sight: "but it doesn't matter much," thought Alice, "as all the arches are gone from this side of the ground." So she tucked it away under her arm, that it might not escape again, and went back to have a little more conversation with her friend.

When she got back to the Cheshire-Cat, she was surprised to find quite a large crowd collected round it: there was a dispute going on between the executioner, the King, and the Queen, who were all talking at once, while all the rest were quite silent, and looked very uncomfortable.

The moment Alice appeared, she was appealed to by all three to settle the question, and they repeated their arguments to her, though, as they all spoke at once, she found it very hard to make out exactly what they said.

The executioner's argument was, that you couldn't cut off a head unless there was a body to cut it off from: that he had never had to do such a thing before, and he wasn't going to begin at *his* time of life.

The King's argument was that anything that had a head could be beheaded, and that you weren't to talk nonsense.

The Queen's argument was that, if something wasn't done about it in less than no time, she'd have everybody executed, all round. (It was this last remark that had made the whole party look so grave and anxious.)

Alice could think of nothing else to say but "It belongs to the Duchess: you'd better ask *her* about it."

"She's in prison," the Queen said to the executioner: "fetch her here." And the executioner went off like an arrow.

The Cat's head began fading away the moment he was gone, and, by the time he had come back with the Duchess, it had entirely disappeared: so the King and the executioner ran wildly up and down, looking for it, while the rest of the party went back to the game.

CHAPTER 9
The Mock Turtle's Story

"Y OU can't think how glad I am to see you again, you dear old thing!" said the Duchess, as she tucked her arm affectionately into Alice's, and they walked off together.

Alice was very glad to find her in such a pleasant temper, and thought to herself that perhaps it was only the pepper that had made her so savage when they met in the kitchen.

"When *I'm* a Duchess," she said to herself (not in a very hopeful tone, though), "I won't have any pepper in my kitchen *at all*. Soup does very well without – Maybe it's always pepper that makes people hot-tempered," she went on, very much pleased at having found out a new kind of rule, "and vinegar that makes them sour – and camomile that makes them bitter – and – and barley-sugar and such things that make children sweet-tempered. I only wish people knew *that*: then they wouldn't be so stingy about it, you know——"

The Duchess took her choice, and was gone in a moment.

"Let's go on with the game," the Queen said to Alice; and Alice was too much frightened to say a word, but slowly followed her back to the croquet-ground.

The other guests had taken advantage of the Queen's absence, and were resting in the shade: however, the moment they saw her, they hurried back to the game, the Queen merely remarking that a moment's delay would cost them their lives.

All the time they were playing the Queen never left off quarrelling with the other players, and shouting "Off with his head!" or "Off with her head!" Those whom she sentenced were taken into custody by the soldiers, who of course had to leave off being arches to do this, so that, by the end of half an hour or so, there were no arches left. and all the players, except the King, the Queen, and Alice, were in custody and under sentence of execution.

Then the Queen left off, quite out of breath, and said to Alice, "Have you seen the Mock Turtle yet?"

"No," said Alice. "I don't even know what a Mock Turtle is."

"It's the thing Mock Turtle Soup is made from," said the Queen.

"I never saw one, or heard of one," said Alice.

"Come on, then," said the Queen, "and he shall tell you his history."

As they walked off together, Alice heard the King say in a low voice, to the company generally, "You are all pardoned." "Come, *that's* a good thing!" she said to herself, for she had felt quite unhappy at the number of executions the Queen had ordered.

They very soon came upon a Gryphon, lying fast asleep in the sun. (If you don't know what a Gryphon is, look at the picture.) "Up, lazy thing!" said the Queen, "and take this young lady to see the Mock Turtle, and to hear his history. I must go back and see after some executions I have ordered"; and she walked off, leaving Alice alone with the Gryphon. Alice did not quite like the look of the creature, but on the whole she thought it would be quite as safe to stay with it as to go after that savage Queen: so she waited.

The Gryphon sat up and rubbed his eyes: then it watched the Queen till she was out of sight: then it chuckled. "What fun!"

said the Gryphon, half to itself, half to Alice.

"What *is* the fun?" said Alice.

"Why, *she*," said the Gryphon. "It's all her fancy, that: they never executes nobody, you know. Come on!"

"Everybody says 'come on!' here," thought Alice, as she went slowly after it: "I never was so ordered about before, in all my life, never!"

They had not gone far before they saw the Mock Turtle in the distance, sitting sad and lonely on a little ledge of rock, and, as they came nearer, Alice could hear him sighing as if his heart would break. She pitied him deeply. "What is his sorrow?" she asked the Gryphon. And the Gryphon answered, very nearly in the same words as before. "It's all his fancy, that: he hasn't got no sorrow, you know. Come on!"

So they went up to the Mock Turtle, who looked at them with large eyes full of tears, but said nothing.

"This here young lady," said the Gryphon, "she wants for to know your history, she do."

"I'll tell it to her," said the Mock Turtle in a deep, hollow tone. "Sit down, both of you, and don't speak a word till I've finished."

So they sat down, and nobody spoke for some minutes. Alice thought to herself "I don't see how he can *ever* finish, if he doesn't begin." But she waited patiently.

"Once," said the Mock Turtle at last, with a deep sigh, "I was a real Turtle."

These words were followed by a very long silence, broken only by an occasional exclamation of "Hjckrrh!" from the Gryphon, and the constant heavy sobbing of the Mock Turtle. Alice was very nearly getting up and saying "Thank you, Sir, for your interesting story," but she could not help thinking there *must* be more to come, so she sat still and said nothing.

"When we were little," the Mock Turtle went on at last, more calmly, though still sobbing a little now and then, "we went to school in the sea. The master was an old Turtle – we used to call him Tortoise——"

"Why did you call him Tortoise, if he wasn't one?" Alice asked.

"We called him Tortoise because he taught us," said the Mock Turtle angrily. "Really you are very dull!"

Alice did not feel encouraged to ask any more questions about it: so she turned to the Mock Turtle, and said "What else had you to learn?"

"Well, there was Mystery," the Mock Turtle replied, counting off the subjects on his flappers, – "Mystery, ancient and modern, with Seaography: then Drawling – The Drawling-master was an old conger-eel, that used to come once a week: *he* taught us Drawling, Stretching, and Fainting in Coils."

"What was *that* like?" said Alice.

"Well, I can't show it you, myself," the Mock Turtle said: "I'm too stiff. And the Gryphon never learnt it."

"Hadn't time," said the Gryphon: "I went to the classical master, though. He was an old crab, *he* was."

"I never went to him," the Mock Turtle said with a sigh. "He taught Laughing and Grief, they used to say."

"So he did, so he did," said the Gryphon, sighing in his turn; and both creatures hid their faces in their paws.

"And how many hours a day did you do lessons?" said Alice, in a hurry to change the subject.

"Ten hours the first day," said the Mock Turtle: "nine the next, and so on."

"What a curious plan!" exclaimed Alice.

"That's the reason they're called lessons," the Gryphon remarked: "because they lessen from day to day."

This was quite a new idea to Alice, and she thought it over a little before she made her next remark. "Then the eleventh day must have been a holiday?"

"Of course it was," said the Mock Turtle.

"And how did you manage on the twelfth?" Alice went on eagerly.

"That's enough about lessons," the Gryphon interrupted in a very decided tone. "Tell her something about the games now."

CHAPTER 10

The Lobster-Quadrille

THE Mock Turtle sighed deeply, and drew the back of one flapper across his eyes. He looked at Alice and tried to speak, but, for a minute or two, sobs choked his voice. "Same as if he had a bone in his throat," said the Gryphon; and it set to work shaking him and punching him in the back. At last the Mock Turtle recovered his voice, and, with tears running down his cheeks, he went on again:—

"You may not have lived much under the sea—" ("I haven't," said Alice) "—and perhaps you were never even introduced to a lobster—" (Alice began to say "I once tasted——" but checked herself hastily, and said "No, never") "—so you can have no idea what a delightful thing a Lobster-Quadrille is!"

"No indeed," said Alice. "What sort of a dance is it?"

"Why," said the Gryphon, "you first form into a line along the seashore——"

"Two lines!" cried the Mock Turtle. "Seals, turtles, salmon, and so on: then, when you've cleared all the jelly-fish out of the way——"

"*That* generally takes some time," interrupted the Gryphon.

"—you advance twice——"

"Each with a lobster as a partner!" cried the Gryphon.

"Of course," the Mock Turtle said: "advance twice, set to partners——"

"—change lobsters, and retire in same order," continued the Gryphon.

"Then, you know," the Mock Turtle went on, "you throw the——"

"The lobsters!" shouted the Gryphon, with a bound into the air.

"—as far out to sea as you can——"

"Swim after them!" screamed the Gryphon.

"Turn a somersault in the sea!" cried the Mock Turtle, capering wildly about.

"Change lobsters again!" yelled the Gryphon at the top of its voice.

"Back to land again, and – that's all the first figure," said the Mock Turtle, suddenly dropping his voice; and the two creatures, who had been jumping about like mad things all this time, sat down again very sadly and quietly, and looked at Alice.

"It must be a very pretty dance," said Alice timidly.

"Would you like to see a little of it?" said the Mock Turtle.

"Very much indeed," said Alice.

"Come, let's try the figure!" said the Mock Turtle to the Gryphon. "We can do it without lobsters, you know. Which shall sing?"

"Oh, *you* sing," said the Gryphon. "I've forgotten the words."

So they began solemnly dancing round and round Alice, every now and then treading on her toes when they passed too close, and waving their fore-paws to mark the time while the Mock Turtle sang this, very slowly and sadly:—

"Will you walk a little faster?" said a whiting to a snail,
"There's a porpoise close behind us, and he's treading
      on my tail.
See how eagerly the lobsters and the turtles all advance!
They are waiting on the shingle – will you come and
      join the dance?
    Will you, won't you, will you, won't you, will you
      join the dance?
    Will you, won't you, will you, won't you, won't you
      join the dance?

"You can really have no notion how delightful it will be
When they take us up and throw us, with the lobsters,
      out to sea!"
But the snail replied "Too far, too far!", and gave a look
      askance—
Said he thanked the whiting kindly, but he would not
      join the dance.
    Would not, could not, would not, could not, would not
      join the dance.
    Would not, could not, would not, could not, could not
      join the dance.

"What matters it how far we go?" his scaly friend replied.
"There is another shore, you know, upon the other side.
Then further off from England the nearer is to France—
Then turn not pale, beloved snail, but come and join the dance.
    Will you, won't you, will you, won't you, will you join the
      dance?
    Will you, won't you, will you, won't you, won't you join the
      dance?

CHAPTER 11

Who Stole the Tarts?

THE King and Queen of Hearts were seated on their throne when they arrived, with a great crowd assembled about them – all sorts of little birds and beasts, as well as the whole pack of cards: the Knave was standing before them, in chains, with a soldier on each side to guard him; and near the King was the White Rabbit, with a trumpet in one hand, and a scroll of parchment in the other. In the very middle of the court was a table, with a large dish of tarts upon it: they looked so good, that it made Alice quite hungry to look at them – "I wish they'd get the trial done," she thought, "and hand round the refreshments!" But there seemed to be no chance of this; so she began looking at everything about her to pass away the time.

WHO STOLE THE TARTS?

Alice had never been in a court of justice before, but she had read about them in books, and she was quite pleased to find that she knew the name of nearly everything there. "That's the judge," she said to herself, "because of his great wig."

The judge, by the way, was the King; and, as he wore his crown over the wig, he did not look at all comfortable, and it was certainly not becoming.

"And that's the jury-box, thought Alice; "and those twelve creatures," (she was obliged to say "creatures," you see, because some of them were animals, and some were birds,) "I suppose they are the jurors." She said this last word two or three times over to herself, being rather proud of it: for she thought, and rightly too, that very few little girls of her age knew the meaning of it at all. However, "jurymen" would have done just as well.

The twelve jurors were all writing very busily on slates. "What are they doing?" Alice whispered to the Gryphon. "They can't have anything to put down yet, before the trial's begun."

"They're putting down their names," the Gryphon whispered in reply, "for fear they should forget them before the end of the trial."

"Stupid things!" Alice began in a loud indignant voice; but she stopped herself hastily, for the White Rabbit cried "Silence in the Court!", and the King put on his looked anxiously round, to make out who was ta

Alice could see, as well as if she were looking shoulders, that all the jurors were writing down "things!" on their slates, and she could even make o of them didn't know how to spell "stupid," and that he had to ask his neighbour to tell him. "A nice muddle their slates'll be in, before the trial's over!" thought Alice.

One of the jurors had a pencil that squeaked. This, of course, Alice could *not* stand, and she went round the court and got behind him, and very soon found an opportunity of taking it away. She did it so quickly that the poor little juror (it was Bill, the Lizard) could not make out at all what had become of it; so, after hunting all about for it, he was obliged to write with one finger for the rest of the day; and this was of very little use, as it left no mark on the slate.

"Herald, read the accusation!" said the King.

On this the White Rabbit blew three blasts on the trumpet, and then unrolled the parchment-scroll, and read as follow:—

> *The Queen of Hearts, she made some tarts*
> *All on a summers day:*
> *The Knave of Hearts, he stole those tarts*
> *And took them quite away!*

"Consider your verdict," the King said to the jury.

"Not yet, not yet!" the Rabbit hastily interrupted. "There's a great deal to come before that!"

"Call the first witness," said the King; and the White Rabbit blew three blasts on the trumpet, and called out "First witness!"

The first witness was the Hatter. He came in with a teacup in one hand and a piece of bread-and-butter in the other. "I beg pardon, your Majesty," he began, "for bringing these in; but I hadn't quite finished my tea when I was sent for."

"You ought to have finished," said the King. "When did you begin?"

The Hatter looked at the March Hare, who had followed him into the court, arm-in-arm with the Dormouse. "Fourteenth of March, I *think* it was," he said.

"Fifteenth," said the March Hare.

"Sixteenth," said the Dormouse.

"Write that down," the King said to the jury; and the jury eagerly wrote down all three dates on their slates, and then added them up, and reduced the answer to shillings and pence.

"Take off your hat," the King said to the Hatter.

"It isn't mine," said the Hatter.

"*Stolen!*" the King exclaimed, turning to the jury, who instantly made a memorandum of the fact.

"I keep them to sell," the Hatter added as an explanation. "I've none of my own. I'm a hatter."

Here the Queen put on her spectacles, and began staring hard at the Hatter, who turned pale and fidgeted.

"Give your evidence," said the King; "and don't be nervous, or I'll have you executed on the spot."

This did not seem to encourage the witness at all: he kept shifting from one foot to the other, looking uneasily at the

WHO STOLE THE TARTS?

Queen, and in his confusion he bit a large piece out of his teacup instead of the bread-and-butter.

Just at this moment Alice felt a very curious sensatio which puzzled her a good deal until she made out what it wa she was beginning to grow larger again, and she thought at fir she would get up and leave the court; but on second though she decided to remain where she was as long as there was roo for her.

"I wish you wouldn't squeeze so," said the Dormouse, who was sitting next to her, "I can hardly breathe."

"I can't help it," said Alice very meekly: "I'm growing."

"You've no right to grow *here*," said the Dormouse.

"Don't talk nonsense," said Alice more boldly: "you know you're growing too."

"Yes, but *I* grow at a reasonable pace," said the Dormouse: "not in that ridiculous fashion." And he got up very sulkily and crossed over to the other side of the court.

All this time the Queen had never left off staring at the Hatter, and ___ ___ ___ormouse crossed the court, she said, to one of th ___ ___ court, "Bring me the list of singers in the last ___ ___ ___the wretched Hatter trembled so, that he sh ___

"Give y ___ ___ng repeated angrily, "or I'll have you ___ ___u're nervous or not."

"I'm a p ___ ___sty," the Hatter began, in a trembling voi ___ ___n't begun my tea – not above a week or so – and what with the bread-and-butter getting so thin – and the twinkling of the tea——"

"The twinkling of *what*?" said the King.

"It *began* with the tea," the Hatter replied.

"Of course twinkling *begins* with a T!" said the King sharply. "Do you take me for a dunce? Go on!"

"I'm a poor man," the Hatter went on, "and most things twinkled after that – only the March Hare said——"

"I didn't!" the March Hare interrupted in a great hurry.

"You did!" said the Hatter.

"I deny it!" said the March Hare.

"He denies it," said the King: "leave out that part."

"Well, at any rate, the Dormouse said——" the Hatter went on, looking anxiously round to see if he would deny it too; but

the Dormouse denied nothing, being fast asleep.

"After that," continued the Hatter, "I cut some more bread-and-butter——"

"But what did the Dormouse say?" one of the jury asked.

"That I can't remember," said the Hatter.

"You *must* remember," remarked the King, "or I'll have you executed."

The miserable Hatter dropped his teacup and bread-and-butter, and went down on one knee. "I'm a poor man, your Majesty," he began.

"You're a *very* poor *speaker*," said the King.

Here one of the guinea-pigs cheered, and was immediately suppressed by the officers of the court. (As that is rather a hard word, I will just explain to you how it is was done. They had a large canvas bag, which tied up at the mouth with strings: into this they slipped the guinea-pig, head first and then sat upon it.)

"I'm glad I've seen that done," thought Alice. "I've so often read in the newspapers, at the end of trials, 'There was some attempt at applause, which was immediately suppressed by the officers of the court,' and I never understood what it meant till now."

"If that's all you know about it, you may stand down," continued the King.

"I can't go no lower," said the Hatter: "I'm on the floor, as it is."

"Then you may *sit* down," the King replied.

Here the other guinea-pig cheered and was suppressed.

"Come, that finishes the guinea-pigs!" thought Alice. "Now we shall get on better."

"I'd rather finish my tea," said the Hatter, with an anxious look at the Queen, who was reading the list of singers.

"You may go," said the King, and the Hatter hurriedly left the court, without even waiting to put his shoes on.

"——and just take his head off outside," the Queen added to one of the officers; but the Hatter was out of sight before the officer could get to the door.

"Call the next witness!" said the King.

The next witness was the Duchess's cook. She carried the pepper-box in her hand, and Alice guessed who it was, even before she got into the court, by the way the people near the door began sneezing all at once.

"Give your evidence," said the King.

"Shan't," said the cook.

The King looked anxiously at the White Rabbit, who said, in a low voice, "Your Majesty must cross-examine *this* witness."

"Well, if I must, I must," the King said with a melancholy air, and, after folding his arms and frowning at the cook till his eyes were nearly out of sight, he said, in a deep voice, "What are tarts made of?"

"Pepper, mostly," said the cook.

"Treacle," said a sleepy voice behind her.

"Collar that Dormouse!" the Queen shrieked out. "Behead that Dormouse! Turn that Dormouse out of court! Suppress him! Pinch him! Off with his whiskers!"

For some minutes the whole court was in confusion, getting the Dormouse turned out, and, by the time they had settled down again, the cook had disappeared.

"Never mind!" said the King, with an air of great relief. "Call the next witness." And, he added, in an under-tone to the Queen, "Really, my dear, *you* must cross-examine the next witness. It quite makes my forehead ache!"

Alice watched the White Rabbit as he fumbled over the list, feeling very curious to see what the next witness would be like, "—for they haven't got much evidence *yet*," she said to herself. Imagine her surprise, when the White Rabbit read out, at the top of his shrill little voice, the name "Alice!"

"It's the oldest rule in the book," said the King.

"Then it ought to be Number One," said Alice.

The King turned pale, and shut his note-book hastily. "Consider your verdict," he said to the jury, in a low trembling voice.

"There's more evidence to come yet, please your Majesty," said the White Rabbit, jumping up in a great hurry: "this paper has just been picked up."

"What's in it?" said the Queen.

"I haven't opened it yet," said the White Rabbit; "but it seems to be a letter, written by the prisoner to – to somebody."

"It must have been that," said the King, "unless it was written to nobody, which isn't usual, you know."

"Who is it directed to?" said one of the jurymen.

"It isn't directed at all," said the White Rabbit: "in fact, there's nothing written on the *outside*." He unfolded the paper as he spoke, and added "It isn't a letter, after all: it's a set of verses."

"Are they in the prisoner's handwriting?" asked another of the jurymen.

"No, they're not," said the White Rabbit, "and that's the queerest thing about it." (The jury all looked puzzled.)

"He must have imitated somebody else's hand," said the King. (The jury all brightened up again.)

"Please your Majesty," said the Knave, "I didn't write it, and they can't prove that I did: there's no name signed at the end."

"If you didn't sign it," said the King, "that only makes the matter worse. You *must* have meant some mischief, or else you'd have signed your name like an honest man."

There was a general clapping of hands at this: it was the first really clever thing the King had said that day.

"That *proves* his guilt, of course," said the Queen: "so, off with——"

"It doesn't prove anything of the sort!" said Alice. "Why, you don't even know what they're about!"

"Read them," said the King.

The White Rabbit put on his spectacles. "Where shall I begin, please your Majesty?" he asked.

"Begin at the beginning," the King said, very gravely, "and

"Begin at the beginning," the King said, very gravely, *"and go on
till you come to the end: then stop."*

go on till you come to the end: then stop."

There was dead silence in the court, whilst the White Rabbit read out these verses:—

> They told me you had been to her,
>   And mentioned me to him:
> She gave me a good character,
>   But said I could not swim.
>
> He sent them word I had not gone
>   (We know it to be true):
> If she should push the matter on,
>   What would become of you?
>
> I gave her one, they gave him two,
>   You gave us three or more;
> They all returned from him to you,
>   Though they were mine before.
>
> If I or she should chance to be
>   Involved in this affair,
> He trusts to you to set them free,
>   Exactly as we were.
>
> My notion was that you had been
>   (Before she had this fit)
> An obstacle that came between
>   Him, and ourselves, and it.
>
> Don't let him know she liked them best,
>   For this must ever be
> A secret, kept from all the rest,
>   Between yourself and me.

"That's the most important piece of evidence we've heard yet," said the King, rubbing his hands; "so now let the jury——"

"If any one of them can explain it," said Alice, (she had grown so large in the last few minutes that she wasn't a bit afraid of interrupting him,) "I'll give him sixpence. *I don't*

believe there's an atom of meaning in it."

The jury all wrote down, on their slates, "*She* doesn't believe there's an atom of meaning in it," but none of them attempted to explain the paper.

"If there's no meaning in it," said the King, "that saves a world of trouble, you know, as we needn't try to find any. And yet I don't know," he went on, spreading out the verses on his knee, and looking at them with one eye; "I seem to see some meaning in them, after all. '—*said I could not swim—*' you can't swim, can you?" he added, turning to the Knave.

The Knave shook his head sadly. "Do I look like it?" he said. (Which he certainly did *not*, being made entirely out of cardboard.)

"All right, so far," said the King; and he went on muttering over the verses to himself: "'*We know it to be true*'—that's the jury, of course—'*If she should push the matter on*' – that must be the Queen – '*What would become of you?* – What, indeed! – '*I gave her one, they gave him two*' – why, that must be what he did with the tarts, you know——"

"But it goes on '*they all returned from him to you,*'" said Alice.

"Why, there they are!" said the King, triumphantly pointing to the tarts on the table. "Nothing can be clearer than *that*. Then again – '*before she had this fit*' – you never had *fits*, my dear, I think?" he said to be the Queen.

"Never!" said the Queen, furiously, throwing an inkstand at the Lizard as she spoke. (The unfortunate little Bill had left off writing on his slate with one finger, as he found it made no mark; but he now hastily began again, using the ink, that was trickling down his face, as long as it lasted.)

"Then the words don't *fit* you," said the King, looking round the court with a smile. There was a dead silence.

"It's a pun!" the King added in an angry tone, and everybody laughed, "Let the jury consider their verdict," the King said, for about the twentieth time that day.

"No, no!" said the Queen. "Sentence first – verdict afterwards."

"Stuff and nonsense!" said Alice loudly. "The idea of having the sentence first!"

"Hold your tongue!" said the Queen, turning purple.

"I won't!" said Alice.

"Off with her head!" the Queen shouted at the top of her voice. Nobody moved.

"Who cares for *you*?" said Alice (she had grown to her full size by this time). "You're nothing but a pack of cards!"

At this the whole pack rose up into the air, and came flying down upon her; she gave a little scream, half of fright and half of anger, and tried to beat them off, and found herself lying on the bank, with her head in the lap of her sister, who was gently brushing away some dead leaves that had fluttered down from the trees upon her face.

"Wake up, Alice dear!" said her sister. "Why, what a long sleep you've had!"

"Oh, I've had such a curious dream!" said Alice. And she told her sister, as well as she could remember them, all these strange Adventures of hers that you have just been reading about; and, when she had finished, her sister kissed her, and said "It *was* a curious dream, dear, certainly; but now run in to your tea: it's getting late." So Alice got up and ran off, thinking while she ran, as well she might, what a wonderful dream it had been.

The Wind in the Willows

by

Kenneth Grahame

Introduction

Kenneth Grahame's *The Wind in the Willows* was first published in 1908. It is easy to see why it has become one of the classics of children's literature and why it continues to appeal today. The characters are individual masterpieces; the setting of the English countryside shown in all its seasons is totally charming; the language is a combination of the poetic and the humourous. *The Wind in the Willows* is a timeless tale that should be a part of everyone's childhood.

With the aim of reaching a wider range of readers, the text has been lightly abridged. Some of the most difficult words have been simplified and the longer sentences split for ease of reading and understanding. Two chapters from the original edition have been omitted. They are self-contained and in no way interrupt the sense of flow of the story.

For those who already know *The Wind in the Willows*, this edition will be a visual delight to return to again and again. For those who are about to discover the world of Mole, Ratty, Toad and Badger for the first time, there is a double treat in store: a marvellous read, beautifully illustrated.

CHAPTER 1

The River Bank

THE Mole had been working very hard all the morning, spring-cleaning his little home. First with brooms, then with dusters; then on ladders and steps and chairs, with a brush and a pail of whitewash; till he had dust in his throat and eyes, and splashes of whitewash all over his black fur, and an aching back and weary arms. Spring was moving in the air above and in the earth below and around him, penetrating even his dark and lowly little house. It was small wonder, then, that he suddenly flung down his brush on the floor, said 'Bother!' and 'O blow!' and also 'Hang spring-cleaning!' and bolted out of the house without even waiting to put on his coat. Something up above seemed to be calling him and he made for his steep little tunnel. He scraped and scratched and scrabbled and scrooged, and then he scrooged again and scrabbled and scratched and scraped, working busily with his little paws and muttering to himself, 'Up we go! Up we go!' till at last, pop! his snout came out into the sunlight, and he found himself rolling in the warm grass of a great meadow.

'This is fine!' he said to himself. 'This is better than whitewashing!' The sunshine struck hot on his fur, soft breezes caressed his heated brow, and after the peace of the underground home he had lived in so long the carol of happy birds fell on his dulled hearing almost like a shout. Jumping off all his four legs at once, in the joy of living and the delight of spring without its cleaning, he went on his way across the meadow till he reached the hedge on the further side.

'Hold up!' said an elderly rabbit at the gap. 'Sixpence for the privilege of passing by the private road!' He was bowled over in an instant by the impatient Mole, who trotted along the side of the hedge chaffing the other rabbits as they peeped hurriedly from their holes to see what the row was about. 'Onion-sauce! Onion-sauce!' he remarked jeeringly, and was gone before they could think of a thoroughly satisfactory reply. Then they all started grumbling at each other. 'How *stupid* you are! Why didn't you tell him——' 'Well, why didn't *you* say——' 'You might have reminded him——' and so on, in the usual way; but of course, it was then much too late, as is always the case.

It all seemed too good to be true. Hither and thither through the meadows he rambled busily, along the hedgerows, across the copses, finding everywhere birds building, flowers budding, leaves thrusting—everything happy, and progressive, and occupied. And instead of having an uneasy conscience pricking him and whispering 'Whitewash!' he somehow could only feel how jolly it was to be the only idle dog among all these busy citizens. After all, the best part of a holiday is perhaps not so much to be resting yourself, as to see all the other fellows busy working.

He thought his happiness was complete when, as he wandered aimlessly along, suddenly he stood by the edge of a full-fed river. Never in his life had he seen a river before— this sleek, twisting, powerful animal, chasing and chuckling, gripping things with a gurgle and leaving them with a laugh, to fling itself on fresh playmates that shook themselves free, and were caught and held again. All was a-shake and a-shiver—glints and gleams and sparkles, rustle and swirl, chatter and bubble. The Mole was bewitched, entranced, fascinated. By the side of the river he trotted; and tired at last, he sat on the bank, while the river chattered on.

As he sat on the grass and looked across the river, a dark hole in the bank opposite, just above the water's edge, caught his eye, and dreamily he fell to considering what a nice snug dwelling-place it would make for an animal with a few wants and fond of a riverside residence, above flood-level and away from noise and dust. As he gazed, something bright and small seemed to twinkle down in the heart of it, vanished, then twinkled once more like a tiny star. But it could hardly be a star in such an unlikely situation; and it was too glittering and small for a glow-worm. Then, as he looked, it winked at him, and so declared itself to be an eye; and a small face began gradually to grow up round it, like a frame round a picture.

A brown little face, with whiskers.

A grave round face, with the same twinkle in its eye that had first attracted his notice.

Small neat ears and thick silky hair.

It was the Water Rat!

Then the two animals stood and regarded each other cautiously.

'Hullo, Mole!' said the Water Rat.

'Hullo, Rat!' said the Mole.

'Would you like to come over?' asked the Rat presently.

'Oh, it's all very well to *talk*,' said the Mole, rather crossly, he being new to a river and riverside life and its ways.

The Rat said nothing, but stooped and unfastened a rope and hauled on it; then lightly stepped into a little boat which the Mole had not observed. It was painted blue outside and white within, and was just the size for two animals; and the Mole's whole heart went out to it at once, even though he did not yet fully understand its uses.

The Rat sculled smartly across and made fast. Then he held up his fore-paw as the Mole stepped gingerly down. 'Lean on that!' he said. 'Now then, step lively!' and the Mole to his surprise and rapture found himself actually seated in the stern of a real boat.

'This has been a wonderful day!' said he, as the Rat

shoved off and took to the sculls again. 'Do you know, I've never been in a boat before in all my life.'

'What?' cried the Rat, open-mouthed. 'Never been in a—you never—well, I—what have you been doing, then?'

'Is it so nice as all that?' asked the Mole shyly, though he was quite prepared to believe it as he leant back in his seat and looked at the cushions, the oars, the rowlocks, and all the fascinating fittings, and felt the boat sway lightly under him.

'Nice? It's the *only* thing,' said the Water Rat solemnly, as he leant forward for his stroke. 'Believe me, my young friend, there is *nothing*—absolutely nothing—half so much worth doing as simply messing about in boats. Simply messing,' he went on dreamily: 'messing—about—in—boats; messing——'

'Look ahead, Rat!' cried the Mole suddenly.

It was too late. The boat struck the bank full tilt. The dreamer, the joyous oarsman, lay on his back at the bottom of the boat, his heels in the air.

'—about in boats—or *with* boats,' the Rat went on, picking himself up with a pleasant laugh. 'In or out of 'em, it doesn't matter. Nothing seems really to matter, that's the charm of it. Whether you get away, or whether you don't; whether you arrive at your destination or whether you reach somewhere else, or whether you never get anywhere at all, you're always busy, and you never do anything in particular; and when you've done it there's always something else to do, and you can do it if you like, but you'd much better not. Look here! If you've really nothing else on hand this morning, supposing we drop down the river together, and have a long day of it?'

The Mole waggled his toes from sheer happiness, spread his chest with a sigh of full contentment, and leaned back blissfully into the soft cushions. '*What* a day I'm having!' he said. 'Let us start at once!'

'Hold hard a minute, then!' said the Rat. He looped the painter through a ring in his landing-stage, climbed up into his hole above, and after a short interval reappeared staggering under a fat, wicker luncheon-basket.

'Shove that under your feet,' he said to the Mole, as he

'Shove that under your feet,' he said to the Mole,
as he passed it down into the boat.

passed it down into the boat. Then he untied the painter and took the sculls again.

'What's inside it?' asked the Mole, wriggling with curiosity.

'There's cold chicken inside it,' replied the Rat briefly; 'coldtonguecoldhamcoldbeefpickledgherkinssaladfrenchrolls cresssandwichespottedmeatgingerbeerlemonadesodawater——'

'O stop, stop,' cried the Mole in ecstasies: 'This is too much!'

'Do you really think so?' inquired the Rat seriously. 'It's only what I always take on these little excursions; and the other animals are always telling me that I'm a mean beast and cut it *very* fine!'

The Mole never heard a word he was saying. Absorbed in the new life he was entering upon, intoxicated with the sparkle, the ripple, the scents and the sounds and the sunlight, he trailed a paw in the water and dreamed long waking dreams. The Water Rat, like the good little fellow he was, sculled steadily on and did not disturb him.

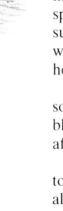

'I like your clothes awfully, old chap,' he remarked after some half an hour or so had passed. 'I'm going to get a black velvet smoking-suit myself some day, as soon as I can afford it.'

'I beg your pardon,' said the Mole, pulling himself together with an effort. 'You must think me very rude; but all this is so new to me. So—this—is—a—River!'

'*The* River,' corrected the Rat.

'And you really live by the river? What a jolly life!'

'By it and with it and on it and in it,' said the Rat. 'It's brother and sister to me, and aunts, and company, and food and drink, and (naturally) washing. It's my world, and I don't want any other. What it hasn't got is not worth having, and what it doesn't know is not worth knowing. Lord! the times we've had together! Whether in winter or summer, spring or autumn, it's always got its fun and its excitements. When the floods are on in February, and my cellars and basement are brimming with drink that's no good to me, and the brown water runs by my best bedroom window; or again when it all drops away and shows patches of mud that smells like plum-cake, and the rushes and weed clog the channels, and I can potter about dry-shod over most of the bed of it and find fresh food to eat, and things careless people have dropped out of boats!'

'But isn't it a bit dull at times?' the Mole ventured to ask. 'Just you and the river, and no one else to pass a word with?'

'No one else to—well, I mustn't be hard on you,' said the Rat patiently. 'You're new to it, and of course you don't know. The bank is so crowded nowadays that many people are moving away altogether. O no, it isn't what it used to be, at all. Otters, kingfishers, dabchicks, moorhens, all of them about all day long and always wanting you to *do* something —as if a fellow had no business of his own to attend to!'

'What lies over *there*?' asked the Mole, waving a paw towards a background of woodland that darkly framed the water-meadows on one side of the river.

'That? O, that's just the Wild Wood,' said the Rat shortly. 'We don't go there very much, we river bankers.'

'Aren't they—aren't they very *nice* people in there?' said the Mole a trifle nervously.

'W-e-ll,' replied the Rat, 'let me see. The squirrels are all right. *And* the rabbits—some of 'em, but rabbits are a mixed lot. And then there's Badger, of course. He lives right in the heart of it; wouldn't live anywhere else, either, if you paid him to do it. Dear old Badger! Nobody interferes with *him*. They'd better not,' he added significantly.

'Why, who *should* interfere with him?' asked the Mole.

'Well, of course—there—are others,' explained the Rat in a hesitating sort of way. 'Weasels—and stoats—and foxes—and so on. They're all right in a way—I'm very good friends with them—pass the time of day when we meet, and all that—but they break out sometimes, there's no denying it, and then—well, you can't really trust them, and that's the fact.'

'And beyond the Wild Wood again?' Mole asked: 'Where it's all blue and dim, and one sees what may be hills or perhaps they mayn't, and something like the smoke of towns, or is it only cloud-drift?'

'Beyond the Wild Wood comes the Wide World,' said the Rat. 'And that's something that doesn't matter, either to you or me. I've never been there, and I'm never going, nor you

either, if you've got any sense at all. Don't ever refer to it again, please. Now then! Here's our backwater at last, where we're going to lunch.'

Leaving the main stream, they now passed into what seemed at first sight like a little landlocked lake. Green turf sloped down to either edge, brown snaky tree-roots gleamed below the surface of the quiet water. Ahead of them the foamy tumble of a weir, arm-in-arm with a restless dripping mill-wheel, that held up a grey-gabled mill-house, filled the air with a soothing murmur of sound. It was so very beautiful that the Mole could only hold up both fore-paws and gasp, 'O my! O my! O my!'

The Rat brought the boat alongside the bank, made her fast, helped the Mole safely ashore, and swung out the luncheon-basket. The Mole begged as a favour to be allowed to unpack it all by himself; and the Rat was very pleased to indulge him, and to sprawl at full length on the grass and rest, while his excited friend shook out the table-cloth and spread it, took out all the mysterious packets one by one and arranged their contents in due order, still gasping, 'O my! O my!' at each fresh revelation. When all was ready, the Rat said, 'Now, pitch in, old fellow!' and the Mole was indeed very glad to obey, for he had started his spring-cleaning at a very early hour that morning, as people *will* do, and had not paused for food or drink; and he had been through a very great deal since that distant time which now seemed so many days ago.

'What are you looking at?' said the Rat presently, when the edge of their hunger was somewhat dulled, and the Mole's eyes were able to wander off the table-cloth a little.

'I am looking,' said the Mole, 'at a streak of bubbles that I see travelling along the surface of the water. That is a thing that strikes me as funny.'

'Bubbles? Oho!' said the Rat, and chirruped cheerily in an inviting sort of way.

A broad glistening muzzle showed itself above the edge of the bank, and the Otter hauled himself out and shook the water from his coat.

'Greedy beggars!' he observed, making for the food. 'Why

The Mole begged as a favour to be allowed to unpack it all by himself.

didn't you invite me, Ratty?'

'This was an unplanned affair,' explained the Rat. 'By the way—my friend, Mr. Mole.'

'Proud, I'm sure,' said the Otter, and the two animals were friends forthwith.

'Such a rumpus everywhere!' continued the Otter. 'All the world seems out on the river today. I came up this backwater to try and get a moment's peace, and then stumble upon you fellows! At least—I beg pardon—I don't exactly mean that, you know.'

There was a rustle behind them, coming from a hedge wherein last year's leaves still clung thick, and a stripy head, with high shoulders behind it, peered forth on them.

'Come on, old Badger!' shouted the Rat.

The Badger trotted forward a pace or two; then grunted, 'H'm! Company,' and turned his back and disappeared from view.

'That's *just* the sort of fellow he is!' observed the disappointed Rat. 'Simply hates Society! Now we shan't see any more of him today. Well, tell us *who's* out on the river?'

'Toad's out, for one,' replied the Otter. 'In his brand-new wager-boat; new togs, new everything!'

The two animals looked at each other and laughed.

'Once, it was nothing but sailing,' said the Rat. 'Then he tired of that and took to punting. Nothing would please him but to punt all day and every day, and a nice mess he made of it. Last year it was house-boating, and we all had to go and stay with him in his house-boat, and pretend we liked it. He was going to spend the rest of his life in a house-boat. It's all the same, whatever he takes up; he gets tired of it, and starts on something fresh.'

'Such a good fellow, too,' remarked the Otter reflectively. 'But no stability—especially in a boat!'

From where they sat they could get a glimpse of the main stream across the island that separated them; and just then a wager-boat flashed into view, the rower—a short, stout figure—splashing badly and rolling a good deal, but working his hardest. The Rat stood up and hailed him, but Toad—for it was he—shook his head and settled sternly to his work.

'He'll be out of the boat in a minute if he rolls like that,' said the Rat, sitting down again.

'Of course he will,' chuckled the Otter. 'Did I ever tell you that good story about Toad and the lock-keeper? It happened this way. Toad . . .'

A May-fly swerved unsteadily across the current. A swirl of water and a 'cloop!' and the May-fly was visible no more.

Neither was the Otter.

The Mole looked down. The voice was still in his ears, but the turf whereon he had sprawled was clearly vacant. Not an Otter to be seen, as far as the distant horizon.

But again there was a streak of bubbles on the surface of the river.

The Rat hummed a tune, and the Mole remembered it was not polite to make any sort of comment on the sudden disappearance of one's friends at any moment, for any reason or no reason whatever.

'Well, well,' said the Rat, 'I suppose we ought to be moving. I wonder which of us had better pack the luncheon-basket?' He did not speak as if he was frightfully eager for the treat.

'O, please let me,' said the Mole. So, of course, the Rat let him.

Packing the basket was not quite such pleasant work as unpacking the basket. It never is. But the Mole was bent on enjoying everything, and although just when he had got the basket packed and strapped up tightly he saw a plate staring up at him from the grass, and when the job had been done again the Rat pointed out a fork which anybody ought to have seen, and last of all, behold! the mustard-pot, which he had been sitting on without knowing it—still, somehow, the thing got finished at last, without much loss of temper.

The afternoon sun was getting low as the Rat sculled gently homewards in a dreamy mood, murmuring poetry-things over to himself, and not paying much attention to Mole. But the Mole was very full of lunch, and self-satisfaction, and already quite at home in a boat (so he thought) and was getting a bit restless besides: and presently he said, 'Ratty! Please, *I* want to row, now!'

The Rat shook his head with a smile. 'Not yet, my young friend,' he said—'wait till you've had a few lessons. It's not so easy as it looks.'

by his considerate host, to the best bedroom, where he soon laid his head on his pillow in great peace and contentment, knowing that his new-found friend the River was lapping the sill of his window.

This day was only the first of many similar ones for the Mole, each of them longer and fuller of interest as the ripening summer moved onward. He learnt to swim and to row, and entered into the joy of running water; and with his ear to the reed-stems he caught, at intervals, something of what the wind was whispering so constantly among them.

CHAPTER 2

The Open Road

'RATTY,' said the Mole suddenly, one bright summer morning, 'if you please, I want to ask you a favour.'

The Rat was sitting on the river bank, singing a little song. He had just composed it himself, so he was very taken up with it, and would not pay proper attention to Mole or anything else. Since early morning he had been swimming in the river, in company with his friends the ducks. And when the ducks stood on their heads suddenly, as ducks will, he would dive down and tickle their necks, just under where their chins would be if ducks had chins, till they were forced to come to the surface again in a hurry, spluttering and angry and shaking their feathers at him, for it is impossible to say quite *all* you feel when your head is under water. At last they implored him to go away and attend to his own affairs and leave them to mind theirs. So the Rat went away, and sat on the river bank in the sun, and made up a song about them, which he called:

splendid!' He shook the paws of both of them warmly, never waiting for an introduction to the Mole. 'How *kind* of you!' he went on, dancing round them. 'I was just going to send a boat down the river for you, Ratty, with strict orders that you were to be fetched up here at once, whatever you were doing. I want you badly—both of you. Now what will you take? Come inside and have something! You don't know how lucky it is, your turning up just now!'

'Let's sit quiet a bit, Toady!' said the Rat, throwing himself into an easy chair, while the Mole took another by the side of him and made some civil remark about Toad's 'delightful residence'.

'Finest house on the whole river,' cried Toad boisterously. 'Or anywhere else, for that matter,' he could not help adding.

Here the Rat nudged the Mole. Unfortunately the Toad saw him do it, and turned very red. There was a moment's painful silence. Then Toad burst out laughing. 'All right, Ratty,' he said. 'It's only my way, you know. And it's not such a very bad house, is it? You know you rather like it yourself. Now, look here. Let's be sensible. You are the very animals I wanted. You've got to help me. It's most important!'

'It's about your rowing, I suppose,' said the Rat, with an innocent air. 'You're getting on fairly well, though you splash a good bit still. With a great deal of patience, and a certain amount of coaching, you may——'

'O, pooh! boating!' interrupted the Toad, in great disgust. 'Silly boyish amusement. I've given that up *long* ago. Sheer waste of time, that's what it is. It makes me downright sorry to see you fellows, who ought to know better, spending all your energies in that aimless manner. No, I've discovered the real thing, the only genuine occupation for a lifetime. I propose to devote the remainder of mine to it, and can only regret the wasted years that lie behind me, squandered in trivialities. Come with me, dear Ratty, and your amiable friend also, if he will be so very good, just as far as the stable-yard, and you shall see what you shall see!'

He led the way to the stable-yard, the Rat following with a most mistrustful expression; and there, drawn out of the coach-house into the open, they saw a gipsy caravan, shining

They saw a gipsy caravan, shining with newness,
painted a canary-yellow picked out with green . . .

with newness, painted a canary-yellow picked out with green, and red wheels.

'There you are!' cried the Toad, standing before them legs apart, chest out. 'There's real life for you, embodied in that little cart. The open road, the dusty highway, the heath, the common, the hedgerows, the rolling downs! Camps, villages, towns, cities! Here today, up and off to somewhere else tomorrow! Travel, change, interest, excitement! The whole world before you, and a horizon that's always changing! And mind, this is the very finest cart of its sort that was ever built, without any exception. Come inside and look. Planned it all myself, I did!'

The Mole was tremendously interested and excited, and followed him eagerly up the steps and into the caravan. The Rat only snorted and thrust his hands deep into his pockets, remaining where he was.

It was indeed very compact and comfortable. Little sleeping-bunks—a little table that folded up against the wall—a cooking-stove, lockers, bookshelves, a bird cage with a bird in it; and pots, pans, jugs and kettles of every size and variety.

'All complete!' said the Toad triumphantly, pulling open a locker. 'You see—biscuits, potted lobster, sardines— everything you can possibly want. Soda-water here— tobacco there—letter-paper, bacon, jam, cards and dominoes—you'll find,' he continued, as they descended the steps again, 'you'll find that nothing whatever has been forgotten, when we make our start this afternoon.'

'I beg your pardon,' said the Rat slowly, as he chewed a straw, 'but did I overhear you say something about "*we*", and "*start*", and "*this afternoon*"?'

'Now, you dear good old Ratty,' said Toad imploringly, 'don't begin talking in that stiff and sniffy sort of way, because you know you've *got* to come. I can't possibly manage without you, so please consider it settled, and don't argue—it's the one thing I can't stand. You surely don't mean to stick to your dull smelly old river all your life, and just live in a hole in a bank, and *boat*? I want to show you the world! I'm going to make an *animal* of you, my boy!'

'I don't care,' said the Rat doggedly. 'I'm not coming,

and that's flat. And I *am* going to stick to my old river, *and* live in a hole, *and* boat, as I've always done. And what's more, Mole's going to stick to me and do as I do, aren't you, Mole?'

'Of course I am,' said the Mole loyally. 'I'll always stick to you, Rat, and what you say is to be—has got to be. All the same, it sounds as if it might have been—well, rather fun, you know!' he added wistfully. Poor Mole! The Life Adventurous was so new a thing to him and so thrilling; and this fresh aspect of it was so tempting; and he had fallen in love at first sight with the canary-coloured cart and all its little fitments.

The Rat saw what was passing in his mind, and wavered. He hated disappointing people, and he was fond of the Mole, and would do almost anything to oblige him. Toad was watching both of them closely.

'Come along in and have some lunch,' he said diplomatically, 'and we'll talk it over. We needn't decide anything in a hurry. Of course, *I* don't really care. I only want to give pleasure to you fellows. "Live for others!" That's my motto in life.'

During lunch—which was excellent, of course, as everything at Toad Hall always was—the Toad simply let himself go. Ignoring the Rat, he painted the prospects of the trip and the joys of the open life and the road-side in such glowing colours that the Mole could hardly sit in his chair for excitement. Somehow, it soon seemed taken for granted by all three of them that the trip was a settled thing; and the Rat, though still unconvinced in his mind, allowed his good-nature to over-ride his personal objections. He could not bear to disappoint his two friends, who were already planning out each day's separate occupation for several weeks ahead.

When they were quite ready, the now triumphant Toad led his companions to the paddock and set them to capture the old grey horse, who, without having been consulted, and to his own extreme annoyance, had been chosen by Toad for the dustiest job in this dusty expedition. He frankly preferred the paddock, and took a deal of catching. Meantime Toad packed the lockers still tighter with necessaries, and

hung nose-bags, nets of onions, bundles of hay, and baskets from the bottom of the cart. At last the horse was caught and harnessed, and they set off, all talking at once, each animal either trudging by the side of the cart or sitting on the shaft, as the mood took him. It was a golden afternoon. The smell of the dust they kicked up was rich and satisfying; out of thick orchards on either side of the road, birds called and whistled to them cheerily; good-natured wayfarers, passing them, gave them 'Good day', or stopped to say nice things about their beautiful cart; and rabbits, sitting at their front doors in the hedgerows, held up their fore-paws, and said, 'O my! O my! O my!'

Late in the evening, tired and happy and miles from home, they drew up on a remote common far from any houses, turned the horse loose to graze, and ate their simple supper sitting on the grass by the side of the cart. Toad talked big about all he was going to do in the days to come, while stars grew fuller and larger all around them, and a yellow moon, appearing suddenly and silently from nowhere in particular, came to keep them company and listen to their talk. At last they turned into their little bunks in the cart; and Toad, kicking out his legs, sleepily said, 'Well, good night, you fellows! This is the real life for a gentleman! Talk about your old river!'

'I *don't* talk about my river,' replied the patient Rat. 'You *know* I don't, Toad. But I *think* about it,' he added pathetically, in a lower tone: 'I think about it—all the time!'

The Mole reached out from under his blanket, felt for the Rat's paw in the darkness, and gave it a squeeze. 'I'll do whatever you like, Ratty,' he whispered. 'Shall we run away tomorrow morning, quite early—*very* early—and go back to our dear old hole on the river?'

'No, no, we'll see it out,' whispered back the Rat. 'Thanks awfully, but I ought to stick by Toad till this trip is ended. It wouldn't be safe for him to be left to himself. It won't take very long. His fads never do. Good night!'

The end was indeed nearer than even the Rat suspected.

After so much open air and excitement the Toad slept very soundly, and no amount of shaking could rouse him out of bed next morning. So the Mole and Rat set to work,

quietly and manfully, and while the Rat saw to the horse, and lit a fire, and cleaned last night's cups and plates, and got things ready for breakfast, the Mole trudged off to the nearest village, a long way off, for milk and eggs and various necessaries the Toad had, of course, forgotten to provide. The hard work had all been done, and the two animals were resting, thoroughly exhausted, by the time Toad appeared on the scene, fresh and gay, remarking what a pleasant easy life it was they were all leading now, after the cares and worries of house-keeping at home.

They had a pleasant ramble that day over grassy downs and along narrow by-lanes, and camped, as before, on a common, only this time the two guests took care that Toad should do his fair share of work. In consequence, when the time came for starting next morning, Toad was by no means so happy about the simplicity of the primitive life, and indeed attempted to resume his place in his bunk, from where he was hauled by force. Their way lay, as before, across country by narrow lanes, and it was not till the afternoon that they came out on the high road, their first high road; and there disaster, sudden and unexpected, sprang out on them— disaster that was momentous indeed to their expedition, but simply overwhelming in its effect on the future career of Toad.

They were strolling along the high road easily, the Mole by the horse's head, talking to him, since the horse had complained that he was being frightfully left out of it, and nobody considered him in the least; the Toad and the Water Rat walking behind the cart talking together—at least Toad was talking, and Rat was saying at intervals, 'Yes, precisely; and what did *you* say to *him*?'—and thinking all the time of something very different, when far behind them they heard a faint warning hum, like the drone of a distant bee. Glancing back, they saw a small cloud of dust, with a dark centre, advancing on them at incredible speed, while from out of the dust a faint 'Poop-poop!' wailed like an uneasy animal in pain. Hardly regarding it, they turned to resume their conversation, when in an instant (as it seemed) the peaceful scene was changed, and with a blast of wind and a whirl of sound that made them jump for the nearest ditch, it was on

them! The 'poop-poop' rang with a blaring shout in their ears, they had a moment's glimpse of an interior of glittering plate-glass and rich leather, and the magnificent motor-car, immense, breath-snatching, passionate, with its driver tense and hugging his wheel, claimed all earth and air for a fraction of a second. It flung a cloud of dust that blinded and enwrapped them utterly, and then dwindled to a speck in the far distance, changed back into a droning bee once more.

The old grey horse, dreaming, as he plodded along, of his quiet paddock, in a new situation such as this simply abandoned himself to his natural emotions. Rearing, plunging, backing steadily, in spite of all the Mole's efforts at his head, and all the Mole's lively language appealing to his better nature, he drove the cart backwards towards the deep ditch at the side of the road. It wavered an instant— then there was a heartrending crash—and the canary-coloured cart, their pride and their joy, lay on its side in the ditch, a complete wreck.

The Rat danced up and down in the road, simply transported with passion. 'You villains!' he shouted, shaking both fists, 'You scoundrels, you highwaymen, you—you—road-hogs!—I'll have the law on you! I'll report you! I'll take you through all the Courts!' His home-sickness had quite slipped away from him.

Toad sat straight down in the middle of the dusty road, his legs stretched out before him, and stared fixedly in the direction of the disappearing motor-car. He breathed short, his face wore a placid, satisfied expression, and at intervals he faintly murmured, 'Poop-poop!'

The Mole was busy trying to quiet the horse, which he succeeded in doing after a time. Then he went to look at the cart, on its side in the ditch. It was indeed a sorry sight. Panels and windows smashed, axles hopelessly bent, one wheel off, sardine-tins scattered over the wide world, and the bird in the bird-cage sobbing pitifully and calling to be let out.

The Rat came to help him, but their united efforts were not sufficient to right the cart. 'Hi! Toad!' they cried. 'Come and bear a hand, can't you?'

The Rat danced up and down in the road,
simply transported with passion.

The Toad never answered a word, or budged from his seat in the road; so they went to see what was the matter with him. They found him in a sort of trance, a happy smile on his face, his eyes still fixed on the dusty wake of their destroyer. At intervals he was still heard to murmur 'Poop-poop!'

The Rat shook him by the shoulder. 'Are you coming to help us, Toad?' he demanded sternly.

'Glorious, stirring sight!' murmured Toad, never offering to move. 'The poetry of motion! The *real* way to travel! The *only* way to travel! Here today—in next week tomorrow! Villages skipped, towns and cities jumped! O bliss! O poop-poop! O my! O my!'

'O *stop* being a fool, Toad!' cried the Mole despairingly.

'And to think I never *knew*!' the Toad went on. 'All those wasted years that lie behind me, I never knew, never even *dreamt*! But *now*—but now that I know, now that I fully realise! O what a flowery track lies spread before me now! What dust-clouds shall spring up behind me as I speed on my reckless way! What carts I shall fling carelessly into the ditch in the wake of my magnificent charge! Horrid little carts—common carts—canary-coloured carts!'

'What are we to do with him?' asked the Mole of the Water Rat.

'Nothing at all,' replied the Rat firmly. 'Because there is really nothing to be done. You see, I know him of old. He is now possessed. He has got a new craze, and it always takes him that way, in its first stage. He'll continue like that for days now, like an animal walking in a happy dream. Never mind him. Let's go and see what there is to be done about the cart.'

A careful inspection showed them that, even if they succeeded in righting it by themselves, the cart would travel no longer. The axles were in a hopeless state, and the missing wheel was shattered into pieces.

The Rat knotted the horse's reins over his back and took him by the head, carrying the bird-cage in the other hand. 'Come on!' he said grimly to the Mole. 'It's five or six miles to the nearest town, and we shall just have to walk it. The sooner we make a start the better.'

'But what about Toad?' asked the Mole anxiously, as they

set off together. 'We can't leave him here, sitting in the middle of the road by himself, in the state he's in! It's not safe. Supposing another Thing were to come along?'

'O, *bother* Toad,' said the Rat savagely; 'I've done with him!'

They had not proceeded very far on their way, however, when there was a pattering of feet behind them, and Toad caught them up and thrust a paw inside the elbow of each of them; still breathing short and staring into vacancy.

'Now, look here, Toad!' said the Rat sharply: 'as soon as we get to the town, you'll have to go straight to the police-station, and see if they know anything about that motor-car and who it belongs to, and lodge a complaint against it. And then you'll have to go to a blacksmith's or a wheelwright's and arrange for the cart to be fetched and mended and put to rights. It'll take time, but it's not quite a hopeless smash. Meanwhile, the Mole and I will go to an inn and find comfortable rooms where we can stay till the cart's ready, and till your nerves have recovered their shock.'

'Police-station! Complaint!' murmured Toad dreamily. 'Me *complain* of that beautiful, that heavenly vision! *Mend* the *cart*! I've done with carts for ever. I never want to see the cart, or to hear of it again. O Ratty! You can't think how obliged I am to you for consenting to come on this trip! I wouldn't have gone without you, and then I might never have seen that—that swan, that sunbeam, that thunderbolt! I might never have heard that entrancing sound, or smelt that bewitching smell! I owe it all to you, my best of friends!'

The Rat turned from him in despair. 'You see what it is?' he said to the Mole, addressing him across Toad's head: 'He's quite hopeless. I give it up—when we get to the town we'll go to the railway station, and with luck we may pick up a train there that'll get us back to River Bank tonight. And if ever you catch me going out with this provoking animal again!'—He snorted, and during the rest of that weary trudge addressed his remarks exclusively to Mole.

On reaching the town they went straight to the station and deposited Toad in the second-class waiting-room, giving a porter twopence to keep a strict eye on him. They then left the horse at an inn stable, and gave what directions

they could about the cart and its contents. Eventually, a slow train having landed them at a station not very far from Toad Hall, they escorted the spellbound, sleep-walking Toad to his door, put him inside it, and instructed his house-keeper to feed him, undress him, and put him to bed. Then they got out their boat from the boat-house, sculled down the river home, and at a very late hour sat down to supper in their own snug little riverside parlour, to the Rat's great joy and contentment.

The following evening the Mole, who had got up late and taken things very easy all day, was sitting on the bank fishing, when the Rat, who had been looking up his friends and gossiping, came strolling along to find him. 'Heard the news?' he said. 'There's nothing else being talked about, all along the river bank. Toad went up to Town by an early train this morning. And he has ordered a large and very expensive motor-car.'

CHAPTER 3

The Wild Wood

THE Mole had long wanted to meet the Badger. He
seemed, by all accounts, to be such an important person
and, though rarely seen, to have an influence on everybody
about the place. But whenever the Mole mentioned his wish
to the Water Rat he always found himself put off. 'It's all
right,' the Rat would say. 'Badger'll turn up some day or
other—he's always turning up—and then I'll introduce you.
The best of fellows! But you must not only take him *as*
you find him, but *when* you find him.'

'Couldn't you ask him here—dinner or something?' said
the Mole.

'He wouldn't come,' replied the Rat simply. 'Badger hates
Society, and invitations, and dinner, and all that sort of thing.

'Well, then, supposing we go and call on *him*?' suggested
the Mole.

'O, I'm sure he wouldn't like that at *all*,' said the Rat, quite alarmed. 'He's so very shy, he'd be sure to be offended. I've never even ventured to call on him at his own home myself, though I know him so well. Besides, we can't. It's quite out of the question, because he lives in the very middle of the Wild Wood.'

'Well, supposing he does,' said the Mole. 'You told me the Wild Wood was all right, you know.'

'O, I know, I know, so it is,' replied the Rat. 'But I think we won't go there just now. Not *just* yet. It's a long way, and he wouldn't be at home at this time of year anyhow, and he'll be coming along some day, if you'll wait quietly.'

The Mole had to be content with this. But the Badger never came along, and every day brought its amusements, and it was not till summer was long over, and cold and frost kept them much indoors, and the swollen river raced past outside their windows with a speed that made boating impossible, that he found his thoughts dwelling again on the grey Badger, who lived his own life by himself, in his hole in the middle of the Wild Wood.

In the winter time the Rat slept a great deal, retiring early and rising late. During his short day he sometimes scribbled poetry or did other small jobs about the house; and, of course, there were always animals dropping in for a chat, and so there was a good deal of story-telling and comparing notes on the past summer and all its doings.

There was plenty to talk about on those short winter days when the animals found themselves round the fire; still, the Mole had a good deal of spare time on his hands, and so one afternoon, when the Rat in his armchair before the blaze was alternately dozing and trying over rhymes that wouldn't fit, he decided to go out by himself and explore the Wild Wood, and perhaps strike up an acquaintance with Mr. Badger.

It was a cold still afternoon with a hard steely sky overhead, when he slipped out of the warm parlour into the open air. The country lay bare and entirely leafless around him as he pushed on towards the Wild Wood, which lay before him low and threatening, like a black reef in some still southern sea.

There was nothing to alarm him at first. Twigs crackled under his feet, logs tripped him, funguses on stumps looked like faces, and startled him for the moment; but that was all fun, and exciting. It led him on, and he went deeper to where the light was less, and trees crouched nearer and nearer, and holes made ugly mouths at him on either side.

Everything was very still now. The dusk advanced on him steadily, rapidly, gathering in behind and in front; and the light seemed to be draining away like flood-water.

Then the faces began.

It was over his shoulder that he first thought he saw a face: a little evil wedge-shaped face, looking out at him from a hole. When he turned and confronted it, the thing had vanished.

He quickened his pace, telling himself cheerfully not to begin imagining things, or there would be simply no end to it. He passed another hole, and another, and another; and then—yes!—no!—yes! certainly a little narrow face, with hard eyes, had flashed up for an instant from a hole, and was gone. He hesitated—braced himself up for an effort and strode on. Then suddenly, and as if it had been so all the time, every hole, far and near, and there were hundreds of them, seemed to possess its face, coming and going rapidly, all fixing on him glances of malice and hatred: all hard-eyed and evil and sharp.

If he could only get away from the holes in the banks, he thought, there would be no more faces. He swung off the path and plunged into the untrodden places of the wood.

Then the whistling began.

Very faint and shrill it was, and far behind him, when first he heard it; but somehow it made him hurry forward. Then, still very faint and shrill, it sounded far ahead of him, and made him hesitate and want to go back. As he halted in indecision it broke out on either side, and seemed to be caught up and passed on throughout the whole length of the wood to its furthest limit. They were up and alert and ready, evidently, whoever they were! And he—he was alone, and unarmed, and far from any help; and the night was closing in.

Then the pattering began.

He thought it was only falling leaves at first, so slight and delicate was the sound of it. Then as it grew it took a regular rhythm, and he knew it for nothing else but the pat-pat-pat of little feet, still a very long way off. Was it in front or behind? It seemed to be first one, then the other, then both. It grew and it multiplied, till from every quarter as he listened anxiously, leaning this way and that, it seemed to be closing in on him. As he stood still to listen, a rabbit came running hard towards him through the trees. He waited, expecting it to slacken pace, or to swerve from him into a different course. Instead, the animal almost brushed him as it dashed past, his face set and hard, his eyes staring. 'Get out of this, you fool; get out!' the Mole heard him mutter as he swung round a stump and disappeared down a friendly burrow.

The pattering increased till it sounded like sudden hail on the dry-leaf carpet spread around him. The whole wood seemed running now, running hard, hunting, chasing, closing in round something or—somebody? In panic, he began to run too, aimlessly, he knew not where. He ran up against things, he fell over things and into things, he darted under things and dodged round things. At last he took refuge in the dark deep hollow of an old beech tree, which offered shelter, a hiding place—perhaps even safety, but who could tell? Anyhow, he was too tired to run any further, and could only snuggle down into the dry leaves which had drifted into the hollow and hope he was safe for the time. And as he lay there panting and trembling, and listened to the whistlings and the patterings outside, he knew it at last, in all its fullness, that dreadful thing which other little dwellers in field and hedgerow had encountered here, and known as their darkest moment—that thing which the Rat had tried to shield him from—the Terror of the Wild Wood!

Meantime the Rat, warm and comfortable, dozed by his fireside. His paper of half-finished verses slipped from his knee, his head fell back, his mouth opened, and he wandered by the grassy banks of dream-rivers. Then a coal slipped, the fire crackled and sent up a spurt of flame, and he woke with a start. Remembering what he had been engaged upon, he reached down to the floor for his verses, pored

At last he took refuge in the dark deep hollow
of an old beech tree . . .

over them for a minute, and then looked round for the Mole to ask him if he knew a good rhyme for something or other.

But the Mole was not there.

He listened for a time. The house seemed very quiet.

Then he called 'Moly!' several times, and, receiving no answer, got up and went out into the hall.

The Mole's cap was missing from its accustomed peg. His goloshes, which always lay by the umbrella-stand, were also gone.

The Rat left the house and carefully examined the muddy surface of the ground outside, hoping to find the Mole's tracks. There they were, sure enough. The goloshes were new, just bought for the winter, and the pimples on their soles were fresh and sharp. He could see the imprints of them in the mud, running along straight and purposeful, leading direct to the Wild Wood.

The Rat looked very grave, and stood in deep thought for a minute or two. Then he re-entered the house, strapped a belt round his waist, shoved a pair of pistols into it, took up a stout cudgel that stood in a corner of the hall, and set off for the Wild Wood at a smart pace.

It was already getting towards dusk when he reached the first fringe of trees and plunged without hesitation into the wood, looking anxiously on either side for any sign of his friend. Here and there wicked little faces popped out of holes, but vanished immediately at sight of the brave animal, his pistols, and the great ugly cudgel in his grasp; and the whistling and pattering, which he had heard quite plainly on his first entry, died away and ceased, and all was very still. He made his way manfully through the length of the wood, to its furthest edge; then, forsaking all paths, he set himself to cross it bit by bit, working over the whole ground, and all the time calling out cheerfully, 'Moly, Moly, Moly! Where are you? It's me—it's old Rat!'

He had patiently hunted through the wood for an hour or more, when at last to his joy he heard a little answering cry. Guiding himself by the sound, he made his way through the gathering darkness to the foot of an old beech tree, with a hole in it, and from out of the hole came a feeble voice, saying, 'Ratty! Is that really you?'

The Rat crept into the hollow, and there he found the Mole, exhausted and still trembling. 'O, Rat!' he cried, 'I've been so frightened, you can't think!'

'O, I quite understand,' said the Rat soothingly. 'You shouldn't really have gone and done it, Mole. I did my best to keep you from it. We river-bankers, we hardly ever come here by ourselves. If we have to come, we come in couples, at least; then we're generally all right. Besides, there are a hundred things one has to know, which we understand all about and you don't, as yet. I mean passwords, and signs, and plants you carry in your pocket, and verses you repeat, and dodges and tricks you can use; all simple enough when you know them, but they've got to be known if you're small, or you'll find yourself in trouble. Of course if you were Badger or Otter, it would be quite another matter.'

'Surely the brave Mr. Toad wouldn't mind coming here by himself, would he?' inquired the Mole.

'Old Toad?' said the Rat, laughing heartily. 'He wouldn't show his face here alone, not for a whole hatful of golden guineas, Toad wouldn't.'

The Mole was greatly cheered by the sound of the Rat's careless laughter, as well as by the sight of his stick and his gleaming pistols, and he stopped shivering and began to feel bolder and more himself again.

'Now then,' said the Rat presently, 'we really must pull ourselves together and make a start for home while there's still a little light left. It will never do to spend the night here, you understand. Too cold, for one thing.'

'Dear Ratty,' said the poor Mole, 'I'm dreadfully sorry, but I'm simply dead beat and that's a fact. You *must* let me rest here a while longer, and get my strength back, if I'm to get home at all.'

'O, all right,' said the good-natured Rat, 'rest away. It's pretty nearly pitch dark now, anyhow; and there ought to be a bit of a moon later.'

So the Mole got well into the dry leaves and stretched himself out, and presently dropped off into sleep, though of a broken and troubled sort; while the Rat covered himself up, too, as best he might, for warmth, and lay patiently

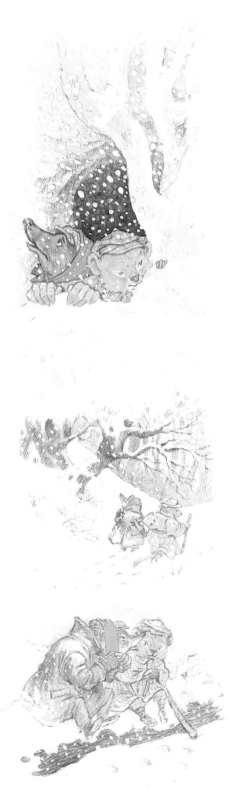

waiting, with a pistol in his paw.

When at last the Mole woke up, much refreshed and in his usual spirits, the Rat said, 'Now then! I'll just take a look outside and see if everything's quiet, and then we really must be off.'

He went to the entrance of their retreat and put his head out. Then the Mole heard him saying quietly to himself, 'Hullo! hullo! here—*is*—a—go!'

'What's up, Ratty?' asked the Mole.

'*Snow* is up,' replied the Rat briefly; 'or rather, *down*. It's snowing hard.'

The Mole came and crouched beside him, and, looking out, saw the wood that had been so dreadful to him in quite a changed aspect. Holes, hollows, pools, pitfalls, and other black menaces to the wayfarer were vanishing fast, and a gleaming carpet of snow was springing up everywhere, that looked too delicate to be trodden upon by rough feet. A fine powder filled the air and caressed the cheek with a tingle in its touch, and the black boles of the trees showed up in a light that seemed to come from below.

'Well, well, it can't be helped,' said the Rat after pondering. 'We must make a start, and take our chance, I suppose. The worst of it is, I don't exactly know where we are. And now this snow makes everything look so very different.'

It did indeed. The Mole would not have known that it was the same wood. However, they set out bravely, and took the line that seemed most promising, holding on to each other and pretending that they recognised an old friend in every fresh tree that grimly and silently greeted them, or saw openings, gaps, or paths with a familiar turn in them, in the endless scene of white space and black tree-trunks that refused to vary.

An hour or two later—they had lost all count of time— they pulled up, downhearted, weary, and hopelessly at sea, and sat down on a fallen tree-trunk to recover their breath and consider what was to be done. They were aching with fatigue and bruised with tumbles; they had fallen into several holes and got wet through; the snow was getting so deep that they could hardly drag their little legs through it, and the trees were thicker and more like each other than ever. There seemed to be no end to this wood, and no beginning, and no difference in it, and, worst of all, no way out.

'We can't sit here very long,' said the Rat. 'We shall have to make another push for it, and do something or other. The cold is too awful for anything, and the snow will soon be too deep for us to wade through.' He peered about him and considered. 'Look here,' he went on, 'this is what occurs to me. There's a sort of dell down there in front of us, where the ground seems all hilly and humpy and hummocky. We'll make our way down into that, and try and find some sort of shelter, a cave or hole with a dry floor to it, out of the snow and the wind, and there we'll have a good rest before we try again, for we're both of us pretty dead beat. Besides, the snow may leave off, or something may turn up.'

So once more they got on their feet, and struggled down into the dell, where they hunted about for a cave or some corner that was dry and a protection from the bitter wind and the whirling snow. They were investigating one of the hummocky bits the Rat had spoken of, when suddenly the Mole tripped up and fell forward on his face with a squeal.

'O, my leg!' he cried. 'O, my poor shin!' and he sat up on the snow and nursed his leg in both his front paws.

'Poor old Mole!' said the Rat kindly. 'You don't seem to be having much luck today, do you? Let's have a look at the leg. Yes,' he went on, going down on his knees to look, 'you've cut your shin, sure enough. Wait till I get at my handkerchief, and I'll tie it up for you.'

'I must have tripped over a hidden branch or a stump,' said the Mole miserably. 'O my! O my!'

'It's a very clean cut,' said the Rat, examining it again attentively. 'That was never done by a branch or a stump. Looks as if it was made by a sharp edge of something in metal. Funny!' He pondered a while, and examined the humps and slopes that surrounded them.

'Well, never mind what done it,' said the Mole, forgetting his grammar in his pain. 'It hurts just the same, whatever done it.'

But the Rat, after carefully tying up the leg with his handkerchief, had left him and was busy scraping in the

There's nothing else remains to be done but to find it!''
Well, I've read about that sort of thing in books, but I've
never come across it before in real life. You ought to go
where you'll be properly appreciated. You're simply wasted
here, among us fellows. If I only had your head, Ratty——'

'But as you haven't,' interrupted the Rat rather unkindly,
'I suppose you're going to sit on the snow all night and
talk? Get up at once and hang on to that bell-pull you see
there, and ring hard, as hard as you can, while I hammer!'

While the Rat attacked the door with his stick, the Mole
sprang up at the bell-pull, clutched it and swung there,
both feet well off the ground, and from quite a long way off
they could faintly hear a deep-toned bell respond.

CHAPTER 4

Mr. Badger

THEY waited patiently for what seemed a very long time, stamping in the snow to keep their feet warm. At last they heard the sound of slow shuffling footsteps approaching the door from the inside. It seemed, as the Mole remarked to the Rat, like some one walking in carpet slippers that were too large for him and down-at-heel; which was clever of Mole, because that was exactly what it was.

There was the noise of a bolt shot back, and the door opened a few inches, enough to show a long snout and a pair of sleepy blinking eyes.

'Now, the *very* next time this happens,' said a gruff voice, 'I shall be exceedingly angry. Who is it *this* time, disturbing people on such a night? Speak up!'

'O, Badger,' cried the Rat, 'let us in, please. It's me, Rat, and my friend Mole, and we've lost our way in the snow.'

'What, Ratty, my dear little man!' exclaimed the Badger, in quite a different voice. 'Come along in, both of you, at once. Why, you must be frozen. Well I never! Lost in the snow! And in the Wild Wood too, and at this time of night! But come in.'

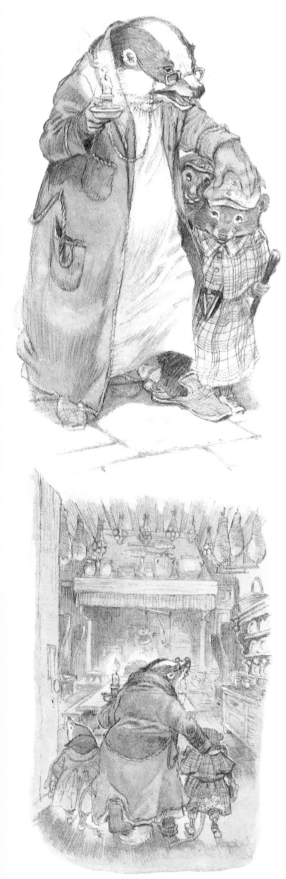

The two animals tumbled over each other in their eagerness to get inside, and with great joy and relief heard the door shut behind them.

The Badger, who wore a long dressing-gown, and whose slippers were indeed very down-at-heel, carried a flat candlestick in his paw and had probably been on his way to bed when he heard their call. He looked kindly down on them and patted both their heads. 'This is not the sort of night for small animals to be out,' he said paternally. 'I'm afraid you've been up to some of your pranks again, Ratty. But come along; come into the kitchen. There's a first-rate fire there, and supper and everything.'

He shuffled on in front of them, carrying the light, and they followed him, nudging each other in an excited sort of way, down a long, gloomy, and to tell the truth, decidedly shabby passage, into a sort of a central hall, out of which they could dimly see other long tunnel-like passages. But there were doors in the hall as well—stout oak doors. One of these the Badger flung open, and at once they found themselves in all the glow and warmth of a large fire-lit kitchen.

The floor was well-worn red brick, and on the wide hearth burnt a fire of logs, between two attractive chimney-corners tucked away in the wall, well out of any draught. A couple of high-backed seats, facing each other on either side of the fire, gave further sitting accommodation. In the middle of the room stood a long table of plain boards placed on trestles, with benches down each side. At one end of it, where an armchair stood pushed back, were spread the remains of the Badger's plain but ample supper. Rows of spotless plates winked from the shelves of the dresser at the far end of the room, and from the rafters overhead hung hams, bundles of dried herbs, nets of onions, and baskets of eggs.

The kindly Badger sat them down on seats to toast themselves at the fire, and made them remove their wet coats and boots. Then he fetched them dressing-gowns and slippers, and bathed the Mole's shin with warm water and mended the cut with sticking-plaster till the whole thing was just as good as new, if not better. In the embracing light and warmth, warm and dry at last, with weary legs propped up in front of them, and the cheering clink of plates being arranged on the table behind, it seemed to the storm-driven animals that the cold and trackless Wild Wood just left outside was miles and miles away, and all that they had suffered in it a half-forgotten dream.

When at last they were thoroughly toasted, the Badger summoned them to the table, where he had been busy laying a meal. They had felt pretty hungry before, but when they actually saw at last the supper that was spread for them, really it seemed only a question of what they should attack first where all was so attractive, and whether the other things would obligingly wait for them till they had time to give them attention. Conversation was impossible for a long time; and when it was slowly resumed, it was that sort of conversation that comes from talking with your mouth full. The Badger did not mind that sort of thing at all, nor did he take any notice of elbows on the table, or everybody speaking at once. He sat in his armchair at the head of the table, and nodded now and then as the animals told their story; and he did not seem surprised or shocked at anything, and he never said, 'I told you so,' or, 'Just what I always said,' or remarked that they ought to have done so-and-so, or ought not to have done something else. The Mole began to feel very friendly towards him.

When supper was really finished at last, and after they had chatted for a time about things in general, the Badger said heartily, 'Now then! tell us the news from your part of the world. How's old Toad going on?'

'O, from bad to worse,' said the Rat, while the Mole, basking in the firelight, his heels higher than his head, tried to look properly mournful. 'Another smash-up only last week, and a bad one. You see, he will insist on driving himself, and he's hopelessly incapable. If he'd only employ a decent, steady, well-trained animal, pay him good wages, and leave everything to him, he'd get on all right. But no; he thinks he's a heaven-born driver, and nobody can teach him anything; and all the rest follows.'

'How many has he had?' asked the Badger gloomily.

'Smashes, or machines?' asked the Rat. 'O, well, after all, it's the same thing—with Toad. This is the seventh.

As for the others—you know that coach-house of his? Well, it's piled up—piled up to the roof—with bits of motor-cars, none of them bigger than your hat! That accounts for the other six—so far as they can be accounted for.'

'He's been in hospital three times,' put in the Mole; 'and as for the fines he's had to pay, it's simply awful to think of.'

'Yes, and that's part of the trouble,' continued the Rat. 'Toad's rich, we all know; but he's not a millionaire. And he's a hopelessly bad driver, and quite regardless of law and order. Killed or ruined—it's got to be one of the two things, sooner or later. Badger! we're his friends—oughtn't we to do something?'

The Badger went through a bit of hard thinking. 'Now look here!' he said at last, rather severely; 'of course you know I can't do anything *now*?'

His two friends agreed, quite understanding his point. No animal is ever expected to do anything strenuous, or heroic, or even moderately active during the off-season of winter. All are sleepy—some actually asleep. All are weather-bound, more or less; and all are resting from hard days and nights, during which every muscle in them has been severely tested, and every energy kept at full stretch.

'Very well then!' continued the Badger. '*But*, when once the year has really turned, and the nights are shorter, and half-way through them one rouses and feels fidgety and wanting to be up and doing by sunrise, if not before—*you* know——!'

Both animals nodded gravely. *They* knew!

'Well, *then*,' went on the Badger, 'we—that is, you and me and our friend the Mole here—we'll take Toad in hand. We'll stand no nonsense whatever. We'll bring him back to reason, by force if need be. We'll *make* him be a sensible Toad. We'll—you're asleep, Rat!'

'Not me!' said the Rat, waking up with a jump.

'He's been asleep two or three times since supper,' said the Mole laughing. He himself was feeling quite wakeful and even lively, though he didn't know why. The reason was, of course, that he being naturally an underground animal by birth and breeding, Badger's house exactly suited him and made him feel at home; but not the Rat, who slept every night in a bedroom the windows of which opened on a breezy river.

'Well, it's time we were all in bed,' said the Badger, getting up and fetching flat candlesticks. 'Come along, you two, and I'll show you your quarters. And take your time tomorrow morning—breakfast at any hour you please!'

He led the two animals to a long room that seemed half bedroom and half loft. The Badger's winter stores, which indeed were visible everywhere, took up half the room— piles of apples, turnips, and potatoes, baskets full of nuts, and jars of honey; but the two little white beds on the remainder of the floor looked soft and inviting, and the linen on them, though coarse, was clean and smelt beautifully of lavender; and the Mole and the Water Rat, shaking off their clothes in some thirty seconds, tumbled in between the sheets in great joy and contentment.

Following the kindly Badger's advice, the two tired animals came down to breakfast very late next morning, and found a bright fire burning in the kitchen, and two young hedgehogs sitting on a bench at the table, eating oatmeal porridge out of wooden bowls. The hedgehogs dropped their spoons, rose to their feet, and ducked their heads respectfully as the two entered.

'There, sit down, sit down,' said the Rat pleasantly, 'and go on with your porridge. Where have you youngsters come from? Lost your way in the snow, I suppose?'

'Yes, please, sir,' said the elder of the two hedgehogs respectfully. 'Me and little Billy here, we was trying to find our way to school—mother *would* have us go—and of course we lost ourselves, sir, and Billy he got frightened and took and cried, being young and faint-hearted. And at last we came to Mr. Badger's back door, and made so bold as to knock, sir, for Mr. Badger he's a kind-hearted gentleman, as everyone knows——'

'I understand,' said the Rat, cutting himself some rashers from a side of bacon, while the Mole dropped some eggs into a saucepan. 'And what's the weather like outside? You needn't "sir" me quite so much,' he added.

'O, terrible bad, sir, terrible deep the snow is,' said the hedgehog. 'No getting out for the likes of you gentlemen today.'

'Where's Mr. Badger?' asked the Mole, as he warmed the coffee-pot before the fire.

'The master's gone into his study, sir,' replied the hedgehog, 'and he said as how he was going to be particular busy this morning, and on no account was he to be disturbed.'

This explanation, of course, was thoroughly understood by every one present. The animals well knew that Badger, having eaten a hearty breakfast, had retired to his study and settled himself in an armchair with his legs up on another and a red cotton handkerchief over his face, and was being 'busy' in the usual way at this time of the year.

The front-door bell clanged loudly, and the Rat, who was very greasy with buttered toast, sent Billy, the smaller hedgehog, to see who it might be. There was a sound of much stamping in the hall, and presently Billy returned in front of the Otter, who threw himself on the Rat with a hug and a shout of affectionate greeting.

'Get off!' spluttered the Rat, with his mouth full.

'Thought I should find you here all right,' said the Otter cheerfully. 'They were all in a great state of alarm along River Bank when I arrived this morning. Rat never been home all night—nor Mole either—something dreadful must have happened, they said; and the snow had covered up all your tracks, of course. But I knew that when people were in any fix they mostly went to Badger, or else Badger got to know of it somehow, so I came straight off here, through the Wild Wood and the snow! My! It was fine, coming through the snow as the red sun was rising and showing against the black tree-trunks! As you went along in the stillness, every now and then masses of snow slid off the branches suddenly with a flop, making you jump and run for cover. Snow-castles and snow-caverns had sprung up out of nowhere in the night—and snow bridges, terraces, ramparts—I could have stayed and played with them for hours. Here and there great branches had been torn away by the sheer weight of the snow, and robins perched and hopped on them in their perky conceited way, just as if they

'Snow-castles and snow-caverns had sprung up
out of nowhere in the night.'

hired lodgings; uncomfortable, in a bad position, and horribly expensive. Take Toad. I say nothing against Toad Hall; quite the best house in these parts, *as* a house. But supposing a fire breaks out—where's Toad? Supposing tiles are blown off, or walls sink or crack, or windows get broken—where's Toad? Supposing the rooms are draughty—I *hate* a draught myself—where's Toad? No, up and out of doors is good enough to roam about and get one's living in; but under-ground to come back to at last—that's my idea of *home!*'

The Mole agreed heartily; and the Badger got very friendly with him. 'When lunch is over,' he said, 'I'll take you all round this little place of mine. I can see you'll appreciate it. You understand what a home ought to be, you do.'

So, after lunch, when the other two had settled themselves into the chimney-corner and had started a heated argument on the subject of *eels*, the Badger lighted a lantern and told the Mole to follow him. Crossing the hall, they passed down one of the principal tunnels, and the wavering light of the lantern gave glimpses on either side of rooms both large and small, some mere cupboards, others nearly as broad and imposing as Toad's dining-hall. A narrow passage at right angles led them into another corridor, and here the same thing was repeated. The Mole was staggered at the size and extent of it all; at the length of the dim passages, the solid ceilings of the crammed store-chambers, the stonework everywhere, the pillars, the arches, the pavements. 'How on earth, Badger,' he said at last, 'did you ever find time and strength to do all this? It's astonishing!'

'It *would* be astonishing indeed,' said the Badger simply, 'if I *had* done it. But as a matter of fact I did none of it— only cleaned out the passages and rooms, as far as I had need of them. There's lots more of it, all round about. I see you don't understand, and I must explain it to you. Well, very long ago, on the spot where the Wild Wood now stands, before ever it had planted itself and grown up to what it now is, there was a city—a city of people, you know. Here, where we are standing, they lived, and walked, and talked, and slept, and carried on their business. Here they stabled their horses and feasted, from here they rode out to fight or drove out to trade. They were a powerful people, and

Crossing the hall,
they passed down one of the principal tunnels . . .

rich, and great builders. They built to last, for they thought their city would last for ever.'

'But what has become of them all?' asked the Mole.

'Who can tell?' said the Badger. 'People come—they stay for a while, they build—and they go. It is their way. But we remain. There were badgers here, I've been told, long before that same city ever came to be. And now there are badgers here again. We keep on going, and we may move out for a time, but we wait, and are patient, and back we come. And so it will ever be.'

'Well, and when they went at last, those people?' said the Mole.

'When they went,' continued the Badger, 'the strong winds and heavy rains took the matter in hand, patiently, year after year. Perhaps we badgers too, in our small way, helped a little—who knows? It was all down, down, down, gradually —ruin and levelling and disappearance. Then it was all up, up, up, gradually, as seeds grew to saplings, and saplings to forest trees, and bramble and fern came creeping in to help. In course of time our home was ready for us again, and we moved in. Up above us, on the surface, the same thing happened. Animals arrived, liked the look of the place, took up their quarters, settled down, and spread. The Wild Wood is pretty well populated by now; with all the usual lot, good, bad, and indifferent—I name no names. It takes all sorts to make a world. But I fancy you know something about them yourself by this time.'

'I do indeed,' said the Mole, with a slight shiver.

'Well, well,' said the Badger, patting him on the shoulder, 'it was your first experience of them, you see. They're not so bad really; and we must all live and let live. But I'll pass the word round tomorrow, and I think you'll have no further trouble. Any friend of *mine* walks where he likes in this country, or I'll know the reason why!'

When they got back to the kitchen again, they found the Rat walking up and down, very restless. The underground atmosphere was getting on his nerves, and he seemed really to be afraid that the river would run away if he wasn't there to look after it. So he had his overcoat on, and his pistols thrust into his belt again. 'Come along, Mole,' he said, as

soon as he caught sight of them. 'We must get off while it's daylight. Don't want to spend another night in the Wild Wood again.'

'It'll be all right, my fine fellow,' said the Otter. 'I'm coming along with you, and I know every path blindfold; and if there's a head that needs to be punched, you can rely upon me to punch it.'

'You really needn't fret, Ratty,' added the Badger placidly. 'My passages run further than you think, and I've bolt-holes to the edge of the wood in several directions, though I don't care for everybody to know about them. When you really have to go, you shall leave by one of my short cuts. Meantime, make yourself easy, and sit down again.'

The Rat was nevertheless still eager to be off and attend to his river, so the Badger, taking up his lantern again, led the way along a damp and airless tunnel that wound and dipped for a weary distance that seemed to be miles. At last daylight began to show itself through tangled growth overhanging the mouth of the passage; and the Badger, bidding them a hasty good-bye, pushed them through the opening, made everything look as natural as possible again, with creepers, brushwood, and dead leaves, and retreated.

They found themselves standing on the very edge of the Wild Wood. Rocks and brambles and tree-roots behind them; in front, a great space of quiet fields, hemmed by lines of hedges black on the snow, and, far ahead, a glint of the familiar old river, while the wintry sun hung red and low on the horizon. The Otter, knowing all the paths, took charge of the party, and they trailed out on a bee-line for a distant stile. Looking back, they saw the whole mass of the Wild Wood, dense, menacing, compact, grimly set in vast white surroundings; together they turned and made swiftly for home, for firelight, and for the voice, sounding cheerily outside their window, of the river that they knew and trusted in all its moods.

CHAPTER 5

Home Sweet Home

THE sheep ran huddling together against the hurdles, blowing out thin nostrils and stamping with delicate fore-feet, their heads thrown back and a light steam rising from the crowded sheep-pen into the frosty air, as the two animals hastened by in high spirits, with much chatter and laughter. They were returning across country after a long day's outing with Otter, hunting and exploring on the wide uplands. The shades of the short winter day were closing in on them, and they had still some distance to go. Plodding across the field, they had heard the sheep and had made for them; and now, leading from the sheep-pen, they found a beaten track that made walking easier.

'It looks as if we were coming to a village,' said the Mole, slowing down, as the track, that had in time become a path and then had developed into a lane, now handed them over to the charge of a well-metalled road. The animals did not hold with villages.

'Oh, never mind!' said the Rat. 'At this season of the year they're all safe indoors by this time, sitting round the fire; men, women, and children, dogs and cats and all. We shall slip through all right, without any bother or unpleasantness, and we can have a look at them through their windows if you like, and see what they're doing.'

The rapid nightfall of mid-December had closed in on the little village as they approached it on soft feet over a first thin fall of powdery snow. Little was visible but squares of a dusky orange-red on either side of the street, where the firelight or lamplight of each cottage overflowed through the windows into the dark world outside. Most of the low windows had no blinds, and the lookers-in from outside saw the inmates, gathered round the tea-table, absorbed in handiwork, or talking and laughing. Moving from one window to another, the two spectators, so far from home themselves, had something of wistfulness in their eyes as they watched a cat being stroked, a sleepy child picked up and huddled off to bed, or a tired man stretch and knock out his pipe on the end of a smouldering log.

Then a gust of bitter wind took them in the back of the neck, a small sting of frozen sleet on the skin woke them as from a dream, and they knew their toes to be cold and their legs tired, and their own home distant a weary way.

Once beyond the village, where the cottages ceased abruptly, on either side of the road they could smell through the darkness the friendly fields again; and they braced themselves for the last long stretch, the home stretch, the stretch that we know is bound to end, some time, in the rattle of the door-latch, the sudden firelight, and the sight of familiar things. They plodded along steadily and silently, each of them thinking his own thoughts. The Mole's thoughts ran a good deal on supper, as it was pitch dark, and it was all a strange country to him as far as he knew, and he was following obediently behind the Rat, leaving the guidance entirely to him. As for the Rat, he was walking a little way ahead, as his habit was, his shoulders humped, his eyes fixed on the straight grey road in front of him; so he did not notice poor Mole when suddenly the call reached him, and took him like an electric shock.

the matter? Tell us your trouble, and let me see what I can do.'

Poor Mole found it difficult to get any words out between the heavings of his chest that followed one upon another so quickly and held back speech and choked it as it came. 'I know it's a—shabby, dingy little place,' he sobbed at last, brokenly: 'not like—your cosy quarters—or Toad's beautiful hall—or Badger's great house—but it was my own little home—and I was fond of it—and I went away and forgot all about it—and then I smelt it suddenly—on the road, when I called and you wouldn't listen, Rat—and everything came back to me with a rush—and I *wanted* it!—O dear, O dear—and when you *wouldn't* turn back, Ratty—and I had to leave it, though I was smelling it all the time—I thought my heart would break.—We might have just gone and had one look at it, Ratty—only one look—it was close by—but you wouldn't turn back, Ratty, you wouldn't turn back! O dear, O dear!'

The memory brought fresh waves of sorrow, and sobs again took full charge of him, preventing further speech.

The Rat stared straight in front of him, saying nothing, only patting Mole gently on the shoulder. After a time he muttered gloomily, 'I see it all now! What a *pig* I have been! A pig—that's me! Just a pig—a plain pig!'

He waited till Mole's sobs became gradually less, till at last sniffs were frequent and sobs came only now and then. Then he rose from his seat, and, remarking carelessly, 'Well, now we'd really better be getting on, old chap!' set off up the road again, over the difficult way they had come.

'Wherever are you (hic) going to (hic), Ratty?' cried the tearful Mole, looking up in alarm.

'We're going to find that home of yours, old fellow,' replied the Rat pleasantly; 'so you had better come along, for it will take some finding, and we shall want your nose.'

'O, come back, Ratty, do!' cried the Mole, getting up and hurrying after him. 'It's no good, I tell you! It's too late, and too dark, and the place is too far off, and the snow's coming! And—and I never meant to let you know I was feeling that way about it—it was all an accident and a mistake! And think of River Bank, and your supper!'

'We're going to find that home of yours, old fellow,'
replied the Rat pleasantly.

He clambered into his bunk and rolled himself well up in the blankets, and sleep soon carried him away.

The weary Mole also was glad to turn in without delay, and soon had his head on his pillow, in great joy and contentment. But before he closed his eyes he let them wander round his old room, mellow in the glow of the firelight that played or rested on all the familiar and friendly things. He was now in just the frame of mind that the tactful Rat had quietly worked to bring about in him. He saw clearly how plain and simple—how narrow, even—it all was; but clearly, too, how much it all meant to him. He did not at all want to abandon the new life and its splendid spaces, to turn his back on sun and air and all they offered him and creep home and stay there; the upper world was all too strong, it called to him still, even down there, and he knew he must return to it. But it was good to think he had this to come back to, this place which was all his own, these things which were so glad to see him again and could always be counted upon for the same simple welcome.

CHAPTER 6

Mr. Toad

It was a bright morning in the early part of summer; the river had sunk back to its normal banks and its usual pace, and a hot sun seemed to be pulling everything green and bushy and spiky up out of the earth towards him, as if by strings. The Mole and the Water Rat had been up since dawn, very busy on matters connected with boats and the opening of the boating season; painting and varnishing, mending paddles, repairing cushions, hunting for missing boat-hooks, and so on; and were finishing breakfast in their little parlour and eagerly discussing their plans for the day, when a heavy knock sounded at the door.

'Bother!' said the Rat, egg all over him. 'See who it is, Mole, like a good fellow, since you've finished.'

The Mole went to answer the door, and the Rat heard him utter a cry of surprise. Then he flung the parlour door open, and announced with much importance, 'Mr. Badger!'

This was a wonderful thing, indeed, that the Badger should pay a call on them, or indeed on anybody. He generally had to be caught, if you wanted him badly, as he slipped quietly along a hedgerow in the early morning or late evening, or else be hunted up in his own house in the middle of the wood.

The Badger strode heavily into the room, and stood looking at the two animals with an expression full of seriousness. The Rat let his egg-spoon fall on the table-cloth, and sat open-mouthed.

'The hour has come!' said the Badger at last.

'What hour?' asked the Rat uneasily, glancing at the clock on the mantelpiece.

'*Whose* hour, you should rather say,' replied the Badger. 'Why, Toad's hour! The hour of Toad! I said I would take him in hand as soon as the winter was well over, and I'm going to take him in hand today!'

'Toad's hour, of course!' cried the Mole delightedly. 'Hooray! I remember now! *We'll* teach him to be a sensible Toad!'

'This very morning,' continued the Badger, taking an armchair, 'as I learnt last night from a trustworthy source, another new and very powerful motor-car will arrive at Toad Hall on approval or return. At this very moment, perhaps, Toad is busily putting on those quite hideous clothes so dear to him, which transform him from a (fairly) good-looking Toad into an Object which throws any decent-minded animal that comes across it into a violent fit. We must be up and doing, before it is too late. You two animals will accompany me instantly to Toad Hall, and the work of rescue shall be accomplished.'

'Right you are!' cried the Rat, starting up. 'We'll rescue the poor unhappy animal! We'll change him! He'll be the most changed Toad that ever was before we've done with him!'

They set off up the road, Badger leading the way. They reached the carriage-drive of Toad Hall to find, as the Badger had expected, a shiny new motor-car, of great size, painted a bright red, standing in front of the house. As they neared the door it was flung open, and Mr. Toad, dressed in goggles, cap, gaiters, and enormous overcoat, came swaggering down the steps, drawing on his gloves.

'Hullo! come on, you fellows!' he cried cheerfully on catching sight of them. 'You're just in time to come with me for a—to come for a—for a—er——'

His hearty voice fell away as he noticed the stern unbending look on the faces of his silent friends, and his invitation remained unfinished.

The Badger strode up the steps. 'Take him inside,' he said sternly to his companions. Then, as Toad was hustled through the door, struggling and protesting, he turned to the chauffeur in charge of the new motor-car.

'I'm afraid you won't be wanted today,' he said. 'Mr. Toad has changed his mind. He will not require the car. Please understand that this is final. You needn't wait.' Then he followed the others inside and shut the door.

'Now, then!' he said to the Toad, when the four of them stood together in the hall, 'first of all, take those ridiculous things off!'

'Shan't!' replied Toad, with great spirit. 'What is the meaning of this outrage? I demand an instant explanation.'

'Take them off him, then, you two,' ordered the Badger briefly.

They had to lay Toad out on the floor, kicking and calling all sorts of names, before they could get to work properly. Then the Rat sat on him, and the Mole got his motor-clothes off him bit by bit, and they stood him up on his legs again. A good deal of his fiery spirit seemed to have disappeared with the removal of his fine clothes. Now that he was merely Toad, and no longer the Terror of the Highway, he giggled feebly and looked from one to the other appealingly.

'You knew it must come to this, sooner or later, Toad,' the Badger explained severely. 'You've disregarded all the warnings we've given you, you've gone on wasting the money your father left you, and you're getting us animals a bad name in the district by your furious driving and your smashes and your rows with the police. Independence is all very well, but we animals never allow our friends to make fools of themselves beyond a certain limit; and that limit you've reached. Now, you're a good fellow in many respects, and

I don't want to be too hard on you. I'll make one more effort to bring you to reason. You will come with me into the smoking-room, and there you will hear some facts about yourself; and we'll see whether you come out of that room the same Toad that you went in.'

He took Toad firmly by the arm, led him into the smoking-room, and closed the door behind them.

'*That's* no good!' said the Rat. '*Talking* to Toad'll never cure him. He'll *say* anything.'

They made themselves comfortable in armchairs and waited patiently. Through the closed door they could just hear the long drone of the Badger's voice, rising and falling in waves; and presently they heard long-drawn sobs, seeming to come from Toad, who was a soft-hearted and affectionate fellow, very easily converted—for the time being—to any point of view.

After some three-quarters of an hour the door opened, and the Badger reappeared, leading by the paw a very limp and dejected Toad. His skin hung baggily about him, his legs wobbled, and his cheeks were lined with tears.

'Sit down there, Toad,' said the Badger kindly, pointing to a chair. 'My friends,' he went on, 'I am pleased to inform you that Toad has at last seen the error of his ways. He is truly sorry for his misguided conduct in the past, and he has agreed to give up motor-cars entirely and for ever. I have his solemn promise to that effect.'

'That is very good news,' said the Mole gravely.

'Very good news indeed,' said the Rat doubtfully, 'if only —*if* only——'

He was looking very hard at Toad as he said this, and could not help thinking he saw something like a twinkle in that animal's still sorrowful eyes.

'There's only one thing more to be done,' continued the Badger. 'Toad, I want you to repeat, before your friends here, what you fully admitted to me in the smoking-room just now. First, you are sorry for what you've done, and you see the folly of it all?'

There was a long, long pause. Toad looked this way and that, while the other animals waited in silence. At last he spoke.

'No!' he said a little sulkily, but stoutly; 'I'm *not* sorry. And it wasn't folly at all! It was simply glorious!'

'What?' cried the Badger, greatly shocked. 'You backsliding animal, didn't you tell me just now, in there——'

'O, yes, yes, in *there*,' said Toad impatiently. 'I'd have said anything in *there*. You're so eloquent, dear Badger, and so moving, and so convincing, and put all your points so very well—you can do what you like with me in *there*, and you know it. But I've been searching my mind since, and going over things in it, and I find that I'm not a bit sorry really, so it's no earthly good saying I am; now, is it?'

'Then you don't promise,' said the Badger, 'never to touch a motor-car again?'

'Certainly not!' replied Toad. 'On the contrary, I faithfully promise that the very first motor-car I see, poop-poop! off I go in it!'

'Told you so, didn't I?' said the Rat to the Mole.

'Very well, then,' said the Badger firmly, rising to his feet. 'Since you won't be reasonable, we'll try what force can do. I feared it would come to this all along. You've often asked us three to come and stay with you, Toad, in this handsome house of yours; well, now we're going to. When we've converted you to a proper point of view we may quit, but not before. Take him upstairs, you two, and lock him up in his bedroom, while we arrange matters between ourselves.'

'It's for your own good, Toady, you know,' said the Rat kindly, as Toad, kicking and struggling, was hauled up the stairs by his two faithful friends.

'Think what fun we shall all have together, just as we used to, when you've quite got over this—this painful attack of yours!'

'We'll take great care of everything for you till you're well, Toad,' said the Mole; 'and we'll see your money isn't wasted, as it has been.'

'No more of those regrettable incidents with the police, Toad,' said the Rat, as they thrust him into his bedroom.

'And no more weeks in hospital, being ordered about by female nurses, Toad,' added the Mole, turning the key on him.

They went downstairs, Toad shouting abuse at them through the keyhole; and the three friends then met in conference on the situation.

'It's going to be a tiresome business,' said the Badger, sighing. 'I've never seen Toad so determined. However, we will see it out. He must never be left an instant unguarded. We shall have to take it in turns to be with him, till the poison has worked itself out of his system.'

They arranged to keep watch over him. Each animal took it in turns to sleep in Toad's room at night, and they divided the day up between them. At first Toad was very trying to his careful guardians. When his violent fits took him he would arrange bedroom chairs to look like a motor-car and would crouch on the front one bent forward and staring ahead, making horrible noises, till the climax was reached, when, turning a complete somersault, he would lie face down among the ruins of the chairs, apparently completely satisfied for the moment. As time passed, however, these painful attacks grew less frequent, and his friends tried hard to make him think of new things. But his interest in other matters did not seem to revive, and he grew weak and depressed.

One fine morning the Rat, whose turn it was to go on duty, went upstairs to relieve Badger, whom he found fidgeting to be off and stretch his legs in a long ramble round his wood and down his earths and burrows. 'Toad's still in bed,' he told the Rat, outside the door. 'Can't get much out of him, except, "O, leave him alone, he wants nothing, perhaps he'll be better presently, it may pass off in time, don't be unduly anxious," and so on. Now, you look out, Rat! When Toad's quiet and obedient, then he's at his most artful. There's sure to be something up. I know him. Well, now I must be off.'

'How are you today, old chap?' asked the Rat cheerfully, as he approached Toad's bedside.

He had to wait some minutes for an answer. At last a feeble voice replied, 'Thank you so much, dear Ratty! So good of you to ask! But first tell me how you are yourself, and the excellent Mole?'

'O, *we're* all right,' replied the Rat. 'Mole,' he added

At last a feeble voice replied, 'Thank you so much, dear Ratty!
So good of you to ask!'

The Clerk scratched his nose with his pen. 'Some people would consider,' he observed, 'that stealing the motor-car was the worst offence; and so it is. But cheeking the police undoubtedly carries the severest penalty; and so it ought. Supposing you were to say twelve months for the theft, which is mild; and three years for the furious driving, which is lenient; and fifteen years for the cheek, which was pretty bad sort of cheek, judging by what we've heard from the witness-box, even if you only believe one-tenth part of what you heard, and I never believe more myself—those figures, if added together correctly, tot up to nineteen years——'

'First rate!' said the Chairman.

'—So you had better make it a round twenty years and be on the safe side,' ended the Clerk.

'An excellent suggestion!' said the Chairman approvingly. 'Prisoner! Pull yourself together and try and stand up straight. It's going to be twenty years for you this time. And mind, if you appear before us again, upon any charge whatever, we shall have to deal with you very seriously!'

Then the brutal minions of the law fell upon the hapless Toad; loaded him with chains, and dragged him from the Court House, shrieking, praying, protesting; across the market-place, where the playful crowd assailed him with jeers, carrots, and popular catch-words; past hooting school children, their innocent faces lit up with the pleasure they ever derive from the sight of a gentleman in difficulties; across the hollow-sounding drawbridge, below the spiky portcullis, under the frowning archway of the grim old castle, whose ancient towers soared high overhead; past guardrooms full of grinning soldiers off duty, past sentries who coughed in a horrid sarcastic way; up time-worn winding stairs, across courtyards, where mastiffs strained at their leash and pawed the air to get at him; past ancient warders, their halberds leant against the wall, dozing over a pasty and a flagon of brown ale; on and on, past the rack-chamber and the thumbscrew-room, past the turning that led to the private scaffold, till they reached the door of the grimmest dungeon that lay in the heart of the innermost keep. There at last they paused, where an ancient gaoler sat fingering a bunch of mighty keys.

'*Prisoner! Pull yourself together and try and stand up straight.*
It's going to be twenty years for you this time.'

'Oddsbodikins!' said the sergeant of police, taking off his helmet and wiping his forehead. 'Get up, old loon, and take over from us this vile Toad, a criminal of deepest guilt and matchless artfulness and resource. Watch and guard him with all your skill; and mark well, grey-beard, should anything untoward befall, your old head shall answer for his!'

The gaoler nodded grimly, laying his withered hand on the shoulder of the miserable Toad. The rusty key creaked in the lock, the great door clanged behind them; and Toad was a helpless prisoner in the remotest dungeon of the best-guarded keep of the stoutest castle in all the length and breadth of Merry England.

CHAPTER 7

Toad's Adventures

WHEN Toad found himself locked away in a damp and evil-smelling dungeon, and knew that all the grim darkness of a medieval fortress lay between him and the outer world of sunshine and high roads where he had lately been so happy, he flung himself at full length on the floor, and shed bitter tears, and abandoned himself to dark despair. 'This is the end of everything' (he said), 'at least it is the end of the career of Toad, which is the same thing; the popular and handsome Toad, the rich and hospitable Toad, the Toad so free and careless and debonair! How can I hope to be ever set at large again' (he said), 'who have been imprisoned so justly for stealing so handsome a motor-car in such an audacious manner, and for such lurid and imaginative cheek, bestowed upon such a number of fat, red-faced policemen!'

(Here his sobs choked him.) 'Stupid animal that I was' (he said), 'now I must languish in this dungeon, till people who were proud to say they knew me, have forgotten the very name of Toad! O wise old Badger!' (he said), 'O clever, intelligent Rat and sensible Mole! What sound judgments, what a knowledge of men and matters you possess! O unhappy and forsaken Toad!' With lamentations such as these he passed his days and nights for several weeks, refusing his meals or light refreshments, though the grim and ancient gaoler, knowing that Toad's pockets were well lined, frequently pointed out that many comforts, and indeed luxuries, could by arrangement be sent in—at a price— from outside.

Now the gaoler had a pleasant and good-hearted daughter, who assisted her father in the lighter duties of his post. She was particularly fond of animals, and, besides her canary, she kept several piebald mice and a restless squirrel. This kind-hearted girl, pitying the misery of Toad, said to her father one day, 'Father! I can't bear to see that poor beast so unhappy, and getting so thin! You let me have the managing of him. You know how fond of animals I am. I'll make him eat from my hand, and sit up, and do all sorts of things.'

Her father replied that she could do what she liked with him. He was tired of Toad, and his sulks and his airs and his meanness. So that day she went on her errand of mercy, and knocked at the door of Toad's cell.

'Now, cheer up, Toad,' she said coaxingly, on entering, 'and sit up and dry your eyes and be a sensible animal. And do try and eat a bit of dinner. See, I've brought you some of mine, hot from the oven!'

It was bubble-and-squeak, between two plates, and its fragrance filled the narrow cell. The penetrating smell of cabbage reached the nose of Toad as he lay in his misery on the floor. It gave him the idea for a moment that perhaps life was not such a blank and desperate thing as he had imagined. But still he wailed, and kicked with his legs, and refused to be comforted. So the wise girl retired for the time, but, of course, a good deal of the smell of hot cabbage remained behind, as it will do, and Toad, between his sobs, sniffed and reflected, and gradually began to think new and inspiring thoughts: of chivalry, and poetry, and deeds still to be done; of broad meadows, and cattle browsing in them, raked by sun and wind; of kitchen-gardens, and straight herb-borders, and warm snap-dragon beset by bees; and of the comforting clink of dishes set down on the table at Toad Hall, and the scrape of chair-legs on the floor as every one pulled himself close up to his work. The air of the narrow cell took on a rosy tinge; he began to think of his friends, and how they would surely be able to do something; of lawyers, and how they would have enjoyed his case, and what a fool he had been not to get in a few; and lastly, he thought of his own great cleverness, and all that he was capable of if he only gave his great mind to it; and the cure was almost complete.

When the girl returned, some hours later, she carried a tray, with a cup of fragrant tea steaming on it; and a plate piled up with very hot buttered toast, cut thick, very brown on both sides, with the butter running through the holes in it in great golden drops, like honey from the honey-comb. The smell of that buttered toast simply talked to Toad, and with no uncertain voice; talked of warm kitchens, of breakfasts on bright frosty mornings, and of snug parlour firesides on winter evenings. Toad sat up on end once more, dried his eyes, sipped his tea and munched his toast, and soon began talking freely about himself, and the house he lived in, and his doings there, and how important he was, and what a lot his friends thought of him.

The gaoler's daughter saw that the topic was doing him as much good as the tea, as indeed it was, and encouraged him to go on.

'Tell me about Toad Hall,' said she. 'It sounds beautiful.'

'Toad Hall,' said the Toad proudly, 'is a self-contained gentleman's residence, very unique; dating in part from the fourteenth century, but with every modern convenience. Up-to-date sanitation. Five minutes from church, post office, and golf-links. Suitable for——'

'Bless the animal,' said the girl, laughing, 'I don't want to *take* it. Tell me something *real* about it. But first wait till I fetch you some more tea and toast.'

a black bonnet; the only demand the old lady made was that she should be gagged and bound and dumped down in a corner. By this trick, she explained, no one would think she had helped Toad escape.

Toad was delighted with the suggestion. It would enable him to leave the prison in some style, and with his reputation for being a desperate and dangerous fellow unharmed; and he readily helped the gaoler's daughter to make her aunt appear as much as possible the victim of circumstances over which she had no control.

'Now it's your turn, Toad,' said the girl. 'Take off that coat and waistcoat of yours; you're fat enough as it is.'

Shaking with laughter, she proceeded to dress him in the cotton print gown, arranged the shawl around him, and tied the strings of the bonnet under his chin.

'You're the very image of her,' she giggled, 'only I'm sure you never looked half so respectable in all your life before. Now, good-bye, Toad, and good luck. Go straight down the way you came up; and if any one says anything to you, as they probably will, being but men, you can answer back a bit, of course, but remember you're a widow woman, quite alone in the world.'

With a quaking heart, but as firm a footstep as he could command, Toad set forth; but he was soon agreeably surprised to find how easy everything was made for him. The washerwoman's dumpy figure in its familiar cotton print seemed a passport for every barred door and grim gateway; even when he hesitated, uncertain as to the right turning to take, he found himself helped out of his difficulty by the warder at the next gate, anxious to be off to his tea.

It seemed hours before he crossed the last courtyard, rejected the pressing invitations from the last guardroom, and dodged the outspread arms of the last warder, pleading for just one farewell embrace. But at last he heard the wicket-gate in the great outer door click behind him, felt the fresh air of the outer world upon his brow, and knew that he was free!

Dizzy with the easy success of his daring exploit, he walked quickly towards the lights of the town, not knowing in the least what he should do next, only quite certain of one thing,

She proceeded to dress him in the cotton print gown . . .

Uses up a power of shirts, it does, till my missus is fair tired of washing 'em. If you'll wash a few shirts for me when you get home, and send 'em along, I'll give you a ride on my engine. It's against the Company's regulations, but we're not so very particular in these out-of-the-way parts.'

The Toad's misery turned into rapture as he eagerly scrambled up into the cab of the engine. Of course, he had never washed a shirt in his life, and couldn't if he tried and, anyhow, he wasn't going to begin; but he thought: 'When I get safely home to Toad Hall, and have money again, and pockets to put it in, I will send the engine-driver enough to pay for quite a quantity of washing, and that will be the same thing, or better.'

The guard waved his welcome flag, the engine-driver whistled, and the train moved out of the station. As the speed increased, and the Toad could see on either side of him real fields, and trees, and hedges, and cows, and horses, all flying past him, and as he thought how every minute was bringing him nearer to Toad Hall, and sympathetic friends, and money to chink in his pocket, and a soft bed to sleep in, and good things to eat, and praise and admiration at the recital of his adventures and his cleverness, he began to skip up and down and shout and sing snatches of song, to the great astonishment of the engine-driver, who had come across washerwomen before, but never one at all like this.

They had covered many and many a mile, and Toad was already considering what he would have for supper as soon as he got home, when he noticed that the engine-driver, with a puzzled expression on his face, was leaning over the side of the engine and listening hard. Then he saw him climb on to the coals and gaze out over the top of the train; then he returned and said to Toad: 'It's very strange; we're the last train running in this direction tonight, yet I could have sworn that I heard another following us!'

Toad stopped his antics at once. He became grave and depressed, and a dull pain in the lower part of his spine, moving down to his legs, made him want to sit down and try desperately not to think of what might happen.

By this time the moon was shining brightly, and the

*Toad could see on either side of him real fields, and trees,
and hedges, and cows, and horses, all flying past him.*

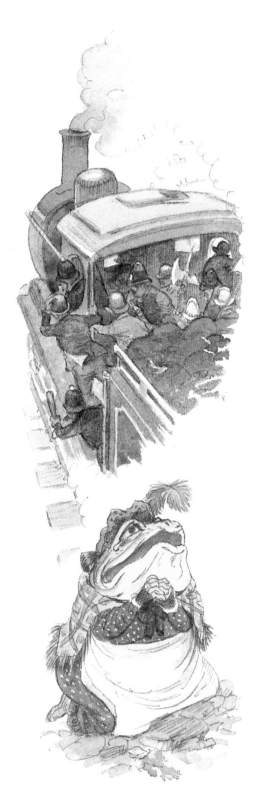

engine-driver, steadying himself on the coal, could see the line behind them for a long distance.

Presently he called out, 'I can see it clearly now! It is an engine, on our rails, coming along at a great speed! It looks as if we are being followed!'

The miserable Toad, crouching in the coal-dust, tried hard to think of something to do, with dismal lack of success.

'They are gaining on us fast!' cried the engine-driver. 'And the engine is crowded with the queerest lot of people! Men like ancient warders; policemen in their helmets, waving truncheons; and shabbily dressed men in pot-hats, unmistakable plain-clothes detectives even at this distance, waving revolvers and walking-sticks; all waving, and all shouting the same thing—"Stop, stop, stop!"'

Then Toad fell on his knees among the coals and, raising his clasped paws in prayer, cried, 'Save me, only save me, dear kind Mr. Engine-driver, and I will confess everything! I am not the simple washerwoman I seem to be! I have no children waiting for me. I am a toad—the well-known and popular Mr. Toad; I have just escaped, by my great daring and cleverness, from a dungeon into which my enemies had flung me; and if those fellows on that engine recapture me, it will be chains and bread-and-water and straw and misery once more for poor, unhappy, innocent Toad!'

The engine-driver looked down upon him very sternly, and said, 'Now tell the truth; what were you put in prison for?'

'It was nothing very much,' said poor Toad, blushing deeply. 'I only borrowed a motor-car while the owners were at lunch; they had no need of it at the time. I didn't mean to steal it, really; but people—especially magistrates —take such harsh views of thoughtless and high-spirited actions.'

The engine-driver looked very grave and said, 'I fear that you have been indeed a wicked toad, and by rights I ought to give you up. But you are evidently in trouble and distress, so I will not desert you. I don't hold with motor-cars, for one thing; and I don't hold with being ordered about by policemen when I'm on my own engine, for another. And the sight of an animal in tears always makes me feel soft-hearted.

So cheer up, Toad! I'll do my best, and we may beat them yet!'

They piled on more coals, shovelling furiously; the furnace roared, the sparks flew, the engine leapt and swung, but still the other engine slowly gained. The engine-driver, with a sigh, wiped his brow with a rag, and said, 'I'm afraid it's no good, Toad. You see, they are running light, and they have the better engine. There's just one thing left for us to do, and it's your only chance, so listen very carefully to what I tell you. A short way ahead of us is a long tunnel, and on the other side of that the line passes through a thick wood. Now, I will put on all the speed I can while we are running through the tunnel, but the other fellows will slow down a bit, for fear of an accident. When we are through, I will shut off steam and put on brakes as hard as I can, and the moment it's safe to do so you must jump and hide in the wood, before they get through the tunnel and see you. Then I will go full speed ahead again, and they can chase *me* if they like, for as long as they like, and as far as they like. Now mind and be ready to jump when I tell you!'

They piled on more coals, and the train shot into the tunnel, and the engine rushed and roared and rattled, till at last they shot out at the other end into fresh air and the peaceful moonlight, and saw the wood lying dark and helpful upon either side of the line. The driver shut off steam and put on brakes, the Toad got down on the step, and as the train slowed down to almost a walking pace he heard the driver call out, 'Now, jump!'

Toad jumped, rolled down a short bank, picked himself up unhurt, scrambled into the wood and hid.

Peeping out, he saw his train get up speed again and disappear at a great pace. Then out of the tunnel burst the other engine, roaring and whistling, her motley crew waving their various weapons and shouting, 'Stop! stop! stop!' When they were past, the Toad had a hearty laugh—for the first time since he was thrown into prison.

But he soon stopped laughing when he came to consider that it was now very late and dark and cold, and he was in an unknown wood, with no money and no chance of supper, and still far from friends and home; and the dead silence of

or Toads; and lost the soap, for the fiftieth time.

A burst of laughter made him straighten himself and look round. The barge-woman was leaning back and laughing, till the tears ran down her cheeks.

'I've been watching you all the time,' she gasped. 'I thought you must be a humbug all along, from the conceited way you talked. Pretty washerwoman you are! Never washed so much as a dish-cloth in your life, I'd say!'

Toad's temper, which had been simmering viciously for some time, now fairly boiled over, and he lost all control of himself.

'You common, low, *fat* barge-woman!' he shouted; 'don't you dare to talk to your betters like that! Washerwoman indeed! I would have you to know that I am a Toad, a very well-known, respected, distinguished Toad! I may be under a bit of a cloud at present, but I will *not* be laughed at by a barge-woman!'

The woman moved nearer to him and peered under his bonnet keenly and closely. 'Why, so you are!' she cried. 'Well, I never! A horrid, nasty, crawly Toad! And in my nice clean barge, too! Now that is a thing that I will *not* have.'

She let go of the tiller for a moment. One big mottled arm shot out and caught Toad by a fore-leg, while the other gripped him fast by a hind-leg. Then the world turned suddenly upside down, the barge seemed to flit lightly across the sky, the wind whistled in his ears, and Toad found himself flying through the air, revolving rapidly as he went.

The water, when he eventually reached it with a loud splash, proved quite cold enough for his taste, though its chill was not sufficient to quell his proud spirit, or slake the heat of his furious temper. He rose to the surface spluttering, and when he had wiped the duckweed out of his eyes the first thing he saw was the fat barge-woman looking back at him over the stern of the barge and laughing; and he vowed, as he coughed and choked, to be even with her.

He struck out for the shore, but the cotton gown greatly impeded his efforts, and when at length he touched land he found it hard to climb up the steep bank. He had to take a minute or two's rest to recover his breath; then, gathering

. . . when he had wiped the duckweed out of his eyes
the first thing he saw was the fat barge-woman.

his wet skirts well over his arms, he started to run after the barge as fast as his legs would carry him, wild with indignation, thirsting for revenge.

The barge-woman was still laughing when he drew up level with her. 'Put yourself through your mangle, washerwoman,' she called out, 'and iron your face and crimp it, and you'll pass for quite a decent-looking Toad!'

Toad never paused to reply. Revenge was what he wanted, not an exchange of words, though he had a thing or two in his mind that he would have liked to say. He saw what he wanted ahead of him. Running swiftly on he overtook the horse, unfastened the tow-rope and cast off, jumped lightly on the horse's back, and urged it to a gallop by kicking it hard in the sides. He steered for the open country, leaving the tow-path, and swinging his steed down a bumpy lane. Once he looked back, and saw that the barge had run aground on the other side of the canal, and the barge-woman was waving her arms wildly and shouting, 'Stop, stop, stop!' 'I've heard that song before,' said Toad, laughing, as he continued to spur his steed onward in its wild gallop.

The barge-horse was not capable of any very sustained effort, and its gallop soon subsided into a trot, and its trot into an easy walk; but Toad was quite contented with this, knowing that he, at any rate, was moving, and the barge was not. He had quite recovered his temper, now that he had done something he thought really clever; and he was satisfied to jog along quietly in the sun, taking advantage of any byways and bridle-paths, and trying to forget how very long it was since he had had a square meal, till the canal had been left very far behind him.

He had travelled some miles, his horse and he, and he was feeling drowsy in the hot sunshine, when the horse stopped, lowered his head, and began to nibble the grass; and Toad, waking up, just saved himself from falling off by an effort. He looked about him and found he was on a wide common, dotted with patches of gorse and bramble as far as he could see. Near him stood a dingy gipsy caravan, and beside it a man was sitting on a bucket turned upside down, very busy smoking and staring into the wide world.

A fire of sticks was burning near by, and over the fire hung an iron pot, and out of that pot came forth bubblings and gurglings. Also smells—warm, rich, and varied smells— that twined and twisted and wreathed themselves at last into one complete, perfect smell. Toad now knew well that he had not been really hungry before. What he had felt earlier in the day had been nothing. This was the real thing at last, and no mistake; and it would have to be dealt with speedily, too, or there would be trouble for somebody or something. He looked the gipsy over carefully, wondering whether it would be easier to fight him or speak nicely to him. So there he sat, and sniffed and sniffed, and looked at the gipsy; and the gipsy sat and smoked, and looked at him.

Presently the gipsy took his pipe out of his mouth and remarked in a careless way, 'Want to sell that there horse of yours?'

Toad was completely taken aback. He did not know that gipsies were very fond of horsedealing, and never missed an opportunity, and he had not reflected that caravans were always on the move and took a deal of drawing. It had not occurred to him to turn the horse into cash, but the gipsy's suggestion seemed to smooth the way towards the two things he wanted so badly—ready money and a solid breakfast.

'What?' he said, 'me sell this beautiful young horse of mine? O no; it's out of the question. Who's going to take the washing home to my customers every week? Besides, I'm too fond of him, and he simply dotes on me.'

'Try and love a donkey,' suggested the gipsy. 'Some people do.'

'You don't seem to see,' continued Toad, 'that this fine horse of mine is a cut above you altogether. He's a blood horse, he is, partly; not the part you see, of course—another part. And he's been a Prize Hackney, too, in his time— that was the time before you knew him, but you can still tell it on him at a glance if you understand anything about horses. No, it's not to be thought of for a moment. All the same, how much would you offer me for this beautiful young horse of mine?'

The gipsy looked the horse over, and then he looked Toad over with equal care, and looked at the horse again.

'Shillin' a leg,' he said briefly, and turned away.

'A shilling a leg?' cried Toad. 'If you please, I must take a little time to work that out, and see just what it comes to.'

He climbed down off his horse, and left it to graze, and sat down by the gipsy, and did sums on his fingers, and at last he said, 'A shilling a leg? Why, that comes to exactly four shillings, and no more. O no; I could not think of accepting four shillings for this beautiful young horse of mine.'

'Well,' said the gipsy, 'I'll tell you what I will do. I'll make it five shillings, and that's three-and-six-pence more than the animal's worth. And that's my last word.'

Then Toad sat and pondered long and deeply. For he was hungry and quite penniless, and still some way—he knew not how far—from home, and enemies might still be looking for him. To one in such a situation, five shillings may very well appear a large sum of money. On the other hand, it did not seem very much to get for a horse. But then, again, the horse hadn't cost him anything; so whatever he got was all clear profit. At last he said firmly, 'Look here, gipsy! I tell you what we will do; and this is *my* last word. You shall hand me over six shillings and sixpence, cash down; and in addition you shall give me as much breakfast as I can possibly eat, at one sitting of course, out of that iron pot of yours that keeps sending forth such delicious and exciting smells. In return, I will make over to you my spirited young horse, with all the beautiful harness and trappings that are on him, freely thrown in. If that's not good enough for you, say so, and I'll be getting on. I know a man near here who's wanted this horse of mine for years.'

The gipsy grumbled, and declared if he did a few more deals of that sort he'd be ruined. But in the end he lugged a dirty canvas bag out of the depths of his trouser-pocket, and counted out six shillings and sixpence into Toad's paw. Then he disappeared into the caravan for an instant, and returned with a large iron plate and a knife, fork, and spoon. He tilted up the pot, and a glorious stream of hot rich stew gurgled into the plate. It was, indeed, the most beautiful stew in the world, being made of partridges, and pheasants, and

He lugged a dirty canvas bag out of the depths of his trouser-pocket . . .

chickens, and hares, and rabbits, and pea-hens, and guinea-fowls, and one or two other things. Toad took the plate on his lap, almost crying, and stuffed, and stuffed, and stuffed, and kept asking for more, and the gipsy never grudged it him. He thought that he had never eaten so good a breakfast in all his life.

When Toad had taken as much stew on board as he thought he could possibly hold, he got up and said good-bye to the gipsy, and took an affectionate farewell of the horse; and the gipsy, who knew the riverside well, gave him directions which way to go, and he set forth on his travels again in the best possible spirits. He was, indeed, a very different Toad from the animal of an hour ago. The sun was shining brightly, his wet clothes were quite dry again, he had money in his pockets once more, he was nearing home and friends and safety, and, most and best of all, he had had a substantial meal, hot and nourishing, and felt big, and strong, and careless, and self-confident.

As he tramped along gaily, he thought of his adventures and escapes, and how when things seemed at their worst he had always managed to find a way out; and his pride and conceit began to swell within him. 'Ho, ho!' he said to himself as he marched along with his chin in the air, 'what a clever Toad I am! There is surely no animal equal to me for cleverness in the whole world! My enemies shut me up in prison, encircled by sentries, watched night and day by warders; I walk out through them all, by sheer ability and courage. They pursue me with engines, and policemen, and revolvers; I snap my fingers at them, and vanish, laughing, into space. I am, unfortunately, thrown into a canal by a woman, fat of body and very evil-minded. What of it? I swim ashore, I seize her horse, I ride off in triumph, and I sell the horse for a whole pocketful of money and an excellent breakfast! Ho, ho! I am The Toad, the handsome, the popular, the successful Toad!' He got so puffed up with conceit that he made up a song as he walked in praise of himself, and sang it at the top of his voice, though there was no one to hear it but him. It was perhaps the most conceited song that any animal ever composed:

The world has held great Heroes,
    As history-books have showed;
But never a name to go down to fame
    Compared with that of Toad!

The clever men at Oxford
    Know all that there is to be knowed.
But they none of them know one half as much
    As intelligent Mr. Toad!

The animals sat in the Ark and cried,
    Their tears in torrents flowed.
Who was it said, 'There's land ahead'?
    Encouraging Mr. Toad!

The Army all saluted
    As they marched along the road.
Was it the King? Or Kitchener?
    No. It was Mr. Toad.

The Queen and her Ladies-in-waiting
    Sat at the window and sewed.
She cried, 'Look! who's that *handsome* man?'
    They answered, 'Mr. Toad.'

He sang as he walked, and he walked as he sang, and got more inflated every minute. But his pride was shortly to have a severe fall.

After some miles of country lanes he reached the high road, and as he turned into it and glanced along its white length, he saw approaching him a speck that turned into a dot and then into a blob, and then into something very familiar; and a double note of warning, only too well known, fell on his delighted ear.

'This is something like!' said the excited Toad. 'This is real life again, this is once more the great world from which I have been missed so long! I will hail them, my brothers of the wheel, and pitch them a yarn, of the sort that has been so successful up to now; and they will give me a lift, of course, and then I will talk to them some more; and, perhaps, with luck, it may even end in my driving up to Toad Hall in a

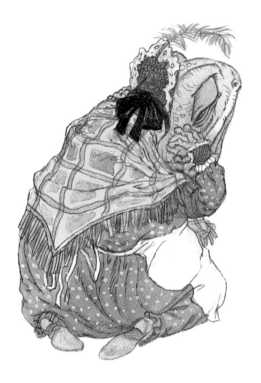

motor-car! That will be one in the eye for Badger!'

He stepped confidently out into the road to hail the motor-car, which came along at an easy pace, slowing down as it neared the lane; when suddenly he became very pale, his heart turned to water, his knees shook, and he doubled up and collapsed with a sickening pain in his insides. And well he might, the unhappy animal; for the approaching car was the very one he had stolen out of the yard of the Red Lion Hotel on that fatal day when all his troubles began! And the people in it were the very same people he had sat and watched at lunch in the coffee-room!

He sank down in a shabby, miserable heap in the road, murmuring to himself in his despair, 'It's all up! It's all over now! Chains and policemen again! Prison again! Dry bread and water again! O, what a fool I have been! What did I want to go strutting about the country for, singing conceited songs, and hailing people in broad daylight on the high road, instead of hiding till nightfall and slipping home quietly by back ways! O hapless Toad! O ill-fated animal!'

The terrible motor-car drew slowly nearer and nearer, till at last he heard it stop just short of him. Two gentlemen got out and walked round the trembling heap of crumpled misery lying in the road, and one of them said, 'O dear! this is very sad! Here is a poor old thing—a washerwoman apparently—who has fainted in the road! Perhaps she is overcome by the heat, poor creature; or possibly she has not had any food today. Let us lift her into the car and take her to the nearest village, where doubtless she has friends.'

They tenderly lifted Toad into the motor-car and propped him up with soft cushions, and went on their way.

When Toad heard them talk in so kind and sympathetic a manner, he knew that he was not recognised, his courage began to revive, and he cautiously opened first one eye and then the other.

'Look!' said one of the gentlemen, 'she is better already. The fresh air is doing her good. How do you feel now, ma'am?'

'Thank you kindly, sir,' said Toad in a feeble voice, 'I'm feeling a great deal better!'

'That's right,' said the gentleman. 'Now keep quite still, and, above all, don't try to talk.'

'I won't,' said Toad. 'I was only thinking, if I might sit on the front seat there, beside the driver, where I could get the fresh air full in my face, I should soon be all right again.'

'What a very sensible woman!' said the gentleman. 'Of course you shall.' So they carefully helped Toad into the front seat beside the driver, and on they went once more.

Toad was almost himself again by now. He sat up, looked about him, and tried to be calm.

'It is fate!' he said to himself. 'Why strive? why struggle?' and he turned to the driver at his side. 'Please, sir,' he said, 'I wish you would kindly let me try and drive the car for a little. I've been watching you carefully, and it looks so easy and so interesting, and I should like to be able to tell my friends that once I had driven a motor-car!'

The driver laughed at the proposal, so heartily that the gentleman asked what the matter was. When he heard, he said, to Toad's delight, 'Bravo, ma'am! I like your spirit. Let her have a try, and look after her. She won't do any harm.'

Toad eagerly scrambled into the driver's seat, took the steering-wheel in his hands, listened with affected humility to the instructions given him, and very slowly and carefully, he set the car in motion.

The gentlemen behind clapped their hands and applauded, and Toad heard them saying, 'How well she does it! Fancy a washerwoman driving a car as well as that, the first time!'

Toad went a little faster; then faster still, and faster.

He heard the gentleman call out warningly, 'Be careful, washerwoman!' This annoyed him, and he began to lose his head.

The driver tried to interfere, but he pinned him down in his seat with one elbow, and put on full speed. The rush of air in his face, the hum of the engine, and the light jump of the car beneath him made him very excited.

'Washerwoman, indeed!' he shouted recklessly. 'Ho, ho! I am the Toad, the motor-car snatcher, the prison-breaker, the Toad who always escapes! Sit still, and you shall know what driving really is, for you are in the hands of the famous, the skilful, the entirely fearless Toad!'

With a cry of horror the whole party rose and flung themselves on him. 'Seize him!' they cried, 'seize the Toad, the wicked animal who stole our motor-car! Bind him, chain him, drag him to the nearest police-station! Down with the desperate and dangerous Toad!'

Alas! they should have thought, they should have remembered to stop the motor-car somehow before playing any pranks of that sort. With a half-turn of the wheel the Toad sent the car crashing through the low hedge that ran along the roadside. One mighty bound, a violent shock, and the wheels of the car were churning up the thick mud of a horse-pond.

Toad found himself flying through the air with the strong upward rush and delicate curve of a swallow. He liked the motion, and was just beginning to wonder whether it would go on, when he landed on his back with a thump, in the soft rich grass of a meadow. Sitting up, he could just see the motor-car in the pond, nearly submerged; the gentlemen and the driver, weighed down by their long coats, were floundering helplessly in the water.

He picked himself up rapidly and set off running across country as hard as he could, scrambling through hedges, jumping ditches, pounding across fields, till he was breathless and weary, and had to settle down into an easy walk. When he had recovered his breath somewhat, and was able to think calmly, he began to giggle, and from giggling he took to laughing, and he laughed till he had to sit down under a hedge. 'Ho, ho!' he cried. 'Toad again! Toad, as usual comes out on the top! Who was it got them to give him a lift? Who managed to get on the front seat for the sake of fresh air? Who persuaded them into letting him see if he could drive? Who landed them all in a horse-pond? Who escaped, flying gaily and unhurt through the air, leaving all of them in the mud where they should rightly be? Why, Toad, of course; clever Toad, great Toad, *good* Toad!'

Then he burst into song again, and chanted with uplifted voice

> The motor-car went Poop-poop-poop,
>   As it raced along the road.
> Who was it steered it into a pond?
>   Ingenious Mr. Toad!

'O, how clever I am! How clever, how clever, how very clev——'

A slight noise at a distance behind him made him turn his head and look. O horror! O misery! O despair!

*He picked himself up rapidly and set off running across country
as hard as he could.*

—swam ashore! Stole a horse—sold him for a large sum of money! Humbugged everybody—made 'em all do exactly what I wanted! O, I *am* a smart Toad, and no mistake! What do you think my last exploit was? Just hold on till I tell you——'

'Toad,' said the Water Rat, gravely and firmly, 'you go off upstairs at once, and take off that old cotton rag that looks as if it might formerly have belonged to some washerwoman, and clean yourself thoroughly, and put on some of my clothes, and try and come down looking like a gentleman if you *can*; for a more shabby, bedraggled, disreputable-looking object than you are I never set eyes on in my whole life! Now, stop swaggering and arguing, and be off! I'll have something to say to you later!'

Toad was at first inclined to stop and do some talking back at him. He had had enough of being ordered about when he was in prison. However, he caught sight of himself in the mirror over the hat-stand, with the black bonnet perched rakishly over one eye, and he changed his mind and went very quickly and humbly upstairs to the Rat's dressing-room. There he had a thorough wash and brush-up, changed his clothes, and stood for a long time before the glass, looking at himself with pride and pleasure, and thinking what utter idiots all the people must have been to have ever mistaken him for one moment for a washerwoman.

By the time he came down again lunch was on the table, and very glad Toad was to see it, for he had been through some trying experiences and had taken much hard exercise since the excellent breakfast provided for him by the gipsy. While they ate Toad told the Rat all his adventures, dwelling chiefly on his own cleverness, and presence of mind in emergencies, and cunning in tight places. But the more he talked and boasted, the more grave and silent the Rat became.

When at last Toad had talked himself to a standstill, there was silence for a while; and then the Rat said, 'Now, Toady, I don't want to give you pain, after all you've been through already; but, seriously, don't you see what an awful idiot you've been making of yourself? On your own admission you have been handcuffed, imprisoned, starved, chased, terrified out of your life, insulted, jeered at, and shamefully

flung into the water—by a woman, too! Where does the fun come in? And all because you must needs go and steal a motor-car. You know that you've never had anything but trouble from motor-cars from the moment you first set eyes on one. But if you *will* be mixed up with them—as you generally are, five minutes after you've started—why *steal* them? Be a bankrupt, for a change, if you've set your mind on it; but why choose to be a convict? When are you going to be sensible, and think of your friends, and try and be a credit to them? Do you suppose it's any pleasure to me, for instance, to hear animals saying, as I go about, that I'm the fellow that keeps company with gaol-birds?'

Now, it was a very comforting point in Toad's character that he was a thoroughly good-hearted animal, and never minded being told off by those who were his real friends. And even when most set upon a thing, he was always able to see the other side of the question. So although, while the Rat was talking so seriously, he kept saying to himself mutinously, 'But it *was* fun, though! Awful fun!' and making strange suppressed noises inside him, k-i-ck-ck-ck, and poop-p-p, and other sounds resembling stifled snorts, or the opening of soda-water bottles, yet when the Rat had quite finished, he heaved a deep sigh and said, very nicely and humbly, 'Quite right, Ratty! How *sound* you always are! Yes, I've been a conceited old fool, I can quite see that; but now I'm going to be a good Toad, and not do it any more. As for motor-cars, I've not been at all so keen about them since my last ducking in that river of yours. The fact is, while I was hanging on to the edge of your hole and getting my breath, I had a sudden idea—a really brilliant idea— connected with motor-boats—there, there! don't take on so and stamp, and upset things; it was only an idea, and we won't talk any more about it now. We'll have our coffee, *and* a smoke, and a quiet chat, and then I'm going to stroll gently down to Toad Hall, and get into clothes of my own, and set things going again on the old lines. I've had enough of adventures. I shall lead a quiet, steady, respectable life, pottering about my property, and improving it, and doing a little landscape gardening at times. There will always be a bit of dinner for my friends when they come to see me;

and I shall keep a pony-chaise to jog about the country in, just as I used to in the good old days, before I got restless, and wanted to *do* things.'

'Stroll gently down to Toad Hall?' cried the Rat, greatly excited. 'What are you talking about? Do you mean to say you haven't *heard*?'

'Heard what?' said Toad, turning rather pale. 'Go on, Ratty! Quick! Don't spare me! What haven't I heard?'

'Do you mean to tell me,' shouted the Rat, thumping with his little fist upon the table, 'that you've heard nothing about the Stoats and Weasels?'

'What, the Wild Wooders?' cried Toad, trembling in every limb. 'No, not a word! What have they been doing?'

'—And how they've been and taken Toad Hall?' continued the Rat.

Toad leaned his elbows on the table, and his chin on his paws; and a large tear welled up in each of his eyes, overflowed and splashed on the table, plop! plop!

'Go on, Ratty,' he murmured presently; 'tell me all. The worst is over. I am an animal again. I can bear it.'

'When you—got—into that—that—trouble of yours,' said the Rat slowly and impressively; 'I mean, when you—disappeared for a time, over that misunderstanding about a —a machine, you know——'

Toad merely nodded.

'Well, it was a good deal talked about down here, naturally,' continued the Rat, 'not only along the riverside, but even in the Wild Wood. Animals took sides, as always happens. The River-bankers stuck up for you, and said you had been wickedly treated, and there was no justice to be had in the land nowadays. But the Wild Wood animals said hard things, and served you right, and it was time this sort of thing was stopped. And they went about saying you were done for this time! You would never come back again, never, never!'

Toad nodded once more, keeping silence.

'That's the sort of little beasts they are,' the Rat went on. 'But Mole and Badger, they stuck out, through thick and thin, that you would come back again soon, somehow. They didn't know exactly how, but somehow!'

Toad began to sit up in his chair again, and to smirk a little.

'They argued from history,' continued the Rat. 'They said that no criminal laws had ever been known to win the day against cheek and a good case such as yours, combined with the power of a deep purse. So they arranged to move their things into Toad Hall, and sleep there, and keep it aired, and have it all ready for you when you turned up. They didn't guess what was going to happen, of course; still, they had their suspicions of the Wild Wood animals. Now I come to the most painful and tragic part of my story. One dark night —it was a *very* dark night, and blowing hard, too, and raining simply cats and dogs—a band of weasels, armed to the teeth, crept silently up the carriage-drive to the front entrance. At the same time, a body of desperate ferrets, advancing through the kitchen-garden, possessed themselves of the back-yard and offices; while a company of skirmishing stoats who stopped at nothing occupied the conservatory and the billiard-room, and held the French windows opening on to the lawn.

'The Mole and the Badger were sitting by the fire in the smoking-room, telling stories and suspecting nothing, for it wasn't a night for any animals to be out in, when those bloodthirsty villains broke down the doors and rushed in upon them from every side. They made the best fight they could, but what was the good? They were unarmed, and taken by surprise, and what can two animals do against hundreds? They took and beat them severely with sticks, those two poor faithful creatures, and turned them out into the cold and the wet, with many insulting and uncalled-for remarks!'

Here the unfeeling Toad broke into a snigger, and then pulled himself together and tried to look particularly solemn.

'And the Wild Wooders have been living in Toad Hall ever since,' continued the Rat; 'and going on simply anyhow! Lying in bed half the day, and breakfast at all hours, and the place in such a mess (I'm told) it's not fit to be seen! Eating your grub, and drinking your drink, and making bad jokes about you, and singing vulgar songs, about—well, about prisons, and magistrates, and policemen; horrid personal songs, with no humour in them. And they're

telling the tradespeople and everybody that they've come to stay for good.'

'O, have they!' said Toad, getting up and seizing a stick. 'I'll soon see about that!'

'It's no good, Toad!' called the Rat after him. 'You'd better come back and sit down; you'll only get into trouble.'

But the Toad was off, and there was no holding him. He marched rapidly down the road, his stick over his shoulder, fuming and muttering to himself in his anger, till he got near his front gate, when suddenly there popped up from behind the palings a long yellow ferret with a gun.

'Who comes there?' said the ferret sharply.

'Stuff and nonsense!' said Toad very angrily. 'What do you mean by talking like that to me? Come out of it at once, or I'll——'

The ferret said never a word, but he brought his gun up to his shoulder. Toad dropped flat in the road, and *Bang!* a bullet whistled over his head.

The startled Toad scrambled to his feet and scampered off down the road as hard as he could; and as he ran he heard the ferret laughing, and other horrid thin little laughs taking it up and carrying on the sound.

He went back, very crestfallen, and told the Water Rat.

'What did I tell you?' said the Rat. 'It's no good. They've got sentries posted, and they are all armed. You must just wait.'

Still, Toad was not going to give in all at once. So he got out the boat, and set off rowing up the river to where the garden front of Toad Hall came down to the waterside.

Arriving within sight of his old home, he rested on his oars and looked around carefully. All seemed very peaceful and deserted and quiet. He could see the whole front of Toad Hall, glowing in the evening sunshine, the pigeons settling by twos and threes along the straight line of the roof; the garden, a blaze of flowers; the creek that led up to the boat-house, the little wooden bridge that crossed it; all tranquil, uninhabited, apparently waiting for his return. He would try the boat-house first, he thought. Very warily he paddled up to the mouth of the creek, and was just passing under the bridge, when . . . *Crash!*

*Very warily he paddled up to the mouth of the creek,
and was just passing under the bridge, when . . . Crash!*

A great stone, dropped from above, smashed through the bottom of the boat. It filled and sank, and Toad found himself struggling in deep water. Looking up, he saw two stoats leaning over the bridge and watching him with great glee. 'It will be your head next time, Toady!' they called out to him. The indignant Toad swam to shore, while the stoats laughed and laughed, supporting each other, and laughed again, till they nearly had two fits—that is, one fit each, of course.

The Toad retraced his weary way on foot, and related his disappointing experiences to the Water Rat once more.

'Well, *what* did I tell you?' said the Rat very crossly. 'And, now, look here! See what you've been and done! Lost me my boat that I was so fond of, that's what you've done! And simply ruined that nice suit of clothes that I lent you! Really, Toad, of all the trying animals—I wonder you manage to keep any friends at all!'

The Toad saw at once how wrongly and foolishly he had acted. He admitted his errors and made a full apology to Rat for losing his boat and spoiling his clothes. And he wound up by saying, 'Ratty! I see that I have been a headstrong and a wilful Toad! Henceforth, believe me, I will be humble and submissive, and will take no action without your kind advice and full approval!'

'If that is really so,' said the good-natured Rat, 'then my advice to you is, considering the lateness of the hour, to sit down and have your supper, which will be on the table in a minute, and be very patient. For I am convinced that we can do nothing until we have seen the Mole and the Badger, and heard their latest news, and held conference and taken their advice in this difficult matter.'

'O, ah, yes, of course, the Mole and the Badger,' said Toad lightly. 'What's become of them, the dear fellows? I had forgotten all about them.'

'Well may you ask!' said the Rat sharply. 'While you were riding about the country in expensive motor-cars, and galloping proudly on blood-horses, and breakfasting on the fat of the land, those two poor devoted animals have been camping out in the open, in every sort of weather, living very rough by day and lying very hard by night; watching over your house, keeping a constant eye on the stoats and the weasels, scheming and planning how to get your property back for you. You don't deserve to have such true and loyal friends, Toad, you don't, really. Some day, when it's too late, you'll be sorry you didn't value them more while you had them!'

'I'm an ungrateful beast, I know,' sobbed Toad, shedding bitter tears. 'Let me go out and find them, out into the cold, dark night and share their hardships, and try and prove by—Hold on a bit! Surely I heard the chink of dishes on a tray! Supper's here at last, hooray! Come on, Ratty!'

The Rat remembered that poor Toad had been on prison rations for a considerable time, and that large allowances had therefore to be made. He followed him to the table and encouraged him in his gallant efforts to make up for past hardships.

They had just finished their meal and returned to their armchairs, when there came a heavy knock at the door.

Toad was nervous, but the Rat, nodding mysteriously at him, went straight up to the door and opened it, and in walked Mr. Badger.

He had all the appearance of one who for some nights had been kept away from home and all its little comforts and conveniences. His shoes were covered with mud, and he was looking very rough and untidy; but then he had never been a very smart man, the Badger, at the best of times. He came solemnly up to Toad, shook him by the paw, and said, 'Welcome home, Toad! Alas! what am I saying? Home, indeed! This is a poor home-coming. Unhappy Toad!' Then he turned his back on him, sat down to the table, drew his chair up, and helped himself to a large slice of cold pie.

Toad was quite alarmed at this very serious style of greeting; but the Rat whispered to him, 'Never mind; don't take any notice; and don't say anything to him just yet. He's always rather low when he's hungry. In half an hour's time he'll be quite a different animal.'

So they waited in silence, and presently there came another and a lighter knock. The Rat, with a nod to Toad, went to the door and ushered in the Mole, very shabby and unwashed, with bits of hay and straw sticking in his fur.

'O, *Moly*, how could you?' said the Rat, dismayed.

The Badger laid down his paper.

'I could see them pricking up their ears and looking at each other,' went on the Mole; 'and the sergeant said to them, "Never mind *her*; she doesn't know what she's talking about."

' "O! don't I?" said I. "Well, let me tell you this. My daughter, she washes for Mr. Badger, and that'll show you whether I know what I'm talking about; and *you'll* know pretty soon, too! A hundred bloodthirsty badgers, armed with rifles, are going to attack Toad Hall this very night, by way of the paddock. Six boat-loads of rats with pistols and cutlasses, will come up the river and land in the garden; while a picked body of toads, known as the Die-hards, or the Death-or-Glory Toads, will storm the orchard and carry everything before them, yelling for vengeance. There won't be much left of you to wash, by the time they've done with you, unless you clear out while you have the chance!" Then I ran away, and when I was out of sight I hid; and presently I came creeping back along the ditch and took a peep at them through the hedge. They were all as nervous and flustered as could be, running all ways at once, and falling over each other, and every one giving orders to everybody else and not listening; and the sergeant kept sending off parties of stoats to distant parts of the grounds, and then sending other fellows to fetch 'em back again: and I heard them saying to each other, "That's *just* like the weasels; they're to stop comfortably in the banqueting-hall, and have feasting and toasts and songs and all sorts of fun, while we must stay on guard in the cold and the dark, and in the end be cut to pieces by bloodthirsty Badgers!" '

'O, you silly fool, Mole!' cried Toad. 'You've been and spoilt everything!'

'Mole,' said the Badger, in his dry, quiet way, 'I can see you have more sense in your little finger than some other animals have in the whole of their fat bodies. You have managed excellently, and I begin to have great hopes of you. Good Mole! Clever Mole!'

The Toad was simply wild with jealousy, more especially as he couldn't make out for the life of him what the Mole had

done that was so particularly clever; but, fortunately for him, before he could show temper or expose himself to the Badger's sarcasm, the bell rang for lunch.

It was a simple meal—bacon and broad beans, and a macaroni pudding; and when they had quite done, the Badger settled himself into an armchair, and said, 'Well, we've got our work cut out for us tonight, and it will probably be pretty late before we're quite through with it; so I'm just going to take forty winks, while I can.' And he drew a handkerchief over his face and was soon snoring.

The hard-working Rat at once resumed his preparations, and started running between his four little heaps, muttering, 'Here's-a-belt-for-the-Rat, here's-a-belt-for-the-Mole, here's-a-belt-for-the-Toad, here's-a-belt-for-the-Badger!' and so on, with every fresh item he produced, to which there seemed really no end; so the Mole drew his arm through Toad's, led him out into the open air, shoved him into a wicker chair, and made him tell him all his adventures from beginning to end, which Toad was only too willing to do. The Mole was a good listener, and Toad, with no one to check his statements or to criticise in an unfriendly spirit, rather let himself go. Indeed, much that he related belonged more properly to the category of what-might-have-happened-had-I-only-thought-of-it-in-time-instead-of-ten-minutes-afterwards. Those are always the best adventures; and why should they not be truly ours, as much as the somewhat inadequate things that really come off?

CHAPTER 10

The Return of
The Hero

WHEN it began to grow dark, the Rat, with an air
of excitement and mystery, called them back into the
parlour, stood each of them up alongside his little heap, and
proceeded to dress them up for the coming expedition.
He was very earnest and thoroughgoing about it, and the
affair took quite a long time. First, there was a belt to go
round each animal, and then a sword to be stuck into each
belt, and then a cutlass on the other side to balance it.
Then a pair of pistols, a policeman's truncheon, several sets
of handcuffs, some bandages and sticking-plaster, and a
flask and a sandwich-case. The Badger laughed and said,
'All right, Ratty! It amuses you and it doesn't hurt me.
I'm going to do all I've got to do with this here stick.' But
the Rat only said, '*Please*, Badger! You know I shouldn't
like you to blame me afterwards and say I had forgotten
anything!'

When all was quite ready, the Badger took a dark lantern in one paw, grasped his great stick with the other, and said, 'Now then, follow me! Mole first, 'cos I'm very pleased with him; Rat next; Toad last. And look here, Toady! Don't you chatter so much as usual, or you'll be sent back, as sure as fate!'

The Toad was so anxious not to be left out that he took up the lowly position given to him without a murmur, and the animals set off. The Badger led them along by the river for a little way, and then suddenly swung himself over the edge into a hole in the river bank, a little above the water. The Mole and the Rat followed silently, swinging themselves successfully into the hole as they had seen the Badger do; but when it came to Toad's turn, of course he managed to slip and fall into the water with a loud splash and a squeal of alarm. He was hauled out by his friends, rubbed down and wrung out hastily, comforted, and set on his legs; but the Badger was angry, and told him that the very next time he made a fool of himself he would most certainly be left behind.

So at last they were in the secret passage, and the driving-out expedition had really begun!

It was cold, and dark, and damp, and low, and narrow, and poor Toad began to shiver, partly from dread of what might be before him, partly because he was wet through. The lantern was far ahead, and he could not help lagging behind a little in the darkness. Then he heard the Rat call out warningly, '*Come* on, Toad!' and a terror seized him of being left behind, alone in the darkness, and he 'came on' with such a rush that he upset the Rat into the Mole and the Mole into the Badger, and for a moment all was confusion. The Badger thought they were being attacked from behind, and, as there was no room to use a stick or a cutlass, drew a pistol, and was on the point of putting a bullet into Toad. When he found out what had really happened he was very angry indeed, and said, 'Now this time that tiresome Toad *shall* be left behind!'

But Toad whimpered, and the other two promised that they would be answerable for his good conduct, and at last the Badger was pacified, and the procession moved on; only

Introduction

Rudyard Kipling's *The Jungle Book* is a classic of children's literature. First published in 1894, it tells the story of Mowgli, the little boy adopted by a family of wolves and brought up in the Indian jungle. Mowgli makes many friends in the jungle, including Bagheera the black panther and Baloo the bear, who together teach him the ways and laws of jungle life. Mowgli also makes a dangerous enemy of Shere Khan, the tiger who is hungry for Mowgli's blood but is constantly out-witted by the boy's clever tricks and ploys.

Many other wonderful tales of men and animals unfold within *The Jungle Book*. Children can read how Kotick, the white seal, finds a safe place to live, far away from Man; how Ricki-ticki-tavi, the red-eyed Mongoose, protects his human family from two deadly cobras and how Toomai, the Indian boy, witnesses the magical dance of the elephants.

Rudyard Kipling was born in India in 1865. He was educated in England and returned to India in 1882, where he began writing short stories. By 1889, he was the popular writer of his day. *The Jungle Book* is the most famous and best-loved of all Kipling's work.

Mowgli's Brothers

Now Chil the Kite brings home the night
    That Mang the Bat sets free –
The herds are shut in byre and hut,
    For loosed till dawn are we.
This is the hour of pride and power,
    Talon and tush and claw.
    Oh, hear the call! – Good hunting all
    That keep the Jungle-Law!

Night-Song in the Jungle

IT was seven o'clock, on a very warm evening in the
Seeonee hills when Father Wolf woke up from his day's rest,
scratched himself, yawned, and spread out his paws one after the
other to get rid of the sleepy feeling in their tips. Mother Wolf lay
with her big grey nose dropped across her four tumbling,
squealing cubs, and the moon shone into the mouth of the cave
where they all lived. 'Augrh!' said Father Wolf. 'It is time to hunt
again.' He was about to spring out of the cave and down the hill
when a little shadow with a bushy tail came up to the entrance
and whined: 'Good luck go with you, Oh Chief of the Wolves;
and good luck and strong white teeth go with your noble children,
that they may never forget the hungry in this world.'

It was the jackal – Tabaqui, the Dish-licker – and the wolves of India despise Tabaqui because he runs about making mischief, and telling tales, and eating rags and pieces of leather from the village rubbish-heaps. But they are afraid of him too, because Tabaqui, more than anyone else in the Jungle, is apt to go mad, and then he forgets that he was ever afraid of anyone, and runs through the forest biting everything in his way. Even the tiger runs and hides when little Tabaqui goes mad, for madness is the most disgraceful thing that can overtake a wild creature. We call it hydrophobia, or rabies, but the animals call it *dewanee* – the madness – and run.

'Enter, then, and look,' said Father Wolf stiffly. 'But there is no food here.'

'For a wolf, no,' said Tabaqui. 'But for so mean a person as myself, a dry bone is a good feast. Who are we, the *Gidur-log* (the Jackal-People), to pick and choose?' He scuttled to the back of the cave, where he found the bone of a buck with some meat on it, and sat cracking the end merrily.

'Many thanks for this good meal,' he said, licking his lips. 'How beautiful are your noble children! How large are their eyes! And so young, too! Indeed, indeed, I might have remembered that the children of Kings are men from the beginning.'

Now, Tabaqui knew as well as anyone else that there is nothing as unlucky as complimenting children to their faces. He was pleased to see Mother and Father Wolf look uncomfortable.

Tabaqui sat there, enjoying the mischief that he had made then he said spitefully:

'Shere Khan, the Big One, has moved his hunting-grounds. He has told me that he will hunt among these hills for the next month or so.'

Shere Khan was the tiger who lived near the Waingunga River, twenty miles away.

'He has no right!' Father Wolf began angrily – 'By the Law of the Jungle, he has no right to change his quarters without due warning. He will frighten every head of game within ten miles, and I – I have to kill for two, these days.'

'His mother did not call him Lungri (the Lame One) for nothing,' said Mother Wolf quietly. 'He has been lame in one foot from his birth. That is why he has only killed cattle. Now the villagers of the Waingunga are angry with him, and he has come here to make *our* villagers angry. They will scour the Jungle for him when he is far away, and we and our children must run when the grass is set alight. Indeed, we are very grateful to Shere Khan!'

'Shall I tell him of your gratitude?' asked Tabaqui.

'Out!' snapped Father Wolf. 'Leave here and go and hunt with your master. You have done enough harm for one night.'

'I'll go,' said Tabaqui quietly. 'But you can hear Shere Khan below in the thickets. I might have saved myself the message.'

Father Wolf listened, and below in the valley that ran down to a little river, he heard the dry, angry, snarly, singsong whine of a tiger who has caught nothing and does not care if all the Jungle knows it.

'The fool!' said Father Wolf. 'To begin a night's work with that noise! Does he think that our buck are like his fat Waingunga bullocks!'

'H'sh! It is neither bullock nor buck that he hunts tonight,' said Mother Wolf. 'It is Man.' The whine had changed to a sort of humming purr that seemed to come from every quarter of the compass. It was the noise that bewilders woodcutters and gipsies sleeping in the open, and makes them run sometimes into the very mouth of the tiger.

'Man!' said Father Wolf, showing all his white teeth. 'Faugh! Are there not enough beetles and frogs in the tanks that he must eat Man, and on our ground too?'

The Law of the Jungle, which never orders anything without a reason, forbids every beast to eat Man except when he is killing to show his children how to kill, and then he must hunt outside the hunting-grounds of his pack or tribe. The real reason for this is that man-killing means, sooner or later, the arrival of men on elephants, with guns, and hundreds of men with gongs and rockets and torches. Then everybody in the Jungle suffers. The reason the beasts give among themselves is that Man is the weakest and most defenceless of all living things, and it is unsportsmanlike to touch him. They say too – and it is true – that man-eaters become mangy, and lose their teeth.

The purr grew louder, and ended in the full-throated 'Aaarh!' of the tiger's charge.

Then there was a howl – an untigerish howl – from Shere Khan.

'He has missed,' said Mother Wolf. 'What is he after?'

Father Wolf ran out a few paces and heard Shere Khan muttering and mumbling savagely, as he tumbled about in the scrub.

'The fool has had no more sense than to jump at a woodcutter's camp-fire, and he has burned his feet,' said Father Wolf, with a grunt. 'Tabaqui is with him.'

'Something is coming uphill,' said Mother Wolf, twitching one

There was a chorus of deep growls, and a young wolf in his fourth year flung back Shere Khan's question to Akela: 'What have the Free People to do with a man's cub?' Now, the Law of the Jungle lays down that if there is any dispute as to the right of a cub to be accepted by the Pack, he must be spoken for by at least two members of the pack who are not his father and mother.

'Who speaks for this cub?' asked Akela. 'Who speaks among the Free People?' There was no answer, and Mother Wolf got ready for what she knew would be her last fight, if things came to fighting.

Then, the only other creature who is allowed at the Pack Council – Baloo, the sleepy brown bear who teaches the wolf-cubs the Law of the Jungle: old Baloo, who can come and go where he pleases because he eats only nuts and roots and honey – rose up on his hindquarters and grunted.

'The man's cub – the man's cub?' he said. '*I* speak for the man's cub. There is no harm in a man's cub. I have no gift of words, but I speak the truth. Let him run with the Pack, and be entered with the others. I myself will teach him.'

'We need another to speak for the man's cub,' said Akela. 'Baloo has spoken, and he is our teacher for the young cubs. Who speaks besides Baloo?'

A black shadow dropped down into the circle. It was Bagheera the Black Panther, inky-black all over, but with the panther markings showing up in certain lights like the pattern of watered silk. Everybody knew Bagheera, and nobody cared to cross his path; for he was as cunning as Tabaqui, as bold as the wild buffalo, and as reckless as the wounded elephant. But he had a voice as soft as wild honey dripping from a tree, and a skin softer than down.

'Oh Akela, and you, the Free People,' he purred, 'I have no say in your assembly; but the Law of the Jungle says that if there is a doubt in regard to a new cub, the life of that cub may be bought at a price. And the Law does not say who may or may not pay that price. Am I right?'

'Good! good!' said the young wolves, who were always hungry. 'Listen to Bagheera. The cub can be bought for a price. It is the Law.'

'Knowing that I have no right to speak here, I ask your permission to do so.'

'Speak then,' cried twenty voices.

'To kill a naked cub is shame. Besides, he may make better sport for you when he is grown. Baloo has spoken on his behalf.

MOWGLI'S BROTHERS

Now to Baloo's word I will add one bull – a fat one, newly killed, not half a mile from here, if you will accept the man's cub according to the Law.'

There was a clamour of scores of voices, saying: 'What does it matter? He will die in the winter rains. He will scorch in the sun. What harm can a naked frog do us? Let him run with the Pack. Where is the bull, Bagheera? Let him be accepted.'

And then came Akela's deep bay, crying: 'Look well – look well, Oh Wolves!'

Mowgli was still deeply interested in the pebbles and he did not notice when the wolves came and looked at him one by one. At last they all went down the hill for the dead bull, and only Akela, Bagheera, Baloo, and Mowgli's own wolves were left. Shere Khan still roared in the night, for he was very angry that Mowgli had not been handed over to him.

'Go on, roar away,' said Bagheera, under his whiskers; 'for the time will come when this naked thing will make you roar to another tune, or I know nothing of Man.'

'It was well done,' said Akela. 'Men and their cubs are very wise. He may be a help in time.'

'Truly, a help in a time of need; for none can hope to lead the Pack for ever,' said Bagheera.

Akela said nothing. He was thinking of the time that comes to every leader of every pack when his strength goes from him and he gets weaker and weaker, until at last he is killed by his own wolves and a new leader comes up – to be killed in his turn.

'Take him away,' he said to Father Wolf, 'and train him as befits one of the Free People.'

And that is how Mowgli was entered into the Seeonee Wolf-Pack at the price of a bull and on Baloo's good word.

*　　*　　*　　*　　*

Now we must skip ten or eleven whole years, and only guess at all the wonderful life that Mowgli led among the wolves, because if it were written out it would fill ever so many books. He grew up with the cubs, though they, of course, were grown wolves almost before he was a child, and Father Wolf taught him his business, and the meaning of things in the Jungle, until every rustle in the grass, every breath of the warm night air, every note of the owls above his head, every scratch of a bat's claws as it roosted for a while in a tree, and every splash of every little fish jumping in a pool, meant just as much to him as the work in an office means to

a business man. When he was not learning, he sat out in the sun and slept, and ate and slept again; when he felt dirty or hot he swam in the forest pools; and when he wanted honey (Baloo told him that honey and nuts were just as pleasant to eat as raw meat) he climbed up for it, and that Bagheera showed him how to do. Bagheera would lie out on a branch and call, 'Come along, Little Brother,' and at first Mowgli would cling like the sloth, but afterwards he would fling himself through the branches almost as boldly as the grey ape. He took his place at the Council Rock, too, when the Pack met, and there he discovered that if he stared hard at any wolf, the wolf would be forced to drop his eyes, and so he used to stare for fun. At other times he would pick the long thorns out of the pads of his friends, for wolves suffer terribly from thorns and burrs in their coats. He would go down the hillside into the cultivated lands by night, and look very curiously at the villagers in their huts, but he had a mistrust of men because Bagheera showed him a square box with a dropgate so cunningly hidden in the Jungle that he nearly walked into it, and told him that it was a trap. He loved better than anything else to go with Bagheera into the dark warm heart of the forest, to sleep all through the drowsy day, and at night to see how Bagheera did his killing. Bagheera killed right and left as he felt hungry, and so did Mowgli – with one exception. As soon as he was old enough to understand things, Bagheera told him that he must never touch cattle because he had been bought into the Pack at the price of a bull's life. 'All the Jungle is yours,' said Bagheera, 'and you can kill everything that you are strong enough to kill; but for the sake of the bull that bought you, you must never kill or eat any cattle young or old. That is the Law of the Jungle.' Mowgli obeyed faithfully.

And he grew and grew strong as a boy must grow who does not know that he is learning any lessons, and who has nothing in the world to think of except things to eat.

Mother Wolf told him once or twice that Shere Khan was not to be trusted, and that some day he would have to kill Shere Khan; but though a young wolf would have remembered that advice every hour, Mowgli forgot it because he was only a boy – though had he been asked, he would have called himself a wolf if he had been able to speak in any human tongue.

Shere Khan was always crossing his path in the Jungle, for as Akela grew older and weaker the lame tiger had become great friends with the younger wolves of the Pack, who followed him for scraps, something that Akela would never have allowed if he had dared to push his authority to the proper bounds. Shere Khan flattered the youngsters and wondered that 'such fine young hunters', were content to be led by a dying wolf and a man's cub.

'They tell me,' Shere Khan would say, 'that at Council you dare not look him between the eyes;' and the young wolves would growl and bristle.

Bagheera, who had eyes and ears everywhere, knew something of this, and once or twice he told Mowgli in so many words that Shere Khan would kill him some day; and Mowgli would laugh and answer: 'I have the Pack and I have you; and Baloo, even though he is so lazy, might strike a blow or two for my sake. Why should I be afraid?'

It was one very warm day that a new notion came to Bagheera – born of something that he had heard. Perhaps Ikki the Porcupine had told him; but he said to Mowgli when they were deep in the Jungle, as the boy lay with his head on Bagheera's beautiful black skin: 'Little Brother, how often have I told you that Shere Khan is your enemy?'

'As many times as there are nuts on that palm,' said Mowgli, who, naturally, could not count. 'What of it? I am sleepy, Bagheera, and Shere Khan is all long tail and loud talk – like Mao, the Peacock.'

'But this is no time for sleeping. Baloo knows it; I know it; the Pack know it; and even the foolish, foolish deer know. Tabaqui has told you too.'

'Ho! ho!' said Mowgli. 'Tabaqui came to me not long ago with some rude talk that I was a naked man's cub and not fit to dig pignuts; but I caught Tabaqui by the tail and swung him twice against a palm tree to teach him better manners.'

'That was a stupid thing to do; for although Tabaqui is a mischief-maker, he would have told you something that concerns you. Open those eyes, Little Brother. Shere Khan would not dare to kill you in the Jungle; but remember, Akela is very old and soon the day will come when he cannot kill his buck, and then he will be leader no more. Many of the wolves that looked you over when you were first brought to the Council are old too, and the young wolves believe, as Shere Khan has taught them, that a man-cub has no place with the Pack. In a little while you will be a man.'

'And what is a man that he should not run with his brothers?' said Mowgli. 'I was born in the Jungle. I have obeyed the Law of the Jungle, and there is no wolf of ours from whose paws I have not pulled a thorn. Surely they are my brothers!'

'No man's cub can run with the people of the Jungle,' howled Shere Khan. 'Give him to me!'

'He is our brother in all but blood,' Akela went on; 'and you want to kill him here! I believe I have lived too long. Some of you are eaters of cattle, and I have heard that others, under Shere Khan's teaching, go by dark night and snatch children from the villager's doorstep. Therefore I know you are cowards, and it is to cowards that I speak now. I know that I must die, and my life is worthless now, or I would offer it in the Man-cub's place. But for the sake of the honour of the Pack – a little matter that by being without a leader you all seem to have forgotten – I promise that if you let the Man-cub go to his own place, I will not, when my time comes to die, bare one tooth against you. I will die without fighting. That will at least save the Pack three lives. I cannot do more than this, but if you want, I can save you the shame of killing a brother against whom there is no fault – a brother spoken for and bought into the Pack according to the Law of the Jungle.'

'He is a man – a man – a man!' snarled the Pack; and most of the wolves began to gather round Shere Khan, whose tail was beginning to switch.

'It's up to you now, Mowgli,' said Bagheera to the boy. '*We* can do no more except fight.'

Mowgli stood up – the fire-pot in his hands. Then he stretched out his arms, and yawned in the face of the Council; but he was furious with rage and sorrow, for, wolf-like, the wolves had never told him how they hated him. 'Listen, you!' he cried. 'There is no need for this dog's jabber. You have told me so often tonight that I am a man (even though I would have been a wolf with you to my life's end), that I feel your words are true. So I do not call you my brothers any more, but *sag* (dogs), as a man would. What you will do, and what you will not do, is not up to you. It is up to *me*; and so that we all see the matter more clearly, I, the man, have brought with me a little of the Red Flower which you, dogs, fear.'

He flung the fire-pot on the ground, and some of the red coals lit a tuft of dried moss that flared up, as all the Council drew back in terror before the leaping flames.

Mowgli thrust his dead branch into the fire until the twigs lit and crackled, and then whirled it above his head among the cowering wolves.

'You are now the master,' said Bagheera, softly. 'Save Akela from death. He was always your friend.'

Akela, the grim old wolf who had never asked for mercy in his life, gave one piteous look at Mowgli as the boy stood all naked,

his long black hair tossing over his shoulders in the light of the
blazing branch that made the shadows jump and quiver.

'Good!' said Mowgli, staring round slowly. 'I see that you are
dogs. I go from you to my own people – if they are my own
people. The Jungle is closed to me, and I must forget your talk
and your companionship; but I will be more merciful than you
are. Because I was all but your brother in blood, I promise that
when I am a man among men I will not betray you to men as you
have betrayed me.' He kicked the fire with his foot, and the
sparks flew up. 'There shall be no war between any of us and the
Pack. But there is a debt to pay before I go.' He strode forward
to where Shere Khan sat blinking stupidly at the flames, and
caught him by the tuft on his chin. Bagheera followed in case of
accidents. 'Up, dog!' Mowgli cried. 'Up, when a man speaks, or I
will set that coat ablaze!'

Shere Khan's ears lay flat back on his head, and he shut his
eyes, for the blazing branch was very near.

'This cattle-killer said he would kill me in the Council because
he could not kill me when I was a cub. Here's how we beat dogs
when we are men. Move a whisker, Lungri, and I will ram the
Red Flower down your throat!' He beat Shere Khan over the
head with the branch, and the tiger whimpered and whined in an
agony of fear.

'Pah! Singed jungle-cat – go now! But remember the next time
I come to the Council Rock, as a man should come, it will be with
Shere Khan's hide on my head. For the rest, Akela goes free to
live as he pleases. You will *not* kill him, because that is not my
will. Nor do I think that you will sit here any longer, lolling out
your tongues as though you were somebodies, instead of dogs
whom I drive out – So! Go!' The fire was burning furiously at the
end of the branch, and Mowgli struck right and left round the
circle, and the wolves ran howling with the sparks burning their
fur. At last there were only Akela, Bagheera, and perhaps ten
wolves that had taken Mowgli's part. Then something began to
hurt Mowgli inside him, as he had never been hurt in his life
before, and he caught his breath and sobbed, and the tears ran
down his face.

'What is it? What is it?' he said. 'I don't want to leave the
Jungle, and I don't know what this is. Am I dying, Bagheera?'

'No, Little Brother. Those are only tears such as men use,' said
Bagheera. 'Now I know you are a man, and a man's cub no
longer. The Jungle is indeed closed to you from now on. Let them
fall, Mowgli. They are only tears.' So Mowgli sat and cried as

though his heart would break; and he had never cried in all his life before.

'Now,' he said, 'I will go to men. But first I must say farewell to my mother;' and he went to the cave where she lived with Father Wolf, and he cried on her coat, while the four cubs howled miserably.

'You will not forget me?' said Mowgli.

'Never while we can follow a trail,' said the cubs. 'Come to the foot of the hill when you are a man, and we will talk to you; and we will come into the croplands to play with you at night.'

'Come soon!' said Father Wolf. 'Oh, wise little frog, come again soon; for we are old, your mother and I.'

'Come soon,' said Mother Wolf, 'little naked son of mine; for, listen, child of man, I loved you more than ever I loved my cubs.'

'I will surely come,' said Mowgli; 'and when I come it will be to lay out Shere Khan's hide upon the Council Rock. Do not forget me! Tell them in the Jungle never to forget me!'

The dawn was beginning to break when Mowgli went down the hillside alone, to meet those mysterious things that are called men.

As the dawn was breaking the Sambhur belled
    Once, twice and again!
And a doe leaped up, and a doe leaped up
From the pond in the wood where the wild deer sup.
This I, scouting alone, beheld,
    Once, twice and again!

As the dawn was breaking the Sambhur belled
    Once, twice and again!
And a wolf stole back, and a wolf stole back
To carry the word to the waiting pack,
And we sought and we found and we bayed on his track
    Once, twice and again!

As the dawn was breaking the Wolf-Pack yelled
    Once, twice and again!
Feet in the Jungle that leave no mark!
Eyes that can see in the dark – the dark!
Tongue – give tongue to it! Hark! Oh, hark!
    Once, twice and again!

Kaa's Hunting

THE story of Kaa and Mowgli happened some time before
Mowgli was turned out of the Seeonee Wolf-Pack, or revenged
himself on Shere Khan the tiger. It was in the days when Baloo
was teaching him the Law of the Jungle. The big, serious, old
brown bear was delighted to have so quick a pupil, for the young
wolves will only learn as much of the Law of the Jungle as applies
to their own pack and tribe, and run away as soon as they can
repeat the Hunting Verse: 'Feet that make no noise; eyes that can
see in the dark; ears that can hear the winds in their lairs, and
sharp white teeth, all these things are the marks of our brothers
except Tabaqui the Jackal and the Hyena whom we hate.' But
Mowgli, as a man-cub, had to learn a great deal more than this.

Sometimes Bagheera, the Black Panther, would come lounging through the Jungle to see how his pet was getting on, and would purr with his head against a tree while Mowgli recited the day's lesson to Baloo. The boy could climb almost as well as he could swim, and swim almost as well as he could run; so Baloo, the Teacher of the Law, taught him the Wood and Water Laws; how to tell a rotten branch from a sound one; how to speak politely to the wild bees when he came upon a hive of them fifty feet above ground; what to say to Mang the Bat when he disturbed him in the branches at midday; and how to warn the water-snakes in the pools before he splashed down among them. None of the Jungle-People like being disturbed, and all are very ready to fly at an intruder. Then, too, Mowgli was taught the Stranger's Hunting Call, which must be repeated aloud till it is answered, whenever one of the Jungle-People hunts outside his own grounds. It means, translated: 'Give me permission to hunt here because I am hungry'; and the answer is: 'Hunt then for food, but not for pleasure'.

All this will show you how much Mowgli had to learn by heart, and he grew very tired of saying the same thing over a hundred times. But, as Baloo said to Bagheera, one day when Mowgli had been cuffed and run off in a temper: 'A Man-cub is a Man-cub, and he must learn *all* the Law of the Jungle.'

'But think how small he is,' said the Black Panther, who would have spoiled Mowgli if he had had his own way. 'How can his little head carry all of your long talk?'

'Is there anything in the Jungle too little to be killed? No. That is why I teach him these things, and that is why I hit him, very softly, when he forgets.'

'Softly! What do you know of softness, old Ironfeet?' Bagheera grunted. 'His face is all bruised today by your – softness. Ugh!'

'Better to be bruised from head to foot by me who loves him than that he should come to harm through knowing no better,' Baloo answered very earnestly. 'I am now teaching him the Master-Words of the Jungle that shall protect him with the birds and the Snake-People, and all that hunt on four feet, except his own pack. He can now claim protection, if he will only remember the words, from all in the Jungle. Is not that worth a little beating?'

'Well, make sure that you do not kill the Man-cub. He is not a tree-trunk for you to sharpen your blunt claws upon. But what are those Master-Words? I am more likely to give help than to ask it,' Bagheera stretched out one paw and admired the steel-blue, ripping-chisel talons at the end of it – 'still I should like to know.'

'I will call Mowgli and he shall say them – if he will. Come, Little Brother!'

'My head is ringing like a bee-tree,' said a sullen little voice over their heads, and Mowgli slid down a tree-trunk very angry and indignant, adding as he reached the ground: 'I come for Bagheera and not for *you*, fat old Baloo!'

'That is all one to me,' said Baloo, though he was hurt and grieved. 'Tell Bagheera, then, the Master-Words of the Jungle that I have taught you today.'

'Master-Words for which people?' said Mowgli, delighted to show off. 'The Jungle has many tongues. *I* know them all.'

'You know a little, but not much. Do you see, Bagheera, they never thank their teacher. Not one small wolfling has ever come back to thank old Baloo for his teachings. Say the word for the Hunting-People, then – great scholar.'

'We be of one blood, you and I,' said Mowgli, giving the words the Bear accent which all the Hunting-People use.

'Good. Now for the birds.'

Mowgli repeated, with the Kite's whistle at the end of the sentence.

'Now for the Snake-People,' said Bagheera.

The answer was a perfectly indescribable hiss, and Mowgli kicked up his feet behind, clapped his hands together to applaud himself, and jumped on to Bagheera's back, where he sat sideways, drumming with his heels on the glossy skin and making the worst faces he could think of at Baloo.

'There – there! That was worth a little bruise,' said the brown bear tenderly. 'Some day you will remember me.' Then he turned to tell Bagheera how he had begged the Master-Words from Hathi the Wild Elephant, who knows all about these things, and how Hathi had taken Mowgli down to a pool to get the Snake Word from a water-snake, because Baloo could not pronounce it, and how Mowgli was now reasonably safe against all accidents in the Jungle, because neither snake, bird, nor beast would hurt him.

'No-one, then, is to be feared,' Baloo wound up, patting his big furry stomach with pride.

'Except his own tribe,' said Bagheera, under his breath; and then aloud to Mowgli: 'Have a care for my ribs, Little Brother! What is all this dancing up and down?'

Mowgli had been trying to make himself heard by pulling at

Bagheera's shoulder-fur and kicking hard. When the two listened to him he was shouting at the top of his voice: 'And so I shall have a tribe of my own, and lead them through the branches all day long.'

'What is this new folly, little dreamer of dreams?' said Bagheera.

'Yes, and throw branches and dirt at old Baloo,' Mowgli went on. 'They have promised me this. Ah!'

'*Whoof!*' Baloo's big paw scooped Mowgli off Bagheera's back, and as the boy lay between the big forepaws he could see the bear was angry.

'Mowgli,' said Baloo, 'you have been talking with the *Bandar-log* – the Monkey-People.'

Mowgli looked at Bagheera to see if the Panther was angry too, and Bagheera's eyes were as hard as jade-stones.

'You have been with the Monkey-People – the grey apes – the people without a Law – the eaters of everything. That is great shame.'

'When Baloo hurt my head,' said Mowgli (he was still on his back), 'I went away, and the grey apes came down from the trees and had pity on me. No one else cared.' He snuffled a little.

'The pity of the Monkey-People!' Baloo snorted. 'The stillness of the mountain stream! The cool of the summer sun! There is no such thing! And then, Man-cub?'

'And then, and then, they gave me nuts and pleasant things to eat, and they – they carried me in their arms up to the top of the trees and said I was their blood-brother except that I had no tail, and should be their leader some day!'

'They have *no* leader,' said Bagheera. 'They lie. They have always lied.'

'They were very kind and told me to come again. Why have I never been taken among the Monkey-People? They stand on their feet as I do. They do not hit me with hard paws. They play all day. Let me get up! Bad Baloo, let me up! I will play with them again.'

'Listen, Man-cub,' said the bear, and his voice rumbled like thunder on a hot night. 'I have taught you all the Law of the Jungle for all the peoples of the Jungle – except the Monkey-Folk who live in the trees. They have no Law. They are outcasts. They have no speech of their own, but use the stolen words which they overhear when they listen, and peep, and wait up above in the branches. Their way is not our way. They are without leaders. They have no remembrance. They boast and chatter and pretend

'And so I shall have a tribe of my own,
and lead them through the branches all day long.'

of wood hung to the worn, rusted hinges. Trees had grown into and out of the walls; the battlements were tumbled down and decayed, and wild creepers hung out of the windows of the towers on the walls in bushy hanging clumps.

A great roofless palace crowned the hill, and the marble of the courtyards and the fountains was split, and stained with red and green, and the very cobblestones in the courtyard where the king's elephants used to live had been thrust up and apart by grasses and young trees. From the palace you could see the rows and rows of roofless houses that made up the city looking like empty honeycombs filled with blackness; the shapeless block of stone that had been an idol, in the square where four roads met; the pits and dimples at street-corners where the public wells once stood, and the shattered domes of temples with wild figs sprouting on their sides. The monkeys called the place their city, and pretended to despise the Jungle-People because they lived in the forest. And yet they never knew what the buildings were made for, nor how to use them. They would sit in circles on the floor of the king's council chamber, and scratch for fleas and pretend to be men; or they would run in and out of the roofless houses and collect pieces of plaster and old bricks in a corner, and forget where they had hidden them, and fight and cry in scuffling crowds, and then break off to play up and down the terraces of the king's garden, where they would shake the rose-trees and the oranges in sport to see the fruit and flowers fall. They explored all the passages and dark tunnels in the palace and the hundreds of little dark rooms, but they never remembered what they had seen and what they had not; and so drifted about in ones and twos or crowds telling each other that they were doing as men did. They drank at the tanks and made the water all muddy, and then they fought over it, and then they would all rush together in mobs and shout: 'There is no one in the Jungle so wise and good and clever and strong and gentle as the *Bandar-log*.' Then all would begin again till they grew tired of the city and went back to the tree-tops, hoping the Jungle-People would notice them.

Mowgli, who had been trained under the Law of the Jungle, did not like or understand this kind of life. The monkeys dragged him into the Cold Lairs late in the afternoon, and instead of going to sleep, as Mowgli would have done after a long journey, they joined hands and danced about and sang their foolish songs. One of the monkeys made a speech and told his companions that Mowgli's capture marked a new thing in the history of the *Bandar-log*, for Mowgli was going to show them how to weave

Trees had grown into and out of the walls;
the battlements were tumbled down and decayed.

leave you alive.'

'We be of one blood, you and I,' said Mowgli, quickly giving the Snake's Call. He could hear rustling and hissing in the rubbish all round him and gave the call a second time, to make sure.

'Even ssso! Down hoods all!' said half a dozen low voices (every ruin in India becomes sooner or later a dwelling-place of snakes, and the old summer-house was alive with cobras). 'Stand still, Little Brother, for your feet may do us harm.'

Mowgli stood as quietly as he could, peering through the open-work and listening to the furious din of the fight round the Black Panther – the yells and chatterings and scufflings, and Bagheera's deep, hoarse cough as he backed and bucked and twisted and plunged under the heaps of his enemies. For the first time since he was born, Bagheera was fighting for his life.

'Baloo must be at hand; Bagheera would not have come alone,' Mowgli thought; and then he called aloud: 'To the tank, Bagheera! Roll to the water-tank. Roll and plunge! Get to the water!'

Bagheera heard, and the cry that told him Mowgli was safe gave him new courage. He worked his way desperately, inch by inch, straight for the reservoirs, hitting in silence. Then from the ruined wall nearest the Jungle rose up the rumbling war-shout of Baloo. The old bear had done his best, but he could not get there sooner.

'Bagheera!' he shouted. 'I am here. I climb! I haste! *Ahuwora!* The stones slip under my feet! Wait my coming, Oh most infamous *Bandar-log*!' He panted up the terrace only to disappear to the head in a wave of monkeys, but he threw himself squarely on his haunches, and, spreading out his forepaws, hugged as many as he could hold, and then began to hit with a regular *bat-bat-bat*, like the flipping strokes of a paddle-wheel. A crash and a splash told Mowgli that Bagheera had fought his way to the tank where the monkeys could not follow. The panther lay gasping for breath, his head just out of water, while the monkeys stood three deep on the red steps, dancing up and down with rage, ready to spring upon him from all sides if he came out to help Baloo.

It was then that Bagheera lifted up his dripping chin, and in despair gave the Snake's Call for protection – 'We be of one blood, you and I' – for he believed that Kaa had turned tail at the last minute. Even Baloo, half smothered under the monkeys on the edge of the terrace, could not help chuckling as he heard the Black Panther asking for help.

'Bagheera!' he shouted, 'I am here, I climb! I haste!
Ahuwora! Wait my coming, most infamous Bandar-log!'

our customs, Mowgli.'

Mowgli turned and saw the great python's head swaying a foot above his own.

'So this is the Manling,' said Kaa. 'Very soft is his skin, and he is not so unlike the *Bandar-log*. Have a care, Manling, that I do not mistake you for a monkey some evening when I have newly changed my coat.'

'We be of one blood, you and I,' Mowgli answered. 'I take my life from you, tonight. My kill shall be your kill if ever you are hungry, Oh Kaa.'

'All thanks, Little Brother,' said Kaa, though his eyes twinkled. 'And what may so bold a hunter kill? I ask that I may follow when next he goes abroad.'

'I kill nothing – I am too little – but I drive goats toward such as can use them. When you are empty come to me and see if I speak the truth. I have some skill in these,' he held out his hands – 'and if you are ever in a trap, I may pay the debt which I owe to you, to Bagheera, and to Baloo, here. Good hunting to you all, my masters.'

'Well said,' growled Baloo, for Mowgli had returned thanks very prettily. The python dropped his head lightly for a minute on Mowgli's shoulder. 'A brave heart and a courteous tongue,' said he. 'They shall carry you far through the Jungle, Manling. But now go quickly with your friends. Go and sleep, for the moon sets, and I don't think you should see what follows.'

The moon was sinking behind the hills, and the lines of trembling monkeys huddled together on the walls and battlements looked like ragged, shaky fringes of things. Baloo went down to the tank for a drink, and Bagheera began to put his fur in order, as Kaa glided out into the centre of the terrace and brought his jaws together with a ringing snap that drew all all the monkeys' eyes upon him.

'The moon sets,' he said. 'Is there yet light to see?'

From the walls came a moan like a wind in the treetops: 'We see, Oh Kaa.'

'Good. Begins now the Dance – the Dance of the Hunger of Kaa. Sit still and watch.'

He turned twice or three times in a big circle, weaving his head from right to left. Then he began making loops and figures of eight with his body, and soft, oozy triangles that melted into squares and five-sided figures, and coiled mounds, never resting, never hurrying, and never stopping his low, humming song. It grew darker and darker, till at last the dragging, shifting coils disappeared, but they could hear the rustle of the scales.

Baloo and Bagheera stood still as stone, growling in their throats, their neck-hair bristling, and Mowgli watched and wondered.

'*Bandar-log*,' said the voice of Kaa at last, 'can you move foot or hand without my order? Speak!'

'Without your order we cannot move foot or hand, Oh Kaa!'

'Good! Come all one pace closer to me.'

The lines of the monkeys swayed forward helplessly, and Baloo and Bagheera took one stiff step forward with them.

'Closer!' hissed Kaa, and they all moved again.

Mowgli laid his hands on Baloo and Bagheera to get them away, and the two great beasts started as though they had been woken from a dream.

'Keep your hand on my shoulder,' Bagheera whispered. 'Keep it there, or I must go back – must go back to Kaa. *Aah!*'

'It is only old Kaa making circles on the dust,' said Mowgli; 'Let us go;' and the three slipped off through a gap in the walls to the Jungle.

'*Whoof!*' said Baloo, when he stood under the still trees again. 'Never again will I make an ally of Kaa,' and he shook himself all over.

'He knows more than we,' said Bagheera, trembling. 'In a little time, had I stayed, I should have walked down his throat.'

'Many will walk by that road before the moon rises again,' said Baloo. 'He will have good hunting – after his own fashion.'

'But what was the meaning of it all?' said Mowgli, who did not know anything of a python's powers of fascination. 'I saw no more than a big snake making foolish circles till the dark came. And his nose was all sore. Ho! Ho!'

'Mowgli,' said Bagheera angrily, 'his nose was sore because of you; as my ears and sides and paws and Baloo's neck and shoulders are bitten on your account. Neither Baloo nor Bagheera will be able to hunt with pleasure for many days.'

'It is nothing,' said Baloo; 'we have the Man-cub again.'

'True; but he has cost us heavily in time which might have been spent in good hunting, in wounds, in hair – I am half plucked along my back – and, last of all, in honour. For, remember, Mowgli, I, who am the Black Panther, was forced to call upon Kaa for protection, and Baloo and I were both made stupid as little birds by the Hunger-Dance. All this, Man-cub, came of your playing with the *Bandar-log*.'

'True; it is true,' said Mowgli sorrowfully. 'I am an evil Man-

cub, and my stomach is sad in me.'

'*Mf!* What says the Law of the Jungle, Baloo?'

Baloo did not wish to bring Mowgli into any more trouble, but he could not tamper with the Law, so he mumbled: 'Being sorry never stops punishment. But remember, Bagheera, he is very little.'

'I will remember; but he has done mischief, and blows must be dealt now. Mowgli, have you anything to say?'

'Nothing. I did wrong. Baloo and you are wounded. I deserve to be punished.'

Bagheera gave him half a dozen love-taps; from a panther's point of view they would hardly have waked one of his own cubs, but for a seven-year-old boy they amounted to as severe a beating as you could wish to avoid. When it was all over Mowgli sneezed, and picked himself up without a word.

'Now,' said Bagheera, 'jump on my back, Little Brother, and we will go home.'

One of the beauties of Jungle Law is that punishment settles all scores. There is no nagging afterwards.

Mowgli laid his head down on Bagheera's back and slept so deeply that he didn't even wake up when he was put down by Mother Wolf's side in the home-cave.

His spots are the joy of the Leopard: his horns are the Buffalo's
 pride.
Be clean, for the strength of the hunter is known by the gloss of
 his hide.
If ye find that the bullock can toss you, or the heavy-browed
 Sambhur can gore;
Ye need not stop work to inform us: we knew it ten seasons
 before.
Oppress not the cubs of the stranger, but hail them as Sister and
 Brother,
For though they are little and fubsy, it may be the Bear is their
 mother.
'There is none like to me!' says the Cub in the pride of his earliest
 kill;
But the Jungle is large and the Cub he is small. Let him think and
 be still.

Maxims of Baloo

'Tiger! Tiger!'

What of the hunting, hunter bold?
  Brother, the watch was long and cold.
What of the quarry ye went to kill?
  Brother, he crops in the Jungle still.
Where is the power that made your pride?
  Brother, it ebbs from my flank and side.
Where is the haste that ye hurry by?
  Brother, I go to my lair – to die!

NOW we must go back to the first tale. When Mowgli left the wolf's cave after the fight with the Pack at the Council Rock, he went down to the ploughed lands where the villagers lived, but he would not stop there because it was too near to the Jungle, and he knew that he had made at least one bad enemy at the Council. So he hurried on, keeping to the rough road that ran down the valley, and followed it at a steady jog-trot for nearly twenty miles, till he came to a country that he did not know. The valley opened out into a great plain dotted over with rocks and cut up by ravines. At one end stood a little village, and at the other the thick Jungle came down in a sweep to the grazing-grounds, and stopped there as though it had been cut off with a hoe. All over the plain, cattle and buffaloes were grazing, and when the little boys in charge of the herds saw Mowgli they shouted and ran away, and the yellow pariah dogs that hang about every Indian village barked. Mowgli walked on, for he was feeling hungry, and when he came to the village gate he saw the big thorn-bush that was drawn up before the gate at twilight pushed to one side.

'Umph!' he said, for he had come across more than one such barricade in his night rambles after things to eat. 'So men are afraid of the People of the Jungle here also.' He sat down by the gate, and when a man came out he stood up, opened his mouth, and pointed down it to show that he wanted food. The man stared, and ran back up the one street of the village shouting for the priest, who was a big, fat man dressed in white, with a red-and-yellow mark on his forehead. The priest came to the gate, and with him at least a hundred people, who stared and talked and shouted and pointed at Mowgli.

'They have no manners, these Men-Folk,' said Mowgli to himself. 'Only the grey ape would behave as they do.' So he threw back his long hair and frowned at the crowd.

'What is there to be afraid of?' said the priest. 'Look at the marks on his arms and legs. They are the bites of wolves. He is but a wolf-child run away from the Jungle.'

Of course, in playing together, the cubs had often nipped Mowgli harder than they intended, and there were white scars all over his arms and legs. But he would have been the last person in the world to call these bites, for he knew what real biting meant.

'Arré! Arré!' said two or three women together. 'To be bitten by wolves, poor child! He is a handsome boy. He has eyes like red fire. By my honour, Messua, he is not unlike your boy that was taken by the tiger.'

'Let me look,' said a woman with heavy copper rings on her wrists and ankles, and she peered at Mowgli under the palm of her hand. 'Indeed he is not. He is thinner, but he has the very look of my boy.'

The priest was a clever man, and he knew that Messua was wife to the richest villager in the place. So he looked up at the sky for a minute, and said solemnly: 'What the Jungle has taken the Jungle has restored. Take the boy into your house, my sister, and do not forget to honour the priest who sees so far into the lives of men.'

'By the Bull that bought me,' said Mowgli to himself. 'All this talking is like another looking-over by the Pack! Well, if I am a man, a man I must become.'

The crowd parted as the woman beckoned Mowgli to her hut, where there was a red-lacquered bedstead, a great earthen grain-chest with curious raised patterns on it, half a dozen copper cooking-pots, an image of a Hindu god in a little alcove, and on the wall a real looking-glass, such as they sell at the country fairs.

She gave him a long drink of milk and some bread, and then

*'Let me look,' said a woman with heavy copper rings
on her wrists and ankles.*

she laid her hand on his head and looked into his eyes; for she thought that perhaps he might be her real son come back from the Jungle where the tiger had taken him. So she said: 'Nathoo, Oh Nathoo!' Mowgli did not show that he knew the name. 'Don't you remember the day when I gave you your new shoes?' She touched his foot, and it was almost as hard as horn. 'No,' she said sorrowfully, 'those feet have never worn shoes, but you are very like my Nathoo, and you shall be my son.'

Mowgli was uneasy, because he had never been under a roof before; but as he looked at the thatch, he saw that he could tear it out any time if he wanted to get away, and that the window had no fastenings. 'What is the good of a man,' he said to himself at last, 'if he does not understand man's talk? Now I am as silly and dumb as a man would be with us in the Jungle. I must learn their talk.'

It was not for fun that he had learned while he was with the wolves to imitate the challenge of bucks in the Jungle and the grunt of the little wild pig. So as soon as Messua pronounced a word Mowgli would imitate it almost perfectly, and before dark he had learned the names of many things in the hut.

There was a problem at bedtime, because Mowgli would not sleep under anything that looked so like a panther-trap as that hut, and when they shut the door he went through the window.

'Leave him alone,' said Messua's husband. 'Remember he has probably never slept on a bed. If he has indeed been sent in the place of our son he will not run away.'

So Mowgli stretched himself in some long, clean grass at the edge of the field, but before he had closed his eyes a soft grey nose poked him under the chin.

'Phew!' said Grey Brother (he was the eldest of Mother Wolf's cubs). 'This is a poor reward for following you twenty miles. You smell of wood-smoke and cattle – altogether like a man already. Wake, Little Brother; I bring news.'

'Are all well in the Jungle?' said Mowgli, hugging him.

'All except the wolves that were burned with the Red Flower. Now, listen. Shere Khan has gone away to hunt far off till his coat grows again, for he is badly singed. When he returns he swears that he will lay your bones in the Waingunga.'

'There are two words to that. I also have made a little promise. But news is always good. I am tired tonight – very tired with new things, Grey Brother – but bring me the news always.'

'You will not forget that you are a wolf? Men will not make you forget?' said Grey Brother anxiously.

'Never. I will always remember that I love you and all in our cave; but also I will always remember that I have been cast out of the Pack.'

'And that you may be cast out of another pack. Men are only men, Little Brother, and their talk is like the talk of frogs in a pond. When I come down here again, I will wait for you in the bamboos at the edge of the grazing-ground.'

For three months after that night Mowgli hardly ever left the village gate, he was so busy learning the ways and customs of men. First he had to wear a cloth round him, which annoyed him horribly; and then he had to learn about money, which he did not in the least understand, and about ploughing, of which he did not see the use. Then the little children in the village made him very angry. Luckily, the Law of the Jungle had taught him to keep his temper, for in the Jungle life and food depend on keeping your temper; but when they made fun of him because he would not play games or fly kites, or because he mispronounced some word, only the knowledge that it was unsportsmanlike to kill little naked cubs kept him from picking them up and breaking them in two.

He did not know his own strength in the least. In the Jungle he knew he was weak compared with the beasts, but in the village people said that he was as strong as a bull.

And Mowgli had not the faintest idea of the difference that caste makes between man and man. When the potter's donkey slipped in the clay-pit, Mowgli hauled it out by the tail, and helped to stack the pots for their journey to the market at Khanhiwara. That was very shocking, too, for the potter is a low-caste man, and his donkey is worse. When the priest scolded him, Mowgli threatened to put him on the donkey, too, and the priest told Messua's husband that Mowgli had better be set to work as soon as possible; and the village head-man told Mowgli that he would have to go out with the buffaloes next day, and herd them while they grazed. No one was more pleased than Mowgli; and that night, because he had been appointed, as it were, a servant of the village, he went off to a circle that met every evening on a masonry platform under a great fig-tree. It was the village club, and the head-man and the watchman and the barber (who knew all the gossip of the village), and old Buldeo, the village hunter, who owned a Tower musket, met and smoked. The monkeys sat and talked in the upper branches, and there was a hole under the platform where a cobra lived, and he had his little platter of milk every night because he was sacred; and the old men sat around the tree and talked, and pulled at the big hookahs (waterpipes),

till far into the night. They told wonderful tales of gods and men and ghosts; and Buldeo told even more wonderful ones of the ways of beasts in the Jungle, till the eyes of the children sitting outside the circle bulged out of their heads. Most of the tales were about animals, for the Jungle was always at their door. The deer and the wild pig grubbed up their crops, and now and again the tiger carried off a man at twilight, within sight of the village gates.

Mowgli, who, naturally, knew something about what they were talking of, had to cover his face not to show that he was laughing, while Buldeo, the Tower musket across his knees, climbed on from one wonderful story to another, and Mowgli's shoulders shook.

Buldeo was explaining how the tiger that had carried away Messua's son was a ghost-tiger, and his body was inhabited by the ghost of a wicked old money-lender, who had died some years ago. 'And I know that this is true,' he said, 'because Purun Dass always limped from the blow that he got in a riot when his account-books were burned, and the tiger that I speak of, *he* limps, too, for the tracks of his pads are unequal.'

'True, true; that must be the truth,' said the greybeards, nodding together.

'Are all these tales such cobwebs and moon-talk?' said Mowgli. 'That tiger limps because he was born lame, as every one knows. To talk of the soul of a money-lender in a beast that never had the courage of a jackal is child's talk.'

Buldeo was speechless with surprise for a moment, and the head-man stared.

'Oho! It is the Jungle brat, is it?' said Buldeo. 'If you are so clever, why not bring his hide to Khanhiwara, for the Government has set a hundred rupees on his life. Better still, do not talk when your elders speak.'

Mowgli rose to go. 'All the evening I have lain here listening,' he called back over his shoulder, 'and, except once or twice, Buldeo has not said one word of truth concerning the Jungle, which is at his very doors. How, then, shall I believe the tales of ghosts and gods and goblins which he says he has seen?'

'It is full time that boy went to herding,' said the head-man, while Buldeo puffed and snorted at Mowgli's impertinence.

The custom of most Indian villages is for a few boys to take the cattle and buffaloes out to graze in the early morning, and bring them back at night; and the very cattle that would trample a white man to death allow themselves to be banged and bullied and shouted at by children that hardly come up to their noses. So long

as the boys keep with the herds they are safe, for not even the
tiger will charge a mob of cattle. But if they straggle to pick
flowers or hunt lizards, they are sometimes carried off. Mowgli
went through the village street in the dawn, sitting on the back of
Rama, the great herd bull; and the slaty-blue buffaloes, with their
long, backward-sweeping horns and savage eyes, rose out of their
byres, one by one, and followed him, and Mowgli made it very
clear to the children with him that he was the master. He beat the
buffaloes with a long, polished bamboo, and told Kamya, one of
the boys, to graze the cattle by themselves, while he went on with
the buffaloes, and to be very careful not to stray away from the
herd.

An Indian grazing-ground is all rocks and scrub and tussocks
and little ravines, among which the herds scatter and disappear.
The buffaloes generally keep to the pools and muddy places,
where they lie wallowing or basking in the warm mud for hours.
Mowgli drove them on to the edge of the Jungle; then he dropped
from Rama's neck, trotted off to a bamboo clump, and found
Grey Brother. 'Ah!' said Grey Brother. 'I have waited here very
many days. What is the meaning of this cattle-herding work?'

'It is an order,' said Mowgli. 'I am a village herd for a while.
What news of Shere Khan?'

'He has come back to this country, and has waited here a long
time for you. Now he has gone off again, for the game is scarce.
But he means to kill you.'

'Very good,' said Mowgli. 'So long as he is away, will you or
one of the four brothers sit on that rock, so that I can see you as I
come out of the village. When he comes back wait for me in the
ravine by the *dhâk*-tree in the centre of the plain. We need not
walk into Shere Khan's mouth.'

Then Mowgli picked out a shady place, and lay down and slept
while the buffaloes grazed round him. Herding in India is one of
the laziest things in the world. The cattle move and crunch, and
lie down, and move on again, and they do not even low. They
only grunt, and the buffaloes very seldom say anything, but get
down into the muddy pools one after another, and work their way
into the mud till only their noses and staring china-blue eyes show
above the surface, and there they lie like logs. The sun makes the
rocks dance in the heat, and the herd-children hear one kite
(never any more) whistling almost out of sight overhead, and they
know that if they died, or a cow died, that kite would sweep
down, and the next kite miles away would see him drop and
would follow, and the next, and the next, and almost before they

were dead there would be a score of hungry kites come out of nowhere. Then they sleep and wake and sleep again, and weave little baskets of dried grass and put grasshoppers in them; or catch two praying-mantis and make them fight; or string a necklace of red and black Jungle nuts; or watch a lizard basking on a rock, or a snake hunting a frog near the wallows. Then they sing long, long songs with odd native quavers at the end of them, and the day seems longer than most people's whole lives, and perhaps they make a mud castle with mud figures of men and horses and buffaloes, and put reeds into the men's hands, and pretend that they are kings and the figures are their armies, or that they are gods to be worshipped. Then evening comes, and the children call, and the buffaloes lumber up out of the sticky mud with noises like gunshots going off one after the other, and they all string across the grey plain back to the twinkling village lights.

Day after day Mowgli would lead the buffaloes out to their wallows, and day after day he would see Grey Brother's back a mile and a half away across the plain (so he knew that Shere Khan had not come back), and day after day he would lie on the grass listening to the noises round him, and dreaming of old days in the Jungle. If Shere Khan had made a false step with his lame paw up in the Jungles by the Waingunga, Mowgli would have heard him in those long, still mornings.

At last a day came when he did not see Grey Brother at the signal-place, and he laughed and headed the buffaloes for the ravine by the *dhâk*-tree, which was all covered with golden-red flowers. There sat Grey Brother, every bristle on his back lifted.

'He has hidden for a month to throw you off guard. He crossed the ranges last night with Tabaqui, hotfoot on your trail,' said the wolf, panting.

Mowgli frowned. 'I am not afraid of Shere Khan, but Tabaqui is very cunning.'

'Have no fear,' said Grey Brother, licking his lips a little. 'I met Tabaqui in the dawn. Now he is telling all his wisdom to the kites, but he told *me* everything before I broke his back. Shere Khan's plan is to wait for you at the village gate this evening – for you and for no one else. He is lying up now in the big dry ravine of the Waingunga.'

'Has he eaten today, or does he hunt empty?' said Mowgli, for the answer meant life or death to him.

'He killed at dawn – a pig – and he has drunk too. Remember, Shere Khan could never fast, even for the sake of revenge.'

'Oh! Fool, fool! What a cub's cub it is! Eaten and drunk too, and he thinks that I shall wait till he has slept! Now, where does he lie up? If there were but ten of us we might pull him down as he lies. These buffaloes will not charge unless they wind him, and I cannot speak their language. Can we get behind his track so that they may smell it?'

'He swam far down the Waingunga to cut that off,' said Grey Brother.

'Tabaqui told him that, I know. He would never have thought of it alone.' Mowgli stood with his finger in his mouth, thinking. 'The big ravine of the Waingunga. That opens out on the plain not half a mile from here. I can take the herd round through the Jungle to the head of the ravine and then sweep down – but he would slink out at the foot. We must block that end. Grey Brother, can you cut the herd in two for me?'

'Not I, perhaps – but I have brought a wise helper.' Grey Brother trotted off and dropped into a hole. Then there lifted up a huge grey head that Mowgli knew well, and the hot air was filled with the most desolate cry of all the Jungle – the hunting-howl of a wolf at midday.

'Akela! Akela!' said Mowgli, clapping his hands. 'I might have known that you would not forget me. We have a job to do. Cut the herd in two, Akela. Keep the cows and calves together, and the bulls and the plough-buffaloes by themselves.'

The two wolves ran, ladies'-chain fashion, in and out of the herd, which snorted and threw up its head, and separated into two clumps. In one the cow-buffaloes stood, with their calves in the centre, and glared and pawed, ready, if a wolf would only stay still, to charge down and trample the life out of him. In the other the bulls and the young bulls snorted and stamped; but, though they looked more imposing, they were much less dangerous, for they had no calves to protect. No six men could have divided the herd so neatly.

'What orders?' panted Akela. 'They are trying to join again.'

Mowgli slipped on to Rama's back. 'Drive the bulls away to the left, Akela. Grey Brother, when we are gone, hold the cows together, and drive them into the foot of the ravine.'

'How far?' said Grey Brother, panting and snapping.

'Till the sides are higher than Shere Khan can jump,' shouted Mowgli. 'Keep them there till we come down.' The bulls swept off as Akela bayed, and Grey Brother stopped in front of the cows. They charged down on him and he ran just before them to the foot of the ravine, as Akela drove the bulls far to the left.

'Well done! Another charge and they are fairly started.

Careful, now – careful, Akela. A snap too much, and the bulls will charge. *Huyah!* This is wilder work than driving black-buck. Did you think these creatures could move so swiftly?' Mowgli called.

'I have – have hunted these too in my time,' gasped Akela in the dust. 'Shall I turn them into the Jungle?'

'Ay, turn! Swiftly turn them! Rama is mad with rage. Oh, if I could only tell him what I need of him today!'

The bulls were turned to the right this time, and crashed into the standing thicket. The other herd-children, watching with the cattle half a mile away, hurried to the village as fast as their legs could carry them, crying that the buffaloes had gone mad and run away.

But Mowgli's plan was simple enough. All he wanted to do was to make a big circle uphill and get at the head of the ravine, and then take the bulls down it and catch Shere Khan between the bulls and the cows; for he knew that after a meal and a full drink Shere Khan would not be in any condition to fight or to clamber up the sides of the ravine. He was soothing the buffaloes now by voice, and Akela had dropped far to the rear, only whimpering once or twice to hurry the rear-guard. It was a long, long circle, for they did not wish to get too near the ravine and give Shere Khan warning. At last Mowgli rounded up the bewildered herd at the head of the ravine on a grassy patch that sloped down to the ravine itself. From that height you could see across the tops of the trees down to the plain below; but what Mowgli looked at was the sides of the ravine, and he saw with a great deal of satisfaction that they ran nearly straight up and down, while the vines and creepers that hung over them would give no foothold to a tiger who wanted to get out.

'Let them breathe, Akela,' he said, holding up his hand. 'They have not winded him yet. Let them breathe. I must tell Shere Khan who comes. We have him in the trap.'

He put his hands to his mouth and shouted down the ravine – it was almost like shouting down a tunnel – and the echoes jumped from rock to rock.

After a long time there came back the drawling, sleepy snarl of a full-fed tiger just wakened.

'Who calls?' said Shere Khan, and a splendid peacock fluttered up out of the ravine screeching.

'I, Mowgli. Cattle thief, it is time to come to the Council Rock! Down – hurry them down, Akela! Down, Rama, down!'

The herd paused for an instant at the edge of the slope, but

Akela gave tongue in the full hunting-yell, and they pitched over one after the other, just as steamers shoot rapids, the sand and stones spurting up round them. Once started, there was no chance of stopping, and before they were fairly in the bed of the ravine Rama caught the smell of Shere Khan and bellowed.

'Ha! Ha!' said Mowgli, on his back. 'Now you know!' And the torrent of black horns, foaming muzzles, and staring eyes whirled down the ravine like boulders in flood-time; the weaker buffaloes being shouldered out to the sides of the ravine, where they tore through the creepers. They knew what the business was before them – the terrible charge of the buffalo-herd against which no tiger can hope to stand. Shere Khan heard the thunder of their hoofs, picked himself up, and lumbered down the ravine, looking from side to side for some way of escape; but the walls of the ravine were straight, and he had to keep on, heavy with his dinner and his drink, willing to do anything rather than fight. The herd splashed through the pool he had just left, bellowing till the narrow ravine rang. Mowgli heard an answering bellow from the foot of the ravine, saw Shere Khan turn (the tiger knew if the worst came to the worst it was better to meet the bulls than the cows with their calves), and then Rama tripped, stumbled, and went on again over something soft, and, with the bulls at his heels, crashed full into the other herd, while the weaker buffaloes were lifted clean off their feet by the shock of the meeting. That charge carried both herds out into the plain, goring and stamping and snorting. Mowgli watched his time, and slipped off Rama's neck, laying about him right and left with his stick.

'Quick, Akela! Break them up. Scatter them, or they will be fighting one another. Drive them away, Akela. *Hai*, Rama! *Hai! hai! hai!* my children. Softly now, softly! It is all over.'

Akela and Grey Brother ran to and fro nipping the buffaloes' legs, and though the herd wheeled once to charge up the ravine again, Mowgli managed to turn Rama, and the others followed him to the wallows.

Shere Khan needed no more trampling. He was dead, and the kites were coming for him already.

'Brothers, that was a dog's death,' said Mowgli, feeling for the knife he always carried in a sheath round his neck now that he lived with men. 'But he would never have shown fight. His hide will look well on the Council Rock. We must get to work swiftly.'

A boy trained among men would never have dreamed of skinning a ten-foot tiger alone, but Mowgli knew better than any one else how an animal's skin is fitted on, and how it can be taken

off. But it was hard work, and Mowgli slashed and tore and grunted for an hour, while the wolves lolled out their tongues, or came forward and tugged as he ordered them.

Presently a hand fell on his shoulder, and looking up he saw Buldeo with the Tower musket. The children had told the village about the buffalo stampede, and Buldeo went out angrily, only too anxious to correct Mowgli for not taking better care of the herd. The wolves dropped out of sight as soon as they saw the man coming.

'What is this folly?' said Buldeo angrily. 'To think that you can skin a tiger! Where did the buffaloes kill him? It is the Lame Tiger, too, and there is a hundred rupees on his head. Well, well, we will overlook you letting the herd run off, and perhaps I will give you one of the rupees of the reward when I have taken the skin to Khanhiwara.' He fumbled in his waist-cloth for flint and steel, and stooped down to singe Shere Khan's whiskers. Most native hunters singe a tiger's whiskers to prevent his ghost haunting them.

'Hum!' said Mowgli, half to himself as he ripped back the skin of a forepaw. 'So you will take the hide to Khanhiwara for the reward, and perhaps give me one rupee? Now as far as I'm concerned, I need the skin for my own use. Heh! old man, take away that fire!'

'How can you talk this way to the chief hunter of the village? Your luck and the stupidity of your buffaloes have helped you to this kill. The tiger has just fed, or he would have gone twenty miles by this time. You can not even skin him properly, little beggar-brat, and you tell me, Buldeo, not to singe his whiskers. Mowgli, I will not give you one anna of the reward, but only a very big beating. Leave the carcass!'

'By the Bull that bought me,' said Mowgli, who was trying to get at the shoulder, 'must I stay babbling to an old ape all noon? Here, Akela, this man plagues me.'

Buldeo, who was still stooping over Shere Khan's head, found himself sprawling on the grass, with a grey wolf standing over him, while Mowgli went on skinning as though he were alone in all India.

'Ye-es,' he said, between his teeth. 'You are absolutely right, Buldeo. You will never give me one anna of the reward. There is an old war between this lame tiger and myself – a very old war, and – I have won.'

To do Buldeo justice, if he had been ten years younger he would have taken his chance with Akela had he met the wolf in

the woods; but a wolf who obeyed the orders of this boy who had
private wars with man-eating tigers was not a common animal. It
was sorcery, magic of the worst kind, thought Buldeo, and he
wondered whether the amulet round his neck would protect him.
He lay as still as still, expecting every minute to see Mowgli turn
into a tiger, too.

'Maharaj! Great King!' he said at last, in a husky whisper.

'Yes,' said Mowgli, without turning his head, chuckling a little.

'I am an old man. I did not know that you were anything more
than a herd-boy. May I rise up and go away, or will your servant
tear me to pieces?'

'Go, and peace go with you. Only, another time do not meddle
with my game. Let him go, Akela.'

Buldeo hobbled away to the village as fast as he could, looking
back over his shoulder in case Mowgli should change into
something terrible. When he got to the village he told a tale of
magic and enchantment and sorcery that made the priest look
very grave.

Mowgli went on with his work, but it was nearly twilight before
he and the wolves had drawn the great bright skin clear of the
body.

'Now we must hide this and take the buffaloes home! Help me
to herd them, Akela.'

The herd rounded up in the misty twilight, and when they got
near the village Mowgli saw lights, and heard the conches and
bells blowing and banging. Half the village seemed to be waiting
for him by the gate. 'That is because I have killed Shere Khan,' he
said to himself; but a shower of stones whistled about his ears,
and the villagers shouted: 'Sorcerer! Wolf's brat! Jungle-demon!
Go away! Get away from here quickly, or the priest will turn you
into a wolf again. Shoot, Buldeo, shoot!'

The old Tower musket went off with a bang, and a young
buffalo bellowed in pain.

'More sorcery!' shouted the villagers. 'He can turn bullets.
Buldeo, that was your buffalo.'

'What is the matter?' said Mowgli, bewildered, as the stones
flew thicker.

'They are not unlike the Pack, these brothers of yours,' said
Akela, sitting down composedly. 'It is in my head that, if bullets
mean anything, they would cast you out.'

'Wolf! Wolf's cub! Go away!' shouted the priest, waving a sprig
of the sacred *tulsi* plant.

'Again? Last time it was because I was a man. This time it is

because I am a wolf. Let us go, Akela.'

A woman – it was Messua – ran across to the herd, and cried: 'Oh, my son, my son! They say you are a sorcerer who can turn himself into a beast at will. I do not believe, but go away or they will kill you. Buldeo says you are a wizard, but I know you have avenged Nathoo's death.'

'Come back, Messua!' shouted the crowd. 'Come back, or we will stone you, too.'

Mowgli laughed a little short ugly laugh, for a stone had hit him in the mouth. 'Run back, Messua. This is one of the foolish tales they tell under the big tree at dusk. I have at least paid for your son's life. Farewell; and run quickly, for I shall send the herd in more swiftly than their brickbats. I am no wizard, Messua. Farewell!'

'Now, once more, Akela,' he cried. 'Bring the herd in.'

The buffaloes were anxious enough to get to the village. They hardly needed Akela's yell, but charged through the gate like a whirlwind, scattering the crowd right and left.

'Keep count!' shouted Mowgli scornfully. 'May be I have stolen one of them. Keep count, for I will do your herding no more. Fare you well, children of men, and thank Messua that I do not come in with my wolves and hunt you up and down your street.'

He turned on his heel and walked away with the Lone Wolf; and as he looked up at the stars he felt happy. 'No more sleeping in traps for me, Akela. Let us get Shere Khan's skin and go away. No; we will not hurt the village, for Messua was kind to me.'

When the moon rose over the plain, making it look all milky, the horrified villages saw Mowgli, with two wolves at his heels and a bundle on his head, trotting across at the steady wolf's trot that eats up the long miles like fire. Then they banged the temple bells and blew the conches louder than ever; and Messua cried, and Buldeo embroidered the story of his adventures in the Jungle, till he ended by saying that Akela stood up on his hind legs and talked like a man.

The moon was just going down when Mowgli and the two wolves came to the hill of the Council Rock, and they stopped at Mother Wolf's cave.

'They have cast me out from the Man-Pack, Mother,' shouted Mowgli, 'but I come with the hide of Shere Khan to keep my word.' Mother Wolf walked stiffly from the cave with the cubs behind her, and her eyes glowed as she saw the skin.

'I told him on that day, when he crammed his head and shoulders into this cave, hunting for you, Little Frog – I told him that the hunter would be the hunted. It is well done.'

'Little Brother, it is well done,' said a deep voice in the thicket. 'We were lonely in the Jungle without you,' and Bagheera came running to Mowgli's bare feet. They clambered up the Council Rock together, and Mowgli spread the skin out on the flat stone where Akela used to sit, and pegged it down with four slivers of bamboo, and Akela lay down upon it, and called the old call to the Council, 'Look – look well, Oh Wolves!' exactly as he had called when Mowgli was first brought there.

Ever since Akela had been deposed, the Pack had been without a leader, hunting and fighting at their own pleasure. But they answered the call from habit, and some of them were lame from the traps they had fallen into, and some limped from shot-wounds, and some were mangy from eating bad food, and many were missing; but they came to the Council Rock, all that were left of them, and saw Shere Khan's striped hide on the rock, and the huge claws dangling at the end of the empty, dangling feet. It was then that Mowgli made up a song without any rhymes, a song that came up into his throat all by itself, and he shouted it aloud, leaping up and down on the rattling skin, and beating time with his heels till he had no more breath left, while Grey Brother and Akela howled between the verses.

'Look well, Oh Wolves! Have I kept my word?' said Mowgli when he had finished; and the wolves bayed, 'Yes,' and one tattered wolf howled:

'Lead us again, Oh Akela. Lead us again, Oh Man-cub, for we are sick of this lawlessness, and we want to be the Free People once more.'

'Nay,' purred Bagheera, 'that may not be. When you are well fed, the madness may come upon you again. Not for nothing are you called the Free People. You fought for freedom, and it is yours. Eat it, Oh Wolves.'

'Man-Pack and Wolf-Pack have cast me out,' said Mowgli. 'Now I will hunt alone in the Jungle.'

'And we will hunt with you,' said the four cubs.

So Mowgli went away and hunted with the four cubs in the Jungle from that day on. But he was not always alone, because years afterwards he became a man and married.

But that is a story for grown-ups.

Mowgli's Song
That he sang at the Council Rock when he danced on
Shere Khan's hide

The Song of Mowgli – I, Mowgli, am singing. Let the Jungle
    listen to the things I have done.
Shere Khan said he would kill – would kill! At the gates in the
    twilight he would kill Mowgli, the Frog!
He ate and he drank. Drink deep, Shere Khan, for when wilt
    thou drink again? Sleep and dream of the kill.
I am alone on the grazing-grounds. Grey Brother, come to me!
    Come to me, Lone Wolf, for there is big game afoot.
Bring up the great bull-buffaloes, the blue-skinned herd-bulls
    with the angry eyes. Drive them to and fro as I order.
Sleepest thou still, Shere Khan? Wake, oh, wake! Here come I,
    and the bulls are behind.
Rama, the King of the Buffaloes, stamped with his foot. Waters
    of the Waingunga, whither went Shere Khan?
He is not Ikki to dig holes, nor Mao, the Peacock, that he should
    fly. He is not Mang, the Bat, to hang in the branches. Little
    bamboos that creak together, tell me where he ran.
Ow! He is there. *Ahoo!* He is there. Under the feet of Rama lies
    the Lame One! Up, Shere Khan! Up and kill! Here is meat;
    break the necks of the bulls!
Hsh! He is asleep. We will not wake him, for his strength is very
    great. The kites have come down to see it. The black ants
    have come up to know it. There is a great assembly in his
    honour.
Alala! I have no cloth to wrap me. The kites will see that I am
    naked. I am ashamed to meet all these people.

'TIGER! TIGER!'

Lend me thy coat, Shere Khan. Lend me thy gay striped coat that
 I may go to the Council Rock.
By the Bull that bought me, I have made a promise – a little
 promise. Only thy coat is lacking before I keep my word.
With the knife – with the knife that men use – with the knife of
 the hunter, the man, I will stoop down for my gift.
Waters of the Waingunga, bear witness that Shere Khan gives me
 his coat for the love that he bears me. Pull, Grey Brother!
 Pull, Akela! Heavy is the hide of Shere Khan.
The Man-Pack are angry. They throw stones and talk child's talk.
 My mouth is bleeding. Let us run away.
Through the night, through the hot night, run swiftly with me, my
 brothers. We will leave the lights of the village and go to the
 low moon.
Waters of the Waingunga, the Man-Pack have cast me out. I did
 them no harm, but they were afraid of me. Why?
Wolf-Pack, ye have cast me out too. The Jungle is shut to me and
 the village gates are shut. Why?
As Mang flies between the beasts and the birds, so fly I between
 the village and the Jungle. Why?
I dance on the hide of Shere Khan, but my heart is very heavy.
 My mouth is cut and wounded with the stones from the
 village, but my heart is very light because I have come back
 to the Jungle. Why?
These two things fight together in me as the snakes fight in the
 spring.
The water comes out of my eyes; yet I laugh while it falls. Why?
I am two Mowglis, but the hide of Shere Khan is under my feet.
All the Jungle knows that I have killed Shere Khan. Look – look
 well, Oh Wolves!
Ahae! My heart is heavy with the things that I do not understand.

THE WHITE SEAL

Oh! hush thee, my baby, the night is behind us,
    And black are the waters that sparkled so green.
The moon, o'er the combers, looks downward to find us
    At rest in the hollows that rustle between.
Where billow meets billow, there soft be thy pillow:
    Ah, weary wee flipperling, curl at thy ease!
The storm shall not wake thee, nor shark overtake thee,
    Asleep in the arms of the slow-swinging seas.

Seal Lullaby

ALL these things happened several years ago at a place
called Novastoshnah, or North-East Point, on the Island of St
Paul, far away in the Bering Sea. Limmershin, the Winter Wren,
told me the tale when he was blown on to the rigging of a steamer
going to Japan, and I took him down into my cabin and warmed
and fed him for a couple of days till he was fit to fly back to St
Paul's again. Limmershin is a very odd little bird, but he knows
how to tell the truth.

Nobody comes to Novastoshnah except on business, and the
only people who have regular business there are the seals. They
come in the summer months by hundreds and hundreds of
thousands out of the cold grey sea; for Novastoshnah beach has
the finest accommodation for seals of any place in all the world.

THE WHITE SEAL

Sea Catch knew that, and every spring would swim from whatever place he happened to be in – would swim like a torpedo-boat straight for Novastoshnah, and spend a month fighting with his companions for a good place on the rocks as close to the sea as possible. Sea Catch was fifteen years old, a huge grey fur-seal with almost a mane on his shoulders, and long, wicked dog-teeth. When he heaved himself up on his front flippers he stood more than four feet clear of the ground, and his weight, if any one had been bold enough to weigh him, was nearly seven hundred pounds. He was scarred all over with the marks of savage fights, but he was always ready for just one fight more. He would put his head on one side, as though he were afraid to look his enemy in the face; then he would shoot it out like lightning, and when the big teeth were firmly fixed on the other seal's neck, the other seal might get away if he could, but Sea Catch would not help him.

Yet Sea Catch never chased a beaten seal, for that was against the Rules of the Beach. He only wanted room by the sea for his nursery; but as there were forty or fifty thousand other seals hunting for the same thing each spring, the whistling, bellowing, roaring, and blowing on the beach were something frightful.

From a little hill called Hutchinson's Hill you could look over three and a half miles of ground covered with fighting seals; and the surf was dotted all over with the heads of seals hurrying to land to begin their share of the fighting. They fought in the breakers, they fought in the sand, and they fought on the smooth-worn basalt rocks of the nurseries; for they were just as stupid and unaccommodating as men. Their wives never came to the island until late in May or early in June, for they did not care to be torn to pieces; and the young two-, three-, and four-year-old seals who had not begun housekeeping went inland about half a mile through the ranks of the fighters and played about on the sand-dunes in droves and legions, and rubbed off every single green thing that grew. They were called the holluschickie – the bachelors – and there were perhaps two or three hundred thousand of them at Novastoshnah alone.

Sea Catch had just finished his forty-fifth fight one spring when Matkah, his soft, sleek, gentle-eyed wife, came up out of the sea, and he caught her by the scruff of the neck and dumped her down on his reservation, saying gruffly: 'Late, as usual. Where *have* you been?'

It was not the fashion for Sea Catch to eat anything during the four months he stayed on the beaches, and so his temper was generally bad. Matkah knew better than to answer back.

She looked round and cooed: 'How thoughtful of you! You've taken the old place again.'

'I should think so,' said Sea Catch. 'Look at me!'

He was scratched and bleeding in twenty places; one eye was almost blind, and his sides were torn to ribbons.

'Oh, you men, you men!' Matkah said, fanning herself with her hind flipper. 'Why can't you be sensible and settle your places quietly? You look as though you had been fighting with the Killer Whale.'

'I haven't been doing anything *but* fight since the middle of May. The beach is disgracefully crowded this season. I've met at least a hundred seals from Lukannon Beach, house-hunting. Why can't people stay where they belong?'

'I've often thought we should be much happier if we hauled out at Otter island instead of this crowded place,' said Matkah.

'Bah! Only the holluschickie go to Otter Island. If we went there they would say we were afraid. We must preserve appearances, my dear.'

Sea Catch sunk his head proudly between his fat shoulders and pretended to go to sleep for a few minutes, but all the time he was keeping a sharp look-out for a fight. Now that all the seals and their wives were on the land, you could hear their clamour miles out to sea above the loudest gales. At the lowest counting there were over a million seals on the beach – old seals, mother seals, tiny babies, and holluschickie, fighting, scuffling, bleating, crawling, and playing together – going down to the sea and coming up from it in gangs and regiments, lying over every foot of ground as far as the eye could reach, and skirmishing about in brigades through the fog. It is nearly always foggy at Novastoshnah, except when the sun comes out and makes everything look all pearly and rainbow-coloured for a little while.

Kotick, Matkah's baby, was born in the middle of that confusion, and he was all head and shoulders, with pale, watery-blue eyes, as tiny seals must be; but there was something about his coat that made his mother look at him very closely.

'Sea Catch,' she said at last, 'our baby's going to be white!'

'Empty clam-shells and dry seaweed!' snorted Sea Catch. 'There never has been such a thing in the world as a white seal.'

'I can't help that,' said Matkah; 'there's going to be now;' and she sang the low, crooning seal-song that all the mother seals sing to their babies:

'Empty clam-shells and dry seaweed!' snorted Sea Catch.

You mustn't swim till you're six weeks old,
  Or your head will be sunk by your heels;
And Summer gales and Killer Whales
  Are bad for baby seals.

Are bad for baby seals, dear rat,
  As bad as bad can be;
But splash and grow strong,
And you can't be wrong,
  Child of the Open Sea!

Of course the little fellow did not understand the words at first. He paddled and scrambled about by his mother's side, and learned to scuffle out of the way when his father was fighting with another seal, and the two rolled and roared up and down the slippery rocks. Matkah used to go to sea to get things to eat, and the baby was fed only once in two days; but then he ate all he could, and throve upon it.

The first thing he did was to crawl inland, and there he met tens of thousands of babies of his own age, and they played together like puppies, went to sleep on the clean sand, and played again. The old people in the nurseries took no notice of them, and the holluschickie kept to their own grounds, so the babies had a beautiful playtime.

When Matkah came back from her deep-sea fishing she would go straight to their playground and call as a sheep calls for a lamb, and wait until she heard Kotick bleat. Then she would take the straightest of straight lines in his direction, striking out with her fore flippers and knocking the youngsters head over heels right and left. There were always a few hundred mothers hunting for their children through the playgrounds, and the babies were kept lively; but, as Matkah told Kotick, 'So long as you don't lie in muddy water and get mange, or rub the hard sand into a cut or scratch, and so long as you never go swimming when there is a heavy sea, nothing will hurt you here.'

Little seals can no more swim than little children, but they are unhappy till they learn. The first time that Kotick went down to the sea a wave carried him out beyond his depth, and his big head sank and his little hind flippers flew up exactly as his mother had told him in the song, and if the next wave had not thrown him back again he would have drowned.

After that he learned to lie in a beach-pool and let the wash of the waves just cover him and lift him up while he paddled, but he always kept his eye open for big waves that might hurt. He was two weeks learning to use his flippers; and all that while he floundered in and out of the water, and coughed and grunted and crawled up the beach and took catnaps on the sand, and went back again, until at last he found that he truly belonged to the water.

Then you can imagine the times that he had with his companions, ducking under the rollers; or coming in on top of a comber and landing with a swash and a splutter as the big wave went whirling far up the beach; or standing upon his tail and scratching his head as the old people did; or playing 'I'm the King of the Castle' on slippery, weedy rocks that just stuck out of the wash. Now and then he would see a thin fin, like a big shark's fin, drifting along close to shore, and he knew that that was the Killer Whale, the Grampus, who eats young seals when he can get them; and Kotick would head for the beach like an arrow, and the fin would jig off slowly, as if it were looking for nothing at all.

Late in October the seals began to leave St Paul's for the deep sea, by families and tribes, and there was no more fighting over the nurseries, and the holluschickie played anywhere they liked. 'Next year,' said Matkah to Kotick, 'you will be a holluschickie; but this year you must learn how to catch fish.'

They set out together across the Pacific, and Matkah showed Kotick how to sleep on his back with his flippers tucked down by his side and his little nose just out of the water. No cradle is so comfortable as the long, rocking swell of the Pacific. When Kotick felt his skin tingle all over, Matkah told him he was learning the 'feel of the water', and that tingly, prickly feelings meant bad weather coming, and he must swim hard and get away.

'In a little time,' she said, 'you'll know where to swim to, but just now we'll follow Sea Pig, the Porpoise, for he is very wise.' A school of porpoises were ducking and tearing through the water, and little Kotick followed them as fast as he could.

'How do you know where to go to?' he panted. The leader of the school rolled his white eyes, and ducked under.

'My tail tingles, youngster,' he said. 'That means there's a gale behind me. Come along! When you're south of the Sticky Water (he meant the Equator), and your tail tingles, that means there's a gale in front of you and you must head north. Come along! The water feels bad here.'

This was one of the very many things that Kotick learned, and he was always learning. Matkah taught him to follow the cod and the halibut along the undersea banks, and wrench the rockling out of his hole among the weeds; how to skirt the wrecks lying a hundred fathoms below water, and dart like a rifle-bullet in at one

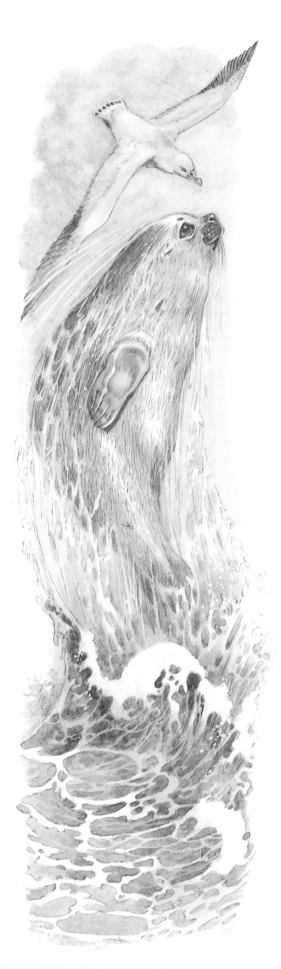

port-hole and out at another as the fishes ran; how to dance on the top of the waves when the lightning was racing all over the sky, and wave his flipper politely to the stumpy-tailed Albatross and the Man-of-war Hawk as they went down the wind; how to jump three or four feet clear of the water, like a dolphin, flippers close to the side and tail curved; to leave the flying-fish alone because they are all bony; to take the shoulder-piece out of a cod at full speed ten fathoms deep; and never to stop and look at a boat or a ship, but particularly a row-boat. At the end of six months, what Kotick did not know about deep-sea fishing was not worth the knowing, and all that time he never set flipper on dry ground.

One day, however, as he was lying half asleep in the warm water somewhere off the Island of Juan Fernandez, he felt faint and lazy all over, just as human people do when the spring is in their legs, and he remembered the good firm beaches of Novastoshnah seven thousand miles away, the games his companions played, the smell of the seaweed, the seal roar, and the fighting. That very minute he turned north, swimming steadily, and as he went on he met scores of his mates, all bound for the same place, and they said: 'Greeting, Kotick! This year we are all holluschickie, and we can dance the Fire-dance in the breakers off Lukannon and play on the new grass. But where did you get that coat?'

Kotick's fur was almost pure white now, and though he felt very proud of it, he only said: 'Swim quickly! My bones are aching for the land.' And so they all came to the beaches where they had been born, and heard the old seals, their fathers, fighting in the rolling mist.

That night Kotick danced the Fire-dance with the yearling seals. The sea is full of fire on summer nights all the way down from Novastoshnah to Lukannon, and each seal leaves a wake like burning oil behind him, and a flaming flash when he jumps, and the waves break in great phosphorescent streaks and swirls. Then they went inland to the holluschickie grounds, and rolled up and down in the new wild wheat, and told stories of what they had done while they had been at sea. They talked about the Pacific as boys would talk about a wood that they had been nutting in, and if any one had understood them, he could have gone away and made such a chart of that ocean as never was. The three- and four-year-old holluschickie romped down from Hutchinson's Hill, crying: 'Out of the way, youngsters! The sea is deep, and you don't know all that's in it yet. Wait till you've rounded the

Dart like a rifle-bullet in at one port-hole
and out at another as fishes ran.

Horn. Hi, you yearling, where did you get that white coat?'

'I didn't get it,' said Kotick; 'it grew.' And just as he was going to roll the speaker over, a couple of black-haired men with flat red faces came from behind a sand-dune, and Kotick, who had never seen a man before, coughed and lowered his head. The holluschickie just bundled off a few yards and sat staring stupidly. The men were no less than Kerick Booterin, the chief of the seal-hunters on the island, and Patalamon, his son. They came from the little village not half a mile from the seal-nurseries, and they were deciding what seals they would drive up to the killing-pens (for the seals were driven just like sheep), to be turned into sealskin jackets later on.

'Ho!' said Patalamon. 'Look! There's a white seal!'

Kerick Booterin turned nearly white under his oil and smoke, for he was an Aleut, and Aleuts are not clean people. Then he began to mutter a prayer. 'Don't touch him, Patalamon. There has never been a white seal since – since I was born. Perhaps it is old Zaharrof's ghost. He was lost last year in the big gale.'

'I'm not going near him,' said Patalamon. 'He's unlucky. Do you really think he is old Zaharrof come back? I owe him for some gulls' eggs.'

'Don't look at him,' said Kerick. 'Head off that drove of four-year-olds. The men ought to skin two hundred today, but it's the beginning of the season, and they are new to the work. A hundred will do. Quick!'

Patalamon rattled a pair of seal's shoulder-bones in front of a herd of holluschickie, and they stopped dead, puffing and blowing. Then he stepped near, and the seals began to move, and Kerick headed them inland, and they never tried to get back to their companions. Hundreds and hundreds of thousands of seals watched them being driven, but they went on playing just the same. Kotick was the only one who asked questions, and none of his companions could tell him anything, except that the men always drove seals in that way for six weeks or two months of every year.

'I am going to follow,' he said, and his eyes nearly popped out of his head as he shuffled along in the wake of the herd.

'The white seal is coming after us,' cried Patalamon. 'That's the first time a seal has ever come to the killing-grounds alone.'

'Hsh! Don't look behind you,' said Kerick. 'It *is* Zaharrof's ghost! I must speak to the priest about this.'

The distance to the killing-grounds was only half a mile, but it took an hour to cover, because if the seals went too fast Kerick

knew that they would get heated and then their fur would come off in patches when they were skinned. So they went on very slowly, past Sea-Lion's Neck, past Webster House, till they came to the Salt House just beyond the sight of the seals on the beach. Kotick followed, panting and wondering. He thought that he was at the world's end, but the roar of the seal-nurseries behind him sounded as loud as the roar of a train in a tunnel. Then Kerick sat down on the moss and pulled out a heavy pewter watch and let the drove cool off for thirty minutes, and Kotick could hear the fog-dew dripping from the brim of his cap. Then ten or twelve men, each with an iron-bound club three or four feet long, came up, and Kerick pointed out one or two of the drove that were bitten by their companions or were too hot, and the men kicked those aside with their heavy boots made of the skin of a walrus's throat, and then Kerick said: 'Let go!' and then the men clubbed the seals on the head as fast as they could.

Ten minutes later little Kotick did not recognize his friends any more, for their skins were ripped off from the nose to the hind flippers – whipped off and thrown down on the ground in a pile.

That was enough for Kotick. He turned and galloped (a seal can gallop very swiftly for a short time) back to the sea, his little new moustache bristling with horror. At Sea-Lion's Neck, where the great sea-lions sit on the edge of the surf, he flung himself flipper over head into the cool water, and rocked there, gasping miserably. 'What's here?' said a sea-lion gruffly; for as a rule the sea-lions keep themselves to themselves.

'*Scoochnie! Ochen scoochnie!* (I'm lonesome, very lonesome!)' said Kotick. 'They're killing all the holluschickie on *all* the beaches!'

The sea-lion turned his head inshore. 'Nonsense!' he said; 'your friends are making as much noise as ever. You must have seen old Kerick polishing off a drove. He's done that for thirty years.'

'It's horrible,' said Kotick, backing water as a wave went over him, and steadying himself with a screwstroke of his flippers that brought him up all standing within three inches of a jagged edge of rock.

'Well done for a yearling!' said the sea-lion, who could appreciate good swimming. 'I suppose it *is* rather awful from your way of looking at it; but if you seals will come here year after year, of course the men get to know of it, and unless you can find an island where no men ever come, you will always be driven.'

'Isn't there any such island?' began Kotick.

'I've followed the *poltoos* (the halibut) for twenty years, and I can't say I've found it yet. But look here – you seem to have a fondness for talking to your betters; suppose you go to Walrus Islet and talk to Sea Vitch. He may know something. Don't flounce off like that. It's a six-mile swim, and if I were you I should haul out and take a nap first, little one.'

Kotick thought that that was good advice, so he swam round to his own beach, hauled out, and slept for half an hour, twitching all over, as seals will. Then he headed straight for Walrus Islet, a little low sheet of rocky island almost due north-east from Novastoshnah, all ledges of rocks and gulls' nests, where the walrus herded by themselves.

He landed close to old Sea Vitch – the big, ugly, bloated, pimpled, fat-necked, longtusked walrus of the North Pacific, who has no manners except when he is asleep – as he was then, with his hind flippers half in and half out of the surf.

'Wake up!' barked Kotick, for the gulls were making a great noise.

'Hah! Ho! Hmph! What's that?' said Sea Vitch, and he struck the next walrus a blow with his tusks and woke him up, and the next struck the next, and so on till they were all awake and staring in every direction but the right one.

'Hi! It's me,' said Kotick, bobbing in the surf and looking like a little white slug.

'Well! May I be – skinned!' said Sea Vitch, and they all looked at Kotick as you can fancy a club full of drowsy old gentlemen would look at a little boy. Kotick did not care to hear any more about skinning just then; he had seen enough of it; so he called out: 'Isn't there any place for seals to go where men don't ever come?'

'Go and find out,' said Sea Vitch, shutting his eyes. 'Run away. We're busy here.'

Kotick made his dolphin-jump in the air and shouted as loud as he could: 'Clam-eater! Clam-eater!' He knew that Sea Vitch never caught a fish in his life, but always rooted for clams and seaweeds, though he pretended to be a very terrible person. Naturally the Chickies and the Gooverooskies and the Epatkas, the Burgomaster Gulls and the Kittiwakes and the Puffins, who were always looking for a chance to be rude, took up the cry, and – so Limmershin told me – for nearly five minutes you could not have heard a gun fired on Walrus Islet. All the population was yelling and screaming: 'Clam-eater! *Stareek!* (old man!)' while Sea Vitch rolled from side to side grunting and coughing.

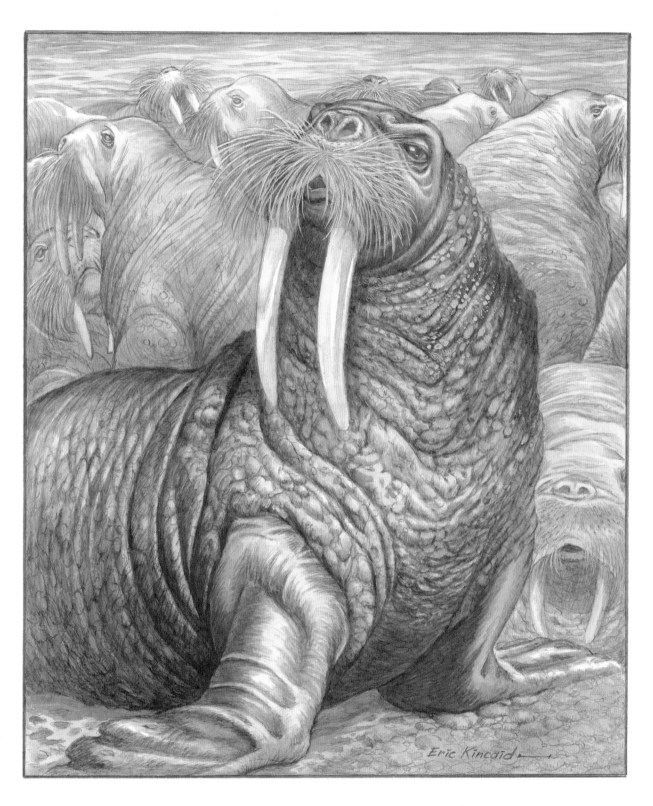

'Hah! Ho! Humph! What's that?' said Sea Vitch.

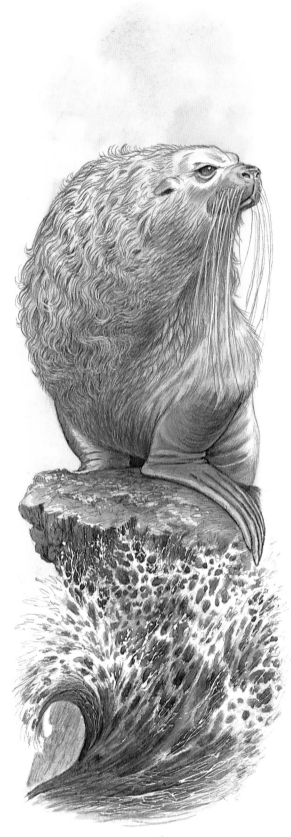

full-grown sea-catch, with a curly white mane on his shoulders, as heavy, as big, and as fierce as his father. 'Give me another season,' he said. 'Remember, mother, it is always the seventh wave that goes farthest up the beach.'

Curiously enough, there was another seal who thought that she would put off marrying till the next year, and Kotick danced the Fire-dance with her all down Lukannon Beach the night before he set off on his last exploration.

This time he went westward, because he had fallen on the trail of a great shoal of halibut, and he needed at least one hundred pounds of fish a day to keep him in good condition. He chased them till he was tired, and then he curled himself up and went to sleep on the hollows of the ground-swell that sets in to Copper Island. He knew the coast perfectly well, so about midnight, when he felt himself gently bumped on a weed-bed, he said, 'Hm, tide's running strong tonight,' and turning over underwater opened his eyes slowly and stretched. Then he jumped like a cat, for he saw huge things nosing about in the shoal water and browsing on the heavy fringes of the weeds.

'By the Great Combers of Magellan!' he said, beneath his moustache. 'Who in the Deep Sea are these people?'

They were like no walrus, sea-lion, seal, bear, whale, shark, fish, squid, or scallop that Kotick had ever seen before. They were between twenty and thirty feet long, and they had no hind flippers, but a shovel-like tail that looked as if it had been whittled out of wet leather. Their heads were the most foolish-looking things you ever saw, and they balanced on the ends of their tails in deep water when they weren't grazing, bowing solemnly to one another and waving their front flippers as a fat man waves his arm.

'Ahem!' said Kotick. 'Good sport, gentlemen?' The big things answered by bowing and waving their flippers like the Frog-Footman. When they began feeding again Kotick saw that their upper lip was split into two pieces that they could twitch apart about a foot and bring together again with a whole bushel of seaweed between the splits. They tucked the stuff into their mouths and chumped solemnly.

'Messy style of feeding, that,' said Kotick. They bowed again, and Kotick began to lose his temper. 'Very good,' he said. 'If you do happen to have an extra joint in your front flipper you needn't show off so. I see you bow gracefully, but I should like to know your names.' The split lips moved and twitched, and the glassy green eyes stared; but they did not speak.

'Well!' said Kotick. 'You're the only people I've ever met uglier than Sea Vitch – and with worse manners.'

Then he remembered in a flash what the Burgomaster Gull had screamed to him when he was a little yearling at Walrus Islet, and he tumbled backward in the water, for he knew that he had found Sea Cow at last.

The sea cows went on schlooping and grazing and chumping in the weed, and Kotick asked them questions in every language that he had picked up in his travels: and the Sea People talk nearly as many languages as human beings. But the Sea Cow did not answer, because Sea Cow cannot talk. He has only six bones in his neck where he ought to have seven, and they say under the sea that that prevents him from speaking even to his companions; but, as you know, he has an extra joint in his fore flipper, and by waving it up and down and about he makes a sort of clumsy telegraphic code.

By daylight Kotick's mane was standing on end and his temper was gone where the dead crabs go. Then the Sea Cow began to travel northward very slowly, stopping to hold absurd bowing councils from time to time, and Kotick followed them, saying to himself: 'People who are such idiots as these are would have been killed long ago if they hadn't found out some safe island; and what is good enough for the Sea Cow is good enough for the Sea Catch. All the same, I wish they'd hurry.'

It was weary work for Kotick. The herd never went more than forty or fifty miles a day, and stopped to feed at night, and kept close to the shore all the time; while Kotick swam round them, and over them, and under them, but he could not hurry them on one half-mile. As they went farther north they held a bowing council every few hours, and Kotick nearly bit off his moustache with impatience till he saw that they were following up a warm current of water, and then he respected them more.

One night they sank through the shiny water – sank like stones – and, for the first time since he had known them, began to swim quickly. Kotick followed, and the pace astonished him, for he never dreamed that Sea Cow was anything of a swimmer. They headed for a cliff by the shore – a cliff that ran down into deep water, and plunged into a dark hole at the foot of it, twenty fathoms under the sea. It was a long, long swim, and Kotick badly wanted fresh air before he was out of the dark tunnel that they led him through.

'My wig!' he said, when he rose, gasping and puffing, into open water at the farther end. 'It was a long dive, but it was worth it.'

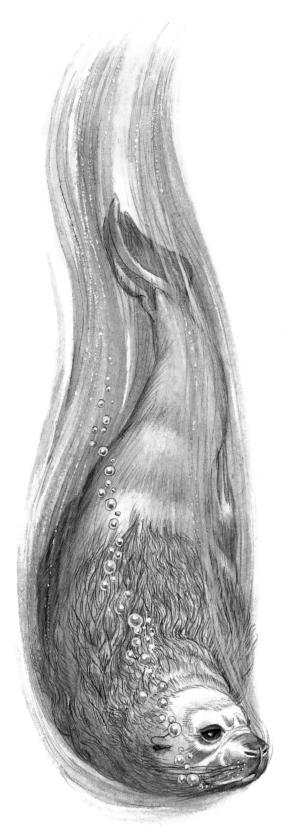

The sea cows had separated, and were browsing lazily along the edges of the finest beaches that Kotick had ever seen. There were long stretches of smooth-worn rock running for miles, exactly fitted to make seal-nurseries, and there were playgrounds of hard sand sloping inland behind them, and there were rollers for seals to dance in, and long grass to roll in, and sand-dunes to climb up and down; and, best of all, Kotick knew by the feel of the water, which never deceives a true Sea Catch, that no men had ever come there.

The first thing he did was to assure himself that the fishing was good, and then he swam along the beaches and counted up the delightful low sandy islands half hidden in the beautiful rolling fog. Away to the northward out to sea ran a line of bars and shoals and rocks that would never let a ship come within six miles of the beach; and between the islands and the mainland was a stretch of deep water that ran up to the perpendicular cliffs, and somewhere below the cliffs was the mouth of the tunnel.

'It's Novastoshnah over again, but ten times better,' said Kotick. 'Sea Cow must be wiser than I thought. Men can't come down the cliffs, even if there were any men; and the shoals to seaward would knock a ship to splinters. If any place in the sea is safe, this is it.'

He began to think of the seal he had left behind him, but though he was in a hurry to go back to Novastoshnah, he thoroughly explored the new country, so that he would be able to answer all questions.

Then he dived and made sure of the mouth of the tunnel, and raced through to the southward. No one but a sea cow or a seal would have dreamed of there being such a place, and when he looked back at the cliffs even Kotick could hardly believe that he had been under them.

He was six days going home, though he was not swimming slowly; and when he hauled out just above Sea-Lion's neck the first person he met was the seal who had been waiting for him, and she saw by the look in his eyes that he had found his island at last.

But the holluschickie and Sea Catch, his father, and all the other seals, laughed at him when he told them what he had discovered, and a young seal about his own age said: 'This is all very well, Kotick, but you can't come from no one knows where and order us off like this. Remember we've been fighting for our nurseries, and that's a thing you never did. You preferred prowling about in the sea.'

THE WHITE SEAL

The other seals laughed at this, and the young seal began twisting his head from side to side. He had just married that year, and was making a great fuss about it.

'I've no nursery to fight for,' said Kotick. 'I want only to show you all a place where you will be safe. What's the use of fighting?'

'Oh, if you're trying to back out, of course I've no more to say,' said the young seal, with an ugly chuckle.

'Will you come with me if I win?' said Kotick; and a green light came into his eyes, for he was very angry at having to fight at all.

'Very good,' said the young seal carelessly. '*If* you win, I'll come.'

He had no time to change his mind, for Kotick's head darted out and his teeth sank in the blubber of the young seal's neck. Then he threw himself back on his haunches and hauled his enemy down the beach, shook him, and knocked him over. Then Kotick roared to the seals: 'I've done my best for you these five seasons past. I've found you the island where you'll be safe, but unless your heads are dragged off your silly necks you won't believe. I'm going to teach you now. Look out for yourselves!'

Limmershin told me that never in his life – and Limmershin sees ten thousand big seals fighting every year – never in all his little life did he see anything like Kotick's charge into the nurseries. He flung himself at the biggest sea-catch he could find, caught him by the throat, choked him and bumped him and banged him till he grunted for mercy, and then threw him aside and attacked the next. You see, Kotick had never fasted for four months as the big seals did every year, and his deep-sea swimming trips kept him in perfect condition, and, best of all, he had never fought before. His curly white mane stood up with rage, and his eyes flamed, and his big dog-teeth glistened, and he was splendid to look at.

Old Sea Catch, his father, saw him tearing past, hauling the grizzled old seals about as though they had been halibut, and upsetting the young bachelors in all directions; and Sea Catch gave one roar and shouted: 'He may be a fool, but he is the best fighter on the Beaches. Don't tackle your father, my son! He's with you!'

Kotick roared in answer, and old Sea Catch waddled in, his moustache on end, blowing like a locomotive, while Matkah and the seal that was going to marry Kotick cowered down and admired their men-folk. It was a gorgeous fight, for the two fought as long as there was a seal that dared lift up his head, and then they paraded grandly up and down the beach side by side, bellowing.

At night, just as the Northern Lights were winking and flashing through the fog, Kotick climbed a bare rock and looked down on the scattered nurseries and the torn and bleeding seals. 'Now,' he said, 'I've taught you your lesson.'

'My wig!' said old Sea Catch, boosting himself up stiffly, for he was fearfully mauled. 'The Killer Whale himself could not have cut them up worse. Son, I'm proud of you, and what's more, I'll come with you to your islands – if there is such a place.'

'Here you, fat pigs of the sea! Who comes with me to the Sea Cow's tunnel? Answer, or I shall teach you again,' roared Kotick.

There was a murmur like the ripple of the tide all up and down the beaches. 'We will come,' said thousands of tired voices. 'We will follow Kotick, the White Seal.'

Then Kotick dropped his head between his shoulders and shut his eyes proudly. He was not a white seal any more, but red from head to tail. All the same, he would have scorned to look at or touch one of his wounds.

A week later he and his army (nearly ten thousand holluschickie and old seals) went away north to the Sea Cow's tunnel, Kotick leading them, and the seals that stayed at Novastoshnah called them idiots. But next spring, when they all met off the fishing-banks of the Pacific, Kotick's seals told such tales of the new beaches beyond Sea Cow's tunnel that more and more seals left Novastoshnah.

Of course it was not all done at once, for the seals need a long time to turn things over in their minds, but year by year more seals went away from Novastoshnah, and Lukannon, and the other nurseries, to the quiet, sheltered beaches where Kotick sits all the summer through, getting bigger and fatter and stronger each year, while the holluschickie play round him, in that sea where no man comes.

RIKKI-TIKKI-TAVI

At the hole where he went in
Red-Eye called to Wrinkle-Skin.
Hear what little Red-Eye saith:
'Nag, come up and dance with death!'

Eye to eye and head to head,
    (Keep the measure, Nag.)
This shall end when one is dead;
    (At thy pleasure, Nag.)
Turn for turn and twist for twist –
    (Run and hide thee, Nag.)
Hah! The hooded Death has missed!
    (Woe betide thee, Nag!)

This is the story of the great war that Rikki-tikki-tavi fought single-handed, through the bathrooms of the big bungalow in Segowlee cantonment. Darzee, the tailor-bird, helped him, and Chuchundra, the musk-rat, who never comes out into the middle of the floor, but always creeps round by the wall, gave him advice; but Rikki-tikki did the real fighting.

  He was a mongoose, rather like a little cat in his fur and his tail, but quite like a weasel in his head and his habits. His eyes and the end of his restless nose were pink; he could scratch himself anywhere he pleased, with any leg, front or back, that he chose to use; he could fluff up his tail till it looked like a bottle-brush, and his war-cry, as he scuttled through the long grass, was: *'Rikk-tikk-tikki-tikki-tchk!'*

One day, a high summer flood washed him out of the burrow where he lived with his father and mother, and carried him, kicking and clucking, down a roadside ditch. He found a little wisp of grass floating there, and clung to it till he lost his senses. When he revived, he was lying in the hot sun on the middle of a garden path, very draggled indeed, and a small boy was saying: 'Here's a dead mongoose. Let's have a funeral.'

'No,' said his mother. 'Let's take him in and dry him. Perhaps he isn't really dead.'

They took him into the house, and a big man picked him up between his finger and thumb, and said he was not dead but half choked; so they wrapped him in cotton-wool, and warmed him, and he opened his eyes and sneezed.

'Now,' said the big man (he was an Englishman who had just moved into the bungalow), 'don't frighten him, and we'll see what he'll do.'

It is the hardest thing in the world to frighten a mongoose, because he is eaten up from nose to tail with curiosity. The motto of all the mongoose family is, 'Run and find out;' and Rikki-tikki was a true mongoose. He looked at the cotton-wool, decided that it was not good to eat, ran all round the table, sat up and put his fur in order, scratched himself, and jumped on the small boy's shoulder.

'Don't be frightened, Teddy,' said his father. 'That's his way of making friends.'

'Ouch! He's tickling my chin,' said Teddy.

Rikki-tikki looked down between the boy's collar and neck, snuffed at his ear, and climbed down to the floor, where he sat rubbing his nose.

'Good gracious,' said Teddy's mother, 'and that's a wild creature! I suppose he's so tame because we've been kind to him.'

'All mongooses are like that,' said her husband. 'If Teddy doesn't pick him up by the tail, or try to put him in a cage, he'll run in and out of the house all day long. Let's give him something to eat.'

They gave him a little piece of raw meat. Rikki-tikki liked it immensely, and when it was finished he went out into the veranda and sat in the sunshine and fluffed up his fur to make it dry to the roots. Then he felt better.

'There are more things to find out about in this house,' he said to himself, 'than all my family could find out in all their lives. I shall certainly stay and find out.'

RIKKI-TIKKI-TAVI

He spent all that day roaming over the house. He nearly
drowned himself in the bathtubs, put his nose into the ink on a
writing-table, and burnt it on the end of the big man's cigar, for
he climbed up in the big man's lap to see how writing was done.
At nightfall he ran into Teddy's nursery to watch how kerosene-
lamps were lighted, and when Teddy went to bed Rikki-tikki
climbed up too; but he was a restless companion, because he had
to get up and attend to every noise all through the night, and find
out what made it. Teddy's mother and father came in, the last
thing, to look at their boy, and Rikki-tikki was awake on the
pillow. 'I don't like that,' said Teddy's mother; 'he may bite the
child.'

'He'll do no such thing,' said the father. 'Teddy's safer with
that little beast than if he had a bloodhound to watch him. If a
snake came into the nursery now.'

But Teddy's mother wouldn't think of anything so awful.

Early in the morning Rikki-tikki came to early breakfast in the
veranda riding on Teddy's shoulder, and they gave him banana
and some boiled egg; and he sat on all their laps one after the
other, because every well-brought-up mongoose always hopes to
be a house-mongoose some day and have rooms to run about in,
and Rikki-tikki's mother (she used to live in the General's house
at Segowlee) had carefully told Rikki what to do if ever he came
across white men.

Then Rikki-tikki went out into the garden to see what was to be
seen. It was a large garden, only half cultivated, with bushes as
big as summer-houses of Marshal Niel roses, lime and orange
trees, clumps of bamboos, and thickets of high grass. Rikki-tikki
licked his lips. 'This is a splendid hunting-ground,' he said, and
his tail grew bottle-brushy at the thought of it, and he scuttled up
and down the garden, snuffing here and there till he heard very
sorrowful voices in a thorn-bush.

It was Darzee, the tailor-bird, and his wife. They had made a
beautiful nest by pulling two big leaves together and stitching
them up the edges with fibres, and had filled the hollow with
cotton and downy fluff. The nest swayed to and fro, as they sat on
the rim and cried.

'What is the matter?' asked Rikki-tikki.

'We are very miserable,' said Darzee. 'One of our babies fell
out of the nest yesterday, and Nag ate him.'

'H'm!' said Rikki-tikki, 'that is very sad – but I am a stranger
here. Who is Nag?'

Darzee and his wife only cowered down in the nest without

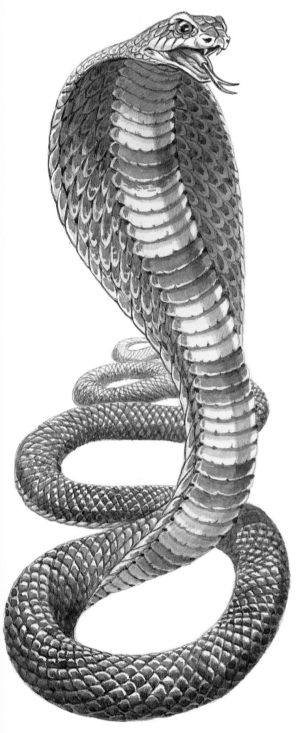

answering, for from the thick grass at the foot of the bush there came a low hiss – a horrid cold sound that made Rikki-tikki jump back two clear feet. Then inch by inch out of the grass rose up the head and spread hood of Nag, the big black cobra, and he was five feet long from tongue to tail. When he had lifted one-third of himself clear of the ground, he stayed balancing to and fro exactly as a dandelion-tuft balances in the wind, and he looked at Rikki-tikki with the wicked snake's eyes that never change their expression, whatever the snake may be thinking of.

'Who is Nag?' said he. '*I* am Nag. The great god Brahm put his mark upon all our people when the first cobra spread his hood to keep the sun off Brahm as he slept. Look, and be afraid!'

He spread out his hood more than ever, and Rikki-tikki saw the spectacle-mark on the back of it that looks exactly like the eye part of a hook and eye fastening. He was afraid for the minute; but it is impossible for a mongoose to stay frightened for any length of time, and though Rikki-tikki had never met a live cobra before, his mother had fed him on dead ones, and he knew that all a grown mongoose's business in life was to fight and eat snakes. Nag knew that too, and at the bottom of his cold heart he was afraid.

'Well,' said Rikki-tikki, and his tail began to fluff up again, 'marks or no marks, do you think it is right for you to eat fledgelings out of a nest?'

Nag was thinking to himself, and watching the least little movement in the grass behind Rikki-tikki. He knew that mongooses in the garden meant death sooner or later for him and his family, but he wanted to get Rikki-tikki off his guard. So he dropped his head a little, and put it on one side.

'Let us talk,' he said. 'You eat eggs. Why should not I eat birds?'

'Behind you! Look behind you!' sang Darzee.

Rikki-tikki knew better than to waste time in staring. He jumped up in the air as high as he could go, and just under him whizzed by the head of Nagaina, Nag's wicked wife. She had crept up behind him as he was talking, to make an end of him; and he heard her savage hiss as the stroke missed. He came down almost across her back, and if he had been an old mongoose he would have known that then was the time to break her back with one bite; but he was afraid of the terrible lashing return-stroke of the cobra. He bit, indeed, but did not bite long enough, and he jumped clear of the whisking tail, leaving Nagaina torn and angry.

'*Behind you! Look behind you!*' sang Darzee.

'Wicked, wicked Darzee!' said Nag, lashing up as high as he could reach toward the nest in the thorn-bush; but Darzee had built it out of reach of snakes, and it only swayed to and fro.

Rikki-tikki felt his eyes growing red and hot (when a mongoose's eyes grow red, he is angry), and he sat back on his tail and hind legs like a little kangaroo, and looked all round him, and chattered with rage. But Nag and Nagaina had disappeared into the grass. When a snake misses its stroke, it never says anything or gives any sign of what it means to do next. Rikki-tikki did not care to follow them, for he did not feel sure that he could manage two snakes at once. So he trotted off to the gravel path near the house, and sat down to think. It was a serious matter for him.

If you read the old books of natural history, you will find they say that when the mongoose fights the snake and happens to get bitten, he runs off and eats some herb that cures him. That is not true. The victory is only a matter of quickness of eye and quickness of foot – snake's blow against mongoose's jump – and as no eye can follow the motion of a snake's head when it strikes, that makes things much more wonderful than any magic herb. Rikki-tikki knew he was a young mongoose, and it made him all the more pleased to think that he had managed to escape a blow from behind. It gave him confidence in himself, and when Teddy came running down the path, Rikki-tikki was ready to be petted.

But just as Teddy was stooping, something flinched a little in the dust, and a tiny voice said: 'Be careful. I am death!' It was Karait, the dusty brown snakeling that lies for choice on the dusty earth; and his bite is as dangerous as the cobra's. But he is so small that nobody thinks of him, and so he does the more harm to people.

Rikki-tikki's eyes grew red again, and he danced up to Karait with the peculiar rocking, swaying motion that he had inherited from his family. It looks very funny, but it is so perfectly balanced a gait that you can fly off from it at any angle you please; and in dealing with snakes this is an advantage. If Rikki-tikki had only known, he was doing a much more dangerous thing than fighting Nag, for Karait is so small, and can turn so quickly, that unless Rikki bit him close to the back of the head, he would get the return-stroke in his eye or lip. But Rikki did not know; his eyes were all red, and he rocked back and forth, looking for a good place to hold. Karait struck out. Rikki jumped sideways and tried to run in, but the wicked little dusty grey head lashed within a fraction of his shoulder, and he had to jump over the body, and the head followed his heels close.

Teddy shouted to the house: 'Oh, look here! Our mongoose is killing a snake;' and Rikki-tikki heard a scream from Teddy's mother. His father ran out with a stick, but by the time he came up, Karait had lunged out once too far, and Rikki-tikki had sprung, jumped on the snake's back, dropped his head far between his forelegs, bitten as high up the back as he could get hold, and rolled away. That bite paralysed Karait, and Rikki-tikki was just going to eat him up from the tail, after the custom of his family at dinner, when he remembered that a full meal makes a slow mongoose, and if he wanted all his strength and quickness ready, he must keep himself thin.

He went away for a dust-bath under the castor-oil bushes, while Teddy's father beat the dead Karait. 'What is the use of that?' thought Rikki-tikki. 'I have settled it all;' and then Teddy's mother picked him up from the dust and hugged him, crying that he had saved Teddy from death, and Teddy's father said that he was a providence, and Teddy looked on with big scared eyes. Rikki-tikki was rather amused at all the fuss, which, of course, he did not understand. Teddy's mother might just as well have petted Teddy for playing in the dust. Rikki was thoroughly enjoying himself.

That night, at dinner, walking to and fro among the wine-glasses on the table, he could have stuffed himself three times over with nice things; but he remembered Nag and Nagaina, and though it was very pleasant to be patted and petted by Teddy's mother, and to sit on Teddy's shoulder, his eyes would get red from time to time, and he would go off into his long war-cry of *'Rikk-tikk-tikki-tikki-tchk!'*

Teddy carried him off to bed, and insisted on Rikki-tikki sleeping under his chin. Rikki-tikki was too well-bred to bite or scratch, but as soon as Teddy was asleep he went off for his nightly walk round the house, and in the dark he ran up against Chuchundra, the musk-rat, creeping round by the wall. Chuchundra is a broken-hearted little beast. He whimpers and cheeps all the night, trying to make up his mind to run into the middle of the room, but he never gets there.

'Don't kill me,' said Chuchundra, almost weeping. 'Rikki-tikki, don't kill me.'

'Do you think a snake-killer kills musk-rats?' said Rikki-tikki scornfully.

'Those who kill snakes get killed by snakes,' said Chuchundra, more sorrowfully than ever. 'And how am I to be sure that Nag

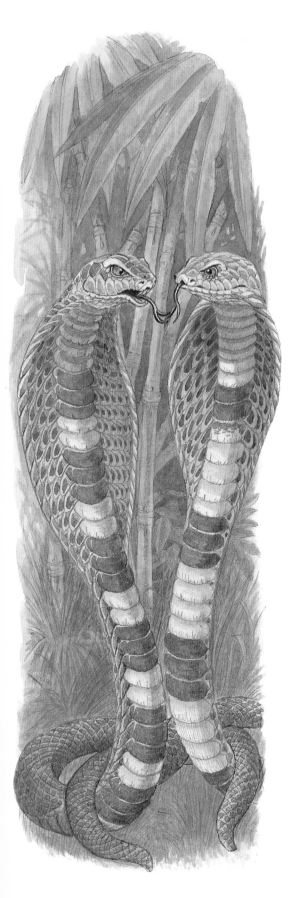

won't mistake me for you some dark night?'

'There's not the least danger,' said Rikki-tikki; 'but Nag is in the garden, and I know you don't go there.'

'My cousin Chua, the rat, told me,' said Chuchundra, and then he stopped.

'Told you what?'

'H'sh! Nag is everywhere, Rikki-tikki. You should have talked to Chua in the garden.'

'I didn't – so you must tell me. Quick, Chuchundra, or I'll bite you!'

Chuchundra sat down and cried till the tears rolled off his whiskers. 'I am a very poor man,' he sobbed. 'I never had spirit enough to run out into the middle of the room. H'sh! I mustn't tell you anything. Can't you *hear*, Rikki-tikki?'

Rikki-tikki listened. The house was as still as still, but he thought he could just catch the faintest *scratch-scratch* in the world – a noise as faint as that of a wasp walking on a window-pane – the dry scratch of a snake's scales on brickwork.

'That's Nag or Nagaina,' he said to himself; 'and he is crawling into the bathroom sluice. You're right, Chuchundra; I should have talked to Chua.'

He stole off to Teddy's bathroom, but there was nothing there, and then to Teddy's mother's bathroom. At the bottom of the smooth plaster wall there was a brick pulled out to make a sluice for the bathwater, and as Rikki-tikki stole in by the masonry curb where the bath is put, he heard Nag and Nagaina whispering together outside in the moonlight.

'When the house is emptied of people,' said Nagaina to her husband, '*he* will have to go away, and then the garden will be our own again. Go in quietly, and remember that the big man who killed Karait is the first one to bite. Then come out and tell me, and we will hunt for Rikki-tikki together.'

'But are you sure that there is anything to be gained by killing the people?' said Nag.

'Everything. When there were no people in the bungalow, did we have any mongoose in the garden? So long as the bungalow is empty, we are king and queen of the garden; and remember that as soon as our eggs in the melon-bed hatch (as they may tomorrow), our children will need room and quiet.'

'I had not thought of that,' said Nag. 'I will go, but there is no need that we should hunt for Rikki-tikki afterwards. I will kill the big man and his wife, and the child if I can, and come away quietly. Then the bungalow will be empty, and Rikki-tikki will go.'

*Chuchundra sat down and cried till the tears
rolled off his whiskers.*

strikes nearly all day. She hid them there weeks ago.'

'And you never thought it worth while to tell me? The end nearest the wall, you said?'

'Rikki-tikki, you are not going to eat her eggs?'

'Not eat exactly; no. Darzee, if you have a grain of sense you will fly off to the stables and pretend that your wing is broken, and let Nagaina chase you away to this bush. I must get to the melon-bed, and if I went there now she'd see me.'

Darzee was a feather-brained little fellow who could never hold more than one idea at a time in his head; and just because he knew that Nagaina's children were born in eggs like his own, he didn't think at first that it was fair to kill them. But his wife was a sensible bird, and she knew that cobra's eggs meant young cobras later on; so she flew off from the nest, and left Darzee to keep the babies warm, and continue his song about the death of Nag. Darzee was very like a man in some ways.

She fluttered in front of Nagaina by the rubbish-heap, and cried out: 'Oh, my wing is broken! The boy in the house threw a stone at me and broke it.' Then she fluttered more desperately than ever.

Nagaina lifted up her head and hissed: 'You warned Rikki-tikki when I would have killed him. Indeed and truly, you've chosen a bad place to be lame in.' And she moved toward Darzee's wife, slipping along over the dust.

'The boy broke it with a stone!' shrieked Darzee's wife.

'Well, it may be some consolation to you when you're dead to know that I shall settle accounts with the boy. My husband lies on the rubbish-heap this morning, but before night the boy in the house will lie very still. What is the use of running away? I am sure to catch you. Little fool, look at me!'

Darzee's wife knew better than to do *that*, for a bird who looks at a snake's eyes gets so frightened that she cannot move. Darzee's wife fluttered on, piping sorrowfully, and never leaving the ground, and Nagaina quickened her pace.

Rikki-tikki heard them going up the path from the stables, and he raced for the end of the melon-patch near the wall. There, in the warm litter about the melons, very cunningly hidden, he found twenty-five eggs, about the size of a bantam's eggs, but with whitish skin instead of shell.

'I was not a day too soon,' he said; for he could see the baby cobras curled up inside the skin, and he knew that the minute they were hatched they could each kill a man or a mongoose. He bit off the tops of the eggs as fast as he could, taking care to crush

Nagaina lifted up her head and hissed:
'You warned Rikki-tikki when I would have killed him.'

moist earth.

Then the grass by the mouth of the hole stopped waving, and Darzee said: 'It is all over with Rikki-tikki! We must sing his death-song. Valiant Rikki-tikki is dead! For Nagaina will surely kill him underground.'

So he sang a very mournful song that he made up on the spur of the minute, and just as he got to the most touching part the grass quivered again, and Rikki-tikki, covered with dirt, dragged himself out of the hole leg by leg, licking his whiskers. Darzee stopped with a little shout. Rikki-tikki shook some of the dust out of his fur and sneezed. 'It is all over,' he said. 'The widow will never come out again.' And the red ants that live between the grass-stems heard him, and began to troop down one after another to see if he had spoken the truth.

Rikki-tikki curled himself up in the grass and slept where he was – slept and slept till it was late in the afternoon, for he had done a hard day's work.

'Now,' he said, when he awoke, 'I will go back to the house. Tell the Coppersmith, Darzee, and he will tell the garden that Nagaina is dead.'

The Coppersmith is a bird who makes a noise exactly like the beating of a little hammer on a copper pot; and the reason he is always making it is because he is the town-crier to every Indian garden, and tells all the news to everybody who cares to listen. As Rikki-tikki went up the path, he heard his 'attention' notes like a tiny dinner-gong; and then the steady *'Ding-dong-tock!* Nag is dead – *dong!* Nagaina is dead! *Ding-dong-tock!'* That set all the birds in the garden singing, and the frogs croaking; for Nag and Nagaina used to eat frogs as well as little birds.

When Rikki got to the house, Teddy and Teddy's mother (she still looked very white, for she had been fainting) and Teddy's father came out and almost cried over him; and that night he ate all that was given him till he could eat no more, and went to bed on Teddy's shoulder, where Teddy's mother saw him when she came to look late at night.

'He saved our lives and Teddy's life,' she said to her husband. 'Just think, he saved all our lives!'

Rikki-tikki woke up with a jump, for all the mongooses are light sleepers.

'Oh, it's you,' said he. 'What are you bothering for? All the cobras are dead; and if they weren't, I'm here.'

Rikki-tikki had a right to be proud of himself; but he did not grow too proud, and he kept that garden as a mongoose should keep it, with tooth and jump and spring and bite, till never a cobra dared show its head inside the walls.

TOOMAI OF THE ELEPHANTS

I will remember what I was. I am sick of rope and chain.
  I will remember my old strength and all my forest affairs.
I will not sell my back to man for a bundle of sugar-cane,
  I will go out to my own kind, and the wood-folk in their lairs.

I will go out until the day, until the morning break,
  Out to the winds' untainted kiss, the waters' clean caress:
I will forget my ankle-ring and snap my picket-stake.
  I will revisit my lost loves, and playmates masterless!

Kala Nag, which means Black Snake, had served the Indian
Government in every way that an elephant could serve it for
forty-seven years, and as he was fully twenty years old when he
was caught, that makes him nearly seventy – a ripe age for an
elephant. He remembered pushing, with a big leather pad on his
forehead, at a gun stuck in deep mud, and that was before the
Afghan War of 1842, and he had not then come to his full
strength. His mother, Radha Pyari – Radha the darling – who had
been caught in the same drive with Kala Nag, told him, before his
little milk-tusks had dropped out, that elephants who were afraid
always got hurt; and Kala Nag knew that that advice was good,

for the first time that he saw a shell burst he backed, screaming, into a stand of piled rifles, and the bayonets pricked him in all his softest places. So before he was twenty-five he gave up being afraid, and so he was the best-loved and the best-looked-after elephant in the service of the Government of India. He had carried tents, twelve hundred pounds' weight of tents, on the march in Upper India; he had been hoisted into a ship at the end of a steam-crane and taken for days across the water, and made to carry a mortar on his back in a strange and rocky country very far from India, and had seen the Emperor Theodore lying dead in Magdala, and had come back again in the steamer, entitled, so the soldiers said, to the Abyssinian War medal. He had seen his fellow-elephants die of cold and epilepsy and starvation and sunstroke up at a place called Ali Musjid, ten years later; and afterwards he had been sent down thousands of miles south to haul and pile big baulks of teak in the timber-yards at Moulmein. There he had half killed an insubordinate young elephant who was shirking his fair share of the work.

After that he was taken off timber-hauling, and employed, with a few score other elephants who were trained to the business, in helping to catch wild elephants among the Garo hills. Elephants are very strictly preserved by the Indian Government. There is one whole department which does nothing else but hunt them, and catch them, and break them in, and send them up and down the country as they are needed for work.

Kala Nag stood ten fair feet at the shoulders, and his tusks had been cut off short at five feet, and bound round the ends, to prevent them splitting, with bands of copper; but he could do more with those stumps than any untrained elephant could do with the real sharpened ones.

When, after weeks and weeks of cautious driving of scattered elephants across the hills, the forty or fifty wild monsters were driven into the last stockade, and the big drop-gate, made of tree-trunks lashed together, jarred down behind them, Kala Nag, at the word of command, would go into that flaring, trumpeting pandemonium (generally at night, when the flicker of the torches made it difficult to judge distances), and, picking out the biggest and wildest tusker of the mob, would hammer him and hustle him into quiet while the men on the backs of the other elephants roped and tied the smaller ones.

There was nothing in the way of fighting that Kala Nag, the old wise Black Snake, did not know, for he had stood up more than once in his time to the charge of the wounded tiger, and, curling

*There was nothing in the way of fighting that Kala Nag,
the old wise Black Snake, did not know.*

up his soft trunk to be out of harm's way, had knocked the springing brute sideways in mid-air with a quick sickle-cut of his head, that he had invented all by himself; had knocked him over, and kneeled upon him with his huge knees till the life went out with a gasp and a howl, and there was only a fluffy striped thing on the ground for Kala Nag to pull by the tail.

'Yes,' said Big Toomai, his driver, the son of Black Toomai who had taken him to Abyssinia, and grandson of Toomai of the Elephants who had seen him caught, 'there is nothing that the Black Snake fears except me. He has seen three generations of us feed him and groom him, and he will live to see four.'

'He is afraid of *me* also,' said Little Toomai, standing up to his full height of four feet, with only one rag upon him. He was ten years old, the eldest son of Big Toomai, and, according to custom, he would take his father's place on Kala Nag's neck when he grew up, and would handle the heavy iron ankus, the elephant-goad that had been worn smooth by his father, and his grandfather, and his great-grandfather. He knew what he was talking of; for he had been born under Kala Nag's shadow, had played with the end of his trunk before he could walk, had taken him down to water as soon as he could walk, and Kala Nag would no more have dreamed of disobeying his shrill little orders than he would have dreamed of killing him on that day when Big Toomai carried the little brown baby under Kala Nag's tusks, and told him to salute his master that was to be.

'Yes,' said Little Toomai, 'he is afraid of *me*,' and he took long strides up to Kala Nag, called him a fat old pig, and made him lift up his feet one after the other.

'Wah!' said Little Toomai, 'you are a big elephant,' and he wagged his fluffy head, quoting his father. 'The Government may pay for elephants, but they belong to us mahouts. When you are old, Kala Nag, there will come some rich raja, and he will buy you from the Government, on account of your size and your manners, and then you will have nothing to do but to carry gold earrings in your ears, and a gold howdah on your back, and a red cloth covered with gold on your sides, and walk at the head of the processions of the King. Then I shall sit on your neck, Oh Kala Nag, with a silver ankus, and men will run before us with golden sticks, crying, "Room for the King's elephant!" That will be good, Kala Nag, but not so good as this hunting in the jungles.'

'Umph!' said Big Toomai. 'You are a boy, and as wild as a buffalo-calf. This running up and down among the hills is not the best Government service. I am getting old, and I do not love wild elephants. Give me brick elephant-lines, one stall to each elephant, and big stumps to tie them to safely, and flat, broad roads to exercise upon, instead of this come-and-go camping. Aha, the Cawnpore barracks were good. There was a bazaar close by, and only three hours' work a day.'

Little Toomai remembered the Cawnpore elephant-lines and said nothing. He very much preferred the camp life, and hated those broad, flat roads, with the daily grubbing for grass in the forage-reserve, and the long hours when there was nothing to do except to watch Kala Nag fidgeting in his pickets.

What Little Toomai liked was the scramble up bridlepaths that only an elephant could take; the dip into the valley below; the glimpses of the wild elephants browsing miles away; the rush of the frightened pig and peacock under Kala Nag's feet; the blinding warm rains, when all the hills and valleys smoked; the beautiful misty mornings when nobody knew where they would camp that night; the steady, cautious drive of the wild elephants, and the mad rush and blaze and hullabaloo of the last night's drive, when the elephants poured into the stockade like boulders in a landslide, found that they could not get out, and flung themselves at the heavy posts only to be driven back by yells and flaring torches and volleys of blank cartridge.

Even a little boy could be of use there, and Toomai was as useful as three boys. He would get his torch and wave it, and yell with the best. But the really good time came when the driving out began, and the Keddah – that is, the stockade – looked like a picture of the end of the world, and men had to make signs to one another, because they could not hear themselves speak. Then Little Toomai would climb up to the top of one of the quivering stockade-posts, his sun-bleached brown hair flying loose all over his shoulders, and he looking like a goblin in the torchlight; and as soon as there was a lull you could hear his high-pitched yells of encouragement to Kala Nag, above the trumpeting and crashing, and snapping of ropes, and groans of the tethered elephants. '*Maîl, maîl, Kala Nag!* (Go on, go on, Black Snake!) *Dant do!* (Give him the tusk!) *Somalo! Somalo!* (Careful, careful!) *Maro! Mar!* (Hit him, hit him!) Mind the post! *Arré! Arré! Hai! Yai! Kya-a-ah!*' he would shout, and the big fight between Kala Nag and the wild elephant would sway to and fro across the Keddah, and the old elephant-catchers would wipe the sweat out of their eyes, and find time to nod to Little Toomai wriggling with joy on the top of the posts.

He did more than wriggle. One night he slid down from the

post and slipped in between the elephants, and threw up the loose end of a rope, which had dropped, to a driver who was trying to get a purchase on the leg of a kicking young calf (calves always give more trouble than full-grown animals). Kala Nag saw him, caught him in his trunk, and handed him up to Big Toomai, who slapped him then and there, and put him back on the post.

Next morning he gave him a scolding, and said: 'Aren't good brick elephant-lines and a little tent-carrying enough? Do you have to go elephant-catching on your own account, little worthless? Now those foolish hunters, whose pay is less than my pay, have spoken to Petersen Sahib of the matter.' Little Toomai was frightened. He did not know much of white men, but Petersen Sahib was the greatest white man in the world to him. He was the head of all the Keddah operations – the man who caught all the elephants for the Government of India, and who knew more about the ways of elephants than any living man.

'What – what will happen?' said Little Toomai.

'Happen! The worst that can happen. Petersen Sahib is a madman. Else why should he go hunting these wild devils? He may even want you to be an elephant-catcher, to sleep anywhere in these fever-filled jungles, and at last to be trampled to death in the Keddah. It is well that this nonsense ends safely. Next week the catching is over, and we of the plains are sent back to our stations. Then we will march on smooth roads, and forget all this hunting. But, son, I am angry that you meddle in the business that belongs to these dirty Assamese jungle-folk. Kala Nag will obey none but me, so I must go with him into the Keddah; but he is only a fighting elephant, and he does not help to rope them. So I sit at my ease, as befits a mahout – not a mere hunter – a mahout, I say, and a man who gets a pension at the end of his service. Is the family of Toomai of the Elephants to be trodden underfoot in the dirt of a Keddah? Bad one! Wicked one! Worthless son! Go and wash Kala Nag and attend to his ears, and see that there are no thorns in his feet; or else Petersen Sahib will surely catch you and make you a wild hunter – a follower of elephants' foot-tracks, a jungle-bear. Bah! Shame! Go!'

Little Toomai went off without saying a word, but he told Kala Nag all his grievances while he was examining his feet. 'No matter,' said Little Toomai, turning up the fringe of Kala Nag's huge right ear. 'They have said my name to Petersen Sahib, and perhaps – and perhaps – and perhaps – who knows? Hai! That is a big thorn that I have pulled out!'

The next few days were spent in getting the elephants together,

in walking the newly caught wild elephants up and down between a couple of tame ones, to prevent them from giving too much trouble on the downward march to the plains, and in taking stock of the blankets and ropes and things that had been worn out or lost in the forest.

Petersen Sahib came in on his clever she-elephant Pudmini. He had been paying off other camps among the hills, for the season was coming to an end, and there was a native clerk sitting at a table under a tree to pay the drivers their wages. As each man was paid he went back to his elephant, and joined the line that stood ready to start. The catchers, and hunters, and beaters, the men of the regular Keddah, who stayed in the jungle year in and year out, sat on the backs of the elephants that belonged to Petersen Sahib's permanent force, or leaned against the trees with their guns across their arms, and made fun of the drivers who were going away, and laughed when the newly caught elephants broke the line and ran about.

Big Toomai went up to the clerk with Little Toomai behind him, and Machua Appa, the head-tracker, said in an undertone to a friend of his, 'There goes one piece of good elephant-stuff at least. 'Tis a pity to send that young jungle-cock to moult in the plains.'

Now Petersen Sahib had ears all over him, as a man must have who listens to the most silent of all living things – the wild elephant. He turned where he was lying all along on Pudmini's back, and said, 'What is that? I did not know of a man among the plains-drivers who had wit enough to rope even a dead elephant.'

'This is not a man, but a boy. He went into the Keddah at the last drive, and threw Barmao there the rope when we were trying to get that young calf with the blotch on his shoulder away from his mother.'

Machua Appa pointed at Little Toomai, and Petersen Sahib looked, and Little Toomai bowed to the earth.

'He throw a rope? He is smaller than a picket-pin. Little one, what is your name?' said Petersen Sahib.

Little Toomai was too frightened to speak, but Kala Nag was behind him, and Toomai made a sign with his hand, and the elephant caught him up in his trunk and held him level with Pudmini's forehead, in front of the great Petersen Sahib. Then Little Toomai covered his face with his hands, for he was only a child, and except where elephants were concerned; he was just as bashful as a child could be.

'Oho!' said Petersen Sahib, smiling underneath his moustache,

'and why did you teach your elephant *that* trick? Was it to help you steal green corn from the roofs of the houses when the ears are put out to dry?'

'Not green corn, Protector of the Poor – melons,' said Little Toomai, and all the men sitting about broke into a roar of laughter. Most of them had taught their elephants that trick when they were boys. Little Toomai was hanging eight feet up in the air, and he wished very much that were eight feet underground.

'He is Toomai, my son, Sahib,' said Big Toomai, scowling. 'He is a very bad boy, and he will end in a jail, Sahib.'

'Of that I have my doubts,' said Petersen Sahib. 'A boy who can face a full Keddah at his age does not end in jails. See, little one, here are four annas to spend in sweetmeats because you have a little head under that great thatch of hair. In time you may become a hunter, too.' Big Toomai scowled more than ever. 'Remember, though, that Keddahs are not good for children to play in.' Petersen Sahib went on.

'Must I never go there, Sahib?' asked Little Toomai, with a big gasp.

'Yes.' Petersen Sahib smiled again. 'When you have seen the elephants dance. That is the proper time. Come to me when you have seen the elephants dance, and then I will let you go into all the Keddahs.'

There was another roar of laughter, for that is an old joke among elephant-catchers, and it means just never. There are great cleared flat places hidden away in the forests that are called elephants' ballrooms, but even these are only found by accident, and no man has ever seen the elephants dance. When a driver boasts of his skill and bravery the other drivers say, 'And when did you see the elephants dance?'

Kala Nag put Little Toomai down, and he bowed to the earth again and went away with his father, and gave the silver four-anna piece to his mother, who was nursing his baby brother, and they all were put up on Kala Nag's back, and the line of grunting, squealing elephants rolled down the hill-path to the plains. It was a very lively march on account of the new elephants, who gave trouble at every ford, and who needed coaxing or beating every other minute.

Big Toomai prodded Kala Nag spitefully, for he was very angry, but Little Toomai was too happy to speak. Petersen Sahib had noticed him, and given him money, so he felt as a private soldier would feel if he had been called out of the ranks and praised by his commander-in-chief.

'What did Petersen Sahib mean by the elephant-dance?' he said, at last, softly to his mother.

Big Toomai heard him and grunted. 'That you should never be one of these hill-buffaloes of trackers. *That* was what he meant. Oh, you in front, what is blocking the way?'

An Assamese driver, two or three elephants ahead, turned round angrily, crying: 'Bring up Kala Nag, and knock this youngster of mine into good behaviour. Why should Petersen Sahib have chosen *me* to go down with you donkeys of the rice-fields? Lay your beast alongside, Toomai, and let him prod with his tusks. By all the gods of the Hills, these new elephants are possessed, or else they can smell their companions in the jungle.'

Kala Nag hit the new elephant in the ribs and knocked the wind out of him, as Big Toomai said, 'We have swept the hills of wild elephants at the last catch. It is only your carelessness in driving. Must I keep order along the whole line?'

'Hear him!' said the other driver. '*We* have swept the hills! Ho! ho! You are very wise, you plainspeople. Anyone but a mud-head who never saw the jungle would know that *they* know that the drives are ended for the season. Therefore all the wild elephants tonight will – but why should I waste wisdom on a river-turtle?'

'What will they do?' Little Toomai called out.

'*Ohé*, little one. Are you there? Well, I will tell you, for you have a cool head. They will dance, and therefore your father, who has swept *all* the hills of *all* the elephants, will have to double-chain his pickets tonight.'

'What talk is this?' said Big Toomai. 'For forty years, father and son, we have tended elephants, and we have never heard such moonshine about dances.'

'Yes; but a plains-man who lives in a hut knows only the four walls of his hut. Well, leave your elephants unshackled tonight and see what comes; as for their dancing, I have seen the place where – *Bapree-Bap!* how many windings has the Dihang River? Here is another ford, and we must swim the calves. Stop still, you behind there.'

And in this way, talking and wrangling and splashing through the rivers, they made their first march to a sort of receiving-camp for the new elephants; but they lost their tempers long before they got there.

Then the elephants were chained by their hind legs to their big stumps of pickets, and extra ropes were fitted to the new elephants, and the fodder was piled before them, and the hill-drivers went back to Petersen Sahib through the afternoon light,

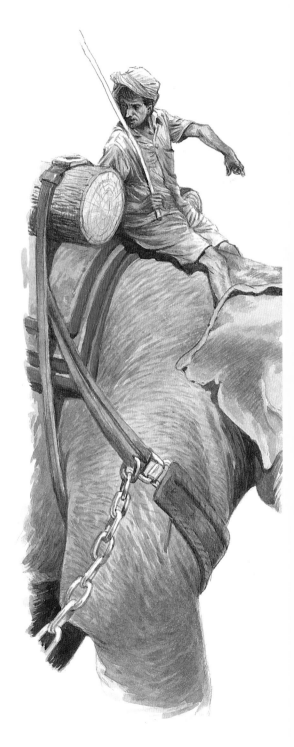

telling the plains-drivers to be extra careful that night, and laughing when the plains-drivers asked the reason.

Little Toomai attended to Kala Nag's supper, and as evening fell wandered through the camp, unspeakably happy, in search of a tom-tom. When an Indian child's heart is full, he does not run about and make a noise in an irregular fashion. He sits down to a sort of revel all by himself. And Little Toomai had been spoken to by Petersen Sahib! If he had not found what he wanted, I believe he would have burst. But the sweetmeat-seller in the camp lent him a little tom-tom – a drum beaten with the flat of the hand – and he sat down, cross-legged, before Kala Nag as the stars began to come out, the tom-tom in his lap, and he thumped and he thumped and he thumped, and the more he thought of the great honour that had been done to him, the more he thumped, all alone among the elephant-fodder. There was no tune and no words, but the thumping made him happy.

The new elephants strained at their ropes, and squealed and trumpeted from time to time, and he could hear his mother in the camp hut putting his small brother to sleep with an old, old song about the great God Shiv, who once told all the animals what they should eat. It is a very soothing lullaby, and the first verse says:

Shiv, who poured the harvest and made the winds to blow,
Sitting at the doorways of a day of long ago,
Gave to each his portion, food and toil and fate,
From the King upon the *guddee* to the Beggar at the gate.
    All things made he – Shiva the Preserver.
    Mahadeo! Mahadeo! He made all –
    Thorn for the camel, fodder for the kine,
    And mother's heart for sleepy head, Oh little son of mine!

Little Toomai came in with a joyous *tunk-a-tunk* at the end of each verse, till he felt sleepy and stretched himself on the fodder at Kala Nag's side.

At last the elephants began to lie down one after another, as is their custom, till only Kala Nag at the right of the line was left standing up; and he rocked slowly from side to side, his ears put forward to listen to the night wind as it blew very slowly across the hills. The air was full of all the night noises that, taken together, make one big silence – the click of one bamboo-stem against the other, the rustle of something alive in the undergrowth, the scratch and squawk of a half-waked bird (birds are awake in the night much more often than we imagine), and

*He sat down, cross-legged, before Kala Nag
as the stars began to come out.*

the fall of water ever so far away. Little Toomai slept for some time, and when he waked it was brilliant moonlight, and Kala Nag was still standing up with his ears cocked. Little Toomai turned, rustling in the fodder, and watched the curve of his big back against half the stars in heaven; and while he watched he heard, so far away that it sounded no more than a pinhole of noise pricked through the stillness, the 'Hoot-toot' of a wild elephant.

All the elephants in the lines jumped up as if they had been shot, and their grunts at last waked the sleeping mahouts, and they came out and drove in the picket-pegs with big mallets, and tightened this rope and knotted that till all was quiet. One new elephant had nearly grubbed up his picket, and Big Toomai took of Kala Nag's leg-chain and shackled that elephant forefoot to hindfoot, but slipped a loop of grass-string round Kala Nag's leg, and told him to remember that he was tied fast. He knew that he and his father and his grandfather had done the very same thing hundreds of times before. Kala Nag did not answer to the order by gurgling, as he usually did. He stood still, looking out across the moonlight, his head a little raised, and his ears spread like fans, up to the great folds of the Garo hills.

'Look to him if he grows restless in the night,' said Big Toomai to Little Toomai, and he went into the hut and slept. Little Toomai was just going to sleep, too, when he heard the coir string snap with a little 'tang', and Kala Nag rolled out of his pickets as slowly and as silently as a cloud rolls out of the mouth of a valley. Little Toomai pattered after him, barefooted, down the road in the moonlight, calling under his breath, 'Kala Nag! Kala Nag! Take me with you, O Kala Nag!' The elephant turned without a sound, took three strides back to the boy in the moonlight, put down his trunk, swung him up to his neck, and almost before Little Toomai had settled his knees slipped into the forest.

There was one blast of furious trumpeting from the lines, and then the silence shut down on everything, and Kala Nag began to move. Sometimes a tuft of high grass washed along his sides as a wave washes along the sides of a ship, and sometimes a cluster of wild-pepper vines would scrape along his back, or a bamboo would creak where his shoulder touched it; but between those times he moved absolutely without any sound, drifting through the thick Garo forest as though it had been smoke. He was going uphill, but though Little Toomai watched the stars in the rifts of the trees, he could not tell in what direction.

Then Kala Nag reached the crest of the ascent and stopped for a minute, and Little Toomai could see the tops of the trees lying all speckled and furry under the moonlight for miles and miles, and the blue-white mist over the river in the hollow. Toomai leaned forward and looked, and he felt that the forest was awake below him – awake and alive and crowded. A big brown fruit-eating bat brushed past his ear; a porcupine's quills rattled in the thicket; and in the darkness between the tree-stems he heard a hog-bear digging hard in the moist, warm earth, snuffing as it dug.

Then the branches closed over his head again, and Kala Nag began to go slowly down into the valley – not quietly this time, but as a runaway gun goes down a steep bank – in one rush. The huge limbs moved as steadily as pistons, eight feet to each stride, and the wrinkled skin of the elbow-points rustled. The undergrowth on either side of him ripped with a noise like torn canvas, and the saplings that he heaved away right and left with his shoulders sprang back again, and banged him on the flank, and great trails of creepers, all matted together, hung from his tusks as he threw his head from side to side and ploughed out his pathway. Then Little Toomai laid himself down close to the great neck, lest a swinging bough should sweep him to the ground, and he wished that he were back in the lines again.

The grass began to get squashy, and Kala Nag's feet sucked and squelched as he put them down, and the night mist at the bottom of the valley chilled Little Toomai. There was a splash and a trample, and the rush of running water, and Kala Nag strode through the bed of a river, feeling his way at each step. Above the noise of the water, as it swirled round the elephant's legs, Little Toomai could hear more splashing and some trumpeting both upstream and down – great grunts and angry snortings, and all the mist about him seemed to be full of rolling, wavy shadows.

'*Ai!*' he said, half-aloud, his teeth chattering. 'The elephant-folk are out tonight. It *is* the dance, then.'

Kala Nag swashed out of the water, blew his trunk clear, and began another climb; but this time he was not alone, and he had not to make his path. That was made already, six-feet wide, in front of him, where the bent jungle-grass was trying to recover itself and stand up. Many elephants must have gone that way only a few minutes before. Little Toomai looked back, and behind him a great wild tusker, with his little pig's eyes glowing like hot coals, was just lifting himself out of the misty river. Then the trees closed up again, and they went on and up, with trumpetings and crashings, and the sound of breaking branches on every side of them.

At last Kala Nag stood still between two tree-trunks at the very top of the hill. They were part of a circle of trees that grew round an irregular space of some three or four acres, and in all that space, as Little Toomai could see, the ground had been trampled down as hard as a brick floor. Some trees grew in the centre of the clearing, but their bark was rubbed away, and the white wood beneath showed all shiny and polished in the patches of moonlight. There were creepers hanging from the upper branches, and the bells of the flowers of the creepers, great waxy white things like convolvuluses, hung down fast asleep; but within the limits of the clearing there was not a single blade of green – nothing but the trampled earth.

The moonlight showed it all iron-grey, except where some elephants stood upon it, and their shadows were inky-black. Little Toomai looked, holding his breath, with his eyes starting out of his head, and as he looked, more and more and more elephants swung out into the open from between the tree-trunks. Little Toomai could count only up to ten, and he counted again and again on his fingers till he lost count of the tens, and his head began to swim. Outside the clearing he could hear them crashing in the undergrowth as they worked their way up the hillside; but as soon as they were within the circle of the tree-trunks they moved like ghosts.

There were white-tusked wild males, with fallen leaves and nuts and twigs lying in the wrinkles of their necks and the folds of their ears; fat, slow-footed she-elephants, with restless little pinky-black calves only three or four-feet high running under their stomachs; young elephants with their tusks just beginning to show, and very proud of them; lanky, scraggy old-maid elephants, with their hollow, anxious faces, and trunks like rough bark; savage old bull-elephants, scarred from shoulder to flank with great weals and cuts of bygone fights, and the caked dirt of their solitary mud-baths dropping from their shoulders; and there was one with a broken tusk and the marks of the full-stroke, the terrible drawing scrape, of a tiger's claws on his side.

They were standing head to head, or walking to and fro across the ground in couples, or rocking and swaying all by themselves – scores and scores of elephants.

Toomai knew that, so long as he lay still on Kala Nag's neck, nothing would happen to him; for even in the rush and scramble of a Keddah-drive a wild elephant does not reach up with his trunk and drag a man off the neck of a tame elephant; and these elephants were not thinking of men that night. Once they started

and put their ears forward when they heard the chinking of a leg-iron in the forest, but it was Pudmini, Petersen Sahib's pet elephant, her chain snapped short off, grunting, snuffling up the hillside. She must have broken her pickets, and come straight from Petersen Sahib's camp; and Little Toomai saw another elephant, one that he did not know, with deep rope-galls on his back and breast. He, too, must have run away from some camp in the hills about.

At last there was no sound of any more elephants moving in the forest, and Kala Nag rolled out from his station between the trees and went into the middle of the crowd, clucking and gurgling, and all the elephants began to talk in their own tongue, and to move about.

Still lying down, Little Toomai looked down upon scores and scores of broad backs, and wagging ears, and tossing trunks, and little rolling eyes. He heard the click of tusks as they crossed other tusks by accident, and the dry rustle of trunks twined together, and the chafing of enormous sides and shoulders in the crowd, and the incessant flick and *hissh* of the great tails. Then a cloud came over the moon, and he sat in black darkness; but the quiet, steady hustling and pushing and gurgling went on just the same. He knew that there were elephants all round Kala Nag, and that there was no chance of backing him out of the assembly; so he set his teeth and shivered. In a Keddah at least there was torchlight and shouting, but here he was all alone in the dark, and once a trunk came up and touched him on the knee.

Then an elephant trumpeted, and they all took it up for five or ten terrible seconds. The dew from the trees above spattered down like rain on the unseen backs, and a dull booming noise began, not very loud at first, and Little Toomai could not tell what it was; but it grew and grew, and Kala Nag lifted up one forefoot and then the other, and brought them down on the ground – one-two, one-two, as steadily as trip-hammers. The elephants were stamping all together now, and it sounded like a war-drum beaten at the mouth of a cave. The dew fell from the trees till there was no more left to fall, and the booming went on, and the ground rocked and shivered, and Little Toomai put his hands up to his ears to shut out the sound. But it was all one gigantic jar that ran through him – this stamp of hundreds of heavy feet on the raw earth. Once or twice he could feel Kala Nag and all the others surge forward a few strides, and the thumping would change to the crushing sound of juicy green things being bruised, but in a minute or two the boom of feet on hard earth

began again. A tree was creaking and groaning somewhere near him. He put out his arm, and felt the bark, but Kala Nag moved forward, still tramping, and he could not tell where he was in the clearing. There was no sound from the elephants, except once, when two or three little calves squeaked together. Then he heard a thump and a shuffle, and the booming went on. It must have lasted fully two hours, and Little Toomai ached in every nerve; but he knew by the smell of the night air that the dawn was coming.

The morning broke in one sheet of pale yellow behind the green hills, and the booming stopped with the first ray, as though the light had been an order. Before Little Toomai had got the ringing out of his head, before even he had shifted his position, there was not an elephant in sight except Kala Nag, Pudmini, and the elephant with the rope-galls, and there was neither sign nor rustle nor whisper down the hillsides to show where the others had gone.

Little Toomai stared again and again. The clearing, as he remembered it, had grown in the night. More trees stood in the middle of it, but the undergrowth and the jungle-grass at the sides had been rolled back. Little Toomai stared once more. Now he understood the trampling. The elephants had stamped out more room – had stamped the thick grass and juicy cane to trash, the trash into slivers, the slivers into tiny fibres, and the fibres into hard earth.

'Wah!' said Little Toomai, and his eyes were very heavy. 'Kala Nag, my lord, let us keep by Pudmini and go to Petersen Sahib's camp, or I shall drop from your neck.'

The third elephant watched the two go away, snorted, wheeled round, and took his own path. He may have belonged to some little native king's establishment, fifty or sixty or a hundred miles away.

Two hours later, as Petersen Sahib was eating early breakfast, the elephants, who had been double-chained that night, began to trumpet, and Pudmini, mired to the shoulders, with Kala Nag, very footsore, shambled into the camp.

Little Toomai's face was grey and pinched, and his hair was full of leaves and drenched with dew; but he tried to salute Petersen Sahib, and cried faintly: 'The dance – the elephant-dance! I have seen it, and – I die!' As Kala Nag sat down, he slid off his neck in a dead faint.

But, since native children have no nerves worth speaking of, in two hours he was lying very contentedly in Petersen Sahib's

hammock with Petersen Sahib's shooting-coat under his head, and a glass of warm milk, a little brandy, with a dash of quinine inside of him; and while the old hairy, scarred hunters of the jungles sat three-deep before him, looking at him as though he were a spirit, he told his tale in short words, as a child will, and wound up with:

'Now, if I lie in one word, send men to see, and they will find that the elephant-folk have trampled down more room in their danceroom, and they will find ten and ten, and many times ten, tracks leading to that danceroom. They made more room with their feet. I have seen it. Kala Nag took me, and I saw. Also Kala Nag is very leg-weary!'

Little Toomai lay back and slept all through the long afternoon and into the twilight, and while he slept Petersen Sahib and Machua Appa followed the track of the two elephants for fifteen miles across the hills. Petersen Sahib had spent eighteen years in catching elephants, and he had only once before found such a dance-place. Machua Appa had no need to look twice at the clearing to see what had been done there, or to scratch with his toe in the packed, rammed earth.

'The child speaks truth,' said he. 'All this was done last night, and I have counted seventy tracks crossing the river. See, Sahib, where Pudmini's leg-iron cut the bark off that tree! Yes; she was there too.'

They looked at each other, and up and down, and they wondered; for the ways of elephants are beyond the wit of any man, black or white, to fathom.

'Forty years and five,' said Machua Appa, 'have I followed my lord the elephant, but never have I heard that any child of man had seen what this child has seen. By all the Gods of the Hills, it is – what can we say?' and he shook his head.

When they got back to camp it was time for the evening meal. Petersen Sahib ate alone in his tent, but he gave orders that the camp should have two sheep and some fowls, as well as a double ration of flour and rice and salt, for he knew that there would be a feast.

Big Toomai had come up hotfoot from the camp in the plains to search for his son and his elephant, and now that he had found them he looked at them as though he were afraid of them both. And there was a feast by the blazing camp-fires in front of the lines of picketed elephants, and Little Toomai was the hero of it all; and the big brown elephant-catchers, the trackers and drivers and ropers, and the men who know all the secrets of breaking the wildest elephants, passed him from one to the other, and they marked his forehead with blood from the breast of a newly killed jungle-cock, to show that he was a forester, initiated and free of all the jungles.

And at last, when the flames died down, and the red light of the logs made the elephants look as though they had been dipped in blood too, Machua Appa, the head of all the drivers of all the Keddahs – Machua Appa, Petersen Sahib's other self, who had never seen a made road in forty years: Machua Appa, who was so great that he had no other name than Machua Appa – leaped to his feet, with Little Toomai held high in the air above his head, and shouted: 'Listen, my brothers. Listen, too, you my lords in the lines there, for I, Machua Appa, am speaking! This little one shall no more be called Little Toomai, but Toomai of the Elephants, as his great-grandfather was called before him. What never man has seen he has seen through the long night, and the favour of the elephant-folk and of the Gods of the Jungles is with him. He shall become a great tracker; he shall become greater than I, even I – Machua Appa! He shall follow the new trail, and the stale trail, and the mixed trail, with a clear eye! He shall take no harm in the Keddah when he runs under their bellies to rope the wild tuskers; and if he slips before the feet of the charging bull-elephant, that bull-elephant shall know who he is and shall not crush him. *Aihai!* my lords in the chains' – he whirled up the line of pickets – 'here is the little one that has seen your dances in your hidden places – the sight that never man saw! Give him honour, my lords! *Salaam karo*, my children! Make your salute to Toomai of the Elephants! Gunga Pershad, ahaa! Hira Guj, Birchi Guj, Kuttar Guj, ahaa! Pudmini – you have seen him at the dance, and you too, Kala Nag, my pearl among elephants! – ahaa! Together! To Toomai of the Elephants. *Barrao!*'

And at that last wild yell the whole line flung up their trunks till the tips touched their foreheads, and broke out into the full salute, the crashing trumpet-peal that only the Viceroy of India hears – the Salaam-ut of the Keddah.

But it was all for the sake of Little Toomai, who had seen what never man had seen before – the dance of the elephants at night and alone in the heart of the Garo hills!